On the Brink
of the World's End

IN THE SAME SERIES

On the Brink
of the World's End
and Other French
Scientific Romances

translated, annotated and introduced by
Brian Stableford

A Black Coat Press Book

ISBN 978-1-61227-474-4. First Printing. February 2016. Published by Black Coat Press, an imprint of Hollywood Comics.com, LLC, P.O. Box 17270, Encino, CA 91416.

TABLE OF CONTENTS

Nounlegos

Roman par R. Bigot

Introduction

This volume continues a series of Black Coat Press anthologies of French *roman scientifique* whose ensemble provides a cross-section of short stories, novellas and short novels illustrating the evolution of that genre from the 18th century to the period between the two world wars.

Le Retour de mon pauvre oncle, ou Relation de son voyage dans la lune, here translated as "My Poor Uncle's Return: The Story of his Voyage to the Moon." was first published as an anonymous booklet in 1784. It was the first work of fiction by the architect and topographer Jacques-Antoine Dulaure (1755-1835), who had previously published *Pogonologie, ou histoire philosophique de la barbe* [Pogonology: A Philosophical History of Beards] (1780) and remained the only one, although he went on to become a prolific writer of non-fiction, including many works of the city of Paris, its monuments and "curiosities," and a provocative work on *Des Divinités génératices, ou du culte du Phallus chez les anciens et les modernes* [Generative Divinities; or, The Cult of the Phallus among the Ancients and Moderns] (1808). He was also a prolific theater critic. He was an enthusiastic supporter of the 1789 Revolution, a prominent Jacobin appointed to the Convention Nationale in 1792, who abandoned politics following Bonaparte's coup, after shouting a farewell "Down with the dictator!" as he left the Chambre. He lost his entire fortune in the early 1800s owing to the bankruptcy of the notary with whom it was deposited, and obtained an administrative position in spite of his opposition to the Emperor, but lost it when the Restoration was effected, and had to live on the produce of his pen thereafter.

There, is of course, little hint of that colorful future to be found in his brief and amiable lunar romance, which is of minor interest in terms of its description of life on the Moon, because it belongs to the well-established tradition of satirical literary works treating the Moon as a Earth-clone in order to poke fun at contemporary human foibles, but is much more interesting and historically significant as a rapid reaction to the development of aerostatics in the wake of the Montgolfier brothers pioneering public demonstration in June 1783. Balloons were to become a key feature of fanciful French fiction for the next hundred years, but Dulaure was the first to seize upon their potential as an imaginative stretching device. He does not take the idea at all seriously—although the protagonist makes his return flight for the Moon in a balloon, he reaches it in the first place, absurdly, by becoming a balloon himself, filling his own body with hydrogen—but Dulaure makes the central character of his amiable farce a "physicist," and his story pays continual homage to the manner in which aerostatics had suddenly made physics an exceedingly fashionable science.

"Paris Futur" by Joseph Méry, here translated as "Future Paris," first published in 1854 and reprinted several times in rapid succession, both in periodicals and as a pamphlet, was one of a series of fictionalized essays kicked of two years previously by a similarly-titled piece by Méry's friend Théophile Gautier. That earlier item and two of the subsequent ones can be found in an earlier anthology in the present series, *Investigations of the Future* (2012).[1] Méry's version picks up one of the themes mentioned in passing by Gautier—weather control—and develops it much more elaborately, featuring a speculative technology that was to become a regular motif in French speculative fiction, greatly encouraged by the fact that a more modest version was tried out in practice over a long period of time, with results sufficiently unclear for no one to be entirely sure, even today, whether or not it has any tangible effect.

"Soeur Marthe" by "Charles Epheyre"—the pseudonym of the Nobel prize-winning physiologist Charles Richet (1850-

---

[1] Black Coat Press, ISBN 978-1-61227-106-4.

1935)—here translated as "Sister Marthe," offers a complete contrast, in being an overwrought melodrama first published in the *Revue des Deux Mondes* in 1889, although it carries forward other themes from Théophile Gautier's work, in this instance from his exotic erotic fantasies. It was written when Richet was the general secretary of the Société de Pyschologie Physiologique [Society of Physiological Psychology], whose president was Jean Charcot, and had a strong interest in the experimental work being carried out at that time in the analytical and therapeutic possibilities of hypnotism.

Although "Soeur Marthe" is by no means the only fictional account of an extraordinary "case study" in "magnetism," there is no other written by a man who was closely involved in such research with a sternly scientific perspective. Although the story it tells is essentially a lurid erotic fantasy, whose closest literary analogues are Gautier's tales of fraught relationships between hapless young men and demanding supernatural women, it nevertheless retains a secure anchorage in scientific skepticism and is possessed of a philosophical ruthlessness that contrasts strongly with Gautier's sentimentality. Indeed, although the narrative voice scrupulously refrains from making any such suggestion, the story carefully excludes any solid objective evidence that the key events of the story are anything but a delusion on the part of its narrator.

Perhaps oddly, there are passages in "Soeur Marthe" that seem remarkably clipped, and there is a temptation to wonder whether the story as printed might have been cut down from a longer text—a suspicion encouraged by the fact that Anatole France, whose novel *Thaïs* was serialized in the *Revue des Deux Mondes* immediately after the appearance there of "Soeur Marthe," complained bitterly about the deep cuts made to his text by the editor. Indeed, a much fuller version of Epheyre's story was subsequently published as a novel by Paul Ollendorf in 1890, and it was also adapted by Octave Houdaille as the libretto for an opera, the music being provided by Frédéric Le Rey, which was produced at the Variétés in 1898. Epheyre's other contributions to *roman scientifique* include "Le Mirosaurus" (1885) and, "Le Microbe de Professeur Bakermann" (1890), both translated—as "The Mirosaurus" and "Professor Bakermann's Microbe"—in *The Supreme Progress and Other Scientific Romances* (2011).[2]

"Paris futur" by Jules Hoche, also translated here as "Future Paris" was a much later contribution to the same series as Méry's piece, first published in 1895, by which time the sequence had become elaborately entangled with a sequence featuring satirical descriptions of the future ruins of Paris, with the result that near-future contributions often tended to the apocalyptic, or at least the disastrous. This particular contribution is as cheerfully farcical as Dulaure's lunar fantasy, and much slighter, but it remains an interesting minor item by a prolific journalist who had first dabbled in speculative fiction when his name was still Jules Hosch, and went on to produce one of the outstanding works of Wellsian *roman scientifique* in *Le Faiseur d'hommes et sa formule* (1905).[3]

"Le Fer qui meurt" by Raoul Bigot, here translated as "The Iron that Died" was originally published in the 15 December 1918 issue of the popular magazine *Lectures Pour Tous*, only a month after the armistice that brought the Great War to a close. It had obviously been written while the war was still raging, and clearly belongs to the glut of propagandistic speculative fiction that began production in 1917, evidently with the active encouragement of George Clemenceau. On publication, therefore, it became something of a curious anomaly: an accidental "alternative history." It was by no means the only story of the period to meet that fate, to which all speculative fictions dealing with contemporary events are exceedingly vulnerable, but it is one of the most extravagant. It is also notable for introducing a motif that had the distinction of being taken up subsequently by writers in all three of the nations that developed a robust tradition of speculative

[2] Black Coat Press, ISBN 978-1-935558-82-8
[3] tr. as *The Maker of Men and His Formula*, Black Coat Press, ISBN 978-1-61227-426-3.

fiction, in France by S. S. Held in *Le Mort du fer* (1931; tr. as "The Death of Iron"), and the U.S.A. by David H. Keller in "The Metal Doom" (1932) and in England by "Wayland Smith" (Victor Bayley) in *The Machine Stops* (1936), thus permitting an intriguing comparison of cultural attitudes.

Raoul Bigot went on to publish a two longer works of speculative fiction in *Lectures Pour Tous*, one of them in collaboration with E. M. Laumann. "Le Fer qui meurt" was rapidly followed by "Nounlegos" (1919) a novella that offers an unusually detailed account of a literal kind of "mind-reading," applying the hypothetical technology to the melodramatic unraveling of an audacious and exceptionally well-planned crime. Although the story is a relatively crude item of downmarket "pulp fiction," those two features give it a particular thematic interest as well as a certain baroque charm, and it is a significant, if decidedly eccentric, contribution to the subgenre of "police procedural" fiction. Its depiction of the eponymous character is a stereotypical addition to a long series of fictional analyses of the supposed psychology of scientific genius.

The final item in the anthology, the short novel *À deux doigts de la fin du monde* by "Colonel Royet"—who also wrote as Max Colroy, although that was probably not, as some sources suggest, his real name—here translated as "On the Brink of the World's End," was published in 1928 by Ferenczi as a "roman inédit" [previously-unpublished novel] although it appears to have been designed for publication as a feuilleton, and might well have been written some years before its publication. The Royet signature initially appeared in tandem with that of Paul d'Ivoi on feuilletons produced prior to the Great War, which he presumably helped the more experienced author to keep going during problematic periods, and then reappeared during the war on jingoistic propaganda pieces before continuing to feature thereafter on various garish thrillers as well as a twenty-part future war epic, *La Guerre est déclarée* [War is Declared] issued by Tallandier in 1931. Little seems to be known about the person behind the name, which might or might not have been borrowed from Colonel Hippolyte Royet of the National Guard, who played a significant role in the suppression of the Lyon insurgency of 1834.

Like "Nounlegos," *À deux doigts de la fin du monde* belongs to the pulpish phase of the evolution of *roman scientifique*, but it warrants particular attention within that arena by virtue of the manner in which it stretches its melodrama to an unusual extreme, and also because of the feverishly colorful fashion in which it deploys the popular notion of the "mad scientist" as a threat to the relative stability of the world. The scientific background of the story is extremely dubious—a frequent feature of popular thrillers of the period—but the nettle is grasped in with an unusually firm hand that adds to the story's vivacity.

The translation of *Le Retour de mon pauvre oncle* was made from the copy of the 1784 Lejay edition reproduced on the Bibliothèque Nationale's *gallica* website. The translations of the two "Paris futur" stories were made from the Kindle edition of the ArcheoSF anthology *Paris futurs* (2014). The translation of "Soeur Marthe" was made from the *gallica* copy of the relevant volume of the *Revue des Deux Mondes*. The translations of the two Raoul Bigot stories were made from the *gallica* copies of the relevant issues of *Lectures Pour Tous* and the translation of *À deux doigts de la fin du monde* from the *gallica* reproduction of the 1928 Ferenczi volume.

Brian Stableford

Jacques-Antoine Dulaure: *My Poor Uncle's Return: The Story of his Voyage to the Moon*
(1784)

Preface

My poor uncle, as all Europe knows, having had lunch after quarreling violently with one of his friends, a fellow physicist, was afflicted by a colic so violent that my sister and I were greatly alarmed. Thinking that an enema might relieve him, troubled as I was, I prepared a syringe and fitted it to my uncle's posterior, but instead of an emollient liquid it was inflammable air that I introduced into his bowels. Suddenly, I saw my dear uncle rose up from his bed by degrees, fly up to the ceiling, make two or three circuits of it, and then escape through the window, I tried to catch hold of his feet, but his shoe came off in my hand, and, stripped of his trousers, he flew majestically up to the clouds. I was still gazing when my eyes could no longer perceive him.

After an absence of three months, that poor uncle has returned. The tender interest that Parisians, his compatriots, have taken in that marvelous event, the works they have produced in order to represent all its circumstances and to eternalize the memory of it, have forced my gratitude to publish this narration.[4]

---

[4] Author's note: "Several Engravings, and a Comedy entirely devoted to this subject, are testimony to the enthusiasm of Parisians for events of this importance."

I. *My Departure from the Earth*

Unfortunately, my window was open; my remedy of inflammable gas caused me, involuntarily, to pass through it, and I was soon carried into the highest atmospheric region. Neither the memory of the adventure of the late Icarus, nor that of another idiot who broke his legs on the way, nor the danger of my perilous voyage, caused me any anxiety. Physicists, as everyone knows, are never afraid; on the contrary, the disposition of my body leaving my face turned toward the Earth, I contemplated in security the most magnificent scene that Nature has ever offered to mortal eyes.

A sweet sensation spread through all my limbs; the air was so pure and so calm, and I was floating in a profound peace, that I thought I was breathing in wellbeing.

It's necessary to climb very high to find this wellbeing, I thought then. *Until cabals, luxury and antisocial behavior have been banished from the earth, humans will no longer encounter it there, and it requires nothing less than an enema of inflammable air to be able to enjoy it.*

For want of a writing-desk and a thermometer, I was unable to calculate the various heights at which I found myself. That is a pity, because I would have been able to provide results of a very rigorous precision.

Pride follows us everywhere; I felt singularly flattered to see myself so rapidly elevated above all other men; like so many highly-placed individuals, I gloried in my elevation, even though it was only the work of an enema.[5]

---

[5] Author's note: "My poor uncle is not the only aerial Voyager to have been sensible of that vainglorious thought. See Monsieur Charles' letter after his ascent from the Tuileries." Jacques Charles (1746-1823) launched the first hydrogen balloon in August 1783, and he and Nicolas-Louis Robert made the first manned flight in a balloon of that kind in December 1783, taking off from the Jardin des Tuileries before a crowd estimated at 400,000 people, including Benjamin Franklin and

During those reflections, which still reeked of the ground, the surface of the Earth gradually disappeared from my eyes and I saw the rotundity of the globe. It was then that I began to tremble; the danger presented itself with all that it had of the most frightening. Privately cursing Physicists and inflammable gas, I abandoned myself entirely to the disturbance that was agitating me. Imagine a Parisian, who has never in his travels lost sight of the towers of Notre-Dame, and who sees himself lifted into the immensities of the skies, and you will be able to estimate my state of mind.

I doubtless found myself in the region of scientific vapors,[6] for I was suddenly plunged into such a great lethargy that the tail of a comet, which singed one of my coat-tails as it passed by, could not succeed in waking me. That is what deprived me of observation during the rest of the journey, to my great displeasure and the great prejudice of the Sciences. My observations would have been bound to clarify many astronomical verities, which are so sublime in their obscurity that the eyes of the vulgar cannot penetrate them.

II. My Awakening

In traversing the air that contains the exhalations of all the brains of the Orators, Eulogists, Calculators and Plagiarists of the Earth, I had respired such a strong dose of soporific that my fall was absolutely insensible to me. Hazard, as you shall see, favored that final accident of my voyage.[7]

---

one of the Montgolfier brothers. Charles made a solo flight soon thereafter, ascending to 3,000 meters and then (wisely) gave up the dangerous practice.

[6] Author's note: "My uncle is preparing a voluminous Work on the vapors that compose the different layers or regions of the atmosphere, as will be seen at the end of this Book."

[7] Author's note: "The day after his experiment at the Champ-du-Mars, Monsieur Blanchard wrote that he had experienced a very violent desire to go to sleep; that proves that my poor

Several pockets of inflammable air that escaped from my body at the same place that they had been introduced into it, doubtless eventually subjugated the ascensional force to gravitation. It was dark; I found myself in the air above a small town, and I was about to land on the cobblestones of a street when, luckily, some poor devil who was changing residence secretly—and doing so very quietly in order not to trouble the slumber of his landlord, who liked to sleep—threw a mattress out of the window. I found myself directly above it at the moment when it was thrown, and followed it down, without the commotion extracting me from my lethargy.

I stayed there until someone came to place me in a small cart where, amid old furniture, I was transported out of the town. The darkness of the night, and the precipitation that always accompanies changes of residence of that sort, prevented me from being perceived.

Far from thinking then that I was such a great distance from my homeland, I believed that I was still in my bedroom; I was dreaming that I was still arguing with my Physicist, who was the most fervent anti-Attractionary seen since Newton. While my mind was working to convert that heterodox scholar, my body was traveling the roads of the Moon.

Yes, dear reader, the Moon; nothing is more true. Without being aware of it, I had reached the Earth's satellite.

Today, as everyone knows, there is no longer anything difficult for Physicists. One has discovered the universal agent, another makes rain and fine weather, and yet another, much cleverer, has stolen the Mysterious Art of the Adepts, by

---

uncle is worthy of faith, and that Monsieur Blanchard found himself in the same region in which my poor uncle went to sleep." Jean-Pierre Blanchard (1753-1809), who made his first flight in a hydrogen balloon launched from the Champ de Mars on 2 March 1784, went on to become a very enthusiastic balloonist, making a profession as a showman, touring America as well as Europe, and eventually dying in a fall.

making gold—and it is with the aid of simples that he accomplishes his Great Work.

The carriage that was carrying me had already left the little town from which it had brought me some way behind when an event finally extracted me from my profound torpor. The landlord, having discovered his tenant's flight, arrived very rapidly, shouting and striving to extract from the vehicle the only guarantees of his rent. The owner of the furniture did his best to defend it with a great deal of ardor.

During that cruel conflict, I felt my head so violently bumped that, believing that I had received a blow from the fist of my anti-Attractionary Physicist, I got up furiously, in order to make a response that was no less striking. In leaping to my feet, however, instead of the Physicist, I knocked over the landlord, who was getting ready to remove the mattress on which I was lying. Uttering a frightful cry, he got up again and took flight, along with his adversary. My sudden and unexpected appearance, the prevailing darkness and my gigantic stature by comparison with that of the inhabitants of the Moon, which does not exceed four feet,[8] had easily made them believe that I was at least a phantom, if I was not a Devil.

Oh, with what astonishment I was gripped by the sight of so many extraordinary things, and how the memory of my aerial voyage was rendered more extraordinary still!

Am I still in the air? I wondered. *How did I fall without feeling it? And how do I come to be on this cart? Why was I asleep? Why, on awakening did I frighten those two little men so much?*

I suspected that I was still asleep; I even doubted that I existed.

---

[8] Author's note: "Scholars will not fail to object to me that the difference between the height of the inhabitants of the Moon and those of Earth is not in proportion to the difference of the diameters of the two planets; so much the worse for those who find geometrical relationships everywhere. But my uncle has seen; there is no reply to that."

Where am I? Is this Montmartre or Gonesse?[9] Alas, I can no longer see the Seine! I can no longer see the towers of Notre-Dame. Perhaps I'm in China, or even in the land of dwarfs to which Gulliver once traveled. The small stature of the men I've seen seems to incline me to think so. (A Physicist is not obliged to be a perfect Geographer.)

That suspicion appeared to me to be confirmed when, seeking to get down from the vehicle, my hand naturally fell upon a small human figure, which I immediately took for an inhabitant of the country. As it was making no movement I thought I had stifled the individual, but I soon recovered from my error when I perceived, by courtesy of the dawn that was beginning to break, that it was only a marionette.

I had scarcely recovered from my astonishment when I perceived one of my little men in the distance. I employed voice and gesture to reassure him and invite him to join me. He approached, but it was with the slowness that fear imparts. Less timid, however, than his adversary, who did not reappear, he accosted me, albeit tremulously. I greeted him so amicably that he was no longer afraid, and we went on together.

---

[9] Author's note: "The first Balloon that rose up from Paris came down in Gonesse. People made fun of the alarm that its fall caused that population of bakers, but the bakers of Gonesse can be excused for a lack of understanding of Physics, since one sees Physicists in Paris who are so scholarly in their lack of understanding of bakery. That is what my good friend César Bucquet, former miller of the Hôtel-Dieu, has demonstrated in his observations on that Art." The balloon that came down in Gonesse in August 1783 was the Montgolfiers'; there is now a street there named after them. César Buquet—or, more commonly, Bucquet—published numerous books, including a manual of milling and mill-construction, although a collection of *Obervations intéressantes et amusantes* credited to his wisdom and issued in 1783 by the same publisher who issued Dulaure's booklet, appears to have been written by Edme Beguillet.

III. Sequel to the preceding.

The furniture and the vehicle belonged to him. He soon got used to me. In my capacity as a Physicist I attempted to seek his heart in his face, but it appeared to me to be indecipherable, so vague was its expression. It resembled the physiognomy of those honest rogues and schemers in whom the habit of masking their knavery entirely effaces the characteristic features of their visage. Once one knew a man by his face, nowadays, a species of hypocrisy known as politeness has completely obscured the mirror of the soul.

The idiom of that region of the Moon, if one excepts the scant usage that is made of consonants, has much in common with the French language; with a little study, I soon succeeded in speaking and understanding it. It was then that my curiosity was assuaged by an infinity of questions of all kinds.

I learned that my traveling companion was the director of a troupe of wooden actors, known in France as marionettes. I learned, by means of the story of his change and residence and nocturnal flight, how I had been able to fall and how I had come to find myself in the vehicle. Nor did I forget to enquire as to whether universal attraction was as clearly demonstrated to the Physicists of the Moon as it is to those of the Earth. As he did not make me any satisfactory reply on that subject, I consoled myself by questioning him about the mores and customs of his land.

"In truth," he replied, "although I have lived in high society I have not made a record of those things , but what I would have more pleasure in recounting to you, which would answer the majority of your questions, is my story."

The estate of the man, his comfortable manners, which announced that he had once held a more distinguished rank, and his tone of frankness and insouciance, almost always accompanied by a philosophical gravity, caused me to judge that the story in question might contain piquant features. I listened to him.

He began thus:

IV. The Marionette Man's Story

I am the son of an honest laborer, an inhabitant of a village situated on the border of a neighboring realm. I might have been happy if my father had taught me the ancient and respectable art of cultivating the field of his ancestors; I would then have been ignorant of the enjoyments of vainglory and the tortures consequent upon it. I would have conserved my name, Kirkerdorf, which I abandoned in order to take that of Oë. Unfortunately, I was able to read and write at an early age, and, persuaded by the Magister of my village that I was a child of genius, I directed my ambition toward the capital of this realm.

There I was in a new world, seeking to understand the customs and manners that, in this country, are sciences of the foremost necessity. I soon perceived that the different fashions of societies can be reduced to three or four sorts, at the most. Be able to adopt, in appropriate circumstances, the mask of foolishness, hypocrisy or importance, and you possess the cardinal points of the means of success. Every society demands that one plays one of those characters, but in order that there should never be an error and that one should not take one role for another, I think that it would not be bad if one were to find in every antechamber the mask of the character of the house. One day, I would like to write a long book about the utility of such a custom.

I spared neither travels nor efforts in order to put myself on the road to fortune. After several futile endeavors I was advised to present myself to a Great Man of the century, a protector of young men revered as a sage, an Apostle of Humanity and, in sum, a kind of Patriarch of Philosophy. I declared to him that I knew Ancient Languages, History, Geography and Mathematics. I was almost completely ignorant of all those sciences, but I had been assured that in such circumstances, the means of making a rapid fortune was to lie brazenly.

Without any other examination, the Great Man replied to me in a pedantically honeyed tone: "I am sorry not to be able to be of any utility to you, but the circle of your knowledge is too circumscribed."

I presented myself to a man who was the Counsel of all men with projects, whose sentiment was always preponderant. He had once been the leader of a party and was in despair at seeing that, for a long time, he was no longer in fashion.

I said to him, following my custom: "I know Ancient Languages, History, Geography and Mathematics."

"You only know that?" said my new Protector, coldly. "Can you not copy the manners of an imbecile, of a simpleton, and amuse all the Lords of the Court by imitating the conversation of a Porter? Or if you could bark like a dog—that is what is known as imitating beautiful nature. If you could eat stones, swallow daggers or razors?"[10]

"In truth, no, Monsieur."

"Can you read cards, tell the fortunes of our coquettes? If, by chance you have eyes good enough to see through twenty feet of earth or see as clearly in the dark as in broad daylight?"[11]

"No, Monsieur."

"Well then, write Vaudevilles or bad Tragedies. I can see no other way for you to get out of difficulty."

"I don't believe I'm able to do any of those things."

"I'm sorry, but you're ignorant of everything that leads to fortune."

---

[10] Author's note: "There was a man in London who made a brilliant fortune by swallowing daggers and razors."

[11] Author's note: "An Academy has proposed the discovery of an instrument that can enable its bearer to see clearly in the dark, a very useful discovery when the habit of making candles has been lost."

Ashamed, I took my leave of that terrible man, saying to myself: *No one told me about that. I am very ignorant, then? That was not what the Magister of my village told me, however.*

A few days later I was introduced to a banal protector. He was a unique man for resources; he possessed, to the extent that it is possible, the marvelous talent of commanding the caprices of fortune; he created favorites, he was the dispenser of graces. By means of his secret, one flatfoot had become a powerful Financier, another a Minister, others a poet of the beauties of the antechamber, a grave individual, a genius of the first order. He was a great man.

"I know," I said to him, "Ancient Languages, History, Geography and Mathematics."

"That has nothing to do with it," he replied. "Just tell me what position would suit you best."

At that unexpected question, I felt penetrated by the keen joy that the hope of happiness gives. *I'm going to cease to be miserable, then,* I told himself. *Fortune has tired of persecuting me.*

My Magister had told me that I was made to distinguish myself in the world. In that agreeable persuasion I thought that it was appropriate to display my frankness, by confessing right away that I did not know how to counterfeit the manners of a porter, that my eyes were not good enough to see twenty feet underground, and that I was absolutely ignorant of the useful art of reading cards.

"That might have had its advantages," he replied, "but it's a question now of knowing what position you desire. Is it in Finance?"

"Oh yes, in Finance; that is surely the high road to fortune."

"Well, I have one all ready and I promise it to you."

I did not know how to thank my benefactor; I was prodigal, as is usual, with words of obligation and gratitude.

"You're quite right," he told me, "for it's an excellent position; before long, I see you with a carriage that will splash the entire world, exceedingly insolent lackeys, and a mistress whose sumptuousness will efface all the ladies of the Court."

"Oh, Monsieur!" I exclaimed, transported by joy. "How can one recognize such a generous service?"

"With ten thousand pieces of gold," he replied, "which you will give me, and I guarantee that your fortune will be made. It's not too much, in truth, if you consider what it will be necessary for me to give to secretaries, valets, and the mistresses of both—do you imagine that after that I'll have much left?"

Scarcely had he finished than I took my leave, ashamedly, in despair at not having ten thousand pieces of gold for the secretaries, the lackeys and the mistresses, in order to become a great Lord at a stroke.

Finally, I had to go to men with projects, who, in making me glimpse a brilliant fortune from afar, completed removing the little that remained to me, and stealing the price of my labor. I became poor, and, in consequence, scorned.

I still had the noble pride that elevates the soul of the unfortunate man and consoles him, but that fruitless virtue succumbed by degrees to the afflictions of need. I acquired debts, I broke my promises, I accustomed myself to borrowing, and my face was insensibly armored against the darts of my creditors.

Gambling offered me resources; my scruples were diminished thereby; I became a cheat, as is usual, and I made a fortune. I became important; I was a gallant man; I was cherished and idolized; I had gold.

The consideration that the possession of that metal gives was not yet sufficient for my ambition; I wanted to merit the esteem of a few honest men. I knew that for that, it was necessary to be the husband of a very coquettish, very gallant and very amiable woman. I had no difficulty finding one who had all those social virtues to an eminent degree. My chaste spouse, who did the honors of her house very well, became for me an inexhaustible source of honor and wealth.

Having had for some time, in the mind of the best society, the reputation of an important person, the whim took me to become one. My wife, all of whose caprices I let pass with a good heart, willingly granted me that one. I therefore set myself at the head of making projects, of changing the face of things and renewing the Administration. With the aid of an intelligence that I hired, I wrote pompous Prospectuses and admirable Memoirs, in favor of which I went to the Great in quest of applause and subscriptions.[12]

Everything went as I desired; my project was miraculous, divine and inconceivable, no one had any idea of it; that is what was said in good company. I was a vast genius, a profound man; it was sufficient to name me to make a eulogy of my Works; that was what the majority of the newspapers said.

Nothing is more easily convinced than self-esteem; I had no difficulty in believing myself to be endowed with all the good qualities with which I was gratified. It was then that it was necessary for me to put on an entire philosophical exterior: a sententious and reserved tone, a distracted and occupied manner, simple attire, a grave tread, eyebrows always furrowed; nothing was neglected. When I opened my mouth it was to talk about beneficence, justice, the happiness of peoples and humankind. You can see that I was a philosopher of the finest carat, so my glory was complete and my reputation reached its highest phase.

"That surprises you," my traveling companion said, on seeing me smile. "You're astonished to see that having played

---

[12] Author's note: "If the Public cared to take the trouble to look closely at the great enterprises proposed by subscription, they would find that the secret agents of the great machine are either an ardent and learned but unknown young Physicist, an estimable but poor Writer, or a clever but unknown young Geographer. At the head of these people, always poorly paid, they will find thereafter a polished ignoramus devoid of modesty and delicacy."

such a great role among men, I'm reduced to playing such a small one with marionettes! That's the law of fate."

As he finished that speech, we arrived in a town, where we spent the night. The next day, we continued our journey toward the capital of the realm, and Oë continued his story as follows:

V. Continuation of Oë's Story

O inconstancy of things of this world! Was it necessary that the great philosopher that I was should be reduced to throwing his furniture out of a window in order to avoid paying the rent? Was it necessary that a genius capable of indoctrinating an entire people should be forced to direct marionettes? You shall see how that happened to me.

Abundance, successes and consideration crowned my complaisance for my faithful wife; she was my sole resource. As soon as I tried to oppose her disorders, quarrels and perfidies, scorn and misery became the fruits of my reform.

The customary funds were lacking; my works experienced delays; I broke my word. My collaborators were no longer paid, my subscribers were murmuring. Gradually, I lost their confidence and the consideration that I had acquired. People took advantage of that momentary distress to bring to light my conduct, my charlatanism and my incapacity. I was doomed, without resource.

It was then that my philosophy inspired me with a simple means of getting myself out of that predicament. My wife had a great many valuable jewels—between us, they were the product of favors she placed at honest interest in the hands of her lovers. By virtue of a perfectly natural reasoning, I concluded that I had an incontestable right to those jewels; in consequence of that right, I took advantage of a favorable night to remove all the most precious ones she had and I departed very swiftly, abandoning my projects, my wife and my disastrous affairs, as one abandons a bad habit of which one rids oneself for the last time.

I arrived in the capital of a neighboring real, where I initially put on a pompous display. Then I embarked on extravagant projects, very difficult to carry out; in spite of that, they were not welcomed. I perceived, a little belatedly, that I was no longer in my homeland; the national character was quite different.

Eventually, my funds ran out, and my ambition with them. I was only too glad to acquire from an operator of marionettes, who had made a considerable fortune, his wooden actors, his portable theater and the stock of his dramatic Works. The inhabitants of that country had a decided taste for spectacles: cock-fighting and brawling charmed them infinitely, as well as scenes in which the executioner played the principal role. I put the inclinations of the people to profit; I wrote new plays, and held the inhabitants up to ridicule with my marionettes; when pleasantries are general in import, they please all individuals.

At first I only had spectators among the rabble, but one day, the maidservant of a kept woman honored my spectacle with her presence, and my affairs took on a more advantageous aspect. Charmed by the witticisms, puns and lewd equivocations that my wooden actors produced, the girl assured her mistress that my spectacle was charming and divine. The kept woman, the principal tenant of her charms, her friend, her dressmaker, her seamstress, her hairdresser and her priest—one might even say her parrot—were persuaded after half an hour that I was an astonishing man for marionettes; that was what each of those individuals assured a hundred others. My reputation spread in such a manner that by the end of the day a large fraction of the inhabitants knew that I was a prodigy.

My glory was brilliantly sustained; I became the man of the moment. People talked about nothing but me, and dressed in accordance with my example. I was engraved and sculpted; my portrait feature alongside those of Great Men and the heroes of the nation. That is how reputations are made.

(I interrupted my storyteller to tell him that it was the same on Earth.)

Glory makes enemies, Oë continued. A heap of men starved of reputation wanted to diminish mine, and published pamphlets and epigrams of all kinds against me. They claimed that my marionettes did not imitate beautiful nature, that their faces lacked soul and expression, and a thousand other calumnies of that sort, which only served to increase my renown.

It was then that a performer of pirouettes caused all heads to turn in his direction; no man had ever pirouetted with so much genius. The novelty removed the favor of the public from me; I was forgotten. The efforts that I made to compete with my adversary drew me into ruinous expenditure, which did not bring me any success, but a great deal of ridicule and scorn. I was no longer fashionable.

Too proud to display my defeat after such a fine triumph, I made the decision to abandon that country to return to my dear homeland, where genius as fecund as mine never lacks resources. I initially arrived in that small town to which Heaven sent you expressly, I believe, to save me from the persecutions of my creditor, whom my misfortunes obliged me to quit without paying.

Having finished his story, Oë questioned me ardently about the event of my voyage; I replied that I would not delay long in satisfying his curiosity, and we continued our route.

VI. My Arrival in the Capital of the Realm and the Encounter we had there

We finally arrived in the famous capital. At that sight, I experienced a secret emotion; I thought I was entering my Paris, the good city of Paris. Alas, my dear nephew and my poor niece, I was very far from finding you there; you were very far from being able to embrace your poor uncle! That memory caused me to shed a torrent of tears.

While I was weeping in that fashion we perceived a brilliant carriage coming toward us at high speed. Everyone was getting out of its way precipitately; the crowd of pedestrians seemed to be escaping the danger of its rapid course miraculously, and were quite happy only to find themselves covered in mud. In spite of our promptitude and our cries, the elegant carriage pitilessly overturned my traveling companion's humble and frail vehicle, as well as the baggage it contained, and we were bruised and wounded in various places by the repercussions.

While we were still stunned by our accident, and the murderous carriage drew away as if nothing had happened, eight or ten vigorous arms, which seemed to have been waiting at the street corner for an opportunity to exercise themselves, came to our aid and repair the disorder of our vehicle in a trice. By their activity and disinterest, one might have thought that they were avenging an outrage they had suffered.

One man, as remarkable by the simplicity of his clothing as the vivacity of his manners, approached and offered us his house and the assistance required by our injuries. We accepted that service with all the more gratitude because it was necessary. A witness to the event, he knew the master of the vehicle and was indignant to see unfortunate strangers run over by arrogant opulence.

I asked him whether the individual having himself transported with so much diligence was not an Envoy of the Court changed with important dispatches, or perhaps a rich benefactor taking assistance to unfortunates.

"No," he replied, "the man who maltreated you has no business and no concerns other than avoiding tedium. Half priest and half secular, he is not charged with any duty by either estate. He is only held to the priesthood by the riches he draws therefrom, and to society by the pleasures that it procures him. He is an egotist by estate."

"It's necessary, however," I said, "that these hybrid individuals are endowed with some distinguished merit, or that they have rendered important services to the fatherland, in order to be so well gratified."

"That is not a reason," he told me. "True merit does not think of gratifications; one sometimes perceives it but it never displays itself. The honest man who renders a service to his fatherland or his compatriots finds his recompense in his heart; but similar dignities, whose advent is arbitrary, are always the price of intrigue and the vilest cabals."

"It's quite astonishing," I went on, "that such great benefits are destined to maintain ambition, futility and vice."

"Unphilosophical founders," the man relies, "have piously sacrificed their fortunes in the praiseworthy intention of honoring Religion and offering relief to the poor; their generosity has had an opposite effect, the usual effect of wealth. These kinds of Minister of Religion have dishonored it by their licentious life and effeminate luxury, and have made money destined to relieve the poor serve their libertinage."

I judged, according to what the Sage told me, that the priests in question bore a close resemblance to those abbés with a simple tonsure who have acquired such a great reputation in France in ladies' alcoves and dressing-rooms.

That benevolent Sage invited us to stay in his home until we were fully recovered; we could not refuse such a kind offer. During that time, I never ceased questioning him about the mores of his homeland, and although he was not an excellent Physicist, as I soon perceived, his responses were so sensible and announced such an accurate observer, that I accorded him all my confidence.

Oë amused us sometimes with his humorous stories, and confessed in good faith that he had known many Philosophers, and had followed the métier himself, but that no Philosopher of reputation had ever resembled the Philosopher who remained in obscurity; that those who make a profession of the former only do good when they are sure of publicity, whereas those who profess the latter, do good at every opportunity—a rare Philosopher, he said, in whom he had never believed!

VII. How Oë Left Us

"It was an enema," I said to my host one day, "that procured me the pleasure of hearing you—yes, an enema of inflammable air, which caused me to cross the immense space that separates the Earth from the Moon. The gratitude that I owe you, as well as Oë, makes it a duty for me to tell you the marvelous story of my voyage."

Then I told them how I had argued with a Physicist who did not want to believe in universal attraction; how that dispute had caused me a violent colic, and how I had been administered the fatal remedy of inflammable air that had caused me to pass through the widow, fly through the air and finally arrive on the Moon, where I had fallen on to a mattress that Oë had thrown into the street.

Then I talked to them about the miracles that inflammable air operated: how it elevated Physicists and their fortunes; how it changed paper into gold and gold into smoke, and a thousand other things as astonishing. Oë would have joked about it abundantly if he had thought that he would generate laughter, but he contented himself with smiling.

Our wise host was not one of those familiar scholars whose reputation gives them the right to limit human understanding, and who reprove, as despots, all the innovations that they have not been able to imagine. Nor did he have the credulity of the vulgar, but doubted like a Sage.

I assured him that if he cared to assist me, an experiment would banish his doubts entirely. He agreed to do so, and I constructed an aerostatic Balloon, which flew away and was lost in the air.

At the sight of that marvel, I read in my host's face the delight, the pure joy, that success engenders, whereas Oë, while admiring it, appeared agitated and reflective. Shortly thereafter he became somber and pensive, and ended up leaving us abruptly, without our knowing the cause of that impolite action or the place of his retreat.

While the rumor of my experiment spread by word of mouth and became the news of the day, I found myself sufficiently recovered from my injuries to travel around the city and take advantage of the observations that my sage had been kind enough to make to me regarding the mores of his homeland.

VIII. The Lottery and the Poor

What, then, etc…?

………………………...

………………………...

But it's time for the spectacle; let's go in.

IX. Spectacles

In spite of the grandeur of the hall, it could not contain the number of people who presented themselves.

"That," said my Sage, "is because a new Tragedy is being performed today. One is assured that it is very black, very atrocious—in sum, that it is superb. At one time, gaiety and the frolicsome, or the tender and the sublime, attracted spectators. At one time, dramatic authors, after having come to know the human heart and the mechanisms of grand passions, submitted the impetus of their genus to rules prescribed by reason. Today, it's no longer the same; it is cries of despair, heartrending remorse and atrocities that charm.

"Melpomene and Thalia are no longer anything but old prostitutes who, knowing the impotence of their charms, have the complaisance to lend themselves to all their lovers' caprices. Some, with a severe and sententious tone, have made a theater into a pulpit; others, combining rascality with bad taste, have made it a revolting slaughterhouse. The latter make excessive depictions of the ravages of the passions, which leave in excited brains the impression of a somber melancholy, or the seed of frenzies dangerous to society. One is no longer made to laugh in the theater, or to shed tears of com-

31

miseration, but one is frightened there—and like children, we love the tales that frighten us."

Meanwhile, the play commenced.

After entries and exists of which only the author knew the cause, the Hero appears. Covered in glory by defeating the enemies of his king, he has returned to the Court to receive the honors due to his courage.

Unfortunately, that Great Man, that Hero—that Sage even—has all the weakness of mind of a badly brought-up girl. He has visions; he believes in dreams and sorceries, and you can see that he is also afraid of ghosts.

His wife, who does not have visions, and is strong-minded by comparison with him, has a rather strange caprice; she is gripped by the desire to become queen. For that, however, it will be necessary to put her husband on the throne, and to succeed in that, it will be necessary to have the king—whom she believes to have no heirs—murdered.

She therefore proposes to her husband that he commit that atrocity. She renews her solicitations through two interminable acts. The latter, after having opposed superb maxims, tells her, as his final word: "If ever the king were attacked by his enemies, he would not fail to summon me to his aid, and I would run to defend him."

That happens at a given time. Assassins introduce themselves by night into the king's bedroom; the unfortunate prince calls to the Hero for help, and the latter runs to defend him. In spite of that initial impulse of his heart, however, in spite of his promise and in spite of the circumstances, his sage maxims and the laws of hospitality, that Hero, that Great Man, suddenly changes his sentiment. Instead of helping his master against the assassins, it is him who delivers the dagger to his breast and takes his life in a cowardly manner—and all of that in order not to displease a woman who is only his wife.

That unexpected and treacherous rascality is followed, as is reasonable, by violent remorse. For a novice criminal, that trial blow is a little too much, so our Hero expresses his remorse in a voice so uncontrolled that an old man listening at the door at the time hears the confession of the crime from the criminal's own mouth. He goes away, and goes to dispose the king's son, who had thus far been unknown, to avenge the murder of his father.

Meanwhile, the Hero, still agitated by remorse, tries to take the throne in order to receive the oath of his new servants, but—who would have believed it?—he is suddenly stopped by a ghost. Seized by fear, weakened by further remorse, he seems demented. His wife reproaches him for his pusillanimity and says to the people, to excuse her husband, that the human species is unfortunately subject to such fancies.

Finally, he is king. He learns that the old man who was listening at the door has raised a party of his subjects against him; he has him put in irons and then summons him to the theater. The prisoner reproaches him for his crime; the new king advances to stab the wise old man again, but the latter is cunning enough to undo his buttons very quickly and show him his belt, which is stained with blood.

Our Hero does not fail to recognize the color of the royal blood that he has shed. His remorse and his visions are reborn, and he throws himself at the feet of the old man. It is then that he takes it into his head—a trifle belatedly—to go against his wife. He renounces the crown, shows his people the veritable sovereign and ends up, as usual, by stabbing himself fatally.

Although I had neglected the theaters of Paris for some time, because they proved nothing in Physics, I nevertheless remembered having once seen the masterpieces of Corneille and Racine there. I attributed the great difference that existed between what I had just seen and the tragedies of those famous authors to the differences necessarily to be found between the mores of two nations as distant from one another as France is from that land of the Moon, and dared not voice my sentiment, My comrade, however, whom I asked for his, uttered a profound sigh and made no reply.

"Have you other spectacles?" I asked then.

"Yes," he replied, "but sorrow and bad taste have introduced themselves insensibly thereto. There is one that is famous for the pleasure of the eyes and eyes, in which intelligence plays no part; it is the most constantly followed. Another theater was once consecrated absolutely to laughter and pastorals, but it is very proud of having obtained some time ago the right to be tearful and lugubrious. There are a few others, less celebrated and less ancient, the last refuges in which Momus makes his bells heard; it is gaiety with grace, wisdom under the mantle of folly: infant theaters where old age comes to forget its antiquity, and men preoccupied by their affairs."

X. The Sciences and Arts of the Moon

One morning, as we were disposed to continue the course of our observations, we arrived in a street renowned as the abode of merchants of pictures, books, wallpaper, geography and almanacs. Those kinds of profiteers were so degraded that it was sufficient to name the street that had seen them born to satirize it.

My guide needed a calendar, and we went into a shop, but I stopped dead.

"This is the study of a scholar; you're mistaken," I said to him. "Read that inscription: *Engineer-Geographer*. Is it possible that an engineer-geographer is reduced to selling almanacs?"

"Rather ask," my Sage replied, "how it is possible for a merchant of almanacs to entitle himself an engineer-geographer."

We made a few purchases, after which my comrade asked the merchant a few questions. He replied to us by showing us piles of illuminated maps, and we left.

As we went along, my Sage did not allow anything to escape me. He pointed out temples, spectacle halls and private houses. There was the same kind of architecture everywhere. Magistrates, High Priests, Financiers and Acrobats had temples erected in order to live in them. Everyone wanted to be his own God, and everyone received in his sanctuary, on a daily basis, a vile troop of worshipers. It had often happened that architects, who did not intend mockery to be the price of their work, devoid of respect for apotheosis, had the furniture of a God sold, because he had wanted to be one a little more than the others.

We went into a celebrated cabinet of curiosities. It contained masterpieces of all kinds. That rare collection cost immense sums. I admired it, like everyone else, with the good faith of a Physicist who is not an initiate in the Arts.

"One very interesting item is missing from this cabinet," said my comrade. "It's the inscription of these words: *The vanity of one man retains here the wellbeing of a hundred families.*

"In fact," he continued, "a hundred families could live happily with the price of this sumptuous and useless old junk. The owner, who soon wearied of admiring it, has taken possession of the wellbeing of so many individuals for the unique satisfaction of hearing someone say: 'You have a precious original there, a superb paining.' Oh, the superb painting that the wellbeing of a hundred families..."

Eventually, we arrived at an assembly of litterateurs, scientists, artists, etc. etc.

"This gathering of men of talent," I said, "is a very praiseworthy institution; by correcting one another, and communicating with one another, taste is purified and people cooperate mutually in the progress of human knowledge."

"It's not exactly like that," my Sage told me. "The least literomaniac, for a modest sum, can buy the privilege of being a member of this Academy of sorts, with the right to demand the applause of his colleagues once a week, and that of four hundred complaisant listeners once a month. It's a tribunal of indulgence, in which the self-esteem that has erected it condemns the jaws and ears of its judges to torture."

"Tell me about scientific societies," I said. "Are there many of them in this country?"

"Too few to reduce the arrogance of their members, and too many to honor talent. The Academic throne is for some the tomb of their genius and for others the proof of the genius they do not have. The latter reason in this manner: the members of the Society ought to have a distinguished merit; I am a member, therefore I have a distinguished merit. It isn't talent that these Messieurs demand in their new member, but he is obliged to prove that he has never written or voiced any maxims contrary to those received in the august Society; it is necessary that he finds the means of pleasing the preponderant members, of cajoling them, of being very attentive to them. Like a man flirting with a coquette, he has to smile at their puns, like their friends, detest their antagonists; in sum, wipe his nose, spit, cough and applaud like them."

"Are you a member of any Academies?" I asked my Sage.

"No," he replied. "But I'd rather people ask me why I'm not than have them ask me why I am..."

We were interrupted by the sound of a bell, which announced the opening of the session. The first reader spoke for a long time about apportionment, commodities, net product, taxes, etc. Another reader appeared, triumphant at having demonstrated that $a + b = x - y$. People were succumbing to the weight of ennui when a distinguished scientist came forward. Everyone's attention reawakened. He spoke about a science unknown to the majority of his listeners, a mysterious science, renewed for some time, of an ancient people. He spoke a great deal about "pure fire," the "humid radical," number, the "universal tree," "pure and intermediary agents," the "intellectual center," the "amalgamated essence" etc. I could not resist the learned and overwhelming dissertation, and fell asleep to the sound of "the reaction of beings and secondary powers."[13]

---

[13] Author's note: "If my uncle had read the book of *La Verité* in two volumes, and that of *Le Tableau naturel des rapports qui existent entre Dieu, l'Homme et l'Univers, etc.*, also in two volumes, he would have noticed that that renewed science of the Greeks and Egyptians is beginning to be reintroduced into France." Although it is not the only possible contender, the

I was still asleep when the sound of several instruments woke me up with a start. Fearing that the audience might go away discontented, and to banish from their brains the soporific vapors that Science had introduced, someone had had the good idea of concluding the session with pleasant music. It is what is known as sending people away with a pleasant taste in the mouth.

"With regard to music," I asked my Sage, "what is its condition in this land of the Moon?"

"A man who made music himself," he told me, "sustained some time ago that there is none. Two famous musicians came after him; they gave rise to sects and occasioned long quarrels. Those discords between people who make a profession of harmony offer evidence against the perfection of their Art..."

XI. The Mores of the Moon

The aerostatic experiment that I had carried out caused a great sensation in the capital. Among scientists it was talked about either as something insane or something very ordinary, among reasonable people as an interesting discovery, and among people belongs to what is known as high society as a curiosity, a new fashion. Everyone wanted to make my acquaintance; everyone claimed to have eaten with me and conversed with my in a familiar fashion, although many had not.

---

first reference might be to *La Verité sortant du puits heretique* (1753), which bears the unlikely signature Cosmocole Philovite. The other work cited appears in several secondary lists as a text dealing with Freemasonry; the citation in a 1786 book of *Observations sure la franc-maçonnerie, le martinisme, etc.* is not the only one to cite it immediately after a text entitled *Des Erreurs & de la Vérité*, which suggests that Dulaure might have accidentally abridged the earlier title, had he found it in an earlier list of a similar sort.

My Sage and I were invited to several Societies. One day, we went to one that was reputed to be very fashionable.

"An Observer ought to see everything," I said. "Let's go to observe."

On the way we went through a superb garden; the luxury and elegance of the people walking there were its finest ornament.

"Everything here respires wellbeing, ease or wealth," I said to my Sage.

"The wellbeing that you attribute to this brilliant crowd," he said, "is only apparent; it is to that appearance that people sacrifice, without examination, the laws of decency and Nature. That striking exterior and luxury is the parent of vices; it has taken the place of virtues; the consideration they attract has usurped them entirely. A man is not respected either for his probity or his morals, but for his carriages and his lackeys. It is not only among the opulent that evil dominates; among people of mediocre fortune it damages both the moral and physical faculties; to satisfy the requirements of opinion, the less fortunate man cuts back on the most pressing needs of Nature. A hairdresser or a merchant of fashionable clothing often takes home the supper of our most frugal housewives. Fops deceive some by means of a false glamour, and ruin others by means of obligatory credit; such a man makes himself considered by his attire and is greatly proud of its merit; it is the only one he has, and he owes it all to his tailor..."

Scarcely had we arrived at the house where we were expected than the Lady had us introduced into her dressing-room; she absolutely wished it. The Divinity of that lovely Temple, while putting the final touches to the fashioning of her beauty, was receiving the incense of a few admirers. She responded to it by exercising the fortunate art of laughter, becoming impatient and being distracted, at will.

"This hat is good for me," she said, standing up to go out. "It gives me a girlish air which suits me infinitely."

Playing the simpleton, she ran into the drawing room where the company was, and threw her arms around the necks of all the ladies, embracing them very tenderly.

"What amity and cordiality the women of this country show to one another!" I said in a low voice to my comrade.

"These demonstrations," he replied, "are scenes that the women have agreed among themselves to play. They want to give the men who see them a specimen of their tenderness, and the women they caress a proof of their talent for artifice. The majority of women detest one another; those that they like the most are those that they hate the least."

After having distributed general compliments, everyone wanted news, and everyone promised to tell a scandalous story. It was a tribute that was paid on a daily basis for the right to be admitted there.

"Yesterday," said a man, "I was with Madame   ; she is crazier than one can imagine. One of her creditors came to paint the picture of his parlous state. 'I'm ruined and without resource, the unfortunate told her, if you don't pay right away. It's not so much for me as for my wife and children; they'll be reduced to the utmost poverty. You will be rendering life to a desperate family of you pay me what you owe.'

"Initially moved by the unfortunate fellow's tears, she was about to satisfy him when a reflection stopped her. 'I'm in despair, she said, 'at being unable to give you that sum, but I need it to buy fashionable earrings for the ball.'"

Everyone started laughing except my comrade and me.

A self-important little person took the floor. "You know Madame ***? There are few people who know her as well as her dear husband. Recently, in her boudoir with one of her lovers, she was so busy receiving the testimonies of his ardor that she neglected the precautions demanded by the mysteries of amour. All the doors were open.

"The woman is entirely wrapped up in what she is doing. Her husband comes in without being heard and, seeing the breach that is being made in conjugal honor, cries, furiously: 'My God, Madame, you ought to close the doors! To what would you be exposing yourself is someone other than me had come in?'"

A man with a clerical collar and a short cloak announced an adventure in which he had played a role; after apologizing for the obligation in which he found himself to recount his good fortune, he commenced:

"It is in the village, our poets say, that innocence and candor reign; you shall judge whether the gentlemen in question are mistaken. I was in a small provincial burg where, to pass the time, I was paying court to the charming wife of the local Aesculapius. Without much difficulty I persuaded that village beauty that nothing was more tedious and provincial than being faithful to her husband, which was not the custom in elegant society. Everyone knows how passionate provincial women are to copy rigorously all the manners of the capital.

"One evening, reassured by the absence of her husband, my beauty wanted to try out the manners in question. I had already compared her favorably several times to women in high society, and the night was advanced during that sweet exercise when, by an inconceivable fatality, the husband arrived and obliged me to tear myself away from the arms of pleasure.

"This was the cause of my disappointment. Under the pretext of caring for the invalids of the vicinity, the doctor had announced that he would not be home that night, but he was actually due to relieve his amorous ardor in the arms of the local president's wife, who believed that the president was away dealing with affairs of the magistracy. The latter, however, had deceived his chaste spouse in order to fly to his tender beloved, the lieutenant's wife, whose husband really was absent on more serious business.

"The lieutenant's wife was savoring securely, with her dear president, a pleasure that prohibition rendered more piquant; the president's wife was happy in the arms of the doctor, and the doctor's wife, without being aware of it, was avenging herself in mine for her husband's infidelity. That chain of infidelities, that mutual displacement, that triple exchange of pleasure, would have been an impenetrable mystery for each of its initiates, but for one of those blows of fate that human prudence cannot anticipate. Expect the most terrible catastrophe.

"The lieutenant had forgotten a document essential to his voyage; he arrives unexpectedly, and sees with his own eyes…how dangerous unexpected returns by husbands are to a household. Men of law rarely launch suits against one another; the lieutenant placidly sent the president away, who, on returning home, expelled the doctor, who came to expel me in his turn.

"I can say in praise of the interested parties, that everything was returned to its place without overmuch fuss. Fortunately my estate as a bachelor did not permit me to find a wife on going home; I would have experienced the same fate as the husbands, and that series of incontinences would doubtless have been perpetuated to the lowest orders of the inhabitants."

The abbé,[14] seeing that his story had amused, did not stop talking. He was a charming man, that abbé!

"I can no longer write verses," he said. "Poetry impassions me too much and that gives me bad nerves." He assured us that he was working on a big book on an entirely new subject. "Artful politeness," he continued, in the gravest tone, "and gallant knavery make women into actresses who are always on stage, and conceal the depths of their hearts. I want, however, to decipher their veritable sentiments and put their

---

[14] Author's note: "In order to be more laconic I have translated the words of the Lunar idiom into equivalents in the French language. For instance, a man who lives at the expense of public credulity, who knows nothing and undertakes everything, who obtains by importunity that which ought to be the recompense of merit, who does nothing but solicit, I have called a "man of projects, a schemer." A priest who fulfils no other function than that of transporting the pleasure of his coquetry and insipidity to the homes of all the priestesses I have called an "abbé," and so on. [Note by my poor uncle.]"

soul in evidence. In order to succeed in that I seize the brief instants when women are themselves; I extract Nature from the fact.

"For example, while the keen sensations of voluptuousness plunge a beauty into the delirium of amour, among the sobs and surges to pleasure, the mouth babbles halting words, which are the language of Nature and gratitude. Those flashes of sincerity are too precious not to focus the attention of the Philosopher, so I have copied faithfully all the pretty exclamations that my good fortune has permitted me to collect. Such a Work has a right to lease the most severe public; I propose to submit it to the censure of the Academy. It will not fail to have its approval, as well as the red stamp. The production will bring me a great deal of honor..."

After the chatter had continued for a long time in the same tone, the conversation came round to spectacles. The women permitted themselves to judge the actors and the authors at the whim of their caprices; extravagance and bad taste seemed to dictate their judgments, and yet the men who were listening to them, far from sustaining the cause of reason, allowed it to be outraged by the ladies in question and applauded their decisions.

We left then, and I asked my companion why the men took pleasure in deceiving the women thus, avoiding enlightening them.

"That's not the point," he replied. "That would be to contradict them, and one never contradicts the ladies. Besides which, it's an established axiom of Society that a pretty woman is permitted to be unreasonable, to say and do foolish things, which are more gallantly described as caprices. As many of them believe themselves to be pretty, many of them use that permission, and it is a capital crime of lèse-gallantry for a man to suggest to a lady that she is not completely right. There are few men who would risk being criminal to that extent, and the majority prefer to applaud the imaginative vertigos of the fair sex..."

XII. How I met Oë again, and what happened

"O unique motor of souls! O most powerful of the Gods of the Earth! Sacred metal gold, you separate friends, you corrupt innocence, you give importance to the stupid, consideration to the wicked; you breed and embellish vice, you cover virtue in opprobrium, you make ingrates. Sacred metal gold, in spite of your prodigies, you never make the ambitious man wise, nor the schemer into an honest man..."

It was thus that my sage comrade spoke, after having received the news of a treason even stranger for him than it was for me.

I had been occupied for some time in the construction of an aerostatic machine for my departure for the Earth, before which I counted on carrying out a public experiment that ought to ensure me the honor of the discovery in that country, when I learned that my traveling companion Oë, the perfidious Oë, had stolen that sweet satisfaction from me and had eclipsed all my projects of glory.

Having remembered the method that I had employed in his presence, he had succeeded, with the aid of a few Physicists, in fabricating a Balloon, and had amassed an immense sum by subscription.

I wanted to tempt his honesty, so I presented myself during his experiment. He had the audacity to refuse to see me or recognize me.

I eventually encountered him in a Society; I was about to heap him with reproaches but he admitted himself, without blushing, the irregularity of his conduct—which, according to him, was nothing but perfectly ordinary. In declaring to me that his only objective had been the fortune rather than the glory, he promised to publish authentically that it was to me that the discovery belonged. Thus the prize was divided into two lots: money and honor, and each of us was served in accordance with his inclination: the money for Oë and the honor for me.

XIII. My Departure from the Moon

Let us flee this ingrate planet, I said to myself; *let us fly back to Earth and regain my homeland, the good city of Paris. One does not find schemers by prospectus there, ignorant men of projects who elevate their fortune and glory at the expense of the labor of others. There is not so much decency, but there is virtue; there is not so much honesty, but it is probity that reigns in that good city of Paris. Wives are faithful to their husbands there, and one cannot reproach the latter for the cowardly complaisance, the shameful traffic in conjugal honor that plunges the husbands of the Moon into abysms of turpitude. One does not encounter priests there whose carriages splash or run over pedestrians; it is a good city, the city of Paris. The abbés, in conformity with their holy institutions, live there with a surprising regularity of conduct; they are neither gallants not fops. None are seen who employ revenues consecrated to alms and divine services in the propagation of luxury and debauchery. Monks are new at odds there; they are united like brothers. Bishops only come there for indispensable matters of business; they normally stay in their Dioceses, where they are models of humility, sobriety and disinterest. For morals, long live our good city of Paris! Let's fly back there.*[15]

In consequence, I had constructed four aerostatic balloons, which I had attached to the four corners of a kind of

---

[15] Author's note: "It is evident that my poor uncle was scarcely well-informed about the mores of his own country; he had not taken the trouble to observe Paris. He thought he was at the center of the capital when he was at the Luxembourg, in the midst of a committee of bourgeois in full dress, where he played politics all afternoon. It is excusable not to know one's own country, and praiseworthy to speak well of it; too many people slander it. For instance, a satirical poet has dared to say of elegant abbés: 'All radiant with vice, from boudoir to boudoir, the benefits flow.'"

boat, in which there was an enormous bellows, the force of whose wind acting inside the machine ought to overcome the atmospheric wind, or at least resist it and serve for steering.[16]

All the dispositions for my departure having been concluded, I announced publicly that I was about to make an atmospheric journey. That announcement stirred all minds; some treated my enterprise as folly, while other regarded its execution as possible. Numerous bets were laid and the newspapers wearied their readers with the boasts of those who offered to lose their money for or against the success of my voyage.

A host of Astronomers, Physicists, Moralists and Poets came to solicit ardently the pleasure of being my traveling companions. Each wanted to acquire in the air a reputation that he could not have merited on the ground: ambitious people, whose frenetic enthusiasm excites laughter and pity! To expose one's life audaciously in order to attract the gaze of a curious public momentarily, is the height of vanity. To glorify oneself and raise oneself up higher than one's competitors is to ornament oneself with the merit of a performer of feats of strength. Oh, how I prefer the virtuous ardor of the citizen who precipitates himself into agitated waves, at the peril of his life, to rescue one of his fellows! The great actions of virtue carry their own recompense; those of self-regard wait for publicity. The conduct of those aerial Don Quixotes convinced me of that; when I had told them that I had no intention of returning among them, seeing their hope of collecting the prize of their temerity from their compatriots eclipsed, they suddenly renounced going with me.

I did not have to go to any trouble making my provision of books; every author hastened to pay me the tribute of his

---

[16] Author's note: "Let people refrain from laughing at this means of steering aerostats; it is not as ridiculous as many others that have been proposed. In any case, this one enabled the voyage of my uncle, who had, in truth, neither money nor subscribers."

productions. One would like to be talked about in a country to which one will never go, just as one would like to exist in a time when one is no longer alive.

Poets brought me pretty volumes in a small format, gilded on the edges, ornamented with vignettes and engravings; they bore some resemblance to the elegant individuals who based their merit on their attire.

"Take them anyway," my Sage said to me, who was helping me to choose. "Their lovely covers and images will amuse your nephews' children."

Scholars brought me voluminous quartos and heavy folios.

"Those," he told me, "might be very useful to you in your journey; their specific weight will serve you as ballast."

I made the decision to take off incognito, although I was warned that if some event forced me to come down, the curious would not fail to testify their satisfaction by unusual extravagances;[17] but I was afraid of being assailed at the moment

---

[17] Author's note: "In spite of the pour success of the Lyon aerostat, all the extravagances that a stupid admiration can produce were seen after its fall. One individual got down from his horse, invited the aerial voyagers to mount up and led them away on foot, bridle in hand. Another took of his cloak to cover them. There was a deep and muddy ditch on the rod; several citizens bent down in the ditch and invited another aerial voyager to pass over their backs. Exclamations accompanied their triumphal entry; a spectacle was recommenced for them, people sang to them, they were crowned with laurels, feasts were held in their honor. What service had they rendered their fatherland, those heroes? What fine deeds had they done? A balloon had lifted them up, and their own weight had immediately brought it down to earth." Seven people took off from Lyon in a Montgolfier balloon called *Le Flesselles* on 17 January 1784. More than 100,000 people were said to have watched the ascent, but the balloon tore when it reached 3,000 feet and made a rapid descent, although the passengers es-

of my departure by armed numbskulls who were capable of disturbing the order of my voyage by wanting to share in its glory.[18]

With tears in my eyes I quit the sage observer, the benevolent host who had been such a great help to me. I regretted no one but him in that country; as for Oë, who was so despicable in my eyes, I never heard any further mention of him.

I traversed without accident, by courtesy of the night, the vast reaches of the air, and arrived at my house via the skylight. I embrace my dear nephew and my niece, who were scarcely expecting their poor uncle.

On the way, I made observations of great interest to the Scientists of Earth, to which I intend to impart to my compatriots very soon, as well as an aerographic map on which the different layers of the atmosphere will be represented. I shall prove geometrically that each of those layers is composed of different species of spirits exhaled by the inhabitants of Earth. I shall indicate in a separate article the dangers one runs in traversing those regions of the air, as well as the remedies that it is appropriate to carry there. For example, in traveling

---

caped without serious injury. A commemorative medal was struck bearing the legend: *Que ne peut le Génie* [What can Genius not achieve?]

[18] Author's note: "At the moment when the Lyon aerostat rose up, a vigorous aeromane ran forward, climbed up to the gallery and forced the modern Argonauts to accept him for their travelling companion. Another, more furious, presented himself with two pistols, ready to kill anyone who wanted to go down. In Paris, when Monsieur Blanchard was ready to rise from the Champ-de-Mars, a young fanatic threw himself at the nacelle and attached himself to it so forcefully that several arms could not tear him away. The shocks that the machine experienced broke its wings and allowed a great deal of inflammable air to escape. Finally, he yielded to force and was taken away, in despair not to have been able to participate in the glory of one of our aerostaticians by subscription."

through the region that is composed by the exhalations of cold critics, austere moralists and icy poets, one should be careful to don a thick cloak and a fur bonnet, and to plug one's ears with cotton. For the region of orators, erudites and chronologists, one should equip oneself with volatile alkali and the most violent sternutatories. For that of the jolly abbés, elegant individuals and fops, one should make a provision of gherkins, pepper and all the acids and salts with which insipid and sickly dishes are normally seasoned, etc. etc. etc.

I shall not take long to distribute a reasoned prospectus for that curious Work, which I shall offer to the public by subscription, as is the custom on the Moon. To begin with I shall promise the finest things in the world, and when I have my subscribers' money, the Work will proceed as best I can.

Joseph Méry: *Future Paris*
(1854)

Paris will only truly be Paris in the twentieth century.

One can demolish the old Medieval city, pierce new streets, combine palaces with hyphens, build kilometers of boutiques, plant promenades, invent rivers and hollow out artificial ponds, but Paris, in spite of these fortunate masonic revolutions, will still remain the rainy city, the somber city, the muddy city, the city embarrassed by Henri IV and Boileau.

It necessary, in the end, to render Paris habitable, and above all to institute the divorce of man and the umbrella.

Man was not born to open and close an umbrella until he dies.

The rain has been, since Pharamond was elected under a *pavois*—an umbrella[19]—the jailer of Parisians. Every Parisian is condemned from birth by the rain to ten years in prison.

That has lasted for fourteen centuries.

There have been insurgencies against all tyrannies and they have all been overturned; only two tyrannies still remain: rain and the porter.

"It is the sun of Austerlitz," Napoléon said, several times. Those six words give pause for reflection. There was, therefore, sunshine at Austerlitz, a battle fought on the second of December in the north

We also read, in the history books: "It was a beautiful spectacle: the cuirassiers of Caulaincourt hurling themselves upon the great redoubt, defended by sixty cannons, at the same

---

[19] A *pavois* is actually a kind of rectangular shield or buckler, although it was doubtless sometimes used to fend off raindrops rather than slings and arrows.

49

moment the sun, veiled since the morning, made breastplates of the cavalrymen resplendent."

That scene occurred in the month of September, at Borodino, near Moscow, in a land where the sun is only known by reputation, which has obliged all the tsars, since Peter the Great, always to gaze eastwards, like icy Tantaluses.

Austerlitz, Borodino and Moscow thus prove to us that there is an ingenious method for obtaining sunlight, even in midwinter, even in the heart of the north.

It is a matter of firing numerous cannons.

On the second of December 1805 and the seventh of September 1812, Austerlitz and Borodino would have kept their eternal cupola of rainy mist; fortunately, France passed that way, fired a few thousand cannon shots, and showed the sun to the bewildered Muscovites.

The Russian general Pyotr Bagration, wounded on the great redoubt, pronounced as he fell these memorable words: I die content; I have seen the sun!" He owed that joy to us.

Will these great historic examples be wasted for the future of Paris? No. The remedy will at first be greeted as a paradox; then it will have the fate of all paradoxes; it will emerge from is well, mirror in hand.

The future aediles, exonerated of loans of fifty million, will one day erect twelve cyclopean towers, one per arrondissement: towers a hundred meters high, which will already be superb as viewpoints. The summit of each tower will be equipped with a circular battery of a hundred cannons, and if the slightest could rises at any of the cardinal points, fire away!

The cloud will hold its assembly somewhere other than the Portes Saint-Martin or Saint-Denis; it will burst over the countryside, and fecundate gardens; no trace of it will ever again be seen over Paris.

It is war declared against the enemies of the air.

Too bad for the merchants of umbrellas, successors of Pharamond; they will change métier, like coaching inns and postillions.

Parisians will say every day, as they pass the Vendôme column with dry feet: "There is the sun of Austerlitz! Three hundred and sixty-five suns of Austerlitz per year!

The merchants of umbrellas can sell parasols, if they do not want to change their estate.

But that is not the only service that the twelve towers might render the twelve arrondissements.

Under the last years of the idle reign of Louis Philippe, one saw on the Place du Carrousel a beacon that resembled a miniature sun. A simple trial: the modest germ of something immense that will one day—which is to say, one night—be resplendent over the twenty thousand roofs of the capital.

The luminous power of the beacon of the Carrousel will be multiplied a hundred fold, ten times that if necessary; twelve suns of electric flame will rotate at the summits of the twelve imbrifuginous towers, and every evening the daylight will be reignited after sunset; the odious night, *nox atra*, that mother of crimes, accomplice of thieves and murderers, will be suppressed.

It will be possible to see clearly at midnight.

No more drunken patrols; no more wheezing sentinels; no more rounds; no more gas explosions; no more national guard....

What benefits!

Let us pursue this work of the future.

Another paradox: there are no fountains in Paris. The naiad who believes that the waves sculpted by Jean Goujon belong to her, *fluctus credidit esse suos*, is mistaken.

A naiad is obliged by her profession to make water clear, and the water-carriers only fish in troubled waters in the fountains of Paris.

How is it that Paris, an essentially academic city, a city that imitates the Romans in comedies, tragedies, triumphal arches, votive columns, temples and popular sedition to such an extent that Paris would have lived for fourteen centuries with its arms crossed if Rome had not invented columns, tragedies, battles, Places Vendôme, Chambre des Députés, full cisterns, geniuses suspended on the right foot, Renown, circuses, the seditions of the forum, Brutuses, Cassiuses, civil wars. Alexandrine verses, advocates, triumphal arches, porters, Academicians, Champs-de-Mars, insulting slaves, rostral columns, garden statues, liberated women and saturnalia...how is it, I repeat, that Paris has forgotten aqueducts of spring-water in its innumerable imitations?

Aqueducts! What a lacuna!

The Romans had a river too, a yellow river like the Seine; they could have caused specimens of the unfiltered Tiber to run through artificial fountains, but their aediles had too much respect for the lips of the sovereign people. They constructed, at enormous expense, infinite successions of monumental lines, which brought water to the sovereign people over triumphal arches, according to Chateaubriand's beautiful expression.

As soon as a spring of superior quality was discovered, an Eau Laffite, a Naiad Chambertin, like virgin water, that liquid treasure was captured, and dispatched to the thirsty lips of the Romans across thirty kilometers of aqueducts.

Too bad for the merchants of adulterated Falernian, or the ungodly substance baptized lustral water! The people, in love with the new naiad, intoxicated themselves in a hydraulic orgy, and deserted the altars of the false Bacchuses, crowned with ivy, at the corn-stalk crossroads.

The Parisian imitation will be belated, but it will come.

Paris will have serious fountains, like the Barcaccia, the Trevi and the Piazza Navona.

It is time that water was drunk in the département of the Seine.

The false Bacchus has done enough harm to the lovers of liquefied campeachy.[20]

The Seine, like the Tiber, is a purveyor of bathing stations or a school of natation. It does not flow in order to slake

---

[20] Campeachy is an American shrub from whose dark heartwood dark red and black dyes used to be extracted.

the thirst of human throats; if one saw in a solar microscope the infamous atoms it ferries, one would die of thirst rather than drink a glass of its water.

In the Midi, the flavorsome bounty of spring water renders people sober and spares them the vice of drunkenness.

The hideous locution *pourboire*,[21] passed into the mores of the North, would cause a southern worker to wilt, if he made use of it. One does not fortify oneself there with alcoholized campeachy.

In Rome, the athletes drank water; Milo of Crotona never went into a wine-merchant's shop, and he could stun a bull with a blow of his fist. If we think that hyperbole, let us say a calf, and that is still not bad.

The hills surrounding Paris are immense reservoirs, which are only awaiting aqueducts and joint-stock companies to inundate our fountains with virgin naiads. They will come from the heights of Meudon, Franconville, Ermont, Saint-Leu-Taverny and all the other hills and petty mountains neighboring Paris, as the heights of Soratte and Tibur neighbored Rome at an almost equal distance.

Providence never places reservoirs too far distant from thirsty lips, having said: Give to them who are thirsty to drink. That order was not addressed to wine-merchants.

That same good Providence watches over Paris with a thoroughly maternal care, and its vigilance increases as the paths of circulation are encumbered with wheels, horses and pedestrians.

Another thing that the future promises

What we see today on our boulevards cannot last long; it imposes too many cares on Providence, the economical guardian of public cobblestones and macadam. Choose a point of observation on the boulevard—for example, the area that separates the Passage Jouffroy from the Passage des Panoramas. One bears witness, for hours on end, to a strange spectacle.

---

[21] Literally "for a drink"—the conventional way of referring to a tip.

In the middle roll, march, fly and gallop, in a frightful pell-mell, fiacres, omnibuses, coupés, citizens, milords, rigs, handcarts, big carts, diligences, tilburys, artillery trains, and every machine ever invented for breaking cobblestones, crushing toes, killing horses, deafening ears and stopping traffic.

In that turbulence, hardy pedestrians, on tiptoe, umbrellas in hand, fight madly, in greater danger than Turks during a sortie from Silistra.[22]

On the threshold of the passages men and women, as immobile as the shades of the Styx, *ripae ulterioris amore*,[23] await the least dangerous moment traverse the boulevard bristling with perils: that Strait of Magellan where the mobile reefs cross paths; that long archipelago of harnessed Cyclades pursuing travelers; that dark gulf in which two eyes are insufficient to see Charybdis to the left and Scylla to the right.

And we are still in the first epoch of Aurelian Paris! The Appian Way has not yet planted its two boundary markers on the two seas. Come a complete railway, merely come the year 1854, and we shall see pedestrians who are too prudent or pusillanimous retained for entire days on one of the two sides of the boulevard, without finding a faint momentary clearing to promise them a fortunate crossing.

The shades of the Styx sometimes waited for a century to pass over to the other side, but they had the patience that death and the absence of business bring. The day that sees a distraction of Providence over that section of the boulevard will also see a proposal burst forth from the bosom of the Parisian aediles. A municipal voice will say: "Since bridges are thrown over dead rivers, it is necessary to throw them over living rivers."

---

[22] Silistra was an Ottoman fortified town besieged and bombarded by the Russians in 1854 during the Crimean War.
[23] "longing for the further bank"—the quotation is from Virgil's *Aeneid.*

Perhaps shareholders will come together to build those bridges at their expense, and they will make fortunes if they are authorized.

The first bridge, which will serve as a model, will be constructed between the Passages Jouffroy and les Panoramas, at the confluence of two enormous cities, one of which always has urgent business in the other.

That bridge will have a colossal arch; people will cross it by mounting two broad staircases; it will be surmounted by a covered gallery with restaurants, cafes and reading rooms, with windows opening on to the two horizons of the boulevard, The success of the first bridge will determine other shareholders to operate at other points.

The boulevards will be traversed as the Seine is traversed, from the Invalides to the Jardin des Plantes; the perils of the crossing will be suppressed over land and over water, and Providence will breaths again.

Those bridges thrown over the boulevards will create a new kind of monumental architecture; they will unite their great lines with the infinite roofs of edifices and the majestic perspectives of horizons. But of all these ameliorations promised for the future, the most important is incontrovertibly the one that will purify the Parisian atmosphere, render rain less frequent and maintain at a distance the intolerable cloud that spits eternally in the face of an honest population.

Since Pharamond committed the enormous fault of founding a city on terrain always exposed to the overflow of the urn of the sad Hyades, it is necessary to think of doing our best to correct the topographical blunder of that royal industrialist, manufacturer of bucklers.

So, I am glad to return to the topic of those twelve imbrifuginous towers that ought to dissipate, without notice, assemblages of cloud over the city of Paris.

Artillery, like all poisons, caries within itself a mysterious remedy.

God would not have permitted gunpowder to be invented if it were only to serve eternally for the destruction of human beings.

The future of the world is the extinction of war; it is peace.

Great cities have their maladies, like individuals; rain is the greatest of urban scourges; it soaks edifices, undermines walls, pierces roofs and produces annoyance, rheumatism and damp. It pleases half a dozen theater directors, and that is all; it ruins all other public establishments. The Tivoli gardens disappeared after a summer of a hundred and fifty rainy days.

It is therefore necessary to master that scourge, as has been done for lightning; since Franklin has snatched lightning from the sky, *eripuit coelo fulmen*, one can send the rain back to the clouds; it is easier.

By consulting a collection of the *Moniteur* from the year 1792 one can see this sentence reproduced repeatedly, almost identically: "As soon as the cortege set off, the heavens, which until then had been pluvious, resumed their serenity, and the sun shone with all its brightness."

The sun has illuminated the solemn entrance to Paris on horseback of all governments; the entrance of kings, of dictators, republic, provisional governments, quasi-legitimate monarchs, presidents and emperors. Is the sun glad to see such ceremonies and to give them all the same approval? Not in the least. That is all same to the sun.

The fact is that at the moment when equestrian governments enter Paris, a hundred cannon shots are fired, and the clouds take flight, like rioters.

Like it or not, the sun is then obliged to watch the cortege pass by, and cover it with radiance.

Now, imagine the effect of the imbrifuginous artillery when it operates, no longer in the flower-bed of the Invalides, but on towers a hundred meters high, firing on the clouds at point-blank range!

The Académie des Sciences excepted, does the result seem to anyone to be in doubt?

Let us imagine the worst-case scenario and suppose that those twelve towers never do work as umbrellas, that they have less efficacy than the cannons of Austerlitz, Moscow and the Invalides and that, in sum, they remain standing, in their monumental inutility, like the fortifications built by Louis Philippe around Paris.

Well, they can be given other purposes: first of all, that of serving as cyclopean candelabras for nocturnal suns of electric gas, and, if necessary, of announcing veridically, by the hand of an artillerist timekeeper, the four divisions of the hours to those worthy Parisians who spend half their lives asking what time it is.

Invalid watches and deceptive clocks would then find a sonorous corrective every fifteen minutes throughout the day.

Finally, if, as we imagine, those twelve towers do respond to the triple destination of chasing away the clouds, illuminating Paris and keeping time, the good people will have, there, before them, a continual amusement, less costly and just as exciting as the lottery.

That aerial warfare, the only one possible in a very near future, will be of ever-renewed and never-exhausted interest,

The people will not have to consult bulletins and telegraphic dispatches; they will read every battle on the great page of the sky.

In summer, the southerly wind, the generalissimo of the clouds, will lead its army, out of habitude, toward the frontiers of Paris. The tower of the tenth arrondissement will sound the alarm cannon, and the response will come all along the line, with the voices of Austerlitz.

It will always be very short, but always very decisive.

If the battle were prolonged, the people would waste too much time in the public squares and on the rooftops.

Why did Louis Philippe not employ to combat the ever-present rain a fraction of the millions consecrated circularly to combat enemies who never presented themselves?

The future, which always comes too late for the living, will see these things, and many others too, for the world is born, nowadays, of the union of steam and the railways. Everything that existed the day before yesterday no longer has any reason for being; the new order is already the antipodes of the old; the impossible will regenerate the world; interests are never disunited, they combine; Nelson fraternizes with d'Estaing, there is no longer any distance; wheels are wings, mountains corridors, ships bridges, oceans streams.

What, then, will come to pass after our generation?

It is permissible to suppose the incredible, to dream of the marvelous, to admit the infinite. Our fortunate children will recommence Genesis

Let us be our children!

Charles Epheyre: *Sister Marthe*
(1899)

I

On returning home that evening, at five o'clock, Laurent Verdine found a telegram thus conceived: *My grandmother dead at the Château de Plancheuille. Come. George Olivier.*

Immediately, Laurent went to consult a railway timetable. Plancheuille is a few kilometers from Moulins. By leaving Paris that evening, he could arrive there in the morning.

He did not hesitate for a moment. Was he not George's best friend, his only friend? So, without losing a minute, he got ready to leave. Three or four books, a few clothes, a good blanket, the final instructions to the old maidservant who served as his housekeeper, and that was it: *en route*. Here he is in the carriage.

George de Plancheuille! Yes, certainly, he is his best friend.

And he remembered the great voyage they had made together, eight years ago already, across the Atlantic, into the immense Brazilian forests, from Rio to the Cordilleras, through perils and emotions of all kinds.

Since school, their amity had been very tender. Laurent Verdine, the son of a petty provincial physician, and George, the son of General Olivier de Plancheuille, conceived for one another, at the beginning of life, one of those profound and precocious sympathies that lasts a lifetime and resists all storms. One day, not long after receiving their baccalaureates, they had left together for America.

For that sudden impulse, Laurent was criticized by everyone, but he was recalcitrant to all discipline. He dared to adopt insouciance as a principle, and he had the enormous and unforgivable audacity to think for himself. Now, in order to succeed it is necessary to pay much less heed to one's own opinion than those of others. Laurent was, in consequence, an eccentric, and he would have merited being punished for his escapade.

He was not punished, though. Far from it. Having returned to France he had quickly acquired one of the first ranks among the students, his contemporaries. A hospital intern, and now a doctor. How time flies! A doctor already. But that is only a first step; there are other grades to conquer. Above all, before him, a world of facts, all mysterious, all interesting, to investigate and analyze.

And Laurent sensed himself gripped by a kind of amorous passion for his art, uncommon in our skeptical and positive era.

At full steam, the train took Laurent far from Paris. He saw filing past, by the fantastic light of the moon, fields, rivers, bridges, hills, long roads planted with trees, villages with their small houses and thatched cottages; and while looking at them, Laurent recalled the events that had traversed his life, almost as fleetingly as those passing silhouettes: his voyage, his endeavors, his friendships, his amours. He stirred in his mind the adventurous studies he had undertaken of the strange forms of human intelligence, that mystery of mysteries; and he felt himself attracted, and simultaneously frightened, but those extraordinary depths, bottomless abysms where everything is unknown. He mingled the past and the future, hopes and regrets. Where would his curiosity end? In other worlds, perhaps...

He woke up at Moulins.

Still half asleep, he gets down from the carriage and, in the courtyard of the station, hails a carriage hitched to two small, vigorous horses; and, briskly, at a crack of the whip that envelops them, the two small hoses go through the town.

Now Laurent is no longer dreaming about magnetism and medicine; he is thinking about the people he will find at Plancheuille: his friend George; the old grandmother who has just died, George's father, General Olivier de Plancheuille, the simplest and most honest of men.

In spite of everything, he will not remain long in that family in mourning. What endeavors await him! In two days for sure, Laurent will return to Paris.

II

At the Château de Plancheuille, the first person Laurent saw was his friend George, who embraced him tenderly, with tears in his eyes.

"Poor grandmother," he said. "She died every peacefully. At her age, death has no shock. How good you are to have come. But you're going to stay here for a few days; you'll keep my father company—he's very sad. And I'll introduce you to my wife; you saw her on our wedding day, a few months ago, but since then…but I'll take you to your room first."

Laurent's room was on the ground floor. A glazed door illuminated it, from which one could go directly into the park. Close by, slightly to the rear, was a chapel that seemed to be attached to the château. A path planted with linden trees departed from the chapel to end at a small gate. Beyond that gate the village commenced: an assemblage of houses, whose thatch-covered pitched roofs Laurent could make out.

A few moments later, in the drawing room, the General shook Laurent's hand forcefully, as if he wanted to break it.

"Thank you, my dear Laurent, thank you! Oh, we're suffering a cruel ordeal. We've seen many things, we old ones. I've seen my wife die…I've seen Sedan…I've seen many other horrors too. Well, the death of my poor old mother has moved me more than all the rest. Once again, thank you, for George and myself."

The funeral ceremony was to take place the following day. Laurent told himself that he would leave thereafter, but he had a long day to spend at Plancheuille. How should he employ it that interminable day?

To remove himself from the heavy atmosphere of a mortuary house, he set out alone, wandering through the park and its surrounding area. He walked in that fashion all day, following the meanders of the stream that snaked through the meadows.

Although he was a Parisian, and a skeptic, Laurent was something of a poet. Every generous spirit has a particle of poetry vibrating within it. That beautiful September day inflated his heart with a sort of vague tenderness for things and for people.

Perhaps happiness is here. Why struggle and strive, battle back there in Paris, lost in that whirlwind of hatreds jealousies and rivalries? Why not live here, in the bosom of this beneficent nature? Here, one can love people freely, without worrying about their ambitions and their disputes. One loves them all the more because one is further away from them.

When he returned to the château, a little fatigued, the sun had just set. It seemed that the horizon was ablaze with an immense and magnificent conflagration, a grandiose spectacle that Laurent contemplated amorously for a long time. But the shadows fell rapidly, and the contours of the trees, the chapel and the village were lost in the increasing gloom.

Suddenly, in the midst of the silence, Laurent heard the sounds of an organ vibrating nearby. Laurent recognized Gounod's *Ave Maria*. The melodious and pure song, which resounded in the shadow and silence of the dusk, was powerfully harmonious. Laurent listened delightedly.

Who can play the organ here at Plancheuille, he thought. *Doubtless it's George's wife.*

Fundamentally, however, he did not care about knowing the name of the organist. He abandoned himself to the charm of the delightful music, and, leaning on the window-sill, breathed in all the scents of the autumn, drawing life and youth into his lungs, allowing his emotion to increase.

The *Ave Maria* concluded. Laurent heard the door of the chapel close. He leaned out in order to see who came out, but he only saw a shadow gliding through the trees of the pathway. Then, everything returned to silence. So it was not George's wife. Who, then?

That evening, at supper, in the main hall of the château, he made the acquaintance of a new guest, the village curé. Abbé Lenègre, a slightly rustic individual, but paternal and acute.

A fine type specimen of the country curé! George thought.

During the dinner, he had a desire to ask the name of the man or woman he had head playing the organ so well, but a kind of false shame restrained him. He was afraid of revealing the extent to which he had been moved. Sometimes, one has a modesty regarding one's emotions; one hides them as if one ought to blush at them.

The General and his son, anxious to render their hospitality amiable, sought to make their guest forget the sad duty that he had come to accomplish. They chatted cordially, with simplicity, but they separated at an early hour.

"Will you permit me to walk back to the presbytery with you?" Laurent said to the old priest.

"Oh, the presbytery isn't far, but I'll accept, in order to have the pleasure of chatting with you for a few minutes more."

After leaving the château, they went past the chapel. Laurent could not help asking: "Is that your church, Monsieur le Curé?"

"Yes," the man said, "that's my church. The old one burned down twenty years ago; it was the General who had this one built, until we're given a veritable parish church. We've been waiting for twenty years, without yet being able to find the necessary funds. We are, alas, living in impious times…and doubtless you yourself…"

"No, Monsieur," said Laurent, smiling. "Not as much as you suppose. The sentiments of poor physicians are greatly calumniated. Truly, we're able to respect people everywhere they're found. And then, how can one not be moved when one sees, as in the de Plancheuille family, the patriarchal traditions of old revived? In fact, since we're talking about the chapel, I heard the sounds of an organ there before dinner. You have an organ and an organist, then? A talented organist, in fact!"

"Oh, you noticed…," said the curé. "It was doubtless Sister Marthe."

"Sister Marthe?"

"Yes, one of our nuns. I say nun, although she's only a novice as yet—but she's going to make her vows in a few weeks. She does have talent, doesn't she?"

"A great deal of talent, Monsieur le Curé. I can say that to you with some knowledge of the case, because, such as you see me and although you take me for an impious individual, I can play the organ. It would take too long to tell you by what series of hazards I was provided with that talent to please, but in sum, as well as I can, I too play the organ. Well, truly, Sister Marthe has a great deal of talent. So you have a convent here?"

"A convent, certainly not, but a school. We owe that to the General too. The school is maintained by the Sisters of Saint Vincent de Paul—this is their domicile, here."

Laurent and the curé had passed through the gate that terminated the park and were passing a large white house, on the roof of which was a cross that was outlined in black against the starry sky.

"Well, my young friend, that Sister Marthe who comes every evening to play in the chapel is very ill, poor child, and even…by what stupidity, unworthy of my age, have I not thought of talking to you about her? You must examine her— you might perhaps have some good medical advice to give her. Yes, that's right! Come to collect me at the presbytery tomorrow morning, before the ceremony, at eight o'clock. I'll bring you here, to the sisters' house. You'll see Sister Marthe, and you'll be able to tell us whether anything can be done to save her."

"She's consumptive I assume?"

"Consumptive? Alas I fear so. That's a great sadness for us, because Sister Marthe is one of our most valiant nuns. It requires great courage, young man, to get the alphabet into the reluctant heads of our little montagnards. Well, Sister Marthe spends her day in that ingrate task. When she has a free moment, in the evening, after class, she goes to play the organ in the chapel. In any case, at tomorrow's sad ceremony, you'll hear her young pupils, and you'll observe that they have good voices and can sing in tune. Oh, my dear doctor, if you could save Sister Marthe, you would be doing a very good deed!"

"We can do very little, alas, but I promise you that I shall do my best. Tell me, Monsieur le Curé, how did she learn to play the organ? Is it you who gave her lessons?"

"No, indeed. I'm only a layman...in musical terms, that is...incapable of teaching anything but the catechism. But Sister Marthe has been to Paris; she received an excellent education, and between ourselves, her life has even been a trifle romantic. I'd tell you about it if it weren't so late." He fished out his watch, lost in the pocket of his soutane. "I thought so! Eleven o'clock! It's practically debauchery. Here we are at the presbytery, young man. *Au revoir*—until tomorrow morning. I'm counting on you."

With that, Laurent returned to the château. He went to bed and to sleep—a peaceful sleep—without giving any further thought to the curé or to Sister Marthe. The mystery of the organ was clarified; there was no longer anything interesting about it.

III

Early the next morning, Laurent got up. A light mist covered the depths of the valley like a fine gauze. Feeling fine, Laurent opened his window, stepped through and went to the village rapidly. When he arrived at the presbytery he saw the aged curé walking in his garden, his breviary in his hand.

"Ah! You're punctual, it appears, Doctor. Well, come in, and come and look at my roses. But that scarcely interests you, I see—you'd rather hear the story of Sister Marthe. Look, sit down here, under this honeysuckle bower...

"Sister Marthe was brought up in Paris, in a large convent, very famous, which she had entered as a child. She was an orphan, it's said, and no one came to see her. In the vacations, when the other little girls returned joyfully to the paternal hearth, she stayed at the convent, all alone, with the superior and the other nuns. She wasn't entirely abandoned, though, for she had a guardian, a very rich and very serious gentleman, who came to visit her at rare intervals to inform himself regarding her work, her pleasures and her troubles, bringing her bonbons, toys and books.

"One day, the superior called Angèle—that was Sister Marthe's name prior to her novitiate—and said: 'My child, a great misfortune has struck you. Your guardian has died suddenly. Have courage, my dear daughter, and pray for him.'

"The next day, the superior summoned Angèle again. 'My daughter, the destines of God are impenetrable. You are not a orphan, because your mother is not dead. She is unfortunate; she is poor; she is asking for you. Would you like to go and live with her?'

"'Oh yes!' Angèle cried.

"The superior sighed sadly, embraced Angèle, and Angèle left."

"Well, we're now in the heart of romanticism," said Laurent.

"Alas, the rest is not at all romantic. Angèle's mother was a peasant woman, a true peasant woman who had once been quite pretty and flighty. You understand me, don't you? And you understand who Angèle's guardian was? With him dead, having died without a testament, Angèle and her mother were abandoned. The two of them lived thus in black poverty, especially harsh for Angèle, who was not used to working in the fields or to domestic chores. Think of it! To pass from the richest convent in Paris to a miserable thatched cottage!"

"Does Sister Marthe know that her guardian was her father?"

"Oh, great God, no!" said the curé. "Her mother's honor must be sacred in the eyes of a child. No one has ever had the courage to tell her the truth, and I wouldn't have told you the whole story if I didn't take you for a gallant man, incapable of an indiscretion. The superior of the convent in Paris told me everything, but Sister Marthe doesn't know, and has no need to know, any more...

"To conclude, I'll tell you that Angèle's mother soon died. The poor child, entirely abandoned, wrote to the superior of the convent, declaring that she wanted to be a nun. And, in fact, what other future was there for her? She had received the education of a great lady; could she become a peasant again? So young Angèle went back to the convent, and she was sent to us here in order to complete her novitiate.

"Unfortunately, her health is very fragile. Each of the dolorous events of her life has taken its toll on her delicate organism. She's very nervous, almost unhealthily nervous, and subject to serious crises that she hides as best she can, and which can't help but make us anxious. Apart from her malady of the chest, there's some affliction of the nervous system—a neurosis, as you say. George has told me that you've studied that kind of malady. Truly, I believe that you might be able to do a great deal for her. Now, let's go to see her, for the ceremony is at ten, and time is a little short."

The superior of the Plancheuille school, a stout, smiling woman, seemed very pleased when the curé announced that he had brought a doctor from Paris to see Sister Marthe.

"Come in, Messieurs; I'll send for our dear sister. Oh, for sure, she takes it very badly when I talk to her about a doctor. She claims that she isn't ill. Alas, how wrong she is, poor child! No matter what I say to her, she doesn't want to be treated. But I'll decide that anyway, and it's necessary for her to take some care of her health. Wait here for a moment, Messieurs; I'll bring her to you her momentarily."

Laurent and the curé remained standing in a large, cold, damp and somber room. The sole ornament was a large rustic crucifix. No chairs, just wooden benches set against the walls, and a geographical map of France hanging alongside the crucifix.

When Sister Marthe came in, it was as if a ray of sunlight were penetrating.

Laurent started in surprise.

Sister Marthe was chastity and grace personified. The severe costume of a nun brought out, with an astonishing imagistic vigor, the pensive eyes, the pale and pure forehead, the blonde hair which, at the back, overflowed the white nimbus of the bonnet, and the pale, diaphanous hands...

It was almost an apparition. Laurent felt troubled, moved, and charmed.

"But Monsieur le Curé," she said, "you're really too kind. You know that I'm not ill."

"On the contrary, my child, I know that you're suffering. You have a fever every evening, and it's high time to think about seeking treatment. My young friend Doctor Laurent Verdine, here, is going to examine you, to question you, and he'll tell you what you need to do in order to get better."

"Very well, Monsieur le Curé," said Sister Marthe, blushing slightly. "I'll submit, for the sake of obedience."

Then Laurent, slightly emotional, took Sister Marthe's hand. She really did have a slight fever. Then he placed his ear lightly against her chest, and asked a few questions to which the young nun replied in a low voice.

"That's good, Sister," he said eventually. "It's nothing serious, I assure you. I'll tell your superior what it's necessary to do."

She raised her beautiful eyes to look at him. "Thank you, Monsieur," she said

Laurent bowed.

"May I go now, Monsieur le Curé?" she added. "My little girls are waiting for me."

"Yes, my child," said the priest. "You can go."

Laurent followed her with his eyes until the door had closed. At that moment, the superior came in through another door.

"Well, Doctor, what do you think of our Sister Marthe?"

"Alas, she seems to me to be quite ill. I can prescribe a few medicaments for her, but I confess that I don't have much confidence. What can we do with drugs against a pulmonary lesion? Let's try, though. Here's a prescription, which it's necessary to have filled: sachets of tannin, and two drops of this arsenical liquor every morning. But what the poor girl needs is vivifying sea air. Not the foggy Ocean but the Mediterranean, with a mild and comforting climate. It's already nearly autumn; it's necessary that Sister Marthe doesn't spend the winter here. Send her to Algiers, Nice or Malta. She must go—her life depends on it."

The superior sighed. "We'll try, Monsieur le Docteur. A voyage…that's really not very easy; it needs money, a lot of money…but we'll do our best..."

IV

In villages, burials are touching celebrations, both more solemn and simpler than the sumptuous and pretentious ceremonies of towns.

Peasants of both sexes and all ages had arrived at the Château de Plancheuille. They had put on their Sunday clothes, and, slightly awkwardly, they filed into the chapel, timid and respectful, fearful of being observed but parading their observant eyes in all directions.

A few relatives of the deceased had come from Paris. They came in after the General and George and sat in the front benches. Laurent was sitting to one side, very close to the organ. He saw Sister Marthe arrive, followed by little girls. The naïve and curious gazes of the children paused on Laurent for a few seconds. As for Sister Marthe, she went past him without looking at him. However, Laurent thought he saw her blush. Then he blushed too, stupidly and nonsensically, without knowing why. But the more indignant he became at his stupidity, the deeper he sensed his blush becoming.

Immediately, Sister Marthe sat down at the organ, and the children sang a hymn. Laurent, placed slightly behind her, admired the chaste profile of the young woman, obliquely illuminated obliquely by the sun's rays coming through the stained glass windows. Angèle's pure beauty, the voices of the young children, the song of the organ, the meditation of the audience, and the semi-contained tears of the General and George, were more than sufficient to stir the soul of a poet.

A contained emotion gripped Laurent—and the hardened and impenitent skeptic sensed religious sentiments vibrating within him: the vague and sublime aspiration toward the unknown that is in the depths of every human being.

As soon as the mass had finished, Laurent approached Sister Marthe and said a few words to her in a low voice. She got up immediately, and Laurent took her place at the organ. He felt as if he were inspired, and he played with an extraordinary passion the hymn that he had heard Sister Marthe play the previous evening, Gounod's *Ave Maria*.

The little chapel of Plancheuille had never resounded with such pathetic, heart-rending tones; the entire audience was profoundly moved. Sister Marthe, standing beside the organ, listened as if transported by ecstasy. The General and George wept.

V

Laurent had sworn to himself that he would leave for Paris that evening, but they insisted so forcefully that he must stay that he could not tear himself away. The General had taken him aside after lunch and said to him, with tears in his eyes: "No, my friend, you can't abandon us like that. Look, my dear Maman's nephews and cousins don't care about us—they've already flown away to their business and their pleasures, and we're alone again, alone with our grief. How empty the château will be now! What sadness, what lugubrious sadness! Oh, I'm not talking about George. She was his grandmother, not his mother, so the heartbreak is less great. Then again, he's young, he adores his wife, he has his future ahead of him; his life is just beginning—but my life is finishing, and without amity…come on! It's settled. You'll stay. You'll keep me company for a few days more. We'll talk about my poor Maman; we'll go hunting; we'll philosophize together."

Laurent stayed.

That same day he went for a long walk with George and the General, but he was distracted, preoccupied and anxious. He tried to pull himself together, to arrest the crazy course of the dreams that were traversing his mind. Sister Marthe! Sister Marthe! What folly it was to think about Sister Marthe! Why had he stayed? Was it in order to see her again, to abandon himself to absurd dreams, a thousand times absurd? Well, no, it was to yield to the General's pleas…and yet, in the depths of his consciousness, he understood that it was for Sister Marthe that he had stayed: in order to see her again, perhaps to cure her. But he knew full well that she could not be cured. Can consumption be cured? And a bitter anguish gripped him at the thought that the poor girl was condemned to death.

Truly, he said to himself, *there's nothing in that to make one sad; I've already seen so many poor consumptive young women!*

That fine reasoning remained completely futile; the image of Sister Marthe did not quit him once during the walk.

It was long, that walk. They did not get back until nightfall. As they went past the chapel, Laurent noticed that the door was closed. Doubtless Sister Marthe had come, as usual, to play the organ, and then she had gone again. What a pity to have got back so late! Instead of that insipid stroll through the meadows and the forests, similar to all the meadows and forests in the world, he might have been able to talk to Sister Marthe, to see her, to sit down beside her. What a pity!

Dinner was less silent than the previous day. Making an effort to be cheerful, George attempted to dissipate the sadness that weighed upon the foreheads of his young wife and his father. The General lent himself to his efforts with a good grace; he chatted, as he was able to chat, with grace and bonhomie. But Laurent did not cheer up.

"Come on, Laurent," the General said to him, "tell us where and how you learned to play the organ. Was it in the forests of the Amazon or the pavilions of the École de Médecine?"

"Oh, Father," said George, "don't you know that Laurent has all the talents? He's a voyager, a hunter, a musician, a physician, and even a magnetizer."

"What!" said the General. "You believe in magnetism?"

"I'm obliged to believe in it," said Laurent, smiling.

"That must be very interesting," said Claire.

"Interesting Madame, certainly," said Laurent, "and even a little more than interesting—but there are harsh compensations. Believe me, it's a painful torture, and ever new, to witness marvelous phenomena that one doesn't understand, and is aware that one might never understand. How many times, also, have I stopped before a mystery too great and a shadow too profound? A German poet tells the story of a certain sorcerer who discovers the magic word that would make a gnome appear. The gnome arrives and brings water, as any correctly-summoned gnome must do—but the poor sorcerer does not know the other magic word necessary to stop the spell commenced, with the result that the infernal gnome continues to pour out water, He pours and pour without end; it's impossible to suspend his work, so the unfortunate magician ends up drowned. That's our history, Madame. We evoke, somewhat at hazard, forces that we don't understand, and when it's a matter of putting them back in order, we're impotent."

"In sum, what can you do?" George asked.

"Not much, but something. For example, we can create personalities."

"Personalities!" said the general. "In fact, I've heard talk of that, but I've never understood it very well."

"Oh, it's not very complicated. There are multiple existences within us, within our soul, which seems unique. Within each of us, a number of different persons are active, each of whom has their own thoughts and their particular character. If one searched hard, one would find that each of us has the cloth

72

of a saint, and adventurer, a debauchee or a criminal. Well, by means of magnetism, we can cause all those latent individuals hidden within us, concealed by the principal personality that is oneself, to appear. In any case, all those individuals that hide within us are also oneself, and our self is the ensemble of all those individuals...

"In truth, I don't know whether I'm making myself comprehensible, but it appears quite clear to me. I know a lady who is the simplest bourgeois wife in the world, who knows nothing but her knitting and her cooking. She likes intercourse and thinks of nothing but her husband and children. But as soon as she is in a magnetic trace, she has a horror of those base occupations. Away with all those vile things! She detests domesticity, her children and husband, wants to see the Eternal face to face and laments no longer being able to be a virgin and martyr."

"In that case," said Claire, "which is the more authentic of the two women? Is it the saint or the housewife?"

"They're both authentic, and all the more so because they're unaware of one another. On awakening, all is forgotten. Nothing remains—absolutely nothing—in the memory. It's a complete forgetfulness, a profound destruction of all memories, an immense ignorance that is always surprising, so absolute is it. On the other hand, I don't know why it's surprising, because we all resemble that somnambulist to some degree. Yes, truly, Madame, we carry within us, without knowing it, the seeds of all the sentiments and al the passions, and we don't know the true springs of our life much better than the somnambulists know the characters they play."

When the curé arrived, at the end of the meal, they were still talking about magnetism.

"Say what you like," the worthy man affirmed, "but those are unhealthy experiments, which are sooner or later deadly to those who carry them out. Oh, be wary, young man! There's some diabolical perfidy beneath that invention. Perhaps you don't believe in the devil, but I believe in him firmly.

73

Quaerens quem devoret,[24] the tempter prowls around us, and he sometimes adopts the mask of science, the better to abuse us."

Laurent smiled without responding. He was thinking that the tempter can take all forms, including that of a chaste nun.

VI

The next day, Laurent performed prodigies of diplomacy to ensure that they return to the château at an early hour. He succeeded, one way and another. At four o'clock, everyone was back. But he did not go to his room, and headed for the chapel. He looked around prudently, as if he feared that he might be under surveillance, but he did not see anyone, and he went in.

He had no thought of hiding, but he did not want to be seen. He sat down in the shadows, on a bench placed behind the pulpit, and waited there, his throat constructed and his heart palpitating with emotion, neither more nor less than if it were a matter of an amorous rendezvous. The setting sun cast red, blue and green rays through the stained glass windows, and the humble church was bathed in a great calm, a religious silence.

This is the way the worst follies commence, Laurent thought. *Will she come? Why shouldn't she come, since she has the habit of coming here every evening?*

Suddenly, the chapel door closed. Yes, it really was Sister Marthe. She advanced toward the organ.

Then Laurent stood up and took a step forward.

She uttered a slight cry of surprise.

"Oh! Pardon me! I thought I was alone."

"It's me, Sister, who ought to beg your pardon," Laurent murmured, rather emotionally. "Yesterday morning you played the organ admirably, and I'd be happy to hear you

---

[24] "Seeking someone to devour."

74

again this evening. Is that indiscreet? If it is indiscreet, I'll go."

"Oh, Monsieur!" she said, smiling. "I believe you're making fun of me. You play so well, so very well, that I'm scarcely a schoolgirl by comparison."

"Truly, no, I don't play as well as you think—but I've had the rare good fortune to receive lessons from an excellent master, a great artist, and it's to him that I owe the little I know."

He sat down at the organ. "If you'll permit, Sister," he said, "let me begin; that will embolden you. Didn't you play *Ave Maria* the other evening? Well, this is how to approach that piece. It's necessary that from the very start, one hears vibrating something akin to a supreme invocation, a cry of gratitude, a surge of infinite tenderness. It's a solemn sacrifice; the incense of a humble and tender prayer that rises, and rises, solely and majestically, toward the blue sky. There is every-thing in that hymn, but above all, there is admiration and love."

Laurent was no longer preoccupied with Sister Marthe now; he allowed himself to be drawn away by inspiration; and again, in the silence of the evening, the Ave *Maria* shook the walls of the chapel, a song of almost-divine love, into which Laurent put his entire soul.

Suddenly, he looked at Sister Marthe. She was immobile, standing next to him, her eyes staring, as if lost in the void.

Laurent recognized that attitude, that ecstatic immobility. What? Could it be somnambulism? He knew that music can sometimes determine such crises, in nervous organizations. But how could he suppose that this nun…?

He pulled himself together quickly. With a prompt and energetic gesture he extended his hand before Sister Marthe's face. Immediately, she uttered a profound sigh, and her eyes closed.

"Sister Marthe?" he said, very softly.

"My name isn't Sister Marthe," she said, straightening up proudly. "My name is Angèle de Mérande."

As Laurent, amazed, made no response, she added: "What do you want with me?"

Laurent was deeply embarrassed. Certainly, Angèle was in a somnambulistic trance. But what should he do? What should he say?

"I want to cure you. I want to save you."

"Ah! You're talking to the nun," she said, with a supreme disdain. "But you know full well that she's consumptive and is going to die."

"No, it's necessary that she doesn't die. I want her to die. It's necessary that she lives."

Angèle reflected for a moment, and shook her head indifferently. "What does it matter to you?"

Then she came very close to Laurent, put her hand on his shoulder, and said, in an imploring tone: "Play again, I beg you."

"No," said Laurent, "I won't play anymore. I want to save her."

"Again, what does it matter to you? You know full well that she can't love you."

Laurent sensed that he had gone very pale. He perceived that his hands were trembling, and he understood the extent to which he was disturbed—profoundly disturbed. But he avoided replying to Angèle, and contented himself with repeating, as if mechanically, what he had said before.

"I don't want her to die. We'll save her, won't we? We'll save her."

"If you wish," said Angèle, taking Laurent's trembling hand between hers. "If you wish. Don't you know that I will always obey you?"

"Always," murmured Laurent, as if speaking to himself.

He was almost no longer conscious of what he was saying. He felt invaded by the dream; he dared not even take his hand away from Angèle's burning hands. How many times, curiously leaning over the faces of his magnetized subjects, had he not monitored their words, their gestures and their attitudes, in the hope of surprising some of the grandiose mysteries of intelligence that revealed themselves then in sudden and fleeting gleams? But today, it was not the sacred fire of science that made his heart beat and oppressed his breast. To love Sister Marthe, to love Angèle—had he, then, reached that degree of folly?

Angèle took his hand and kissed it.

He snatched it away abruptly.

"No! I don't want that," he said, in a firm voice. "I don't want that. Listen to me, now, and think about obeying me."

"Oh!" she cried, bring her two hands back to her breast. "I beg you, don't speak to me harshly. You'll make me ill."

"Forgive me! Forgive me!" He had already renounced the role of master. He was at her knees, and tears stifled his voice.

"Angèle," he said, "Angèle, understand me. I won't speak to you harshly again; I won't cause you any more pain. It's not a matter of you but the other, the nun, Sister Marthe, who will soon pronounce her vows. It's necessary to cure her, to save her. You alone can stop the terrible disease that is threatening her, and I want you to save her."

There was a long silence. Angèle seemed to be reflecting profoundly.

"So be it," she said, finally. "I promise you that she won't die."

"Oh, thank you, thank you!"

It was him, now, who held Angèle's hands clasped between his own. With her eyes closed, she smiled, as if that chaste caress had rendered her happy, all the way to the utmost depths of her being.

And Laurent, allowing himself to be carried away by the vision that had entered his life, could not detach his gaze from that charming face, illuminated by a delicate and tender smile.

Then, suddenly regaining possession of himself, he dropped the young woman's hands.

She sought now to retain them in his, but he resisted.

"Adieu, Angèle, adieu! It's late; it's necessary to recall Sister Marthe."

"No—I don't want her to come back. What need do we have of her?"

"It's necessary," Laurent repeated. "It's necessary."

He could see the shadows of dusk increasing by the minute. Already, the grooves between the flagstones of the church were no longer discernible, and the crucifix on the holy altar was half-drowned in the darkness.

He understood that it was necessary to finish it. With an energetic effort he took hold of Angèle's two hands and blew sharply on her forehead.

She uttered a slight sigh, and immediately opened her eyes. Then she looked around and, after a brief moment of indecision, headed for the door.

"Thank you, Monsieur le Docteur," said Sister Marthe, gravely. "The next time I play the *Ave Maria*, I'll remember the lesson you've given me."

Then she went out. Laurent, standing at the chapel door, followed her with his eyes until she went through the gate of the park.

As is understandable, that evening, at dinner, Laurent was distracted, and he did not lend a very attentive ear to the conversation of his hosts.

They were talking about magnetism again. Laurent got carried away.

"Fundamentally, magnetism is an enormous ineptitude, and I shall henceforth hold it in horror. I shall never occupy myself with that nonsense again; it's a waste of time—and I'd give ten years of my life never to have entered into that accursed study."

"What!" said George. "Don't you know more about it than others?"

"On the contrary, I know less than the others. Oh, my friend, what depresses me is that I'm always working in vain, in order not to understand anything. Look at its history! Magnetism is neither more nor less than the question of the beyond. When has it been resolved? When has anyone even approached a solution? For three thousand years people have been studying it, and they're no further forward than they were three thousand years ago. The priests of Isis sought for twenty-five dynasties of kings; they didn't find anything. For twenty centuries, in the mountains of Tibet, the fakirs have been mortifying and mutilating themselves. What have they achieved? And we, in our savant Europe, are as impotent as those old bonzes. What consoles me for my pains, is thinking that, after us, others will seek without finding any more. No, truly, the best thing is to let all that rest in the folderol of old errors. Let's sleep, eat, drink, walk, live, and not rack our brains searching for a solution to the insoluble."

"Good," said the General. "All that's talk, and you don't believe a word of it. You'd be the first to complain if tranquility were imposed on you."

"No, General, I swear to you. Oh, I believe that the curé was right, and that they're infernal problems. By delving into them I've lost—and completely lost, alas—the divine peace of the heart."

"The peace of the heart, the peace of the heart—a fine affair! It's only snails that possess it, the peace of the heart."

That evening, on the terrace of the château, smoking their cigars, Laurent and the general talked again. They talked about happiness, that ungraspable dream of every human being, a hollow dream, a vain imagination, a frightful and harrowing pursuit.

The general's conclusion was that happiness is neither repose or action, but action with the hope of repose.

Laurent, by contrast, claimed that the greatest stupidity is necessary to happiness. "A very modest ease, a tenacious passion, moderate and easy to satisfy, like collecting postage stamps or butterflies; a petty monotonous employment, which occupies the day without fatigue; an irreproachable stomach that nothing upsets; a ferocious egotism that nothing disturbs—those are the conditions of a true and solid happiness."

Poor Laurent! He sensed that happiness was not made for him. He could not go back, to efface the images and memories that imposed themselves upon him. One is not the master of one's thoughts; one cannot say to oneself: "Let's forget; let's stop." Even in the midst of follies, one can neither forget nor stop.

This ridiculous adventure can only degenerate into an odious scandal. So it's necessary to go, and to go right away. But to go is never to see her again. What a cruelty of fate!

He spends the entire night without sleep. Standing on the balcony of his window, he gazes out into the countryside. The moon illuminates the chapel; a profound silence reins everywhere.

Sister Marthe is asleep now. But the other, that adorable Angèle, where is she? In what shadow is she plunged? If I wanted, she would appear again. And why shouldn't I want it? Can I not find true love there, the pure and profound love that no woman in the world can give me? And then again, if it's love, it's power too, power so great that no man can dream of its like. Love and power—what more is necessary to make the human heart beat?

Happiness, love, science, power, the future! What truth is there behind all those big words?

It is only at dawn that Laurent is able to fall asleep.

VII

The next day was to be spent hunting. George and the General had promised Laurent to enable him to kill a few pheasants, perhaps even a capercaillie, an entirely exceptional game-bird scarcely found anywhere but France. All three of them left early in the morning.

Laurent was seeking to stun himself, to distract himself, to rid himself of the unhealthy agitation that had stirred him during the night. He walked all day, and had the good fortune to kill a few pheasants, to the great joy of the General, who was astonished to find such an intrepid hunter in that Parisian.

George was the first to want to go back. Then the General followed his example. Laurent thus fund himself in the wood alone, in the company of a twelve-year-old boy who was carrying his cartridges and his game-bag.

Until then he had put on a brave face, but when he saw that he was left to his own devices, all his hunter's courage suddenly disappeared. On the slope of the valley, between the clearings in the chestnut trees, the turrets of the château were visible in the distance, and, nearby, the little white chapel where, yesterday, Sister Marthe...

Angèle or Sister Marthe; he no longer distinguishes them from one another. He is in love.

In love! Is he that mad? Certainly, he has been in love before—twice, counting accurately. The first time, at twenty-two, it was with a cheerful, insouciant, elegant seamstress, also very affectionate, whom he had loved madly for months on end. Then, a second time, at twenty-eight, there was a charming woman, pretty and amiable. But those two amorous caprices, perhaps more sensual than loving, bore no resemblance to the palpitation full of anguish, both delightful and fatiguing, with which the mere memory of Angèle obsesses his breast.

Then he perceived that he had taken a path that was bringing him closer instead of further away from the village. He also recognized that, instead of descending slowly and serenely, in the manner of a hunter whose is looking in all directions, he was striding past the brushwood on the stony paths, as if he were in a tearing hurry to get back. His young companion was entirely out of breath.

"Hey there, Doctor!" someone called to him, a few paces from the path.

He stopped dead. Under an oak, the old curé was reading is breviary.

"You're going back to the village, young man, I can see. It's nearly five o'clock—time to go back to our lodgings."

"Give me your arm, Monsieur le Curé."

"Why? The legs are still solid. But, from what I see, you've had good hunting at Plancheuille."

"Well, yes, Monsieur le Curé, the day has been quite good. Not for capercaillie though."

"Ah, they're wily, the vagabonds. It's necessary to get up very early to see them."

There as a moment of silence. The curé was marching ahead of Laurent, and they had a lot to do to steer between the stones and the brambles.

"By the way," said the curé, turning round, "are you giving another organ lesson to our Sister Marthe this evening?"

"I don't know," said Laurent, perplexed.

"She was delighted by yesterday's lesson. You have a rare musical talent, my dear Doctor. Have I told you that you transported us all with admiration on the day of the burial, with your *Ave Maria*? Certainly, Sister Marthe has dispositions for music, but she's still far from you, and I'm sure that that a few lessons with such an artist would do more for her than two years of solitary work. Two years! Will she even live two years, poor child?"

"I certainly hope so, Monsieur le Curé, I must confess— and I fear that I might have alarmed you the other day by telling you that the disease has no remedy. Yes, truly, nature has unexpected resources."

"So has Providence, young man," said the curé, gravely.

Laurent made no reply; he did not want an argument. He allowed the curé to sing the praises of Sister Marthe—and on that matter, the worthy man never ran dry. Sister Marthe was the best teacher that had ever been encountered in Plancheuille.

"All the little girls adore her, and if there's a sick person to be helped, a chagrin to be consoled, it's always Sister Marthe who arrives first. And there are people who talk about laywomen! No, truly, my friend, find me among your communal teachers a woman like Sister Marthe... Look, I'll call in at the school and send you your pupil..."

It was five o'clock when Laurent went into the chapel. A few moments later, he saw Sister Marthe arrive.

"I want to thank you again, Monsieur, for your kindness. Monsieur le Curé told me that you were waiting for me, and I've come..."

"Yes, Sister, as often as you wish. I'm glad to be able to be useful to you. Come on, sit down beside me. Today, if you don't mind, it won't be the *Ave Maria* but Rossini's *Stabat*. See how, from the very first measures, the song reveals the solemn and profound dolor that invaded the soul of the mother of Christ..."

Laurent had promised himself that he would not evoke Angèle, but he did not have the courage to keep his word, and when he saw Angèle's gaze become fixed, he extended his hand over her forehead. As on the previous day, she uttered a profound sight, and her eyes closed. Immediately, a smile animated her visage, previously serious and cold.

She got up, moved toward Laurent, and took his hands.

"Oh, thank you for having called me back. If you knew how I've been waiting for you. All night I was thinking about you—for I dream during the night, and I go in search of those I love. Well, last night, I saw you: you were standing by the window, and you were gazing at the chapel."

"That's true," Laurent murmured.

"And the other, the nun, how can she understand anything? She doesn't know that I've come. She doesn't know that I can see you at night. She doesn't know that I can read your thoughts."

"What! Read my thoughts?"

She smiled with pride. "Didn't you know that, you who have studied magnetism so much? Yes, I can see what is going through your imagination and your will. I don't even need to make an effort; everything presents itself to me with perfect clarity, as if in a mirror. Would you like me to tell you what you were thinking last night, and what you're thinking now?"

She smiled with a sort of malice. Laurent, nonplussed, made no reply.

Then, in a very low voice, leaning close to Laurent's ear, she said to him: "Thank you for loving me amorously."

"Angèle, don't talk like that. Don't pronounce the word love. You can't understand it."

She stood up and placed her hand on Laurent's shoulder.

"Now we're united forever, and nothing can separate us. From now on, whatever you think, whatever you do, I'll always be there, nearby. I even want to protect you. See how obedient I am to the orders you give me. I can't do otherwise, for I'm proud to obey you. Didn't you tell me that it was necessary to cure Sister Marthe? Well, yesterday evening, Sister Marthe was much better, and I promise you that in three months, she'll no longer be ill, and won't cough any more. Are you content with me, my lord and master?"

Laurent did not reply. What could he say? Angèle's hand was resting gently on his shoulder. How could he defend himself.

He said to himself: *A few more moments and I'll wake her. We'll return to the reality of things, to cruel and implacable reality. Then, there'll no longer be anyone but Sister Marthe, unknown to me, as I'm unknown to her.*

Already, Angèle had penetrated Laurent's thought. "If you wanted, my love, I could remain with you always; Sister Marthe would no longer reappear. You could leave here, taking me with you. No one would know. I'd depart enveloped in a big cloak, and I'd never leave you again. I'd be your slave, your thing, I'd follow you everywhere: to Paris, to Italy, to England, everywhere. Who could stop us? You wouldn't let Sister Marthe come back, and perhaps she'd end up not being able to come back any more. There wouldn't be anyone any longer but your Angèle. Poor Sister Marthe! She hasn't yet pronounced her vows. It's not for three months. She didn't want to be a nun. Cruel events were required to force her vocation. Certainly, she suffered a great deal once, but she's no longer suffering now. What would you like me to tell you, Laurent? She only knew her mother; she didn't know her father—he was…the Comte de Mérande."

Angèle pronounced that name so quietly that Laurent could hardly hear it. "He's dead now, and as he didn't write anything, no one can know or prove that he's her father. It was him who came to see her in the convent. Sister Marthe believes that he was her guardian, but he wasn't her guardian, was he? He was her father, her true father. Promise me, my friend, that you won't reveal that secret to Sister Marthe. It would add too much pain to the memory of her mother."

"I promise you that," said Laurent.

He was listening with an indescribable amazement. Yes, not only did Angèle read his most secret thoughts, but she was also able to know facts that no one else knew. How many times had Laurent sought in magnetized subjects for proof of lucidity? And now Angèle was providing a striking demonstration of it, effortlessly.

In any case, Laurent was no longer thinking about lucidity or about science; he was moved to the utmost depths of his soul, Angèle's tender voice and amorous words had cast a great disturbance into him. And then again, that small hand, leaning on him and quivering at all emotions, was like a caress, of an infinite chastity and softness. His reason escaped him.

To leave, to flee with her…why not? What was the point of worrying about the future? The dolorous days, the regrets, the remorse would come later.

At present, since she's here, since she loves me, let's not think of anything but her, and leave all the rest...

Meanwhile, Angèle seemed to be following, with a penetrating attention, the confused thoughts that presented themselves to him. Suddenly, she extracted the conclusion therefrom.

"Oh! Thank you! We're leaving, we're leaving together."

She headed for the door. But already, Laurent had got a grip on himself again, entirely.

No, that's impossible. Leave with Sister Marthe! What would they say in Plancheuille? What would the General say? Who could tell whether a tribunal wouldn't see it as an illicit seduction?

Laurent shivered in terror. The gendarmes, the court of assizes, are enough to make the bravest man tremble.

No decidedly, it's impossible. There are certain follies it isn't permissible to commit.

He stood up and took Angèle by the hand. "I don't want that," he said, gazing at hr fixedly.

She tried to get away and turned her head away, but he spoke to her forcefully.

"Remember this, Angèle. It's necessary that she be cured, and she will be cured."

Then, without giving her time to respond, he blew lightly on her forehead. She uttered a slight sigh.

Sister Marthe had returned.

"Thank you, Monsieur," she said. "Tomorrow, I'll play the *Stabat* that you've taught me."

VIII

Laurent spent a night even more agitated than the previous one, but this time, insomnia inspired him with wisdom. The idea of the court of assizes, which, until then, had scarcely occurred to him, had taken on proportions that frightened him. There was much talk then, in the newspapers and in the tribunals, of seduction by hypnotism. Now, if he were to run away with Angèle, he would not be able to prove that hypnotism was not the cause of it. That pious and charitable nun, leaving with him after having seen him twice, could only be explained by a crime. All the severity of the law would fall upon him. He would be annihilated under the weight of the enormous scandal.

Thus, it's necessary to renounce all these follies, to leave, to leave Angèle and flee, far, far away.

Yes, it's necessary to forget everything. Everything can be forgotten, for nothing has happened that is irreparable. Today, his thoughts are full of Angèle, but in a few days, in a few months, at the most, Angèle will be no more to him than a vague memory. It's necessary that this romantic adventure, sketched in a chapel, ends there. Nothing will remain of that delicious and fugitive apparition than a charming distant memory, such as young men ought to have in order to enchant the somber hours of their old age.

Unfortunately, he could not leave that day. A large hunting-party had been arranged. They were to go to the woods of Serpes, ten kilometers from Plancheuille. It was there that they hoped to find a capercaillie, that myth of hunters.

Laurent did not want to cause the General and his friend any pain by leaving. In any case, there was no inconvenience in staying for one more day; they would not return to Plancheuille until eight o'clock in the evening, which would render any meeting with Sister Marthe impossible. That night would therefore be the last spent at the château. At six o'clock the following morning, a carriage would take him to Moulins.

He would be in Paris the same day, and once in Paris, no more organ, no more Sister Marthe, no more romance. Active life would take hold of him again without division. Adieu these crazy chimeras and absurd adventures, for which he already felt that he was too old.

The day was as it should be, like any other hunting party. Laurent tried to amuse himself, and he did, in fact, seem quite joyful. But whatever ardor he tried to put into the pursuit of game, he could not take an interest in the pheasants that flew up in front of him or the capercaillies that were heard calling in the distance. No, he was elsewhere; he saw Angèle again; he heard her charming voice...

Finished, all that is finished! He will never see that adorable creature again; never again will he hear that harmonious voice, which invokes in him all the sweetness of amour.

I appeal to all those who are capable of thought. Is there anything more dolorous than an eternal rupture with that which has existed, the irremediably and definitive adieu to someone who will never be seen again? And yet, alas, is our existence anything else? What is living, if not a perpetual series of irreparable adieux?

Laurent, however, applauded his own resolution, and it was with a great relief that he saw the sun progress toward the horizon, decline and then descend, and finally attain the limit of the hills. Six o'clock! Dusk was already falling. He would not be at Plancheuille until eight o'clock, in darkness, and the following morning, on the way to Paris. Paris! Paris! That was his safeguard at present.

When Laurent told his hosts that he wanted to depart so soon, they pressed him to stay. He was inflexible—but he promised to return.

"So be it," said the General. "I'll take note of your promise; you're giving me pain, but after all...tomorrow morning, at six o'clock, since you insist, the carriage will be ready and will take you to Moulins. Embrace me, my friend, and *à bientôt!*"

Laurent returned to his room. Before going to sleep, he darted a last glance over the park and opened the window wide. The silence was solemn. Then an immense sadness invaded him.

What! He will not see her again, that Angèle, whose heart has beaten so close to his own! To what vain idols is he sacrificing so much love? Who will be grateful to him for that abnegation, that heroism of virtue? Is it really abnegation? And is that virtue not the mask of cowardice?

Suddenly, on the path, he thought he perceived a white form heading toward the château. A great frisson shook him from head to toe. A hallucination, perhaps an apparition! He threw himself backwards, not daring to look at the phantom; he was afraid, and his heart was beating with so much force that he could hear its tumultuous vibrations striking the walls of his pulmonary cavity.

Soon, mastering his fear, he approached the window and, leaning against the wall, looked out, leaning slightly forward, as if plunging his gaze into the abyss.

Yes, it was really Angèle; the gravel crackling under her feel was audible.

No apparition has that clarity of image. No, it isn't an apparition, for Laurent senses all his intelligence, and the full possession of himself.

She is not wearing her nun's head-dress. Her beautiful hair, which tongs have not yet curled, is thrown backwards. A white dress envelops her, and over that white dress, a long, thick mantle like those the local shepherds wear, trailing on the ground.

Without hesitation, Angèle heads for Laurent's window.

"Laurent," she says, in a low voice, "it's me—don't be afraid."

"You, Angèle, you!"

Her eyes are closed, but she is walking with assurance, as if she were able to distinguish all the objects around her.

"Well, yes, it's me. You didn't want to come to the chapel today? So, you see, it's me who is coming to you. Give me your hand to help me come up. Someone might see me, and you'll understand that I don't want to be seen."

"What imprudence!" Laurent murmured. Nevertheless, he gave her his hand. Then, lightly, Angèle leapt into the room, scarcely leaning on Laurent's arm.

"It's cold," she said, pressing herself against him. "Warm me up a little" And before he could defend himself, she was next to him, shivering all over.

She laid her head gently on the young man's breast.

"Isn't it as well that I came?" she said. "You intended to leave…without bidding me adieu, ingrate! As soon as you opened the window, I saw you. The other, the nun, was fast asleep. Then I got up, without making a sound. Everything was silent. In haste, I put on a dress and this mantle. In our house, the doors aren't locked, so I was able to get out without difficulty. No one is in the streets of the village at midnight, and besides, who would have recognized me? At any rate, no one saw or heard me. I'm close to you now, and I'm very happy."

"What imprudence!" Laurent repeated. "What imprudence!"

Angèle's head was resting on his bosom, and, involuntarily, intoxicated by amour, he covered her forehead and her hair with burning kisses. She smiled, and allowed herself to be kissed.

"You were there, at the window, and you called to me. I wouldn't have come if you hadn't called me. But you said to me: 'Come!' Oh, I heard you; I understood; here I am."

"No," said Laurent, "I didn't call to you. No!" And he tried to push her away. But she took his hands, obstinately, and clung on to him.

"I beg you," she said, in an imploring tone, "I beg you, Laurent, don't be nasty to me. Alas, I'm neither as beautiful nor as seductive as the women you've loved, but I love you so much! Remember that you're everything to me: my master, my king, my god. Laurent, for pity's sake, love me!"

Certainly, Laurent was aware of the full extent of his power over Angèle. He knew that with his powerful hand he could evoke images in her soul, gentle or bloody, terrifying or pleasant; wake her up or plunge her into a profound lethargy; perhaps even—who knows?—make her forget everything; change that love into hatred. That charming being who had come to him, almost without being summoned, was under his absolute dependence: a phantom that, with a word or a sign, he could compel to return to oblivion. But he did not resign himself to that dolorous sacrifice.

The cold air of autumn nights penetrated into the room; he shivered, and he closed the widow, because he felt chilled to the marrow of his bones. Then he lit a candle, whose vacillating light cast a pale and fantastic glare over Angèle.

Standing with her back against the mantelpiece, he listened to Angèle without replying, without even thinking. He felt devoid of courage. Yes, this was true love, absolute love, the only one that merits being lived. He had never been loved with that self-abandonment, with that limitless tenderness. Who can tell whether that is not the key to the great mystery? The priests of Isis, the dervishes of Tibet and the savants of Europe were unable to clarify it because they did not have that which alone can work miracles: the annihilation of the will in amour.

And then, all his youth quivered within him. The amorous fever had taken hold. That adorable and chaste young woman who was delivering herself to him, pressing herself against his breast, wrapping her delicate arms around him, in his room, in the midst of the silence of the night…what a redoubtable temptation! He dared not surrender to it, nor resist...

He did resist, albeit telling himself that the very resistance was perhaps the worst of follies.

As for her, she seemed happy, and she smiled.

"You see, Laurent, how easy it will be. I'll depart on foot for Moulins. I'll walk all night; I'll still arrive at the station before you. You take the carriage and we meet out there, in Moulins. With my mantle and a veil over my head, no one will recognize Sister Marthe. Then, we'll depart for Paris together. Do you understand? Together! And we won't be separated again. How lovely, isn't it? To leave with you, not to be separated from you again, never to be separated…to love one another without remorse, without fear. Oh, I can see what you're thinking. You're afraid that someone might hear noises in our room—but out there, in Paris, we'll have nothing to fear.

"For a few days here, people will occupy themselves with Sister Marthe. They'll try to discover what has become of her, but they won't find any trace of her. And then they'll no longer think about her. Sister Marthe will have disappeared. Who, in any case, is interested in Sister Marthe? My name isn't Sister Marthe, I'm Angèle de Mérande. My father was the Comte de Mérande, and I'm his heir, for he's left me all his fortune. There's a testament, I know, although that testament hasn't been found. Oh, if I wanted to be, I could be rich. Perhaps I'll tell you one day where my father hid that testament...

"But what do riches matter to me? What does my birth matter? I only want your love, Laurent. Yes, I want your love, all of your love. I want you to give it to me entirely, just as I'm giving everything, body and soul, to you. I want to be

91

your Angèle, as you'll be my Laurent. Everything, everything for you! You don't know what I can do, but, oh, my love, you'll see what I can do for you, and because of you. I'll unveil secrets to you, unknown to humans, to feeble humans. I'll teach you how, sometimes, the veils of the future will be torn apart for us. I'll show you how, in the rapid lightning-flashes that illuminate the soul, time and space no longer exist for us. Yes, because of me, Laurent, because of me, you'll have knowledge; I promise you that, my love. People will put themselves at your knees; amazed men will adore you almost like a god. And I'll do that to please you; I'll be at your orders, to render you powerful, because all that science is irrelevant to me, and I don't want anything except your tenderness."

Without saying anything, Laurent gently pushed Angèle away, as she was offering him her forehead. He no longer knew what he was going to do, and he was half-vanquished, half lost, when suddenly, in the silence, he heard the chiming of an old clock.

"Shh!" said Angèle, putting a finger over his lips. And she counted: "One, two, three. Three o'clock; three o'clock already. I have to go."

And abruptly, she opened the window.

"Go! Go where?" exclaimed Laurent.

"To Moulins, where you'll come to join me shortly."

"No," he said, forcefully, "no! You shan't go. And since that's the way it is, let it be finished forever, finished forever."

Then, with an abrupt gesture, he extended his hand over Angèle's forehead. She tottered, uttered a faint cry, and fell backwards. Laurent was only able to retain her partially in his arms.

Suddenly, the scene had changed. Angèle was lying on the floor, almost inanimate, as pale as a corpse, in the frightful inertia of a cadaver.

Laurent placed his hand on Angèle's breast; the heart was still beating, slowly, slowly and faintly.

"Lethargy," he murmured.

He knew that in spite of that immobility, Angèle, in that profound lethargy, could still hear and understand him.

He got down on his knees on the floor and, taking Angèle's cold hand between his, he spoke to her in a low voice, so close to her that his lips were almost touching the young woman's pale cheeks.

"Angèle, listen to me carefully. This is my formal will; I want it to be accomplished. It's necessary that Sister Marthe be cured. Sister Marthe cured: I want that. In six months, it's necessary that no trace of her malady remains. And as for you, Angèle, you who have given me your tender and sweet love, know that I love you, that I adore you...

"Whatever happens to me in future, everything in my life will pale by comparison with the unforgettable hour in which we have loved one another. Yes, my Angèle, I'm weeping because it is my entire youth, my entire life that is going away with you...

"Listen to me again, Angèle, for you can hear me, I know; your chaste and loving soul understands me. Although your lips are pale and cold, although the regular alternation of your breath and the slow beating of your heart betray no emotion, you can hear me Angèle. Well, I don't want, I don't want you to come back. Your memory will live in my heart, but never, understand me well, Angèle, never come back again. You will not respond to any appeal, from me or from anyone else. Nothing will be able make you come back. I want that, and I know that that solemn order will be carried out...

"And now, adieu, adieu forever, dear soul that I adore, adieu!"

She was still lying on the floor, immobile. He leaned over, and kissed her forehead.

Then he tried to wake her up. It was not without dread, that moment of awakening. What would Sister Marthe say when she found herself here? How could he make her understand that a mysterious force had made her get out of bed to bring her here, into this room, in the middle of the night, alone with Laurent? What stupor! What terror! What shame, perhaps!

Even so, he tried to wake her. But he soon perceived that his efforts were utterly futile. There was no sign of a return to consciousness. The more he saw the impotence of his efforts, in fact, the more he sensed that his will-power was escaping him—the will-power that as more necessary than ever. His distracted attention could no longer lend itself to any effort, and still, on the floor beside him, Angèle, pale and insensible, was breathing with the same serenity.

Habituated as he was to the alarming spectacle of lethargy, Laurent was frightened. That woman lying on the floor, unmoving, was almost the image of death. Was he going to be unable to recall her to life? The shock had been too abrupt, the emotion too profound. In extraordinary, almost supernatural, human organisms there are delicate springs that the slightest damage is capable of breaking forever.

Angèle, Angèle is going to die, to die here, to die because of me!

That sinister idea passed back and forth through Laurent's mind with a vertiginous rapidity. In vain he told himself that lethargy of this sort never leads to death, that these crises, although terrifying, are fundamentally devoid of danger. He had forgotten al the lessons of science; he saw before him a cadaver, and the more afraid he was, the more impotent he became. Sinister ideas whirled in his head, tracing redoubtable circles that became ever more restricted, like the immense orbits, always spiraling inwards, that vultures describe when they are about to fall upon their prey.

A cold sweat beaded Laurent's forehead.

"Angèle," he said, "Wake up! Wake up!"

But there was nothing, nothing at all. Still that deathly immobility, that terrible mortal silence.

He lifted up her eyelid; the eye was dull, devoid of gaze.

"Angèle, Angèle, wake up!"

Suddenly, in the country, far away, a cock crowed. Another cock replied. A pale, scarcely visible light fringed the horizon.

Laurent had a sudden inspiration. He understood. Yes, if Angèle is asleep with that profound lethargy, it is in order that Sister Marthe will never know that she has been in Laurent's room. The mystery of that night of amour must remain unknown to Sister Marthe, unknown to everyone.

Then, Laurent regained courage. He no longer made any effort to wake Angèle. He took her in his arms and, stepping through the window, went down into the park. He carried her gently, barefoot, in order that no one would hear the gravel creaking. He arrived thus at the door of the chapel, which, fortunately, was not locked.

When Laurent opened the door, the rusty hinges grated with a noise that seemed resounding. Laurent stopped, his heart palpitating with anguish. He remained thus for a few minutes, holding Angèle's body in his arms, and dared not move forward.

Although dawn was beginning to break outside, the church was in profound darkness. The main altar could, however, be vaguely discerned

Laurent advanced slowly, bearing his precious burden. When he was in front of the gate of the choir, he laid Angèle down on the flagstones, very gently, as one might have laid a cadaver down. He covered her with the thick mantle that she had brought; then, leaning over her, he kissed her chastely on the forehead.

Adieu, my Angèle, adieu. If there is another existence somewhere—alas, why is it necessary for me not to believe it!—we shall see one another again, my Angèle... Adieu forever, down here.

But Angèle remained motionless, inert: still that frightful monotony of an impassive respiration, that pallor and that rigidity of the features. Laurent was speaking to her as one might speak to the dead.

On the threshold of the chapel he looked back. He saw, confusedly, the white form lying on the ground, like a distant specter. He made a desperate gesture, and closed the door.

IX

When he was back in his room, he had the sensation of a man who has emerged alive from a great peril. Alive, but torn apart: be bore in his heart one of those profound wounds that time soothes, but never effaces. Nevertheless, he was alive. No shame or scandal would tarnish his life. After all, why should he not resume his work, his hopes of old? Life is still for him what it was three days ago, before the deadly music of the *Ave Maria* resounded in the silence of the dusk.

Then again, it is necessary to do something, and in great dolors, action is a consolation.

At six o'clock in the morning, the General's victoria was waiting for Laurent at the perron. It departed at a rapid trot. After half an hour, however, Laurent perceived that he had forgotten his valise, containing papers of the utmost importance.

"Let's go back," he said to the coachman. "I'll take the evening train."

"Oh, good God!" George said to him, "how fortunately you've arrived! It's a true stroke of luck that you forgot your manuscript. Can you imagine that Sister Marthe has been found half-dead, lying in the church. She was unconscious. They tried to wake her, but haven't yet succeeded. Now she's at the convent; the superior and the curé are with her. Come quickly, you might perhaps be able to revive her."

"But how did Sister Marthe come to be in the church like that, at six o'clock in the morning?"

"In truth, no one knows," said George. "She must have got up during the night—it appears that she walks in her sleep—to go and say her prayers; then the cold must have seized her, and she lost consciousness."

They had arrived at the school. They found a small gathering of women and children there. George and Laurent went in.

The lethargy was as profound as before. Nothing could give any indication of whether it would last for days, months or minutes. But Laurent had recovered his composure; he knew that lethargies are inoffensive, in spite of the terror they inspire. For Sister Marthe, there was no danger. It was a matter of a few hours. And assuredly, Sister Marthe would come back, utterly unconscious of the events that Angèle had lived.

So, in spite of the insistences of all the people surrounding Sister Marthe's bed, he did not want to employ any means to awaken her.

"Anything we do," he said, "can only have inconveniences. She will wake up on her own. If we allow her lethargy to dissipate, Sister Marthe, when she wakes up, will be neither fatigued nor ill; whereas, by provoking an abrupt awakening, we would risk bringing on a long and redoubtable crisis."

Toward midday, suddenly, Sister Marthe made a movement. Her respiration, absolutely regular until then, was suspended momentarily. She uttered a long and profound sigh; then, opening her eyes, she looked around. She was still clad in her white dress; her first movement was to palpate and look at the dress.

"What!" she said dazedly, intimidated by the sight of all the people around her. "What is it? What's happened? In the name of Heaven, what is it?"

"Thank God, my daughter," the superior said to her. "You've escaped a great peril."

"What peril? I don't understand."

The superior asked the others to leave. Then, when she was alone with Sister Marthe, she told her that at six-thirty in the morning, she had not been found in her bed, and that they had searched everywhere; finally, she had been found lying on the floor in the chapel, as if dead.

Sister Marthe was nonplussed. Her gaze lost in space, she tried to understand, to remember, to grasp some shred of all that had happened of which she was unaware, and which fled before her—but she could not recover anything. She remembered that, the previous night, as usual, she had lain down in her little bed. She had slept tranquilly, and yet, something strange and inexplicable must have happened, since she found herself, at midday, dressed in white, with all those strange people round her bed.

"Thank God, my daughter. God has worked a miracle for you and saved you."

"Not only am I saved," said Sister Marthe, smiling, "but I'm no longer ill, and I feel well enough to take the class today."

At that moment, Laurent came in. He tried in vain to make Sister Marthe understand that it would be better for her to rest. She claimed that she was no longer suffering, that she was not ill, that people had already been too occupied with her and that it really was not worth the trouble of continuing to talk about that ridiculous incident.

With that, Laurent ceased his exhortations. That same evening, entirely reassured, he left for Paris—and this time, he did not leave any manuscript behind in his room.

X

Which of us has not amused himself by throwing a stone into the tranquil mirror of a lake? The water splashes up, and all around, a wave forms, and then another, and then yet another. They spread rapidly, reach the bank, rebound there, return to the center, and then, again, in tightly-packed circles, return to the edge. And that agitation continues for a long time. For a long time, the serenity of the water is lost.

Is our soul not like the pure water of that lake? Let an unexpected event—an amorous passion, for example—fall upon us, and that is it, forever, for the serenity of the soul. But we are more unfortunate than the stupid lake. The lake forgets, but for us, it is necessary to remember. The odious power of memory! An ancient dolor bites as cruelly as a recent dolor.

Laurent had the rude experience of that. He had said: "I shall forget; I shall work," but work can only bring forgetfulness when one is already indifferent.

So, Laurent tried to go back to work. He recommenced his scientific research, went to the theater, visited his friends; but science, friends and the theater seemed equally unsupportable to him.

Once, he had paid court to a certain young widow, very flirtatious, who had sent him away. In order to distract himself, he wanted to attempt the adventure again. At the first visit, he was well received—perhaps even too well received. Although he was far from being conceited, he was not blind. He understood easily that if he persisted…but he did not persist. He did not care to play the comedy of amour. Had he not, in the chapel of Plancheuille, felt the palpitation of true love? His caprice for the young widow had suddenly flown away, as soon as he realized that she would yield to his persistence.

He spent two months thus, very sad, with the heavy sadness that weighs upon us all the more, the more we find the cause to be absurd. He could not think about anything but Angèle. He could not forgive himself for having been so prudent, so reserved, so sage. What good had it done him, that sagacity? He had wanted to avoid being unhappy, and now he was more unhappy than ever. No, truly, it was necessary to put an end to it. It was necessary not to allow himself to be eaten away by an inept torment that was taking the best part of life. At all costs, he had to free himself from that obsession, and for that, he had to see Angèle again.

On the first of November, abruptly, he set off once again for Plancheuille.

The General uttered a cry of joy when he saw Laurent. He was alone, entirely alone, because George was traveling in Italy with his young wife.

"Decidedly," he said to Laurent, "you have it in for my pheasants. Well, we'll have a word with them. But truly, you've had an admirable idea, all the more so because you'll be able to collect yourself here, work, put your documents in order. Here, complete liberty. Perhaps you've brought a few books? Yes—well, that's perfect. You'll be able to work at your ease. Why don't you stay with me until the first of January?"

"I won't say no, General, unless my patients call me back."

"Your patients! Your principal patient is me. I have gout and rheumatism—what you physicians call gouty rheumatism. Then again, I cough like a damned soul. Now, I only want to be cared for by you, and it would be lacking in duty and in friendship to abandon me. Besides which, don't imagine that you'll have any lack of patients in Plancheuille? You have some reputation in the locality, since you cured Sister Marthe."

"In fact, that's true," said Laurent, affecting a detached manner. "How has Sister Marthe been these last two months?"

"As well as can be. I don't know what you prescribed for her, but your prescription has worked marvels. She was very ill—consumptive, it's said—but now she's cured, or very nearly. In any case, in order that you have news of her, I'll invite our worthy curé to dine with us at the château this evening. He's an excellent fellow, who speaks of you with a genuine sympathy. We'll play a game of whist this evening. Confess that you've done well to come."

"In truth, General, I left Paris in quite a bad way. I had a host of black butterflies in my head, making a diabolical racket. But now I'm here, they've flown away, is if by a miracle, and the appetite for broad daylight has returned."

In fact, as soon as he had seen the turrets of Plancheuille and the white wall of the little again, Laurent had suddenly felt as if transformed.

He was almost frightened by that sudden change, which revealed a most abnormal state of mind, and a more profound disturbance than he had been able to suspect. What! That history of Angèle, that romantic adventure, which ought to have been one of the fleeting episodes of his life, takes such a vast place?

Why that tremor, that frisson, that gleam of hope on find-ing this room again? It is by that window that Angèle entered; it was in that armchair that she sat down. There is the chapel where I heard her for the first time. There is the path where her white form, in the night, came toward me. Further away is the village, and she is there, and if I wanted...

But he did not want to. He imposed that sacrifice upon himself. He kept the General company all day, and went walk-ing with him.

They came back at five o'clock. While they were playing a game of billiards, the sound of the organ suddenly became audible. Laurent went pale, and then blushed.

"Well," said the General, "that's your pupil playing the organ. It's the same every evening. It seems that she's made progress since your last lessons. Tomorrow, if you like, you can recommence."

During dinner, they talked again about Sister Marthe. It was like a universal conspiracy; everyone at Plancheuille seemed to want to sing the praises of the young nun to Lau-rent, as if he had any need to be reminded of her. The curé never stopped talking about her, marveling at her recovery, and he repeated in the smallest details everything he knew about the famous episode of the lethargy.

"If you wish, Doctor, we'll go to see her tomorrow, after her class. You can see for yourself that she's much better."

"Is it with arsenic that you treated her?" the General asked.

"Oh, truly," said Laurent, "it's necessary not to cry victo-ry too soon. And you'll recall, Monsieur le Curé, that a great physician, living in a century less skeptical than ours, was accustomed to say when he saved a patient: 'I bandaged him; God has healed him.'"

"Bravo," said the curé. "Well said and well thought, without wordplay."

The next day, outside the school, Laurent found the curé in conversation with the superior.

101

"Ah. Monsieur le Docteur," said the excellent woman, "we're very happy to see you again. Your presence has been a benefit for us. You'll see what a miraculous change has taken place in the health of our Sister Marthe. Above all, though, don't talk to her about her crisis of somnambulism, because she's ashamed of it, poor child, and it's a subject of conversation that horrifies her."

Sister Marthe came in. Laurent tried not to appear emotional. He affected the solemn and indifferent gravity of a physician called upon to make a diagnosis. In fact, though, the presence of Sister Marthe moved him profoundly. He devoured her with his gaze, as if he had not dared to hope that he would see her again.

Yes, it's really her. There are her adorable hands, which knotted around my neck. There is the supple body that pressed against mine. Angèle or Sister Marthe or both together? How did that meek nun, so timid, so humble, dare to talk to me about love, and demand love of me?

"It appears, Sister, that you're on the way to recovery?"

"Yes, Monsieur le Docteur, thanks to you, and I'm glad to be able to express all my gratitude to you. I carry out your recommendations faithfully: two drops of arsenical liquor every morning."

"Well, Sister, it's necessary to continue. But before then, permit me to listen for a moment."

He applied his ear gently to Sister Marthe's chest. She smiled with resignation, perhaps with a slight ennui, thinking that too much attention was being paid to her.

The curé and the superior waited anxiously. "Well?" they said, when Laurent had finished his auscultation.

"Well," said Laurent, "I'm astonished myself to observe such considerable progress. There's still a small lesion here on the right, but it's very slight. The amelioration is striking, unexpected; a few more months of the same regime, and all will be well—even very well."

"Thank you, Monsieur le Docteur," said Sister Marthe.

As she prepared to leave, Laurent stopped her. "And the organ lessons, Sister? Would you like to resume them?"

Sister Marthe looked at the superior, as if to request authorization or advice—but the curé had already replied: "Certainly, my child, it's necessary to continue. And I hope, for my part, that Monsieur Laurent Verdine will stay here long enough for you to be able to play the *Ave Maria* as well as he does himself."

"You trying to make fun of me," said Sister Marthe. "I have no need to be an artiste; it's sufficient that I help the little girls to sing canticles at catechism."

XI

If Laurent thought that, in order to liberate himself from the memory of Angèle, it was sufficient for him to return to Plancheuille, Laurent has made a terrible mistake. Scarcely has he heard Sister Marthe's voice than he has been recaptured entirely. Now he no longer has but one desire, that of recovering Angèle. With an increasing impatience, he waits in the chapel for the moment when Sister Marthe will arrive.

He heard the door opening. It was Sister Marthe; he made out the soft sound of her footsteps on the flagstones, the trailing of her robe, the clicking of the crucifix that was hanging by her side. He did not raise his eyes, but he felt troubled to the utmost depths of his soul. His heart was beating forcefully, and he savored the delicious moment—who has not known it?—when the beloved, adored woman, finally arrives after a long wait.

Two months! He had waited two months! He had lived those two months in the unique hope of this charming hour. Now, the hour has come...

Well, what is he going to do? He does not know, and does not want to know. He dare not confess to himself, what he is going to decide. Or rather, he has not decided anything. He will let Angèle do as she wishes...and he will abandon himself to her. She will pronounce. For the heroic sacrifice that he made before, he no longer feels the courage to recommence.

"Well, Sister," he said, "If you wish, we can set to work right away. We could play, for instance Mozart's *Requiem*? It's also a song of dolor, but the plaint is more solemn and less poignant than in the *Stabat*."

He began. Sister Marthe, standing behind him, listened attentively. When he had finished, it was her who spoke.

"Certainly," she said, "it's an admirable music, but you've played it from memory. Alas, it will be impossible for me to profit from it. If you wish, you can play me the *Ave Maria* again, which I know quite well."

"Very well," said Laurent, slightly astonished.

Then he played the first bars of the *Ave Maria*. After a few moments, he looked at Sister Marthe, but he did not see any change in her; her eyes were not staring. On the contrary, she was following with a keen interest the development of the admirable song, which, under Laurent's experienced fingers, shook the somber vaults of the church with all its passion.

Laurent stopped.

"Why aren't you continuing, Monsieur?" asked Sister Marthe. "For the *Ave Maria*, which I know, I can follow you very well."

Laurent shivered. Yes, he remembered that, on that fatal night, he had solemnly ordered Angèle never to appear again. Is she, perchance, being too faithful to that command? He knew that an order given is absolute. He knew that obedience is servile. Was it, in fact, true that Angèle would never, ever return?

Then he continued. His fingers ran across the keyboard mechanically, but silently he repeated: "Angèle! Angèle! Come, I want it. Come, I order you to. Forget the order I gave you before. You know full well that I love you, and that I love only you. You know that I want to live for you, for you alone."

Involuntarily, however, he remembered having said: "I no longer want you. You will no longer exist, for me or for anyone else." And he understood that he had raised between Angèle and the world of the living a barrier that nothing could cross.

Until then, even in the bitterest hours of great despair, he had always, in the depths of his soul, thought that he could see Angèle again; but in that cruel moment, the atrocious idea that Angèle was lost to him had cut through his intelligence like a flash of lightning, the dazzle of which obliterates everything.

Then he looked at Sister Marthe.

"Oh, Monsieur," she said to him, smiling, "I'm very grateful to you. Will you permit me to play the same song in my turn? You can see whether I've profited from the lesson."

"Try," said Laurent, standing up. He said it with a kind of irritation. His voice, caressant until then, had become a trifle harsh, as if he were annoyed.

Sister Marthe looked at him in surprise for a moment, and then she sat down at the organ.

While she played, Laurent stood behind her. He concentrated all the forces of his will and his intelligence. "Angèle! Angèle! I want, I want you to come." He even made a gesture, and extended his hand over the nun's head.

But it had no effect. Sister Marthe continued playing, tranquilly,

"I really believe that I'm making progress," she said, smiling.

Laurent did not reply. He was humiliated, desperate, with sorrow in the depths of his soul. Tears rose to his eyes.

"Are you in pain, Monsieur?" asked Sister Marthe, standing up.

"No, Sister, it's nothing, I assure you. Perhaps a little emotion."

"In any case, it's getting late. I need to go back. Thank you, Monsieur."

She was about to leave. He made one last effort. "Angèle," he said aloud.

She blushed. "How do you know my former name, Monsieur le Docteur?" she said, slightly hesitant. "Doubtless Monsieur le Curé told you. But Angèle has consecrated herself to God, and there's only Sister Marthe now."

"Forgive me," he said, taking her hand. "Forgive me if I called you Angèle; but I once had a friend, a sister, that I loved tenderly. Her name was Angèle, and she's dead…dead."

Laurent, his head between his hands, was weeping.

"Alas!" murmured Sister Marthe. "Pray to God, Monsieur. All consolations come from God."

XII

The General found, that evening, that Laurent was very whimsical. He came out with a firework display of paradoxes regarding magnetism, science, women and religions.

"In sum," he said, to conclude the argument, "the more I see your Plancheuille, General, the more admirable I find the existence that one can lead here. The peasants, the fields, the hunting, the mountains, the wheat and the sheep: that's the only verity. All the rest is nothing but lies. I truly have a yen to come and live here. I could pay you a small rent to compensate you, and since George—the imprudent fellow!—has thought it good to place his happiness in the hands of a woman, the two of us could live like hermits, as recluses, without asking anything of the gods or of humans but to leave us undisturbed."

At that point, the curé arrived. They started a game of whist, which lasted until eleven o'clock. But when the General had gone up to his room, Laurent took on a grave, almost solemn, expression that made a strange contrast with the artificial and unhealthy joviality that he had affected all evening.

"Forgive me, Monsieur le Curé, if I speak to you again about Sister Marthe, but since she is an orphan and abandoned, are you not her sole protector here? Now, this is truly a matter of grave concern for her, and you would not forgive me if I kept silent. You've told me that Angèle's father is dead. Do you know the name of that father?"

106

"Yes," said the curé. "The superior of the Ursuline convent, without telling me positively, allowed me to understand that Angèle's guardian was really her father."

"And did she tell you the name of that guardian?"

"She told me—but no one here knows it, and Sister Marthe does not know it herself."

"Well, Monsieur le Curé, I can tell you the name of Sister Marthe's father. She would be called Angèle de Mérande if her father had recognized her. Am I not well informed? And what would you say if I succeeded in establishing that Monsieur de Mérande, died without children or nephews, made a will in favor of his daughter?"

"I would say that you're truly something of a sorcerer, because it's nearly a year since Monsieur de Mérande died. His fortune has all been divided today, and nothing resembling a testament has been found."

"Well, Monsieur le Curé, that testament exists."

"Is it one of your somnambulists who made you that revelation?" asked the curé, smiling.

"Yes," said Laurent, coldly, "it's one of my somnambulists. And don't think that I'm joking. Never, at any moment of my life, have I been more serious. Tomorrow morning, I shall leave for Paris, and when I return here, I shall bring you Angèle de Mérande's fortune. Do you understand what that signifies, Monsieur le Curé? Poor, Sister Marthe cannot be cured, but if she is rich, if she is surrounded by luxury and the minute cares that only wealth can acquire, she will live. What is at stake, therefore, is Sister Marthe's life…and also her happiness. Have you not told me that poverty determined her vocation? Now, wish me good luck and *au revoir*."

The curé went back to the presbytery very intrigued, not knowing what to think. Was it a joke or an idle boast?

The next day, at the château, he learned that Laurent had gone.

"He's a very amiable fellow," said the General. "He doesn't seem very serious to me, but what does it matter? After all, serious people are boring, and Laurent isn't boring at all."

XIII

As Laurent drew away from Plancheuille, he measured the difficulty of the enterprise more accurately. To discover Monsieur de Mérande's notary—one of the hundreds of notaries in Paris—was simple enough, but to interrogate him, to question him, to talk to him about little Angèle or Sister Marthe was a much more delicate matter. What entitlement could he invoke for thus defending the interests of the young nun? And above all, what reason could he allege for affirming the existence of a testament? A testament is an authentic, tangible fact, not an airy proposition. When the notary demanded proof, what proof could be offered? Angèle alone could say, in one of her flashes of lucidity, where Monsieur de Mérande had written his last will.

Angèle...oh, misery of miseries! Angèle will not come again. That's finished forever now. Well, so be it, everything is finished. I won't search for the testament. I'll carry out other experiments. I'll find other subjects as brilliant, and easier to handle than Angèle. That's enough of nuns and nonsense.

Sure of that resolution, he reached Paris again. He immediately resumed work on magnetism. A young woman named Lucienne had once lent herself with a good grace to various experiments. She was the lover of Émile D***, one of Laurent's comrades. Émile had left Paris, leaving Lucienne alone; Laurent succeeded in finding her address.

Then he tried a few experiments, which succeeded; but he quickly tired of them, Lucienne only presented vulgar phenomena, the classics of hypnotism, for which Laurent now had an insurmountable aversion.

Then again, he sensed that Lucienne had a stupid amorous passion for him. She became absolutely odious to him. He tried to inspire an aversion in the entranced Lucienne to replace the amour, but he did not succeed; the amour persisted, in spite of all his suggestions. The various commands he formulated were executed irregularly by Lucienne; he became angry then, and abused the poor girl roundly.

He multiplied sessions of catalepsy and ecstasy, prolonging them for several hours. He studied their phases with persevering attention. Docile, like a well-regulated machine, or an ingenious and savant automaton, Lucienne obeyed, but with a word, Laurent could make the entire edifice that he had laboriously constructed disappear.

And always, his thoughts returned to Angèle. *What a difference there is between the stable lucidity of Angèle and the gross, rudimentary mechanism of poor Lucienne. If lucidity exists—and it exists—it is Angèle alone who can give the proof of it.* In an hour, with Angèle, he could learn more than in fifteen years with Lucienne.

One evening, as he was passing the large shop selling musical instruments, he perceived an organ that was for sale for eight hundred francs. He went in, examined the machine, and decided to buy it.

From that moment on he abandoned Lucienne completely. He spent his days at home playing the organ, without paying any heed to the complaints of the tenants, piling up in his drawing room the religious music of the great masters—but it was always Rossini's *Stabat* and Gounod's *Ave Maria* to which he found himself incessantly brought back.

There is an extraordinary, sometimes frightening, logic in things and events. The ignorant speak of chance, but it is probable that there is no chance. One evening, while casting his eyes over the display of a second-hand book dealer who lived nearby, Laurent fell upon a pitifully dilapidated pamphlet entitled *Le Château de Mérande*. He learned thus that there is a Château de Mérande in Picardy, near Abbeville. The pamphlet was dated 1842. It related the beauties of the princely, almost historic, dwelling, the property of a very rich, very ancient and very noble family.

This time, Laurent's ideas have definitively settled. It is no longer a question of an amorous caprice or scientific curiosity. It is a matter of great act of justice to accomplish. Angèle is the heir of the Mérande family. It is necessary to render her the heritage that is her due.

Then he did his research. By consulting a directory he discovered that there were three Mérandes in Paris: a cabinet-maker living in the Faubourg Saint-Antoine, a wine-merchant in Belleville and a Comte de Mérande living a 118 Rue Oudinot. At 118 Rue Oudinot Laurent learned from the concierge that the Comte had died the previous year. He was, it appeared, a man of about fifty, deceased without children leaving only distant heirs. The division of the fortune had not yet taken place and the house was for sale. The advertisement bore the notary's name, Maître Leflèchu, Rue de l'Élysée.

Thus far, everything had been easy, but Laurent could not go any further. Maître Leflèchu, very busy and very distracted, smiled thinly when Laurent talked to him about a heritage and a testament.

"But after all," Laurent said to him, impatiently. "You know full well that Monsieur de Mérande had a natural child. It's almost publicly notorious, and it isn't possible that he didn't leave anything to his daughter."

"Yes, Monsieur," replied Maître Leflèchu, "I know that story as well as you do, perhaps better. The little Angèle that the Comte went to see every month at the convent in the Avenue d'Eylau was the daughter of one of his gamekeepers, a worthy man killed by accident. I don't know any more, and no one knows any more. Certainly, Monsieur de Mérande had taken the poor child under his protection, but that's all. When my noble client died, carried off in a matter of hours, as you doubtless know, by a devastating malady, his heirs wanted to send help to the young woman and her mother. It was, I believe, a considerable sum, but they had the regret of being poorly received."

Then Laurent became angry. He had arrived at the state of nervous exasperation that cannot suffer contradiction. The notary replied to him politely and coldly. Finally, as Laurent continued to argue fervently, Maître Leflèchu stood up.

"Permit me, Monsieur, not to continue this futile conversation. You speak to me about a testament and a deed of acknowledgement. Nothing would be better—but it's up to you to find the proof. Thus far, your protégée has no more rights than you or I, or my most junior clerk, to the Comte de Mérande's succession. If you would authorize me to give you some advice, I would engage you to abandon the pursuit of research that cannot have any result. But that is not my concern. Come to me with the documents, and we'll see what can be done. Until then, the best thing is to remain silent. In the meantime, I have the honor of saluting you, for I have numerous clients waiting for me."

That same evening, Laurent left once again for Plancheuille.

XIV

Nothing is more somber than Plancheuille in winter: snow everywhere; a bitter, glacial north wind that whistles and roars in the denuded branches of the trees; in the distance, making stains on the white ground, the thatch of scattered houses, sending their plums of smoke into the mist; roads kneaded by mud and snow, crows dotting the sky in hungry bands, croaking; somber gray clouds, running very low, chased by the wind, covering the mountains with their damp obscurity.

Laurent's soul was even sadder than the valley of Plancheuille. He understood that he had ruined his life. For every man, there is a fateful moment when his future is determined: the happiness of an entire existence depends on that minuscule point, an imperceptible atom of time. Well, Laurent, at that supreme moment, had been unable to show resolution, energy or perspicacity. He had allowed to pass, without taking advantage of it, the decisive minute that judged his entire life. That minute would never come again, and, so cruel is the fatality of human things, forty years of repentance and tears would not repair that fugitive and irreparable moment.

Yes, Laurent had ruined his life. The poor fellow had re-jected Angèle. And yet, Angèle was love, profound, sweet, immense love, such as poets and great men have conceived it: the love devoid of brake or law that dominates the paltry so-cial conventions in the bosom of which we stifle. She was also knowledge, an infinite and mysterious knowledge that sur-passes the wildest conceptions of intelligence, and which, in one bound, would have placed Laurent among the benefactors of humanity. By virtue of a caprice of fortune, he had held a prodigy in his hands. An almost supernatural revelation had been offered to him, and he had not taken advantage of it.

Idiot, triple idiot! Brute, triple brute!

In the depths of his soul, he has lost all hope. He knows that all is finished between Angèle and him. The rip is pro-found, irreparable; the past never comes back, because it is the past. No human force can recall the minute that has disap-peared, efface the word that has just resounded in space. One word, one alone, like a funeral knell, has resonated in Angèle's ears, and Angèle has reentered oblivion.

At the Château de Plancheuille, the General was alone. He had an attack of gout, and it was with great difficulty that he came down to the dining room at meal times.

"Thank you, my young friend, for this unexpected and unhoped-for visit. You're truly very kind to think about an old recluse like me. Let's see, is it to cure me or distract yourself that you've come? I divine that you have chagrins...amorous chagrins, perhaps?"

Laurent shook his head. "Who knows? Even for the hap-piest man in the world, life is a heavy burden—but in any case, General, I believe that I'll cure you sooner than myself."

"Get away, child that you are, an amorous chagrin isn't mortal; it's not even cruel, and when it is cruel, the sweetness holds sway over the cruelty. Oh, how hard it is no longer to feel the ardent and tender sap of youth rising to the heart! Let's leave all that. What are you going to do here, all alone?"

"I've brought a few books, and I'll work as best I can. Work is still the best thing one can imagine to soothe the ills of the soul."

But Laurent did not set to work. Scarcely was lunch over than he went to the presbytery.

"Why," said the worthy curé, "it's our young doctor; have you brought me good news?"

"I can't tell you anything at present, Monsieur le Curé, but I hope that this evening…first, it's necessary that I talk to Sister Marthe. What I have to reveal to her must remain absolutely secret between her and me. Would you please tell her that I'll expect her at the château in an hour. I'll talk to her, and I'll ask her for formal explanations, and her response will decide her fate."

"Come on, you're talking in mysteries! However, it will be done as you wish. You know that I have entire confidence in you; but you'll be careful, won't you, my friend?"

Laurent waited for Sister Marthe in the drawing room. A large fire was blazing in the vast hearth, while blasts of snow were lashing the windows outside.

He had recovered all his presence of mind, all his composure. He was about to gamble two human lives, his own and Sister Marthe's.

It appears that those condemned to death, when the supreme moment arrives, maintain a terrible calm. Laurent had the calm of the condemned.

Sister Marthe came in.

Ah, there you are, Sister," said Laurent, going to meet her. Here, come close to the fire to dry yourself and warm yourself. Monsieur le Curé has doubtless told you that I want to talk to you about very serious matters?"

"Yes, Monsieur," said Sister Marthe, "but I scarcely understood his language. I assume that it's a matter of my health?"

"Certainly," said Laurent, "it's a matter of your health...and also…something else. Let's talk about your health first."

"Well, Monsieur, thanks to your prescriptions, I'm no longer ill. I no longer cough, in spite of the cold of winter, and I never have a fever anymore."

"Well, Sister, no one is happier than I am at that almost unexpected success."

He looked at Sister Marthe and he sensed himself softening completely. Never had the young woman's eyes shone with such a vivid gleam. The tenderness and candor of that gaze troubled Laurent's soul profoundly, and he felt, on seeing it, all the force of his love.

He gathered all his courage. Whatever happened, he would do his duty to the end.

"Since your health is reestablished, Sister, that's fine. Continue the same treatment, and soon, there'll be no more question of medicine or malady. If I've asked you to come here, it's because I have to give you important news of your family."

"Of my family!" she exclaimed, bewildered.

"Or rather, the family of Monsieur de Mérande. Don't be astonished, Sister, I beg you, and let me explain. Hazard, perhaps Providence, has put me in communication with your guardian's family, and I've come…"

"Oh, Monsieur," said Sister Marthe, getting to her feet. "Don't continue. I divine what you're going to propose to me, and in advance. I refuse. When my guardian died, my mother was offered a small pension, but my mother refused, estimating that no one owed her anything, and that, although it was permissible to accept a benefit from Monsieur de Mérande, our protector, she could not receive alms from his heirs. What my mother has done, Monsieur, I wish to do and ought to do. It will be all the easier for me as I have no need of anything. In a few days, I shall pronounce my vows. That is an irrevocable decision. Thus, I have no further need of the wealth of this world. Sister Marthe only needs to be forgotten."

"You haven't understood me, Sister. It's not a matter of alms but a restitution. What would you say if I told you that Monsieur de Mérande' heirs are not his veritable heirs? What would you say if Monsieur de Mérande had left you his entire fortune?"

"Oh, Monsieur, that isn't possible, and if I didn't know you, I'd think that you were making fun of me."

"Sister, the moment is solemn, Reply to me frankly, honestly. When Monsieur de Mérande came to see you at your convent, did he talk to you about the future and his projects?"

"Never, Monsieur. Why would he have spoken to me about that? What did he have to say to me? Don't you know that he was my guardian, and that my father was one of his gamekeepers?"

"And you know nothing more?"

"No, Monsieur, nothing more."

And Sister Marthe looked at Laurent with an amazement so sincere that he dared not continue.

"Well, Sister, I know—hear me well, I *know*—that Monsieur de Mérande made a testament and that you are his unique heir."

Sister Marthe had gone very pale. "Forgive me, Monsieur, if I interrogate you, but in order for you to say that to me, you must have seen the testament. Perhaps you've brought it to me?"

"Alas, no, I haven't seen it, but I know that it exists."

"But you can't tell me anything more certain?"

"I hoped that you could give me some indications."

"Me, Monsieur? Why is that?" She was genuinely almost angry. She moved toward the door.

Laurent tried to retain her.

"So, Sister, you don't want the wealth that I'm bringing you? If you were rich, what would you do?"

"First of all, Monsieur le Docteur," she said, gravely, "I'm not rich; I can't be. I'm only a humble young woman, an orphan without support. In any case, if I were rich, would be the point of the wealth that you have, I don't know how or why, dreamed of for me? I've made a promise to consecrate myself to God, and I shall keep my promise. Poor, I shall live with the poor."

"Then your resolution is immutable?"

"Yes, Monsieur, immutable. Let me go, I beg you."

"So that's the way it is," he said, in a low voice. "Well, it's necessary to finish it."

The young woman was struggling, and trying to free herself, but he, looking her full in the face, fixedly, said: "Angèle! Angèle! Come! I want it."

Sister Marthe uttered a faint cry, and fell backwards.

"Ah!" cried Laurent. "Finally, here you are, Angèle! Thank you, thank you!"

But Angèle did not move. She remained lying on the carpet, inert, immobile. It was the same mortal silence, the same frightful calm, that had invaded her four months before, when Laurent, in his room, had prevented her from leaving.

Laurent said to himself: *That's the first step taken. When I've dissipated this fit of lethargy, it's Angèle who will appear.*

He was now sure of success. He had rediscovered his power. This might last a long time, but in the end, he knew that Angèle would return.

She was there, breathing slowly. Her pale lips parted slightly at every breath of her respiration. Laurent, on his knees, contemplated her amorously.

Oh! he said to himself. *How I love her! How I love her!*

He leaned over, and gently, with exceedingly tender precaution, passed his hands over the young woman's forehead. He repeated it several times, but he saw no change. Neither his words, nor his gestures, nor his breath changed Angèle's state. She remained immobile.

For half an hour, Laurent exhausted his efforts. Finally, all of a sudden, he understood. A frisson ran through him from head to foot. He had one of the frightful flashes that reveal to us, in less than a second, an entire ruination, an entire annihilation, and reveal to us more woes than one could recount in several days. A blinding light traversed Laurent's soul.

Yes, it is the end, the end of everything. Angèle is dead, forever dead. All the supreme effort he has attempted has ended here, in making himself understood to her. She has come

116

back in order that Laurent can address a supreme adieu to her. She wants to hear it one last time, but she cannot respond to him. Today! Today, once again, and that will be all…and forever. The order that he gave, the other day, back there in his room, will be executed in all its rigor. No remission, no weakness. Angele will not some back again.

An immense despair seized him. There was more than despair, there was remorse. Who, then, if not him, had broken that admirable instrument, annihilated that tender soul, who adored him? Who could he blame if not himself, the imbecile, the wretch?

What do the Mérande testament and heritage matter to him? What he wants is Angèle, the adored Angèle who came to him and whom he rejected, unworthily. He loves her with an ardent, passionate amour, and he can do nothing. And it is his own fault, by virtue of his cynical cowardice, that he can do no more.

On the floor kneeling beside Angèle, he wept. He pressed her inert hand between his burning hands, and he would have given his entire existence to feel a slight inflexion of the fingers responding to his supplications.

But no: nothing. Angèle's fingers remain immobile. Her hand is like that of a cadaver. The pulse is beating, slowly, with an inexorable regularity.

"Angèle! Angèle! If you can't reply to me, at least you can hear me. Yes, Angèle, it's a supreme adieu that I've come to bid you. An adieu and a plea for forgiveness. Forgive me! I dared not live for you, and henceforth, my sin will weigh heavily upon my entire life. How happy we would have been! Rich! Powerful! Rich, you really would have been Angèle de Mérande. You know that there's a testament, you alone know it, and if you don't speak, the secret will die with you. Powerful, for you would have revealed to me knowledge unknown to humans. Happy, for you loved me, oh, my Angèle, you loved me immediately, and I, I loved you so much, and now I love you so much more that I shall no longer live except by means of your memory...

"Forgive me! Forgive me!

"But all hope isn't yet lost. Listen, Angèle. The order that I gave you, that accursed order, I rip it up, I annihilate it. Forget it, and come. Tear it up, as I tear it up. Shake off the heavy chains that are weighing on your limbs. Let me hear your voice, your soft voice; let your hands recover their strength. Just one word, one gesture, and you'll be saved. Get up, walk, take back your power over your charming body, Angèle, Oh, this is frightful! Are you going to separate us forever?"

He thought he saw—was it an effect of the vacillating light of the wood burning in the hearth?—he thought he saw Angèle's lips stir slightly. But it was an illusion, undoubtedly, for the features retained the same serenity, and the heart was beating with the same monotonous regularity.

He hid his head in his hands and wept.

"Oh my Angèle! Adieu, and forgive me!"

He leaned over her, and applied his lips to hers for a long time. But Angèle's lips remained inert, insensible to that caress, without any effort to seek it or to escape it. It was the glacial indifference of death.

Then Laurent stood up.

"Since all is finished, Sister Marthe," he said, "get up."

He extended his hand. Then, slowly, the young woman raised her head, her eyes still closed. Then, propping herself up on her elbows, she struggled to her feet.

When she was upright, she opened her eyes and passed her hand over her eyelids.

"Whatever you can say, Monsieur, my resolution is immutable. I thank you for your good intentions, but I don't want to owe anything to Monsieur de Mérande's heirs. May I go now, if you don't want anything more of me?"

Laurent shook his head, unable to speak.

"Once again, Monsieur, thank you."

XV

Laurent has returned to Plancheuille; it is spring. Back there, in Paris, nothing has succeeded for him; magnetism inspires a profound disgust in him; medicine seems to him to be a métier both fatiguing and frivolous, populated with disappointments and bitterness. As for music, it sickens him.

He has refused the proposition of his father, who would have liked to keep him close to him, in the Franche-Comté, in a large town, where an active physician could easily earn six or eight thousand francs a year. One acquires influence there, and—who can tell—might one day be a député.

Laurent has preferred to accept, at Plancheuille, the hospitality of the General. He spends his time in the mountains, studying natural history. He studies fossils, and collects plants and insects. He claims that he will never leave Plancheuille again. But the General, who believes that it is an amorous chagrin, knows full well that at twenty-eight, an amorous chagrin is not mortal. He knows that science will get the upper hand again, and that Laurent will soon begin to live again, and to hope, and to suffer too, since that, above all, is what life is.

As for Sister Marthe, she has quit Plancheuille.

As soon as she had pronounced her views, she was sent to a little village in Brittany, near Douarnenez, where she is teaching French and the catechism to little Breton girls.

She is very cheerful, very pious, and her health is excellent.

Jules Hoche: *Future Paris*

(1895)

Now, the years 1894 and 1895 had been signaled by various cosmic phenomena, which provoked great alarm among the Parisian population on every occasion.

The Butte Montmartre was gradually shifting—see the papers of June 1895. That was no longer a secret for anyone. It was collapsing, little by little, sliding slowly and invisibly, but surely, toward the center of Paris.

That had been the subject of several interpellations in the Chambre, which has sent several scientific committees, one after another, to the location. They brought back desperate reports.

The Butte was falling, without it being possible to retain it on that wretched slope.

All that could be done was to calculate, to within a few days, the date of its appearance at the corner of the Faubourg Montmartre, and takes measures—as if *measures* had ever prevented a butte from falling.

Parisians are careless of nature. After a few days, the Butte was forgotten, the marriage of the Princesse d'Orléans having captured public attention.

Paris was on the threshold of the twentieth century were approaching; its doors opened at the appointed hour, at the same time as those of the great Exposition.

Floods of strangers rushed into Paris, beneath its one-meter moon, its dirigible balloons and its famous hole, the hole so dear to Paschal Grousset.[25]

---

[25] In 1895 Paschal Grousset (better known under the pseudonym of André Laurie, under which he wrote several notable Vernian novels), who was a député for Paris at the time, pro-

An unparalleled era of prosperity began; food prices were sky high and Parisians were sleeping under bridges because of the rents.

Suddenly, there was a frightful bang and cries:

"It's the Metro blowing up!"

"The Hole has collapsed."

It was worse than that; it was the Butte Montmartre that had just hurled itself bodily on to the Boulevard des Italiens, annihilating a few Sino-Japanese lacquers that had nothing to do with the affair.

In the blink of an eye, the chiefs of police and the firemen, two or three ministers, eleven reporters, the troops of the Château-d'Eau, a dozen pickpockets and as many stray dogs, sandwich-men, coco-merchants and sixty thousand idlers –in brief, the All Paris of great disasters—were gathered at the scene of the catastrophe.

As had been said before, there was no remedy.

It was impossible to take the Butte back up to Montmartre. The best thing to do was to leave it there and await developments.

Paris then had the lamentable experience of the inconveniences that the displacement of a butte brings in its wake.

Public life changed it aspect completely; the coachmen went on strike; the itinerary of the Batignolles-Clichy-Odéon omnibus had to be completely overhauled.

Frightful things!

Several newspapers had been buried alive.

---

posed that by way of a main attraction for the projected exposition of 1900 a deep shaft ought to be excavated extending a mile underground, in order that visitors could undertake a journey at least a little way toward the center of the Earth. The plans were quite elaborate, featuring a series of subterranean galleries, with tropical plants and animals taking advantage of the high temperature and humidity at the bottom. The project never got off the ground (so to speak).

One of them was publishing a feuilleton that had lasted two years, and whose ups and downs found an unexpected conclusion in that occurrence.

The author sued the newspaper, demanding compensation. The newspaper protested, alleging that it was, after all, irrelevant whether the characters of the novel perished in the real catastrophe of the Butte or a cataclysm due to the author's imagination, since they would be exterminated anyway in the final episodes—but that argument did not prevail, and the paper was convicted, and never recovered.

Grave difficulties did not take long to result from the presence of the Butte in the middle of one of the most elegant quarters of Paris.

A host of women, for whom virtue was only a question of distance, took to regularly throwing their bonnets over the windmill of la Galette, which was brandishing its sails directly above their windows.

The dance-halls and drinking dens of the ex-Butte made fortunes.

Finally, calm was gradually reestablished among the Parisian population; people fraternized with the indigenes of the Butte, who began to shave and put on gloves in order to keep up with fashion.

A few weeks later, the fun-lovers of the boulevard were reconciled with the young female immigrants and thus, once more, the misfortune of one group completed the happiness of the other.

Raoul Bigot: *The Iron That Died*
(1918)

For forty-eight hours Lieutenant Jacques had not had a moment's rest. Since the beginning of the attack violently launched by the enemy, his battery, installed not far from the front line, had come under particularly heavy fire from the opposing artillery; he was the sole surviving officer, with a personnel reduced by almost half. The orders were imperative; it was necessary, whatever the cost, to continue the barrage under the hail of the 20s and the 150s.

With his habitual detached expression, the lieutenant was going from gun to gun, inspecting his men and giving advice whenever an incident threatened to stop the fire. Nothing seemed to move him, and his imperturbable calm tempered the courage of his soldiers better than more or less nervous speeches. From time to time he went into his hole in order to take cognizance of the news that he was able to receive thanks to the improvised wireless receiver he had installed there.

Good news was transmitted by him directly to his men, and he took to each gun, personally, the new instructions for firing when orders instructed him to change target.

But his physical resistance was at an end this evening; he perceived that in reading a communication saying:

Enemy attack definitively failed. On target one, a burst every quarter hour. Measures taken to resupply you 23 hours and evacuate your wounded. Your fire very efficacious.

Then he made one last round, spreading the consoling information, gave a few orders, and headed for his mattress, felling exhausted.

Lieutenant Jacques had not been born to be a soldier. Rather delicate in health, repelled by any violent exercise, he only felt alive in the research laboratory that he had entered as soon as his scientific education was complete. He deemed himself fortunate to have been able to penetrate right away into one of the all-too-rare great French industrial enterprises that had understood the technical, economic and moral importance of those research laboratories, so well-developed in certain countries industrially younger than France.

He had found his way, and had rapidly rendered appreciated services. At the outbreak of the war, as a complement officer, he had rejoined his regiment. Patriotic and scrupulous, he did his duty without ostentation; the cerebral labor that it demanded was mere child's play to him; he was able to carry out his functions while leaving his mind to work in much higher spheres. Naturally, his scientific preoccupations were orientated toward means of war, and he had astonished his comrades many a time by describing to them, a year before they made their appearance, new machines that seemed to him to be necessary. He gladly repeated that the means of making war were, in sum, very restricted. The present adversaries only used engines of limited local operation, which, in order to produce their effect, had to be employed in considerable numbers.

In order to beat Germany rapidly, it was necessary to be able to do to it, over the thousands of kilometers of the front, at the rear, among its innumerable armies and even on its own territory, by means of a general catastrophe comparable to a major epidemic of the plague or cholera, what the Bocho-Maximalist[26] virus had done to the old Greater Russia or what a torpedo did to a defenseless steamer. But those points of comparison did not furnish any datum to solve the problem. The creation of a general epidemic in Germany was impossible; it was, in any case, repugnant to the French character, all the more so as Germany had already attempted to employ it.

---

[26] "Maximalist" is an approximate translation of "Bolshevik," "Bocho" is an improvised derivative of Boche, signifying the German origin of Marxist-Leninist theory.

As for interior decomposition originating from politics, it was necessary not to think of it; the entire history of Germany was there to prove that the German people were made to obey; it could not be other than an arm; it needed its government to think for it.

It was also utopian to think of blowing up the enemy country like a poor ship!

And Lieutenant Jacques sank into profound reflections in search of a method that might disarm the abhorred enemy at a stroke.

Gradually, sudden and strange gleams were produced in his mind, unexpected connections between experiments he had carried out on the contexture and fragility of metals and curious anomalous electrical phenomena that he had promised to look into in future.

He forced his mind to follow those two questions in parallel, and an idea of genius slowly crystallized in his mind.

During the frightful attack that had been repelled, thanks in large measure to the conduct of his battery, it seemed to him that the idea took on a definitive form.

And lying down on his bed of straw, he said to himself: *I've found it!* Then he thought he had the strength to reflect— but physical fatigue got the better of him. He murmured: "That's it: I'll write to the President of the Council."[27] Then, worn out, he fell into a profound sleep.

Lieutenant Jacques of the 3rd battery, 10th artillery regiment, to Monsieur the President of the Council of Ministers.

I have the honor of informing you that I have discovered a previously-unknown means of war, capable in a matter of hours of provoking an unprecedented catastrophe over enemy territory, placing our enemies at our mercy. The method requires:

A new material, rather important but not extraordinary;

---

[27] The President of the Council, or Prime Minister, of France in 1918 was Georges Clemenceau.

An ensemble of measures easy to take and to apply simultaneously to all fronts and to neutral frontiers, but the strict execution of which is a vital condition to protect the Allies against a catastrophe identical to the one that must be provoked in the central empires;

Absolute discretion, because, if the enemy were informed of the project, it could not only diminish the magnitude of the result but suppress it completely by a very simple means;

A narrow coordination with the general strategy that would certainly modify the plans presently decided.

For all these reasons, recourse to the usual channels with be absolutely impractical; the number and nature of the questions raised would require the examination of my proposal by a large number of committees and bureaux, which would find it absolutely impossible to reach accord before, by one of the devious means that are unknown to us, but which we sense, the enemy would be informed of the idea and undertake the simple measure to which I have made allusion.

I will add that add that all these preparations for execution should not give, either to our agents or the enemy, if it should become aware of them, any indication of the goal pursued.

Only one man in France can examine the ensemble of these questions and decide on them; that man is you, Monsieur President.

Public opinion has brought your energy to power; I am presenting it with the opportunity to make use of it for the greater good of the country.

                                                        Lieutenant Jacques.

The military office of the President of the Council, to which that letter was sent, did not attach much importance to it; nevertheless, information was sought regarding the officer so scantly respectful of hierarchical channels.

That information was such that the skepticism of the President's entourage was shaken, and in order to avoid any blunder, the letter was presented to the President of the Council. The latter ordered that a senior officer be immediately sent to Lieutenant Jacques to demand the principle of his project and a few details that would permit a judgment as to whether the proposal merited study.

The officer returned swiftly.

The lieutenant had simply replied that, on his honor, he guaranteed the veracity of what he had put forward, but that, for the reasons indicated in the letter, he would only explain his project to the President of the Council in person.

From his short mission, the impression that Jacques had made on him, the conversations he had had with his military superiors and with the director of the Company that had employed him before the war, the officer reported the conviction that the proposal could not be summarily dismissed. The Premier telephoned G.H.Q. to send Lieutenant Jacques to see him.

The first interview between the great clear-sighted and unshakably determined politician and the calm and resolute young scientist was a rapid clash of swords.

"Monsieur, you have sent me this letter; you have refused explanations to the superior officer I sent to you. I want to believe that you are not playing a practical joke and that you've reflected that causing the man who concentrates the energy and will of France in his hands to waste his time is almost a crime. Explain your project to me rapidly."

"Monsieur President, the time has not yet come. I would explain to you what you would not believe. First, it is necessary for me to prove to you that the fundamental idea is sound, and I ought to commence with an experiment."

He took a small container out of his jacket pocket the size of a pocket electric torch.

"With this," he continued, "by borrowing for a few seconds an electric current just sufficient to illuminate an ordinary light bulb, I could destroy the world.

"You're shaking your head, Monsieur President, wondering if I'm not mad. Come with me to a place where I can carry out my experiment without doing any damage, and you'll see, you'll believe, and afterwards, you'll hear and comprehend my project."

The President asked for a telephone connection.

"Colonel, do you have an old building in your arsenal that's a hindrance to you and you'd like to see disappear? Good...I'll come to see you tomorrow then."

As he was about to hang up the receiver, Lieutenant Jacques made a gesture.

"Pardon me, Monsieur President, but a few preliminary precautions are indispensable; will you permit me to indicate them before you?"

In response to an affirmative sign, Jacques took he telephone and gave a few instructions.

When the communication was terminated, the President said: "So, Monsieur, we'll leave from here at ten-thirty tomorrow."

The next day, at ten-thirty precisely, the President of the Council and Lieutenant Jacques climbed into an automobile, which took them to an arsenal situated in a large Parisian suburb. Jacques made sure that the prescribed instructions had been carried out. Satisfied with his examination, he returned to the President, who was talking to the colonel in command.

"I'm ready, Monsieur President. Colonel, you know the conditions. Come back in an hour; you'll be able to observe that the building won't inconvenience you any longer."

At a sign of assent from the great master, the colonel went away. An hour later, when he came back, nothing remained of the large hangar but a layer of dust.

The President, in an attitude of profound reflection, was staring at the accumulation at his feet. Lieutenant Jacques was placidly making notes. The arrival of the director of the arsenal recalled them to reality.

The President showed the Colonel what remained of the large edifice, with an expression that said: *How was it done? I don't know*. Then he addressed himself to Jacques.

"What you've just done is prodigious, but I can't conceive its application to the war. I don't understand."

"Now I can explain to you, Monsieur President."

A few days later, the lieutenant was summoned to the Presidency.

"Monsieur Jacques; as you will have anticipated, my decision is made; we're going to attempt your extraordinary operation. The triumph of civilization and humanity justifies it. But I ought not to be the only one informed. In order to bear all its fruits, your action needs to be intimately linked with that of our armies, and it isn't me who commands them."

"I've thought of that. As you've finally succeeded in convincing all the Allies to name a single generalissimo,[28] it's him that it's necessary to inform. We three alone informed, without saying a word to anyone whatsoever, will ensure triumph. I've brought a plan of organization and execution such that all those who will be involved will have no suspicion of the work that they are preparing."

"That's my opinion too. I've summoned the commander-in-chief."

As he said that, the President opened the door to a small room adjacent to his office. With the door securely closed, the three individuals remained in conference for half a day.

The allied offensive that had been expected did not happen, all the armies receiving strict orders to stay on the defensive and maintain pressure on the enemy by means of an uninterrupted harassment of the front and rear lines. Considerable concentrations of automobile trucks carrying various materiel were, however, organized not far from the lines, as well as large quantities of munitions and provisions of every sort.

The President of the Council had enormous difficulty, politically, defending himself against reproaches for inaction; he repeated incessantly that: "We're waiting for the right mo-

---

[28] Ferdinand Foch was appointed commander-in-chief of the Allied armies in the Spring of 1918.

ment," citing the authority of the decisions of the generalissimo, who, appointed by all the Allies, was shielded from the ill humor of parliamentarians.

In the meantime, Jacques worked. To the Swiss frontier and three points on the western front he brought electric power lines from the nearest large generating stations. He had bizarre electrical machines constructed, which bore no resemblance to those known prior to that day; those machines were set up in armored bunkers instructed at the extremities of new lines.

Crews of sappers carried out various maneuvers at the front.

After a few months of intensive labor, Jacques, in the course of a meeting with his two highly-placed collaborators, declared to them: "I'm ready. It's certain that all the precautions have been taken on the Franco-Anglo-Belgian-American, Italian and Greek fronts. On our front, we have succeeded at three points, taking advantage of watercourses, in establishing the necessary connections. If the order is sent to close the Swiss frontier, in the agreed fashion, both on the French side and the Italian side, the cataclysm can by unleashed within forty-eight hours.

"Half an hour after that release, the observers at the front, the barrage balloons and the airplanes, having been be altered to the phenomena to look for, will inform us as to whether or not that first action has been successful. It is, in fact, necessary to anticipate that the mechanisms established with great difficulty at the front might have suffered deterioration; if the result is negative we shall then be obliged to launch the catastrophe through Switzerland. In that case, you know the measures taken to limit the damage, and those permitting our neighbors to remedy the general upheaval that they will suffer.

"If, on the contrary, as it is necessary to hope, the result is good, our emissaries will act in the agreed fashion to oblige Switzerland to take the measures that will safeguard that country; in addition, reliable men will depart for selected points where, even independently of the Federal Government, they can proceed with simple operations that will protect the country from all contagion. That is the system that will be employed in Holland and Demark. France will have made the maximum efforts to ensure that those who have not intervened in the struggle do not have to suffer the rude blow that her adversaries are going to receive.

"Among the enemy, it will be devastating. They will not be able to carry out any defensive move; their famous methodical organization does not permit the rapid comprehension of new things and the consequent making of the necessary decisions. The unexpected is for them a terrible obstacle that stops them, obliging a laborious cerebral effort, which necessities consultations in order to accommodate the abnormal in a familiar frame. They will not yet have grasped the situation as whole when our endeavor will be complete.

"Squadrons of reconnaissance aircraft will keep us up to date with the progress of the disaster. Then, General, it will be up to you to conclude the task."

Lieutenant Jacques had never made such a long speech; in spite of all his calmness, the frightful grandeur of what was about to occur at a gesture from him had overexcited him a little.

For a few seconds silence reigned between the three men on whom the destiny of the world depended.

The meditation terminated, they settled with a common accord the ultimate details of the execution of the gigantic project. At the moment of separation, they thought that they would not see one another again until "afterwards"—which is to say, after the great victory—brought them together and, moved, they embraced fraternally.

A few days after that meeting, the allied front was abuzz with rumors. It appeared that something gave was happening among the Boches. Fires could be seen in large agglomerations; munitions depots were exploding. The aviators reported that they had observed and absolute cessation of movement on the railways.

131

Messages providing more detailed information signaled that a large number of destructions were visible behind all the enemy lines. The messages multiplied, making the entire world aware of the extraordinary cataclysm that was invading enemy territory. The ruination and conflagrations reached Berlin, Vienna and all the way to Constantinople.

A sentiment of surprise, rapidly turning to amazement, and then changing into rage and utter despair, takes possession of Germany and its allies.

On the other side of the front, the first news is welcomed with calm, people being somewhat suspicious of everything that seems supernaturally favorable, but events hurry on; the terrible epidemic that is ravaging the central empires is recorded step by step; a wild joy takes possession of everyone; people run out into the streets and embrace one another, weeping with joy. The tombs of those "Died for France and the Allies" are covered with flowers, and loud voices declare to the dear departed; "You are avenged!"

Then the great awaited new bursts like a clap of thunder: the entire front moves; the French, the English, the Americans, the Italians, the Serbs and the Greeks plunge forward, reducing to nothing the rare resistances of a completely demoralized enemy.

What, then, has happened?

Three days after the last meeting of those who were about to save the civilized world, General von Schünburg arrived, out of breath, at Nuremburg railway station just in time to take the westbound train.

After having expelled the occupants of a carriage that suited him and rebuked the employees who did not exhibit sufficient urgency with regard to a man of his importance—he was in command of an army corps—he installed himself. Then, with an anxious expression, he took two telegrams out of his pocket and reread them attentively. What could they signify? One of the two telegrams came from the commandant of his army at the front, the other from the Minister of War, giving him the order to return to his post immediately "in view of extraordinary circumstances." He had, therefore, been obliged to interrupt his leave, although he had only arrived in Nuremburg the day before.

Tyrannical with his subordinates, he showed, like all Prussian officers, an absolute discipline with regard to his superiors. Thus, he did not protest against the order that deprived him of the distractions he had promised himself, but preoccupied himself with the reason that had provoked it. What could the extraordinary circumstances in question be?

The train stopped at a small station through which it should have passed at speed. Leaning out of the window, von Schünburg could see an agitated man making broad gestures speaking to the locomotive's driver. He was about to send for news when the train moved off again at a much reduced speed, which it maintained.

The general, his conscience tranquil, made himself comfortable in a corner, and fell asleep shortly thereafter.

A sudden shock wakes him up. The train has stopped abruptly. This time, the general gets down; if the driver has not been warned that he has the honor of conducting the commandant of an army corps, he will go to inform him in energetic terms.

Around the machine there is a circle formed by railway employees and a few passengers. The locomotive has derailed; the accident has been caused the rupture of the rails, which have split over a length of several meters.

Thanks to its low speed, the machine had not traveled far; it has traced a furrow in the gravel and has stopped against a rail of the adjacent track—which, someone remarks, has been split by the impact over a distance of several meters. The machine is obstructing both tracks; circulation will certainly be interrupted for several hours.

The train manager informs the passengers that there is a station only three kilometers further on, and that the simplest thing is to head for it on foot; from there they can telegraph for a train to be formed and come to pick up the passengers stranded by the breakdown.

Von Schünburg sees wan faces peering at him, which might, in emitting the complaints of people who cannot swallow their anger, offend the dignity of the high rank he represents. He therefore contains himself and, responding to the salute addressed to him a moment before by a young officer of pretentious appearance striking the regimental pose, authorizes the latter to accompany him in attaining the advertised station.

At the station there is an extraordinary hubbub; all the station personnel are afflicted by panic. There is good reason; no train has passed through for an hour; the last one to arrive derailed while stopping, the rails having twisted and broken beneath the locomotive at the moment the engineer applied the brake. It is necessary to believe that the shock was rude and had broken the wheels, for they had given way shortly afterwards and the machine is now maintained on the ground by a part of its mechanism and its axles.

The general went directly to the station-master; authorizing himself by his rank, and even exhibiting his two telegrams. He ordered imperatively that a train be formed immediately. The station-master raised his arms to the heavens in a gesture of despair; all the dispatches he had received were incomprehensible; they talked of derailed rains and catastrophes, but nothing precise could be obtained therefrom except that railways circulation appeared to have stopped completely. Furthermore, telegraphic communication had been progressively cut off, without it being possible to determine the cause. At that very moment, information had just arrived that extraordinary phenomena were occurring at the large freight terminal created to serve the munitions factory with which the little town had been honored in 1915: the rails were disappearing and wagons were collapsing.

Exasperated by that verbiage, which he attributed to a fit of madness provoked in a feeble mind by the announcement of a vulgar railway accident, von Schünburg sent the officer accompanying him to request on his behalf the elements necessary to form a train, and headed for the buffet.

For nearly an hour, von Schünburg ate and drank copiously, isolated in a small separate room.

As he lit a cigar he thought about the officer, who had not come back, but his well-garnished stomach inclined him temporarily to indulgence toward the subaltern who seemed to be taking a long time to carry out his orders. Suddenly, a man brought him a note scribbled by his companion, which told him that what the station-master had said was unfortunately correct; he had not been able to find and rolling-stock in s for state to travel. On the indication that he might perhaps find something at the munitions factory, he had gone there.

After having taken cognizance of that message, the general noticed that the man who had brought it seemed to be on the brink of fainting.

"What's happening, then?"

"Frightful things."

"Let's go, then!"

Getting up, with difficulty, von Schünburg decided to make a tour in order to restore order.

At that moment, a cry of "Fire!" resounded. At the door of the buffet, the general stopped, dazedly. A short distance away the deformed locomotive had collapsed completely, and the coals, still incandescent, had set fire to the mass of fuel in the tender, of which nothing remained but vestiges.

The wagons had crumbled; only the planks and drapes seemed intact; the gas reservoir of one was letting out gas through its walls, and a gust of wind had caused the cloud of gas to make contact with the sparks of the fire; in an instant, flames engulfed the train. In a matter of moments, the entire station would be on fire!

The general followed the crowd that was fleeing through the only available exit, toward the freight terminal.

There, he was obliged to admit that the rumors reaching him were accurate. Where the rails had been, nothing could now be seen but streaks of dark dust; nothing remained of wagons but plants and partitions; it was as if the framework had been volatilized.

He stopped in front of a train loaded with munitions and contemplated the large shells that were heaped up pell-mell. He struck one of them with the tip of his cane and stopped, stupefied.

Come on! He was dreaming. It wasn't possible!

He repeated the experiment; his cane had pierced the shell; under the slight impact, the magnificent steel of the German factories had shattered, laying bare the redoubtable explosive.

Mechanically, he did it again, and every time, his stick disaggregated one of the shells of which he was so proud.

As if under the influence of a hallucination, he struck with harder blows, hoping finally to hear the metallic sound usually rendered by those large jewels of death, which only Germany had been able to prepare in advance—but he encountered nothing but soft sounds, which the friable envelopes made as they crumbled, laying bare their hideous yellow souls.

Then, griped by vertigo, he fled. But he did not get far.

A few hundred meters away, and immense whirlwind of flames burst forth. He only just had time to think: *The munitions factory!* before he was swept away and crushed by the torrent of gas, materials and debris of all kinds projected in all directions by the explosion of a considerable mass of munitions and thousands of tons of explosives.

Lieutenant Jacques' method was triumphant.

It really was an idea of genius that he had had, of provoking, by means of a new phenomenon of the electric order, what he called a "molecular disease of iron." Under the impact of that special wave, iron and steel took on an intimate vibratory movement—for nothing was revealed at the outset—that provoked an extreme fragility in the metal. Under the effect of the stresses to which it was subjected, the metal broke; the disintegration continued by virtue of the annihilation of molecular attraction, and the iron was reduced to dust. And the

136

most extraordinary thing was that the malady was eminently contagious; the vibration was transmitted with a speed so reduced that it was difficulty to explain scientifically, but it was transmitted from one piece to another, even when there was only an insignificant contact between them.

What had happened at the station where General Schünburg had had such a tragic end to his dinner was only one small scene in the terrible drama that shook Germany and extended to Austria, Bulgaria and Turkey. The disease progressed, following the facile route of the railway, and multiplied, without any break in continuity, at the inexorable velocity of fifty kilometers and hour, sowing terror everywhere.

The first effects were those already known: the rails broke and disintegrated, leading to frightful derailments; the locomotives and the metal parts of the wagons soon followed, and by means of the fires in the engines, the gas in the wagons and electrical short-circuits, the trains fell prey to flames. In the big stations, above all, the accumulation of materials subject to that extraordinary decomposition led almost immediately to devastating conflagrations.

Metal bridges attained by the epidemic collapsed noisily.

At army railways depots, the accumulation of munitions and cannons offered a magnificent field for the extension of the molecular disease, whose ravages spread, reducing the results of the efforts of Boche industry to nothing.

Near the front, the stations of the various engineering and artillery stores are naturally afflicted; in the munitions depots, the casings of shells disintegrate before the fearful eyes of the personnel, who flee madly in all directions, often with reason, for the fires produced there, as everywhere, lead in places to mighty explosions; the latter spread from one accumulation to another. Projectiles and cartridges of every caliber, grenades, rockets, canisters of incendiary liquids and gas cylinders form gigantic firework displays, of which only those who are able to contemplate the most massive destructions accomplished in the course of the war can have any idea.

Ill. Lelong

The contagion continues; a simple momentary contact between an item attained by the mysterious disease and a healthy piece contaminates the latter, which becomes susceptible in its turn of transmitting the plague. Many bizarre incidents result therefrom.

Projectiles unloaded from a cart at the moment when the fatal wave reaches them carry the germ inexorably into the munitions depots of batteries where they are stored; if those projectiles are immediately employed, it is to the cannons that they communicate the decomposition still latent within them; in that case, it is a rare gun that resists the first shot; at the second, the breech, under the pressure of the gases, explodes with a bang.

In the interior, the railway stations are not the only places attained; industrial communications are a facile route of penetration which the molecular disease comes implant itself in the enemy's factories. By way of wagons, and the conveyor belts that load and unload them, the vibratory shock imperceptible invests the frameworks of the vast proud halls; as time goes by, they collapse noisily, contaminating the machine-tools and the components under construction, reducing the martial and economical equipment so laboriously constructed to nothing.

But that is not all; many tramway rails are connected to those of the railways. By way of them, the funeral frisson reaches the hearts of cities.

Tramway rails, in order to reduce the effects of electrolysis provoked by the currents, are linked to the great cast iron conduits that distribute water and gas; those electrical links, in copper cables prior to the war, have been replaced by pieces of soft iron, because Germany needs to make use of its entire stocks of copper in munitions; those cables are, therefore, further vehicles that tranquilly absorb the electrical wave broadcast from the French front; and those routes offer a magnificent means of fulfilling the mission for which it has been created.

It reaches the electricity stations and water distribution stations and destroys them. It reaches the gas factories, and its destructive power is amply displayed; the apparatus of the manufacture and purification of the gas, and the gasometers, disintegrate under its action. The gas and incandescent hearths are liberated; their encounter produces cataclysms; gigantic flames rise up to enormous heights, as if to underline the amplitude of the punishment for the terrified populations.

The devastating scourge follows its inflexible law; the major conduits that have brought it to the places where gas is produced have not caused it to disdain the secondary iron conduits that aliment certain districts; it arrives to prove its power by provoking conflagrations that the disappearance of the water mains does not allow to be combated.

The fluvial routes do not remain immune; bridges and locks are infected, and break; cisterns empty; their contents produce floods.

Any yet more: the ravages are not only exercised on land, the ports are subject to it as well. Maritime railway stations docks and warehouses are gripped and disappear in the torment. Naval shipyards are not sheltered from the blows of the invisible enemy, which shows no mercy to any of the atoms of iron that it encounters in its path. The gigantic or modest hulls of cruisers under repair and submarines under construction disappear rapidly from the places where they are being prepared for further depredations.

The ships in dock receive the unforgiving flux via the apparatus for loading coal and the embarkation gangways; in a matter of hours they are on the sea-bed. Several large battleships, confronted by the inexplicable disease, decide to leave, but many of them carry away the fatal germ that a fortuitous contact has transmitted to them. At sea, their hulls dissolve and they plunge abruptly beneath the waves.

The initial shock provoked at three points of the enemy railway network by the intermediary connections established with great difficulty had succeeded in reaching the adversary in all its vital and sensitive spots, thanks to the prodigious continuity of the metal components that cover all the civilized or supposedly civilized nations with a slender but tangled network that binds together all toil and production.

Germany, Austria-Hungary, Bulgaria and Turkey were reduced to helplessness. The destruction extended, alas, to the territories occupied by the ferocious aggressors, but that was the ransom of the triumph.

As for neutrals, to the great satisfaction of the three protagonists of the momentous affair, they had not suffered. The molecular disease had been transmitted from the front; the anticipated protective measures had been taken in time; the railway lines linking them to the central empires had been cut.

The task of Lieutenant Jacques was accomplished; he had refused in advance all the flattering proposals made to him. He would return to his cherished laboratory; he had a great problem to solve—to the molecular disease of iron that his genius had created, he needed to find a remedy. That would be his work during the peace, the glorious and just peace that the beaten enemy was now demanding on its knees, and which would be signed the next day.

"Lieutenant! Lieutenant! The colonel has arrived to congratulate the battery!"

It is only at the third announcement of that news, shouted by his orderly, that Lieutenant Jacques, after twelve hours of deep sleep, wakes up.

Raoul Bigot: *Nounlegos*

(1919)

I

Nounlegos. That was the name, written in pencil on a piece of paper in the waiting room, that Monsieur de Landré, examining magistrate of the Court of the Seine, read when he cast a glance at his desk as he handed his hat and coat to the office boy.

Anticipating the question, the boy replied: "He's an old gentleman who's asking to speak to Monsieur the examining magistrate about the Charfland affair; he refuses to give any further explanation. Asked to request an audience in writing, explaining the reason, he replied: 'I've come to offer help in discovering the truth; I'm not asking for anything; I'm making an offer; I won't make it again.' What should I do, Monsieur?"

"Leave me alone for a moment; I'll summon you again."

And Monsieur de Landré, holding in his hand the piece of paper on which the name *Nounlegos* stood out in large letters, irregular but clearly traced, sat down to contemplate it, pensively.

How many times had he been disturbed by importunate individuals affirming that they had information of great importance relative to some affair or other, who ended up wasting his time without adding anything of interest to the cases? That was what had led him only to grant audiences, save for exceptional cases, in response to written requests.

This time, however, although scantly initiated by his profession into the so-called mysteries of graphology, he examined those characters attentively, revealing, he had no doubt, an uncommon will. The verbal response made by the unknown person augmented the magistrate's curiosity to make the acquaintance of an individual that he anticipated to be interesting.

Faithful to his method, which was to leave as little scope as possible to chance and surprise, he telephoned his secretary to carry out immediate research regarding a certain Nounlegos and to inform him immediately.

He knew that all the Bottins and directories, and all the files accumulated by the Court and the Prefecture of Police, would be consulted, and that he would have some indications regarding his visitor in a matter of minutes.

Then, his thoughts going to the object of his visit, he absorbed himself in recalling the details of the famous Charfland affair.

Yes, famous—and threatening to be disastrous for him!

In the heart of Paris, in a first-rate family boarding-house, an American billionaire, A. H. Terrick, his wife, his two children and their governess had been murdered by the injection of a violent poison that the experts had not been able to define exactly.

On the eve of the discovery of the crime, a great financial institution, the Universel Crédit, had paid in cash to someone named Joe Helly a check for ten million francs signed A. H. Terrick, who had informed the bank of that circumstance. It had been impossible to find any trace of that Joe Helly, whose description had been easily reconstituted, in view of the curiosity inspired by the beneficiary of such a large sum withdrawn at a stroke.

On the crime scene there had been no trace of a struggle, no sign of forced entry had been found, and no theft had been committed.

Charged with the investigation of the affair, Monsieur de Landré had been very satisfied; it promised to be sensational, given the number of victims, their notoriety in America, the ten millions collected by the ungraspable Joe Helly and the general mystery suspended over the ensemble.

An accomplished and hard-working magistrate of genuine talent, Monsieur de Landré hoped, by conducting an efficient investigation in such an important case that he might reach the position as a tribunal judge that his professional ambition had set as an objective.

Naturally, to begin with, he had interrogated the people resident in the boarding-house where the crime had taken place. There were only three: the proprietor, a maid and a traveler.

From that first enquiry, he had learned that a month before the event, the proprietor, Madame Durand, a very honorable individual, the widow of a former civil servant, had received a cable from New York signed "Charfland" asking that a room be reserved for him on a particular day; a telegraphic mandate for five hundred francs had been attached. The client thus announced was unknown to Madame Durand, but as her clientele, exclusively composed of Americans, was invariably recommended to her house, she was not astonished by that; she was even delighted, as no guest was then occupying the large and luxuriously furnished apartment that comprised her accommodation. The message being accompanied by a reply coupon, she had cabled that a room had been reserved.

Two days later, another telegram, similarly sent from New York, had arrived retaining the whole apartment; it was signed A. H. Terrick. That one was known to Madame Durand. Almost every year, he came to spend some two months in Paris with his wife and two daughters; to the great caravanserais that are modern hotels that American, a man of taste and discretion, preferred the elegant furnished apartment that Madame Durand maintained very well, and tried every time to retain the entire accommodation for his family, for which he paid five thousand francs a month.

In spite of that windfall, the proprietor had been unable to break her prior arrangement, so, on the arrival of the Terrick family, she had taken great care to apologize for not being able to put one of the rooms at their disposal, occupied two days previously, but retained for some time, by a Mr. Charfland.

In any case, the position of that room left complete liberty to the occupants of the rest of the apartment.

The latter was on situated a broad avenue, with one wall at the junction of two streets. On entering, a large gallery communicated, to the left, with two small rooms, one of which had no windows, which was reserved for Madame Durand, and then a beautiful dining room overlooking the street, and, to the right, with a large cloakroom, a bathroom, WCs, a kitchen and then a small room occupied by Thérèse Vila, Madame Durand's maidservant.

The bedroom to the right of the gallery next to the entrance door had been attributed to Mr. Charfland; apart from the small drawing room, the four bedrooms overlooking the avenue had been given, in the following order, to Mr. Terrick, Mrs. Terrick, the two children and the governess.

The room overlooking the courtyard, occupying the interior angle formed by the gallery and the corridor contiguous with Mr. Charfland's room, had remained free and served as a nursery for the little Terricks.

As permanent staff resident in the apartment, Madame Durand only had Thérèse Vila; she was at the disposal of the clientele at all times. Depending on the number of guests, one or several housemaids came by the day to do the necessary work. When the guests wanted to take their meals in the house, an agreement made between Madame Durand and a good local restaurateur permitted them to be easily satisfied.

As soon as Mr. Terrick arrived, Madame Durand had introduced him to Mr, Charfland; the two men had bowed to one another courteously, no more; they did not appear to know one another.

After that, each of them had led a tranquil life and no incident had occurred.

On the eve of the day of the discovery of the crime, Madame Durand had been obliged to go to the suburbs to visit her aged parents, who were ill. Departing at eight o'clock in the morning, she had not returned until ten o'clock in the evening. When she came in, her maid, Thérèse Vila, had told her that the American family, being indisposed, had not left the drawing room all day.

The proprietor added that when her domestic had made that communication to her regarding her principal tenant, she appeared slightly haggard, but as that fashion of acting afflicted her from time to time, being a woman of overly sensitive nerves, Madame Durand had not paid any particular attention to it at the time.

The following morning, at half past eight, Thérèse had come into the proprietor's room without knocking, prey to an intense emotion, and cried: "Madam! Madame! They're all dead in the drawing room!"

It was true. Upset by the horrible sight, the proprietor had her other tenant alerted, so great was her need for support at such a tragic moment.

The maid had found Mr. Charfland still in bed; he had put on a dressing gown and run to the drawing room. Mr. and Mrs. Terrick, the two children and the governess were slumped in the chairs. Their icy hands and heads attested to the fact that death had done its work. Mr. Charfland, overcoming his emotion, had recommended that nothing should be touched and that the nearest police commissaire should be alerted by telephone. Then he had dressed in haste and was ready when the magistrate in question, accompanied by his secretary and two agents, had arrived. The commissaire had limited himself to putting an agent on sentry duty at the door of the drawing room in order that no one would go in, and another at the door of the apartment, in order that no one would leave, and had immediately alerted the court.

It was at that moment that the public prosecutor, who was summoned personally with a medical examiner, had charged Monsieur de Landré with the investigation of the frightful crime.

When the physicians consulted as experts had affirmed that the death had taken place some thirty hours previously, the magistrate had no hesitation in having Thérèse Vila arrested, who, according to her employer's declarations, must certainly have had knowledge of the facts a day before revealing them.

In spite of that crushing evidence, Monsieur de Landré had been unable to get anything out of the poor girl, who, utterly distraught, swore that she did not know anything at all and did not recall having mentioned the victims to Madame Durand on the eve of the discovery of the crime. The accused, seemingly extremely nervous, had been examined by specialist physicians, who, while recognizing hereditary defects in her, had concluded that she was entirely responsible for her actions—but the investigation could not deduce anything from that.

Charfland, interrogated as a witness, said that he only knew the victims by virtue of having perceived them once or twice on the stairs or in the antechamber. He had given an account of the employment of his time, the verification of which, without leading to certainty—it is so easy for a stranger to pass unperceived in the public life of Paris—did not permit any doubt to be cast on his declaration.

The examining magistrate had immediately sensed a veritable combatant in the man who, he thought, could put him on the right track: he was a cool individual, incapable of letting himself be carried away by a nervous impulse, the master of his words as well as his actions. His prudence was such that one could clearly sense reflection and calculation prior responding even to insignificant questions. Spontaneity was so excluded from everything the man said that Monsieur de Landré said to himself: *If that man is the guilty party, it will be difficult to unmask him; the contest will be hard.*

One day, in order to provoke a movement of protest on the part of the man he vaguely suspected, he said to him point-blank: "What if I were to have you arrested?"

Charfland did not even blink, and replied: "In what way would arresting a innocent person advance your instruction?"

The lack of emotion at the announcement of that redoubtable eventuality, and the tone of the response, indicated

147

that the man expected the question and had reflected in advance as to what reply to make.

From that moment on, the magistrate's suspicions gained substance, but they were only based on imponderables that did not permit any action on the part of the law.

One precious indication was furnished to him by one of his friends, a celebrated doctor at the Salpêtrière, who had been part of the committee charged with examining Thérèse Vila. Informed of the magistrate's suspicions, he asked him to repeat the confrontation, which had produced no result, of the accused and the witness while he the doctor, watched the scene concealed behind a curtain.

This was what the man of the art observed:

Thérèse Vila is sitting in the magistrate's study, facing the door; when, on the ringing of the handbell, Charfland is introduced, she stands up as if moved by a spring, but the witness darts a cold glance at her, which seems to subjugate her, and she sits down quietly, as if resigned. The remainder of the scene presents nothing of interest; Mr. Charfland does not appear to pay any heed to the unfortunate creature who is there; no contradiction is manifest in the responses that the two of them make to the magistrate's questions.

When the confrontation is over, Charfland having left while Thérèse Vila is still there, the doctor lifts the curtain and enters the scene in his turn. With a gesture, he signals to the magistrate not to intervene, and advances quietly toward the accused. He seems to recognize her, enquiries amiably about her health, brings up a chair, sits down beside her, and takes her hands, continuing his conversation in a low voice. Gazing at her fixedly, he makes a few passes over her head...

"She's asleep," he whispers then, attracting the attention of the magistrate. In a voice that is not raised, but insistent, he says: "Do you know Charfland?"

"Yes," she replies, shivering at the name.

"Do you like him?"

"Oh, no!"

"Does he frighten you?"

"Oh, yes!"

"Tell me what he ordered you to do, and what he ordered you so say."

The face of the accused reveals an intense internal struggle; she raises her hands, seemingly want to repel an atrocious vision; then, as if curbed by a superior will, she murmurs: "No, I can't...he's forbidden me to do it."

By means of further passes, the doctor renders the magnetic sleep more profound. He exerts all his psychic will to extract his subject from the anterior grip, but he does not succeed.

Breathlessly, the poor girl can only respond: "No...no!"

To prolong the experiment would be dangerous; the doctor calms the patient and wakes her up gently. He asks the magistrate to have some consolation brought to her.

Then, in a low voice, he says: "You're right, my friend; the girl is innocent. Charfland, who dominates her, is in all probability the guilty party, but my science can do no more; the criminal's emprise is too powerful. The truth will have to come out some other way. In the meantime, it would be kind to ameliorate the material situation of this poor creature, for I understand that, legally, you're not yet able to release her."

"Any more than I can have Charfland arrested," the magistrate replies, still moved, in spite of his professional impassivity, by what has just happened before him.

It was all the more necessary to take precautions with regard to Charfland because the latter claimed to be a United States citizen, although born of French parents. He had shown several documents justifying his claims, incomplete from the legal point of view but generally recognized as sufficient for foreigners traveling in France for pleasure.

Via diplomatic channels, very slow, but which could not be by-passed in the present case, the magistrate had requested complementary information from America at the very start of the investigation, and had even sent an agent of the Sûreté over there with a detailed description along with a photograph of the man he wanted to unmask. Unfortunately, he had not been able to add anthropometric date to it, because subjecting a foreigner who had not been accused of a crime to Bertillonian measurement might have created a diplomatic incident. The envoy was therefore limited to a detailed verbal description made by skillful sleuths who had been able to examine Charfland in the public places he frequented, and photographs taken without the knowledge of the interested party.

A summary of the investigation was added to it.

One morning, Monsieur de Landré found in his post a letter from the Ministry of Foreign Affairs. He opened it immediately, and was astonished to read:

In response to your request for information on the subject of case no. *** (in accordance with the diplomatic habit of classifying affairs of a criminal nature by numbers in order not to have name appear in documents officially exchanged between chancelleries) *we have the honor of informing you that the response will be made to you verbally by an American functionary specially dispatched from New York for that purpose.*

He had not had time to think of drawing deductions from that fact when the usher handed him a folded piece of paper, saying: "The man who has come from New York."

"Send him in," ordered the magistrate, spontaneously.

The door opened, and the usher let through a handsome old man with a white beard, standing very straight, dressed in the latest Parisian fashion.

He bowed to the magistrate "You are Monsieur de Landré, the examining magistrate responsible or the Charfland affair?"

The magistrate replied with an affirmative nod of the head.

"In that case, Monsieur le Juge, would you be kind enough to make sure that no one disturbs us, on any pretext, while our conversation lasts? I don't want to be recognized."

The magistrate rang, gave the instruction to the usher, invited the stranger to sit down, and said: "I'm listening, Monsieur."

The man from New York sits down. Then, briskly disposing of his beard, his moustache and his white wig, he shows his astonished interlocutor a completely clean-shaven face surmounted by black hair. He fixes the examining magistrate with his intelligence gaze and says: "I ought to talk to you with an uncovered face."

Standing up again in order to bow, he introduces himself: "Max Semper, of the New York Police." He takes out some documents from a wallet, which he presents to Monsieur de Landré. "These are my accreditations."

The examination of the latter is rapid; no doubt is permissible; the man really is the celebrated detective Max Semper, officially charged with bringing the French magistrate the response to his request for information concerning the mysterious affair.

Monsieur de Landré extends his hand to his visitor. "Delighted to make your acquaintance, Monsieur Semper, and thank you in advance for your collaboration."

The conversation immediately got to the heart of the subject; it was little more than a monologue by the citizen of free America.

"The examination and connection of the following facts: firstly, that the family of A. H. Terrick was the victim; secondly; that ten millions have been abstracted from the murdered man; and thirdly, that the crime is surrounded by a profound mystery; permit the belief that the crime might—I don't say must—have been carried out by the famous Invisible Gang, of whom you've certainly heard mention, although its exploits have been limited until now to the State of New York.

"The gang only commits crimes that bring in large amounts, like the aforementioned ten million collected by Joe Helly. It accomplishes its crimes in extraordinarily mysterious circumstances, such that, in spite of the finest official and private detectives in the United States, it has not yet been possible to discover them.

"Finally, it was only by a providential hazard that A. H. Terrick escaped a blackmail attempt few months ago, which

151

was for two million dollars, the equivalent of ten million francs.

"It would take too long to explain that hazard in detail. Let it suffice for you to know that, by virtue of it, and, so to speak, independently of A. H. Terrick, we were able to abort the blackmail and lay our hands on two members of the Invisible Gang.

"Those two scoundrels were absolutely determined not to surrender their accomplices and the organization of their association, but in the end, thanks to whisky, one of them let slip, in conversation with his guards, a few petty indications that might be useful. He allowed it to be understood that, the Terrick affair having been aborted, the latter had been condemned to death.

"In several crimes, traces have been found of a bandit whose description, although vague, nevertheless fits the one you have given of Charfland.

"In these circumstances, I can only try to discover whether Charfland is part of the Invisible Gang; following the results of that first investigation, I shall see if I can go any further.

"I have the necessary indications to have Charfland followed from now on; I'll come back tomorrow to bring you up to date. Is that okay with you?"

Although slightly disillusioned, because he had expected more, Monsieur de Landré accepted the proposal.

The detective readjusted his disguise, and the usher, having been summoned, showed his out with all the deference due to a man whose hand had just been shaken cordially by the magistrate.

Twenty-four hours later, Max Semper presented himself before the examining magistrate again and told him the following:

"Among the few useful indications I possess regarding the Invisible Gang, the most important is one related to the signs by which the affiliates recognize one another: rather complex signs in which the general attitude of the body as well as the bearing of the head, the position of the hands and that of the fingers plays a role.

"Yesterday evening, two of my men, who arrived from New York by different routes, played a little comedy in the renowned Frangip bar, which Charfland frequents almost every day.

"One of the men, after making sure of the presence of the quarry, perched on one of the high stools at the bar in such a fashion as to be visible from where Charfland was sitting. I placed myself in gallant company—it's necessary to keep up appearances—in such a manner as not to miss a single one of the individual's movements.

"My man, who was in evening dress, appeared to be absorbed in drinking a cocktail, but from time to time, unable to hide his impatience, as if he were waiting for someone, his eyes examined the whole room with a circular glance and then rapidly resumed their dull aspect. In brief he acted, in such a way as not to attract attention, like someone forewarned of danger or obliged by his situation to keep a close watch on their surroundings.

"Your Charfland—who responds very well, by the way, to the description given by your Sûreté—did not take long to perceive that performance and, without giving any indication of it, keep track of it.

"That was what I was waiting for; I then gave the agreed signal. My other man, also in evening dress, seemingly slightly tipsy, came into the bar. The first stared at him attentively and then, when the other passed close to him, made the rallying signal of the Invisible Gang. The second stopped momentarily, skillfully feigned the movement of a man recovering his composure, and repeated the famous signal. The two men then approached one another frankly, shook hands and sat down on stools side by side.

"At the first signal Charfland, I'm sure, shifted in surprise; at the second, he almost started. He remained thoughtful for more than a quarter of an hour, watching, almost without dissimulation, the actions of my two acolytes. Finally, he

153

stood up and went to sit down on a nearby stool. When he arrived, my two policemen drew closer to one another and continued talking in lower voices, clearly showing that they did not want to be overheard by the newcomer. Charfland continued watching them, now looking directly at the one who had arrived first.

"The comedy was good. Two or three times my man submitted to the inquisitive gaze without appearing to perceive it, and then, at a further attempt, he muttered: 'What can this fellow want, I wonder?'

"My second acolyte then turned round to look at our Charfland in his turn, made a slight movement, as if he had recognized someone, and leaned toward his companion's ear as if he wanted to make him party to his surprise. The latter got up and, passing between his friend and Charfland said in a fashion to be overheard: 'What do you want? I'm looking in the mirror.' Then, looking, as he said it toward the mirror situated on the other side of the bar—a movement that Charfland imitated—he executed the rallying sign of the Invisible Band.

"I was waiting for that moment. Charfland put his body in the position of the sign; his hands began to sketch a movement that might have been that of the sign, but, as if suddenly changing his mind, he didn't finish it and negligently turned his head away.

"The policeman muttered an insult then in a low voice, resumed his seat and said to his comrade, in a fashion to be overheard by our man: 'He's not one of ours; I don't like the look of him.'

"The other immediately replied: 'Take care; no fuss here.'

"Then the latter paid for the drinks and almost forcibly drew his companion away. As he left, the latter darted a furious glance at Charfland.

"Charfland remained absorbed for some time; he seemed very perplexed, but the calm and self-controlled expression that you know soon got the upper hand again. Half an hour later he left in his turn and slowly, as if prey to profound thoughts, made his way home."

After that simple narration Max Semper stopped, as if to concentrate his reflections, and then resumed:

"From all that, Monsieur le Juge, it results that I can't affirm to you that Charfland is a member of the Invisible Gang, but my hunch as a policeman tells me—and me alone—that he is. It's indisputable that he recognized the gang's rallying signal; he sought contact with people who appeared to be in it, and although he didn't finish the signal—if he had done, I could affirm his affiliation—it's because he remembered in time that, to his knowledge, none of the gang except for him was in Paris, and that he was being constantly watched by your police. The fear of a trap held back his revelatory gesture.

"I think you're absolutely right to follow this trail; it's the right one. I regret not being able to bring you any proof. With your permission, I'll consider my mission here concluded. I'll send you a detailed report of the facts I've just brought you."

Monsieur de Landré remained thoughtful for a few moments; then he told the policeman about the scene of the confrontation of Charfland and Thérèse Vila and the session of magnetism that had followed it.

"In that case," said Max Semper, "my conviction is well-founded. Don't you have sufficient elements to have Charfland arrested? You know that if the man really is who we think he is, he'll slip through your fingers one day. If you prevent that, you might be able to assemble enough evidence to confound him."

"If Charfland were a French national, Mr. Semper, he'd already be locked up, but he claims to belong to the great nation of the United States. The man is energetic; he'll be able to combine his voice with that of a top-flight advocate, and our chancellery won't accept a diplomatic incident if the arrest is only based on what, legally, we can only call the commencements of suspicion."

It was the celebrated detective's turn to reflect, and then make his decision.

"If Charfland is who we suppose, it's in the common interests of both our countries to make sure that he can't do any more harm. What I've seen permits me, I think, to smooth out any diplomatic difficulty in advance. I'll go to see the ambassador immediately; I'll come back in an hour."

The agreed delay was just about to elapse when Max Semper presented himself on Monsieur de Landré's study again.

"Monsieur le Juge," he said, "It's agreed. The American embassy won't create any difficulty for you. You know that it wants to punish the Terrick family's murderer as much as you do. You can ask us for a rogatory commission by way of the usual channels; so long as that doesn't come to a conclusion, you can keep your fellow locked up, and I promise you that it won't conclude until your investigation is closed. I'll do everything possible over there; my renown is at stake, but don't hope that I'll be able to find anything capable of helping you; my veritable aid is simply a matter of slowing down the rogatory commission, to give you time. Good luck, then, and *au revoir!*"

That same evening Max Semper and his aide left for America, and a special edition of the newspapers announced that Monsieur Charfland, alleged American citizen, had been arrested on suspicion of the murder of A. H. Terrick, his wife, his two children and their governess.

Six months had already passed since then, and the investigation had made no progress.

It had been quite impossible to make Charfland say anything other than what he had said in his witness statements; it had been quite impossible to get Thérèse Vila to say anything more under hypnosis, although she still expressed the same repulsion for the principal accused.

Several times already, the public prosecutor had summoned Monsieur de Landré to tell him that he was out of time; public opinion, massaged by the intelligent and active defender that Charfland had selected, was beginning to lose patience. Disagreeable comments about the slowness and impotence of the law were appearing with increasing frequency in the leading newspapers. The affair was threatening to turn into a scandal and when the Chambres resumed, several interpellations had been tabled for the Garde des Sceaux.

The American ambassador and Max Semper had kept their promises; no diplomatic action had been taken with regard to the incarceration of the American Charfland, and the rogatory commission sent to America had not yet concluded— but the pretext, now unique, of the commission's delay, could not stand up any longer. Monsieur de Landré saw the moment coming when he would be obliged to sign a release or have the case taken off him, which was the equivalent of a serious punishment.

And yet, all his instincts as an honest man and all his experience as a magistrate told him that Charfland was guilty...

But he still had no proof.

All of that had passed through Monsieur de Landré's mind while he held the piece of paper bearing the name Nounlegos, and time was passing.

When he pulled himself together and saw that nearly an hour had gone by while he was mulling over the past, he was surprised not to have received the information he had requested from his secretary. Summoned, the latter told him that research carried out in all possible sources had had no result. Nounlegos was unknown.

He gave the ordered to show the enigmatic visitor in.

A strange little old man presented himself, his back very curbed, clad in old-fashioned garments. He came forward, not in a timid manner but in a fashion suggesting that he was unaccustomed to taking steps of this kind. His large eyes blinked continually, as if under the effects of fatigue, shielded by large spectacles; his cranium, absolutely bald, was creased by wrinkles.

He gave an impression of weariness, as if worn out by a difficult material existence and an intense mental life. Thus, Monsieur de Landré was surprised by the freshness and clarity of the bizarre individual's voice when he declared, without any preamble:

"Monsieur le Juge, you are charged, are you not, with a curious affair in which the accused, Charfland, whom you believe to be guilty, claims that he is innocent, and against whom you cannot raise any certain proof of guilt. I have come to tell you that I can remove all your doubts."

"How can you do that?" asked the magistrate, interrupting involuntarily.

"I can read minds. I can therefore read Charfland's, and tell you what he is thinking."

Oh! Is he a madman? Monsieur de Landré wondered. Aloud, he said: "Monsieur, before going any further, permit me to ask you a question, with which, in fact, I ought to have begun this conversation. Who are you? Where do you live? What are you occupations, your references? It is only after being enlightened on these points that I can listen to your proposals."

The little man had a smile full of delicious irony, so paltry did those preoccupations appear to him by comparison with what he had to offer. Laconically, he replied:

"My name is Nounlegos. I live at number 17, Rue des Saules, in Bondy. I'm a rentier and I pursue my studies in my private laboratory. Living alone, with no relations, I have no references to cite to you."

Then he fell silent, his thin smile seemingly interested by the embarrassment he read in the magistrate's face.

The latter replied: "For want of personal references, you can still cite me scientific references, of which you can have no lack if, as you say, your studies have led you to be able to realize the extraordinary proposal you have just made to me."

Nounlegos' smile disappeared, and it was in a grave voice that he replied:

"I have been working absolutely alone for between thirty and forty years on the problem that I set myself: to read the human mind. I have never made any communication, and my research is unknown to the scientific world. To make it known, I'm waiting for the moment when I have completely solved the vast problem that I'm investigating; that might take me another ten years, perhaps twenty—perhaps I shall never get there. I have, therefore, no reference among official scientists.

"I have succeeded in being able to decipher the thoughts of a human being obliged to lend himself to the experiment, for it requires a special apparatus. In order to take account for myself, in a genuinely interesting case, of whether my method, such as it is, is susceptible of rendering services, I have come to put my experiment at your disposal to examine Charfland.

"Take note that in doing that, I am not pursuing any particular advantage; the trial that I shall attempt will only profit the law. It's said that you're about to be obliged to sign Charfland's release; if the man is innocent you'll be liberated from any future remorse; if he's guilty, you'll certainly find, in the man's thoughts, what you need to gather the evidence that you lack."

Monsieur de Landré was understandably embarrassed. Nounlegos' proposition appeared to him to be so strange that his mind refused to admit its veracity; but on the other hand, he was disposed to clutch at any hope, even chimerical, susceptible of aiding him in the tenebrous affair.

"Of what does this experiment consist?" he asked.

"I place a special apparatus on the subject's head. I examine the mind and note the thoughts traversing it. The apparatus does not inconvenience the examinee in any way."

"Where can it be done?"

"Here, if you desire. I only need a little electric current, which I can take from the socket of one of your desk-lamps. I will add that if the subject does not want to lend himself to the experiment, I can immobilize him painlessly, with current taken from another socket, while leaving cerebral activity intact."

"But even if I believe what you're telling me, how can you be sure that Charfland will think about the crime?"

"Oh, the mere fact of his presence here before you will oblige his mind to think about the affair. If he orientates it in another direction, it will be sufficient for you to ask him a few questions that will oblige him to return to it. You ought to know better than I do, that a guilty man who pleads innocence, in order not to give himself away in his responses, has to concentrate all his attention on his crime, remembering what he ought to say and what he must hide."

"But what proof would I have that what you tell me has really traversed the mind of the accused?"

"Obviously, I can't oblige you in advance to have faith in my method, but I can submit you to the proof; you'll be able to see whether I'm able to read your thoughts."

"Indeed," murmured the magistrate, prodigiously interested. Then an objection occurred to him. "But even with that proof, your method, not being officially recognized, can't serve as the basis for a legal action; you're reading won't be admissible evidence

"That might be true," Nounlegos replied, "but it will be up to you, as the examining magistrate, once in possession of the thoughts of the accused, to act in the interests of the law to acquire the proof. If Charfland is guilty, might he not think about the instrument of which he made use to commit his crime and the place where he got rid of it? Then you'll be able to recover it. Wouldn't that be a commencement of proof?"

"That's true," Monsieur de Landré could not help saying. Nounlegos' confidence and clarity were beginning to convince him. He started. "But that examination would have to take place in the presence of the advocate; if he refuses, your science not being recognized, the law won't permit me to impose it."

"For my part," Nounlegos replied, "I don't intend to have dealings with anyone but you and Charfland; the moment hasn't yet come to make my discoveries known You alone will know that I, Nounlegos, have given you a means, but I shall not participate in any way in your future actions, inspired by my reading. The offer I'm making to you is only valid if you promise never to reveal what you have witnessed. As for Charfland, you can easily get him to lend himself to the experiment without involving his advocate. In any case, he'll never suspect the truth, and if you convict him of his crime, he'll remain entirely in ignorance of the method that led you to that end."

The question was taking on a procedural aspect for the magistrate. He reflected, visibly attracted by the idea of the trial that had been suggested to him.

"I could tell Charfland that before closing the investigation, I'd like to have him examined by a celebrated phrenologist; I know the man well enough by now to be sure that, convinced of the incompetence of that science..."

"With good reason," Nounlegos articulated, curtly.

"...And, desirous of lending himself without objection to any new investigation that appears devoid of danger, he'll acquiesce without demanding the collaboration of his advocate. He's certainly aware of the present situation, in any case, and his defender has promised him a definitive release any day. He'll think he's hastening the moment of his liberation by not raising any objection to the examination. Besides which, he'll reflect that if the examination reveals anything that could weigh against him, I won't be able to use it because of the absence of his counsel."

"It's not for me to judge those means." After a pause, Nounlegos went on. "Let's conclude: firstly you promise not to reveal to anyone the conversation that we've just had, not the scene that you're going to witness?"

"I promise," replied Monsieur de Landré.

"Secondly, I shall be here tomorrow morning at ten o'clock, and your study will be closed throughout the duration of the experiment."

"Agreed."

161

And the little old man, picking up his hat, which he had placed on the magistrate's desk, stood up, nodded his head and left, while Monsieur de Landré, slightly petrified by a decision so rapidly made, remained pensive, wondering, now that the door had closed on the strange Nounlegos, whether he might have been dreaming, or whether he had just been deceived by a skillful trickster.

II

The next day, Monsieur de Landré, the examining magistrate, slightly discomfited by a sleepless night, incapable of taking any interest whatsoever in his post, which he was opening mechanically, cast frequent glances at his little desk clock.

At nine forty-five, his secretary came to tell him that Charfland was there. The accused had not said anything when the secretary had told him that the magistrate had summoned him; he had not mentioned his defender.

At ten o'clock, the usher, following the orders he had received, opened the door to introduce Nounlegos, without announcing him. The latter, carrying two large valises, seemed even more stooped than the day before.

"I need a few minutes to prepare, Monsieur le Juge."

Then, with a remarkable activity for a man so seemingly worn out, he set to work, accompanying his gestures with various brief explanations.

He cleared half of the magistrate's desk. "To make room for my apparatus."

He took bizarre utensils out of his valises, placed them on the desk and assembled them carefully.

He arranged an armchair with its back to the desk. "For Charfland."

Another armchair was placed on the other side of the desk. "For me."

He connected his apparatus to an electric socket. "For the reading."

He connected another apparatus to another socket. "To impose immobility if necessary."

Then, disposing another armchair: "For you, Monsieur le Juge. Like this, you'll be able to look the accused and he'll be able to see you. If I think it necessary for you to ask him questions, I'll give you a signal simply by raising my hand; you'll ask the questions that, in your opinion, ought to remind Charfland of the phases of the drama, if there was a drama; the order of the question ought to be the chronological order of the supposed events. If I don't raise my hand, don't interrogate— don't say anything."

Then Nounlegos placed a large sheet of paper on the desk, next to the seat he had reserved for himself, secured by a heavy frame, equipped with two transversal rulers, and placed a kind of stylet on it. Casting one last glance over the ensemble, he said: "I'm ready." As the magistrate leaned forward to ring the bell he added: "Above all, no witness."

"Send in the accused," the magistrate ordered the usher

Charfland soon made his entrance, framed by two municipal guards. The latter were dismissed by a gesture.

The magistrate spoke: "Charfland, my investigation is on the brink of being closed, but before signing the order that will either send you for committal or set you free, I've summoned a savant phrenologist"—he indicated Nounlegos with his hand—"who knows how, by examining a skull, to determine whether or not the subject has criminal tendencies. Have you any objection to submitting yourself to that examination?"

At that question, the other looked at the magistrate, then at Nounlegos, and then the bizarre apparatus that was there. After a few moments of reflection, Monsieur de Landré's expectations were realized, and Charfland replied, tranquilly: "None."

"Let's operate, then," declared Nounlegos, indicating to the accused the chair prepared for him. "Will you please it here. Good. I'm going to place this apparatus on your head. Oh, it's weight isn't in proportion to its volume; you'll be able to support it easily."

So saying, Nounlegos coiffed Charfland's cranium with a kind of box.

That box, almost cubical, had large gaps in two faces, with the result that the visage of the patient, once coiffed, remained visible except for the eyebrows. The sides of the head were covered, but for two openings corresponding to the ears; the rest of the head was enveloped. A strap passing under the chin secured the box; two props, adjustable in height, permitted almost all of the weight of the apparatus to rest on the patient's shoulders, in such a way that the head was not subjected to any inconvenient pressure.

"Relax your muscles. You don't feel any discomfort? Good. I'm going to examine you. It might take some time; if the apparatus causes you any fatigue, tell us and we'll take a few moments' rest."

Monsieur de Landré had already taken his place in his armchair. Nounlegos turned a commutator placed on the electric wire connected to the socket, and then placed himself in front of the other apparatus, before a visor analogous to that of a stereoscope, which was incrusted, after a fashion, upon his forehead. With his left hand he stated to manipulate a series of switches disposed on a small inclined panel, while his right hand seized the stylet and supported itself on the metal rulers placed on the frame maintaining the piece of paper.

For a few minutes, no substantial movement was made by the three participants in that mysterious scene. The magistrate looked alternately at Nounlegos and Charfland, wondering anxiously whether the man who said he was a scientist was really capable of reading that which he claimed to be decipherable for him alone.

The accused, wary at first, soon appeared to adapt himself to the bizarre situation, casually resting on the arms of the chair, seemingly absorbed in his reflections.

Nounlegos, his neck extended toward his apparatus, remained motionless, his left hand occasionally maneuvering a few switches; then, suddenly, his right hand agitated, making the stylet trace bizarre little symbols, closely packed, in the interval of white paper left visible by the two metal rulers. His hand arrived at the extremity of the lead; a click made the two rulers slide for a few millimeters, and he continued to inscribe the bizarre symbols, this time going from right to left. At the extremity of the new line, an analogous click caused a new displacement of the rulers, and the docile hand continued to write, but now in the conventional direction, from left to right.

That singular session lasted for nearly an hour.

Yes, for nearly an hour, Monsieur de Landré, prey to a cerebral agitation that nothing revealed, let his gaze wander from the examiner to the examinee, wondering whether the unknown science on which the so-called scientist was relying really did establish a current of unknown forces between the two men: a current so extraordinary that one could read what the other was thinking.

Yes, for nearly an hour, Charfland, resigned to what he considered to be an ultimate formality, patiently supported the thick helmet, without a single complaint, without wanting to take advantage of the faculty that had been offered to him by the phrenologist of asking for a rest.

Yes, for nearly an hour, Nounlegos' forehead remained riveted to the visor of his apparatus. His left hand only rarely manipulated the switches at his disposal, but, by way of compensation, his right hand continued without interruption, alternating its direction, to trace hieroglyphs of some sort on the large white sheet. Only the click of the steel rulers as they were displaced on the metal frame of the white paper troubled the silence.

Finally, Nounlegos' right hand stopped. His face presenting his bulging eyes, he quit his observation post, threw his upper body backwards, rested his weary head on the back of his chair, remained there for a few moments with his eyes half-closed as if to contrive his transition between the immaterial world in which he had just been traveling and the real world to which he was returning, and then rose to his feet painfully and murmured: "I've finished."

Then he cut off the current and liberated Charfland from the yoke of sorts that he had borne for so long.

The accused, his head teeming with sweat, mopped his brow. He could not help saying: "I'm thirsty."

"Me too," added Nounlegos, unconsciously.

At those words, the magistrate, excessively impressed, more by what he expected than what he had seen, without taking account of the strangeness of his decision, rang the bell and ordered the usher to bring a bottle of port and three glasses. Dumbstruck, the usher obeyed, and filled the three glasses he had brought.

The three men, still silent, emptied their glasses rapidly. Their reflections, of very different orders, would have absorbed them for longer still, but Charfland, with a slightly mocking expression, said to Nounlegos: "Well, Monsieur Scientist, what are your conclusions?"

"It's necessary now for me to coordinate my observations. I'll give the results to Monsieur le Juge." As he said those words he looked at the magistrate with an expression that signified: *It's necessary now for the two of us to be alone.*

The magistrate rang; the municipal guards came in and Charfland resumed the road to his prison.

"Well, Monsieur Nounlegos?" pronounced Monsieur de Landré, in a voice that probably did not have all the firmness he would have liked.

"Monsieur le Juge," Nounlegos replied gravely, "the man who has just left is definitely guilty; the proofs abound here." And he pointed at the large sheet of white paper, now covered with a multitude of symbols, each as strange as the next. Then, without waiting to be asked a question, he added: "But it's necessary for me to translate my secret language for you; it's better to do that right away. Give me paper and a pen; it will take me some time."

For nearly three hours, Nounlegos covered numerous sheets of paper with rapid writing.

When he had finished, he began to dismantle his apparatus.

166

Monsieur de Landré interrupted him. "Haven't you promised to give me indisputable proof, for myself, of your science?"

"Oh, that's true—I'd forgotten. Sit down here; I'll put the helmet on. As I'm tired from that long session, I hope five minutes will suffice or you. In any case, to simplify things, I'll translate immediately, aloud, what I read in your mind. I warn you that I can't read proper names."

A few moments later, Nounlegos, his forehead against the apparatus once again, announced:

"My wife…waiting…lunch…knows very well…affair five victims…so no anxiety…I find my wife very agreeable…twenty years together…still young…seems like big sister…our children...

"Strange man divining my thought…try to think about something else...

"Politics…often opposed…general interests…country…recommendations…bad lots…discourage good...will I arrive…superior post..."

Breathless, Monsieur de Landré uttered a cry: "Enough!" And, taking off the mysterious box: "Yes, yes, I believe you. It's true, you read all that I was thinking—but who are you, then, to dispose of a power that humankind has never dared glimpse? Aren't you trying to play God?"

While dismantling his apparatus and carefully arranging the pieces in his valises, the scientist replied: "I'm simply Nounlegos, unknown, as you know; my work will revolutionize the world one day, because it will impose sincerity. But I came here for something else: here is the confession of the wretch Charfland; you'll find a host of indications therein, which will permit you to confound him.

"Now, remember out agreement; I consider that your word of honor has been given; you will not reveal to anyone either our first conversation or what has just happened."

The examining magistrate renewed his promise and politely showed the little man out. He left, bowed down by his diabolical apparatus.

III

It was in a small sub-prefecture of France that the individual who was later to become Nounlegos was born, under a banal name that has not reached us.

The new-born was not handsome; he seemed sickly, and gave many anxieties to his parents, who were well-off shopkeepers in the small town. They surrounded him with the most delicate cares, trembling for their only son, all the more beloved because he had arrived late in life.

If his physique left much to be desired, however, intelligence was manifest early. While very young, bearing on his young head the air of reflection that is generally the prerogative of children of aged parents, he quickly astonished those around him with his repartee—rare, it is true, for he had a reserved temperament, but denoting an observant wit well beyond his years.

At school, although not very assiduous at first, he immediately outshone all his comrades by virtue of his extraordinary faculties of assimilation.

Later, he acquired a taste for study and then became a source of astonishment for his teachers; he could, without any apparent intellectual fatigue, follow two classes at the same time, or even three in the same school year. As it was impossible to obtain the enormous dispensation of age that would have been necessary for him to pass his first baccalaureate when he was ready, he prepared for others and, with the required legal dispensation, he passed three in the same session.

At that moment, the perplexity of his parents reached its maximum. What might such a prodigious young man do? They could not follow the idea they had caressed for so long of making him their successor in running the business, healthy as its profits were. All the great Schools would have been open to him; in view of his physique they could not think of a military career, but the parents thought that he might be a brilliant civil servant—the eternal dream of prosperous petty bourgeois.

When they talked to him for the first time about those future projects, he responded curtly, like a man who knows what he wants: "I shall practice medicine."

The parents gave in; the only son was installed in Paris, with all the usual recommendations. The success continued; the young student passed all his examinations brilliantly, in the minimal time. He had just come first in the competition for young hospital interns when his parents died.

Informed by the family's notary of his exact situation, which was financially secure, he simply replied: "I shall be able to work."

Then commenced a period of intense study, which only a brain out of proportion with those of the epoch could have supported and assimilated.

As a hospital intern, once he was familiar with a service he asked to change it; his merit was so real, and his professors recognized it so clearly, that in a matter of months they had nothing more to teach him. But he was no longer preoccupied with examinations; pressed to complete a thesis that would have obtained him a doctorate, he replied: "I have other things to do."

Knowing all the Medicine could teach him, he threw himself into the sciences. Having assured himself a slid grounding in mathematics, physics, chemistry and natural sciences, he followed, with ease, specialist courses embracing all present scientific knowledge. He even went to spend a few months in provincial and foreign universities where, in accordance with indications, he was able to make new discoveries: a foretaste of what the Science of tomorrow might be.

His mind admirably furnished, he then undertook stints, in the capacity as an aide, in the foremost research laboratories in the world. When he had familiarized himself with the work of one he went to another, refusing the most advantageous and flattering offers that the scientists, recognizing him as an elite intelligence, made him to attach himself to their studies as an associate.

At thirty he knew, thoroughly, what the whole of the scientific world knew; by means of the most specialized journals he kept up to date with current research, and often prognosticated, on the basis of experimental results, what would follow them and what the final outcomes would be.

Outside of his studies life had, so to speak, no purchase on him..

He lived in the heart of the student quarter in a small street on the left bank, in an apartment comprising a small bedroom and a large desk on which books and pamphlets multiplied by the day. The concierge of the building took care of his modest housekeeping. He generally took his meals in a high quality restaurant, not for love of luxury or the attraction of good food, but because he found that the tranquility there permitted him to continue in his mind the elevated speculations with which he was occupied; he had fled modest restaurants because of the noise made by the boisterous youth that frequented them. He had no friends; the frivolous instinctively steered clear of him, and he did not see them, but when serious young people attracted by his intelligence had tried to enter into closer relationship with him he abstained, without brutality, from responding to advances that he appeared not to notice, and discourages all good intentions.

It was at the age of thirty, as we have said, that he considered his studies to be terminated; from the scientific point of view, he had nothing more to learn, and for him, the era of research began.

It was at that point that the learned man took the steps necessary to change his name. By the name he took, he was bold enough to define the problem that was agitating his superior intelligence: Nounlegos, from the Greek *noun*, thought, and *lego*, I read. That was the first manifestation of his nascent genius.

Having obtained that change of name, he returned to the town of his birth, which he had not seen since the death of his parents; he liquidated his entire fortune, invested it in reliable stocks and bonds, and deposited them with a Parisian banker. After a few visits to that suburb of Paris he bought a detached house in Bondy, isolated in a large garden, situated outside the agglomeration.

He spent a considerable sum fitting out a first-rate laboratory, installed an aged maidservant as his housekeeper, and set to work.

His life was henceforth that of a recluse; his laboratory absorbed him for twelve, fourteen or fifteen hours a day. He only went out to go to Paris in order to supervise the construction and take delivery of bizarre items of apparatus whose plans he drew up himself. His door was irremediably closed to all visitors. For some time he occupied the curiosity of the inhabitants of Bondy, who, finally making up their minds, left him to his chimeras and referred to him an eccentric.

As the name he had chosen suggested, it was to the study of the brain that he devoted himself. Firstly, he wanted to clarify certain doubtful points related to the composition of that organ, and he dissected a quantity of human heads that he procured at a high price.

Certain that nothing regarding the dead brain was unknown to him, he passed on to the study of the living brain, but there he was soon arrested. The examination of the cranium could not, in his view, lead to anything; he knew the various symptoms of a nervous order produced when a particular part of an animal brain was excited, via an opened skull, but what he wanted to determine was not the relationship between the superior nervous centers and the various organs of the body, but whether the phenomenon of thought was accompanied by physical phenomena in the brain.

He rapidly arrived at the conclusion that that question could only be studied on condition of being able to see into the interior of the organ under examination. The question therefore passed from physiology to physics; he dared to follow it.

He found the solution to it after a few years, by means of the emissions of two radioactivities obtained exclusively from

171

electrical phenomena. Those two emissions, projected at a certain angle, produced a kind of fluorescence that rendered visible, to a distance of about thirty centimeters, all the substances, organic as well as mineral. The emitted waves, without bringing any permanent modification to the atoms and cells subjected to their action, perhaps deforming them in part, doubtless acted upon their index of refraction in such a way that the cells and atoms passed through all the degrees of translucency and transparency, all the way to invisibility. By the regulation of these emissions, the respective positions of their planes of emission and the angle of those planes, one could obtain the various degrees and determine, over a well-defined section, a clarification permitting a detailed examination.

Later improvements permitted Nounlegos to ensure a uniform illumination over a thickness equal to that of a human head.

With that apparatus, the examination of animals permitted the scientist to verify certain relationships between circumvolutions and sensations and movements, and to invalidate others. The real problem, however, could only be studied in a thinking brain; the observations made, if they were possible, could only have value is there were no doubt about the thoughts to be detected. Nounlegos was therefore led to the sole conclusion that it was himself that he had to examine.

He built an apparatus thanks to which his eyes could see into his own brain and he equipped it with optical equipment permitting a considerable magnification.

From that moment on it was with his head surrounded by a kind of yoke that the prodigious man spent all his time.

In the beginning, his head preoccupied with so many things, avid to divine and observe, was full of confused thoughts; he could only distinguish rapid movements in the gray matter of the cerebral hemisphere, swellings and contractions of a sort, in all directions, without any interconnections: a veritable chaos.

He understood that before anything else, he had to determine his own thought, oblige his head to an absolute repose in putting on the yoke and then, being placed for the observation, to strive only to think of a single simple idea: "I am looking," for example.

When he began that experiment, he believed that he observed something, and, his brain then resuming its activity unconsciously, the multiple undulations recommenced agitating the cells.

He began again many times, obliging himself to extraordinary efforts to master his thoughts. Finally he arrived at a certainty: every time he thought "I am looking," a tiny movement—which the accessory phenomena whose examination was permitted by the illumination translated into a kind of tiny swelling—was produced at a precise point in one of the circumlocutions, the role of which had never been defined at yet..

That day, Nounlegos told himself, gladly: "I shall succeed!"

To avoid any confusion between the physiological phenomena of thought itself and those produced to command in the nerves the most important functions of life, he constrained himself to a detailed study of the latter, and succeeded in determining in an absolute manner the locations on which the respiratory mechanism, the regulation of the heart, the motor incitements, and coordinating forces of movement, and so on, depend.

Then, for his first thought, "I am looking," he substituted others that were equally simple, and succeeded in observing indisputably the kind of phenomenon produced and the location of its production. He thus arrived at being able to grasp in his own brain the manifestation of a series of simple thoughts that he considered as an initial alphabet.

The method that was to lead him to the result thus became more precise. He applied it for twenty-five years and, by dint of determination and patience, his genius succeeded in fixing the physiological manifestation of which the brain is the seat when a concrete or abstract thought passes through it, whether it relates to an object, a fact or an abstraction. By combining several thoughts, little by little, he was able to read rapidly and simultaneously the various thoughts emitted. He even succeeded in distinguishing idea relating to the past, those relative to the present, those relative to the future, those whose situation is independent of the time factor, and even determining whether a thought is new or familiar to the brain.

He had, in fact, observed that the amplitude of the phenomena produced was a function of their antiquity; which is to say that the cells activated—for it was to a veritable movement of turbulence that he attributed the said phenomena—vibrated relatively weakly when they were activated for the first time, when the thought interested the brain for the first time, and that the amplitude of the vibrations increased with the time separating the observed phenomenon from the epoch when the phenomenon had first been produced. He had arrived at that curious observation be make use, as reference points, of memories of his enormous erudition, remembering precisely the epochs in which he had learned particular things.

Thought is rapid, as everyone knows; thus, to succeed in recording it as it was being emitted, he was obliged to invent, not an alphabet but a veritable new writing in which a simple symbol was equivalent to a long sentence. By means of his hieroglyphs, he was able to observe and record while leaving his cerebral mass absolute liberty to operate at its ease. Thus, he was able, after having read an article, for example, to put himself into his apparatus, in order to note via the intermediary of his eyes and his hand, the reflections that the reading had suggested to him.

It was thus possible for him to grasp phenomena not yet observed, thanks to his method of organizing his mental labor; he succeeded in analyzing them like the others and thus enriching the mysterious dictionary of sorts to which he was consigning the "language of the brain."

By the time he reached his sixtieth year, nothing was passing through his own brain that was indecipherable to him.

Curiously enough, until then, he had never observed another brain.

He had certainly thought about it, but by virtue of his physiological knowledge and is multiple observations of himself, he had arrived at the absolute conviction that the locations of various thoughts were absolutely the same in all individuals. The circumvolutions were certainly not identical in dimension in each individual, but in every one, the active cells for a certain idea were always in the same relative position. He therefore found himself certain in advance of being able to read any human brain, although perhaps not as quickly as his own, to begin with, because of the proportions. He also knew, however, that few people were capable of stirring as many thoughts as he was, and that having commenced, in sum, by reading the most arduous and complex mind, other, simpler ones would not cause him any embarrassment.

At that moment he wanted to put his science to the proof on a third party.

He hesitated momentarily, for he wanted to be sure of the greatest discretion. On the other hand, he wanted that experimental intervention to have some utility.

A headline referring to a "judiciary scandal" attracted his attention one day; he scanned the article, which summarized the famous affair, and rapidly concluded that he might perhaps find there the terrain of the experiment that he wanted to carry out.

The next day, he went to see the examining magistrate, Monsieur de Landré; our readers know what followed.

IV

Monsieur de Landré fell upon the manuscript that Nounlegos had handed him, and plunged into its reading.

His physiognomy reflected the impressions he felt; he was exultant…then he calmed down, reflected, recommenced reading, and took notes. Putting away the manuscript and his notes, he telephoned the Sûreté and went out at about eight o'clock in the evening. He had not left his study for eleven hours; he had not had anything to eat or drink except for the glass of port taken in the company of Nounlegos and...Charfland.

His stomach, however, was not demanding anything. He went home primarily to reassure his wife, dined rapidly, returned to his office and drew up a series of mission orders.

At eleven o'clock, the head of the Sûreté arrived, as requested. The two men deliberated for two hours and came out together. As they separated, the magistrate said: "It's agreed, then; the various missions will be carried out as soon as possible; each of them will be completely unaware of the others. I'm expecting you at ten o'clock to carry out the most important of all, about which I haven't yet given you any information. I'm hoping for a resounding success. Until tomorrow."

The following morning, Monsieur de Landré was at work in his study early.

At nine o'clock the telephone rang. "Hello! Monsieur le Juge d'Instruction de Landré?"

"That's me."

"I'm calling from the secretariat of the Court and am instructed to request that you go to see the public prosecutor immediately."

"That's fine. I'm on my way."

When the conversation was concluded, Monsieur de Landré thought bitterly that instead of employing the usual formula—"Would Monsieur X be kind enough to call...," he had just been given an order.

"The public prosecutor has made a decision. There's only just time, then!"

He was not mistaken. Introduced to the prosecutor's office, the latter, instead of extending his hand to him, as usual, remained seated.

"Monsieur," he said to him. "You have not taken account of my numerous indications that have been given to you on the subject of the Chalfrand affair; public opinion considers the latter as an innocent man, and parliament is agitated. Urgently summoned by the Garde des Sceaux yesterday, I've been obliged to recognize, with him, that a measure is imposed to put an end to a scandal from which the prestige of the Law can only suffer. In consequence, I warn you that I have just signed"—he displayed a large sheet of paper bearing the court's heading—"your dismissal from this affair to the advantage of your colleague Monsieur Laumier; you will hand over all your files to him this morning."

Slightly astounded by that decision, and above all by the brutal fashion in which he had been informed of it, Monsieur de Landré pulled himself together swiftly. Was he not on the brink of finally confounding the guilty party?

"Monsieur le Procureur Général, you know how convinced I still am of Charfland's guilt. I understand, in view of the absence of certain proof, the emotion of public opinion. I also understand that this affair might be used to the advantage of the opposition to the present ministry. Be certain, therefore, that I would incline without discussion to the order that you have just signed if..."

The prosecutor started, but the magistrate, without paying any heed to it, continued: "If I were not absolutely certain of unmasking the guilty party very soon; I have come to ask you for a delay of a few days."

"I regret, Monsieur, that that is impossible."

"However, Monsieur le Procureur Général, if I told you that I have just become acquainted with new facts concerning the case and that the delay is simply that necessary to proceed with their verification..."

"It would be futile. The signed order will be carried out."

"But if, to give you proof of the importance I attach to these new facts, I give you my word that if I am mistaken—which is to say that if I do not succeed imminently in proving Charfland's culpability—it is not merely the dossier that I shall return to you but also my resignation as an examining magistrate. With that resignation you would be covered with

177

regard to the Garde des Sceaux, so you can grant me the short respite."

"Impossible," pronounced the public prosecutor, dryly, standing up to signify that the interview was terminated.

Monsieur de Landré went white. So, at the moment when he was about to ring the long investigation to a conclusion, when—he was convinced—he was finally about to demonstrate how exact his intuition had been, it was necessary, under the weight of a decision equivalent to a veritable disgrace, to detach himself from the case in which he had put his heart and soul.

He stiffened, and said in a contained voice: "You know, Monsieur le Procureur Général, that I have always been a faithful servant of the law; for nearly thirty years I have devoted all my strength and all my intelligence to it. You know very well that magistrate de Landré has never made an error, has never convicted an innocent man, and has only sent guilty parties to the tribunal.

"Well, in the name of those thirty years of honorable and devoted service, and in the name of the law that I am proud to serve with the depths of my soul, grant me this delay, Monsieur le Procureur Général…which will astonish you. I implore you!"

Slightly emotional, the prosecutor, knowing that what he heard was true, was silent.

Ten o'clock chimed. De Landré started.

"Monsieur le Procureur Général, the head of the Sûreté is waiting for me in my office; I have to carry out an operation of the highest importance with him relative to the Charfland affair. Please, wait for me to return in two hours, and I'll bring you indisputable proof...

"Keep that order of dismissal on your desk for just two hours…if the truth is not blinding…may God strike me dead!"

Prey to a veritable exaltation, Monsieur de Landré ran out like a madman.

Once the prosecutor was alone he reflected.

All right, I can wait until noon!

And from the file that he was about to hand over to his office, he removed the order relative to the Chalfrand affair.

At quarter past noon, the usher came in.

"Monsieur le Procureur Général, the head of the Sûreté is asking to speak to you urgently."

"Send him in."

The individual in question appeared; he was still under the influence of a profound emotion, which did not escape the magistrate's experienced eye.

"Monsieur le Procureur Général, I have been sent by Monsieur le Juge d'Instruction de Landré to ask you...beg you...to accompany me. I can't tell you anymore, but I give you my word that you won't regret your disturbance. I have a taxi waiting at the door.

Although somewhat intrigued, the other replied, after a brief hesitation: "I'll go with you."

The two men climbed into the vehicle, whose motor was still running. The head of the Sûreté shouted to the driver: "Back to where we came from."

During the short journey, silence reigned in the vehicle. When it stopped, the prosecutor got out and, looking up, perceived that he was in front of the Caisse des Dépôts et Consignations.

What does this mean? he wondered.

Meekly, he followed the head of the Sûreté inside.

In a small room the newcomers joined Monsieur de Landré, who was carrying a large package, accompanied by a clerk and two inspectors from the Prefecture of Police.

The magistrate bowed. "Thank you for coming, Monsieur le Procureur Général, but for the deposit I want to make in your presence one important witness is still lacking; I must ask you to be kind enough to wait for him."

Scarcely had he spoken than the door opened and a gentleman of respectable appearance appeared, accompanied by another inspector who, addressing the magistrate, simply said: "Here he is."

179

Monsieur de Landré spoke. "You recognize me, do you not? Monsieur de Landré, examining magistrate in the Charfland affair."

"Oh, indeed—you've interrogated me sufficiently on the conditions of the cashing of Joe Helly's check for ten millions."

The magistrate, turning then to the public prosecutor, proceeded with the introduction. "Monsieur Alivet, chief of service at the financial establishments of the Universel Crédit."

"Monsieur le Procureur Général!"

The two men bowed to one another.

"Monsieur Alivet," the magistrate continued, "if you were shown the briefcase in which Joe Helly placed the ten thousand thousand-franc bills that you handed over to him, would you recognize it?"

"I believe so—but what I would certainly recognize is the fashion in which the bills are arranged. In the nearly twenty years that I have been at the Universel Crédit it's the first time that I've ever witnessed the withdrawal, in the form, of such a large sum, and, without attaching any importance to it, because the transaction was absolutely in order, I noticed all the details."

"In that case, Monsieur, look."

The magistrate placed the package he was carrying on the table. He removed the newspaper in which it was wrapped, and a rubber envelope stained with patches of mildew appeared. That envelope was stuck; he was obliged to cut through it with a pen-knife. A kind of brown cloth bag emerged, secured by a trap. When the bag was opened he took out a black morocco leather briefcase.

"It was exactly like that!" exclaimed Alivet.

The briefcase was divided into two compartments; large flaps closed each of the two pockets.

"That's extraordinary!" murmured Alivet. Then, as the magistrate was about to open the pockets, he said: "Wait! I remember clearly that the strap of one of the flaps entered very easily into its buckle, whereas Joe Helly had to force the other, the buckle seeming too narrow for the strap."

"We can verify that," the magistrate replied, and proceeded gently with the extraction of the straps; the first resisted; it was tightly held by the buckle in the direction of its width; the other, by contrast, emerged without effort.

The two pockets were opened; the watchers leaned over anxiously…and perceived wads of banknotes.

"That's exactly how Joe Helly arranged the bills: six piles side by side."

"Let's count them," said Monsieur de Landré, addressing Alivet.

"The bills are arranged as we organize them; they're stacked in tens, fastened with a pin; ten packets of ten are fastened together by a red rubber band."

He counted a hundred packets thus defined.

"Are there any other indications you can give me," the magistrate asked, "permitting you to confirm your belief that these bills really are those delivered by the Universel Crédit to the bearer of the check signed A. H. Terrick?"

"Perhaps," Alivet replied. "In every packet of ten thousand-franc bills, we have the habit of placing the third and the ninth in the opposite orientation to the remainder."

Verification made of a few packets chosen at random proved that particularity existed.

"Monsieur Alivet," declared the magistrate, "Would you please make your declaration; clerk, write."

"Monsieur le Juge d'Instruction, save for inexplicable coincidences, I recognize this briefcase as the one in which Joe Helly arranged the ten millions in thousand-franc bills here present, which were handed over in payment of the Terrick check."

"Good. Now, in your presence, Monsieur le Procureur Général, I shall deposit that sum in the Caisse des Dépôts et Consignations; I shall keep the briefcase and the envelopes as pieces of evidence."

A few minutes later, the ten million francs was deposited in the safe; the receipt was drawn up at the magistrate's request as follows:

The Caisse des Dépôts and Consignations has today received, from the hands of Monsieur le Juge d'Instruction de Landré, in the presence of Monsieur le Procureur Général, Monsieur le Chef de la Sûreté and Monsieur Alivet, chief of service at the Universel Crédit, the sum of ten million francs in thousand-franc bills of the Banque de France. That sum, which there is every reason to believe to be that paid out by the financial establishments of the Universel Crédit to someone named Joe Helly in payment of a check signed A. H. Terrick, is consigned to the disposition of the central court.

Then the various actors in the scene separated, after swearing on oath not to divulge anything of it

Monsieur de Landré accompanied his superior to his office.

"Monsieur le Procureur Général, will you permit me now to keep the investigation of the Charfland affair? The results of this morning's enquiry have changed my conviction into indisputable certainty; in a matter of days, I can enable you to witness the confession of the accused. Will you now grant me the delay I am requesting for the good of the law?"

"Monsieur le Juge, the situation has indeed changed since this morning; I recognize that the recovery of the ten millions constitutes a commencement of proof; I'll grant you a week. I'll explain to the Garde des Sceaux."

"Thank you, Monsieur le Procureur Général, but I beg you in the interests of the investigation not to say explicitly what the commencement of proof I've discovered is; that might compromise the success of what I still have to do."

"Agreed."

The two men separated, Monsieur de Landré radiant, the prosecutor thinking about the explanations that he would have to give to the Minister, but fundamentally glad to be able to hope that the magistrate, whom he held personally in high esteem, had every chance of emerging unscathed from the tight spot into which the unfortunate affair had placed him.

Monsieur de Landré sent Max Semper, in New York, a cablegram saying simply: *Take first steamer urgently.*

A few days went by, in the course of which Monsieur de Landré worked tirelessly; he ran hither and yon, saw a great many people, rehearsed veritable roles. He was even seen in the offices of a large cinematograph company.

In the meantime, the accused and his advocate knew nothing about the strange steps that the magistrate was taking. As for public opinion, it had been calmed by a statement from the chancellery affirming that the Charfland affair would be definitely concluded within a week.

Six days after the depositing of the ten millions, Monsieur de Landré notified Charfland by way of a clerk, and his advocate by way of a secretary, that there would be a reconstruction of the crime the following day.

He telephoned the news to the public prosecutor, giving him to understand that the reconstitution in question would be a landmark in the annals of crime. The prosecutor, as the magistrate had expected, manifested his intention to witness it.

"Meet at eight o'clock in the morning at the family boarding-house," the magistrate told him, and added: "It will certainly last all day; lunch is arranged, don't worry about that."

Charfland had not understood the notification that had been made to him; he lost himself in conjectures, but his composure and aplomb did not abandon him. He had received a visit from his bewildered advocate, who told him that the notification had arrived without any prior warning; it could only be a matter of a farce or a crude intimidation, but whatever it might be, he was not to worry about it; his clear conscience would enable him to avoid the trap that they wanted to set for him.

The advocate had then gone to see the magistrate and had expressed his surprise at the unexpected indication, no new facts having emerged so far as he knew.

"Maître," the magistrate had replied, "the manner in which the crime was committed is known, but that knowledge has come to me independently of the accused; the latter has been able to tell you that no interrogation has been addressed to him in your absence; the announced reconstruction will summarize the entire investigation; the truth will be manifest; I can tell you no more."

Slightly angered by what he had just hard, the celebrated advocate adopted a high tone: "Pay attention, Monsieur le Juge. For six months, scornful of all justice, you have been keeping an innocent man in jail. At the moment when, under the pressure of public opinion, you're about to be obliged to release my client or be relieved of the case—you can see that I'm well-informed—you're going to play a comedy of intimidation that can have no result, since you do not have the guilty party in hand.

"Be careful! This latest fashion of acting will considerably augment the moral charges that weigh upon you; you have already been reproached for the weakness with which you have undertaken this investigation; public opinion, when it is fully informed—and it will be, I guarantee—will be manifest in such a fashion that someone stronger than you would be swept away by it. Beware!"

"Maître, this time tomorrow, you will have changed your opinion. The reconstruction of the crime that cost the life of the entire Terrick family will take place tomorrow; I confirm that the rendezvous is at eight o'clock at the house where the murder was committed; I warn you that the reconstruction will take all day. Lunch is arranged. If you want to do us the honor of sharing it with us, you will be welcome."

The advocate eluded that courteous invitation with a gesture, simply replying: I shall be at the boarding-house at eight o'clock tomorrow with my two secretaries."

The magistrate then received the American detective Max Semper, who had already presented himself the day before and had been asked to return.

"Mr. Semper, the moment has come to tell you why I cabled asking you to cross the Atlantic. I have absolute, crushing proof of the culpability of Charfland, but the most curious thing is that neither he nor his advocate knows anything about the evidence in question. It's not possible for me to inform you regarding the circumstances that led me to the great discovery.

"That having been made and verified, instead of recommencing an investigation set by step, which would take time and might permit the accused to concoct a defense as the charges were put to him, I've decided to attempt a reconstruction of the crime on the spot, including the salient facts that preceded and followed it.

"The accused, before that resurrection of all his actions, will not be able to maintain his composure; he will give himself away, confess...because he will not be able to imagine that the detailed scenes could be organized without irrefutable witnesses having been heard.

"It's necessary that he confess. If I insist on that—you'll be astonished—it's because, if he doesn't confess, I shall be defenseless against him, even though I can guarantee to you the veracity of all the details of the affair. When he takes account of the fact that I am even able to know what he was thinking at certain moments of his actions, vertigo will grip him; he'll confess everything.

"I am assured of the collaboration of a phonocinematograph, which will replay the principal scenes; that way, nothing will escape us of the various movements and exclamations provoked in the accused by tomorrow's reenactment.

"It will be very interesting—you'll see. But in sum, it's not for that reason that I permitted myself to cable you to come. After the confession, in the profound depression in which our man will find himself, I believe that something might be obtained from him on the subject of the Invisible Gang of which you suspect him of being a part. That will then be your affair; if the result satisfies you, I shall have thanked

185

you for the great service you rendered me in permitting me to arrest the criminal and keep him in prison, under the pretext of waiting for the famous rogatory commission that you sent."

Delighted, Max Semper thanked Monsieur de Landré and tried, but in vain, to find out how the magistrate had finally discovered the truth. They separated, having agreed to meet again the following morning.

V

This is the story of that fantastic day:

At the appointed time, Charfland, framed by two solid police inspectors, followed by his advocate and the latter's two secretaries, made his entrance into the apartment occupied by the widowed Madame Durand's family boarding-house.

In the antechamber there is no one but an inspector, who indicates that the new arrivals should go into the first room on the right—which was, it will be remembered—the room once reserved for Charfland.

The accused goes in without any apparent concern, but he immediately starts violently and stops, stupefied. He has just perceived, sitting at the little table where he had the habit of reading, facing the door, a man who resembles him in every regard: it is incontestably his double.

The accused's gaze shifts and he perceives, motionless and silent, standing in a corner, a number of men in frock-coats, among whom he recognizes the examining magistrate Monsieur de Landré, his clerk and his secretary, accompanied by the public prosecutor and the detective Max Semper. A cinematograph is installed in another corner of the room.

"What is this comedy?" asks the principal defender, gazing at the individual disguised as Charfland.

Without waiting for a reply, Charfland, recovered from his emotion, calms his advocate. "My dear Maître, if these Messieurs want to amuse themselves with this buffoonery, let them. What would be the result of protesting, if not to create doubt in their minds?"

"All right," said the advocate.

"Then we'll begin," announced Monsieur de Landré, while he pressed the button of a dissimulated bell discreetly.

In order to simplify the story that follows, we shall now designate by the name of "Charfland" the disguised policeman who is about to play the principal role, whereas we shall allude to the true guilty party as "the real Charfland."

Charfland, therefore, his head between his hands and his elbows leaning on the table, thinks aloud:

"Mr. Terrick, since we're now neighbors, it's just the two of us! Ah, you didn't want to conform with the orders of the Invisible Gang! A little more and you'd have had us pinched. You think you're free of the tax of two million dollars that I imposed on you; your account here at the financial establishments of the Universel Crédit is, however, good for that sum!

"I've been able to get ahead of you by two days; with my check, old lady Durand couldn't refuse me this room and I'm now the only other guest, with you, in this apartment. Lady Durand has to absent herself from time to time, but there's still the maid. What shall I do?

"Anyway, let's let a few days go by; I'll succeed in making use of her or rendering it impossible for her to get in my way. It's extraordinary how comfortable I feel. Yes, truly, it's easier to carry out a coup absolutely alone; I'm sheltered from any treason or clumsiness on the part of the Gang's accomplices. Of course, they won't get their full share of the profits, since, alone and without their knowledge, I'm taking the risks of bringing the affair to a successful conclusion."

At the moment when the monologist pronounced the words "Invisible Gang" the real Charfland went pale, in spite of the attention that he sensed he was the object on the part of the witnesses of the scene. He made the brief reflection: *I seem to have seen the man next to the magistrate somewhere in New York.* Then he resumed his habitual self-composure.

And the scene continues:

Charfland rings. Thérèse Vila—a double—knocks on the door, comes in and stops, intimidated by the piercing gaze launched sat her by the client. The examination lasts for a few seconds during which the poor girl seems disconcerted; a nervous frisson runs through her.

"Please bring my tea," says Charfland, finally.

"Yes, Monsieur," stammers the maid.

When she has gone the guest resumes his monologue: "If I'm not mistaken, that woman ought to be an excellent subject; that would be truly lucky; I need to find out right away what I can do."

The maidservant comes back in, carrying a tray that she sets down on the little table. She dare not raise her eyes, so much does the gaze that weighs upon her seem to disturb her. When she has completed her task, she raises her head. Charfland stands up; his fixed gaze expresses a will-power extended to excess. Thérèse Vila seems to vacillate. The man makes a few rapid magnetic passes, and then brings up a chair; the hypnotized woman sits down.

"She's soundly entranced," murmurs the hypnotist. "She's a remarkable subject. It's mere child's play for me to mold her as I please, but it's necessary to proceed in stages." In a low voice, and an authoritarian tone, he goes on: "Thérèse, I forbid you—I forbid you, you understand, ever to repeat what I command you to say and do. Tell me that you'll obey that order."

"Yes," murmurs the sleeper, shuddering.

"Now, tonight you're going to come to say this to me: 'I will obey your will, and I will never speak about your orders.'"

The magnetizer then makes a few passes; the poor neurotic wakes up, and Charfland this time in a soft voice, says: "You have a weakness, my child. It's necessary not to fatigue yourself too much."

And the domestic leaves, accompanying her exit with a faint: "Oh, it's nothing, Monsieur."

The presence of the actress made up as Thérèse Vila did not disturb the accused overmuch. *They must have succeeded in making the poor wretch talk*, he thought. *My defense is easy; the tale of a visionary, subject to several influences, as that seems to be the case, doesn't constitute evidence. I only have to deny it; my advocate will do the rest; it will even be a good subject for his speech, assuming that they drag me to the Assizes.*

The advocate, irritated by the spectacle whose outcome he cannot anticipate, poses his question once again, addressing the public prosecutor: "But in sum, what does this comedy signify?"

The prosecutor simply responds: "Monsieur le Juge d'Instruction is conducting his investigation as he sees fit; you have nothing to say for the moment, since, duly summoned, you are present. Afterwards, you will be able to draw all the conclusions you wish."

There is nothing to reply.

Monsieur de Landré speaks then, declaring: "Now we come to the eve of the crime."

At a sign the electric light is switched on and the blinds lowered.

Charfland resumes his monologue: "The first proof that I imposed on Thérèse succeeded perfectly, as have those which followed. The girl is in my power; I can count on her. She's just told me that her mistress will be leaving early tomorrow morning and will be absent all day. The moment has come to act. Let's first prepare the innocent accomplice for her role."

He rings. Thérèse appears; a single gaze; a single word: "Sleep!" and the subject, remarkable indeed, collapses on a chair, prey to magnetic sleep.

With his muted, commanding voice, the traveler gives her the following orders:

"You will sleep all night.

"Tomorrow, you will not enter the Terrick's apartment before your mistress has departed.

"At one o'clock you will lock the doors of the large drawing room, without going in; you will keep the keys.

"You will instruct the housekeepers not to go into that drawing room, where the Terrick family is gathered.

"When your mistress returns, you will tell her that the members of the Terrick family, being indisposed, have not left the drawing room all day.

In the middle of the following night you will replace the keys in the drawing room doors, unlock them, and go back to bed."

Three times he repeated those orders, assuring himself after each repetition that the subject has understood and will obey.

Thérèse is immediately woken up and leaves.

The accused remains thoughtful and absorbed, but nothing betrays his emotion.

Charfland takes off his boots and puts on light carpet-slippers. He goes to one of his valises, opens a locked compartment with a key and takes out a kind of medical kit, which he places on the table; then he puts bottles, tampons, a small box and a mask in his jacket pockets.

At the sight of those preparations the accused is seized by a kind of tremor, which he has difficulty mastering.

Charfland takes out his watch. "It's ten o'clock; old Durand's asleep; the children and the governess are in bed; the two Terricks are reading in the drawing room. Let's go—it's time." He opens the door cautiously and murmurs, with satisfaction: "An apartment of this sort is delightful; not a single door creaks, and the thick carpets stifle all footfalls."

He turns right and goes along the gallery, guided by rays of light that are escaping from the drawing room do. He turns right into the corridor and stops in front of the cloakroom. He goes in prudently and, switching on a pocket electric torch, climbs on to a stool in order to detach one of the two wires activating all the bells in the apartment. It is evident that he is thinking: *One never knows what might happen.*

Emerging from the cloakroom he retraces his steps. He pauses for breath in front of the drawing room door, covers his face with the mask and, with infinite precaution, turns the handle and pushes the door; no creak is produced.

The witnesses following the leading actor can see, gathered around the large table illuminated by the lamps of the chandelier, the entire Terrick family, reconstituted by skillfully disguised actors.

Mr. and Mrs. Terrick are to the left on entering, comfortably installed in large armchairs; he is reading a newspaper, she a book. Facing the door, the two little girls are on their knees on chairs, to either side on the governess, who is standing up and leafing through a large album of pictures.

The malefactor has entered without anyone noticing his presence. He murmurs: "Ah! I thought I'd only find two here." But as the governess looks up at that moment he does not hesitate, takes out of his pocket a kind of vaporizer and, with a circular movement, launches a jet of liquid into the faces of the five individuals present, who, under the effect of the instantaneous narcotic, appear to go to sleep. The scene has been so rapid that one can easily imagine how a coup thus carried out might succeed.

Charland then takes out a tampon, which he puts over his nose and mouth, closes the door, and then, sprinkling the liquid contained in another bottle on to a second tampon, he applies that one successively to the faces of Mrs. Terrick, the children and the governess. He switches off the electricity and opens a window. After a few moments, he is heard to say: "It's breathable now."

He closes the window, puts the light on again and heads toward Mr. Terrick, who seems to be asleep. He gags him, and ties his hands and feet with cords. He rummages in the inside pocket of his jacket and, radiant, takes out a check book, which he places on the table beside and inkstand, which he fetches from the smaller drawing room.

He watches the movements of his principal victim. "It's been a quarter of an hour; the effect of the narcotic is wearing off."

He then takes a revolver out of his trouser pocket and places his vaporizer within arm's reach.

Mr. Terrick comes round; on perceiving the masked man he tries to stand up, but Charfland forces him to remain seated with a robust hand and, putting the revolver under his nose, says to him in a low voice:

"Terrick, you and yours are in my power. Look at your neighbors; they're chloroformed and incapable of doing anything whatsoever. You're gagged and immobilized; it's futile to try and resist me. Anyway, what I have to ask of you is very little for you. You're simply going to sign me a check for ten million francs, on the Universel Crédit."

The man addressed replies in the negative with a abrupt shake of the head.

Charfland retorts: "I tell you that you'll sign it for me, with a little letter that will permit me to collect it without difficulty. If not"—his eyes become menacing—"I'll proceed with the execution of your wife and children before your eyes; then it will be your turn. I'll give you ten minutes to reflect. In ten minutes, if you're not disposed to sign the two pieces of paper for which I'm asking you—a very little thing for the billionaire A. H. Terrick—you'll have condemned one of your family to death, and I won't show any mercy. I have spoken."

Coldly, Charfland installs himself in a chair on the other side of the table, without taking his eyes off the American, the revolver in one hand and his watch in the other.

Then ten minutes pass in the midst of a silence troubled only by the hoarse breathing of the real Charfland, who is sweating copiously and seems to be on the brink of fainting in the arms of his two guards, and the regular tick-tock of the phonocinematographic apparatus.

At the end of the delay, Charfland stands up.

"Well?" he asks.

Terrick nods his head in a sign of acquiescence.

"That's good," says the wretch. "I'm going to untie your hands, but as you'll be tempted to take action against me, I'm going to place myself like this..." He passes between the American and his wife; with his right hand he places the revolver against the American woman's head and his left hand, drawing a second revolver from his trouser pocket, aims it at Terrick. "At the first untoward movement you make, I'll shoot both of you—that's understood, isn't it?"

He sets down the revolver that he is holding in his right hand and unties the wrists of the head of the family, then picks up the revolver again, which he places as before.

"You have everything that you need in front of you. Write, first of all, your check payable on presentation to Mr. Joe Helly...

"Good; now, a letter on your personal notepaper, as I dictate it to you.:

"Financial establishments of the Universel Crédit,

"Messieurs,

"I have the advantage of informing you that I have just expedited, to the order of Mr. Joe Helly, my check number 0203 for ten million francs, a sum that you will be kind enough to pay on presentation, debiting my account accordingly.

"Please accept, Messieurs, my sincere salutations."

The letter having been dictated, Charfland makes sure that it is duly signed. Then he tells his victim what remains to be done:

"Now, write on the envelope the address of the Universel Crédit (Foreign Services).

"Stick a stamp on but don't seal it.

"On the other side of the envelope write: *Urgent*.

"Everything is fine now, but you can't suppose that I'm going to set you free immediately. No, I'm going to put you to sleep again; when you all wake up I'll have the ten millions and you'll be able to look for me."

As he concludes that speech, Charfland pours a few drops of the contents of his vaporizer on Trick's face; the latter's head falls abruptly on to the back of the armchair.

The wretch takes out of his pocket the little box that he put in there before setting out; it contains a small Pravaz syringe and a little bottle. While preparing those objects for his sinister work he talks to himself:

"Was he stupid, all the same! As if I could leave a single witness to what has just happened! Even those"—he glances at the children—"must never be able to say anything.

"Oh, you won't suffer; it's a miraculous poison, still unknown to your medical examiners; one drop will suffice; the contents of the syringe could serve for several families; you'll pass without a word from sleep to death. No cries, no struggle, no blood."

And the sinister bandit, his preparations complete, lightly pricks the arm of each of the five persons present with the sharp point of the syringe, and presses lightly on the piston.

"It's done!" And, carefully, picking up all the objects of which he has made use, including the tampons and the bonds, he adds: "That really is good work."

He scans the scene with a glance, perceives the inkstand, and takes it back to the small drawing room.

At that moment, the examining magistrate, who was following the play of the real Charfland's physiology carefully, believing, based on the lividity of the latter's face, that he was ready to confess, asked him, abruptly; "It was really like that that you acted, Charfland, wasn't it?"

The wretch shuddered, without being able to pronounce a single word.

The advocate, who did not understand that mutism, exclaimed: "Defend yourself, then!"

And under the effect of that admonition, which gave him courage, the accused replied, albeit without his usual calmness: "I don't understand any of what happened here; my emotion is perfectly comprehensible when one sees oneself passed off as the author of the frightful crime that you've just simulated."

"You deny it?" says Monsieur de Landré. "That's your business. It only remains for us to continue.

Charfland switches off the light, goes out, and leaves the door ajar. In his room he places his various instruments on a table, takes another small vaporizer from his medical kit, returns to the drawing room and spreads a cloud. He takes precaution as far as to inspect his own garments and hands. He checks that the keys to the three doors giving access to the drawing room are all on the outside.

He finally goes out, for the last time, He returns to the cloakroom and replaces the wire connecting the bells to the batteries.

He is soon back in his room. Drawing the bolt of his bedroom as a precaution, he proceeds carefully to make up a little packet in which he assembles all the tools and various ingredients of which he had just made use.

He sits down and contemplates, delightedly, the check and the letter signed by A. H. Terrick. He draws pen and ink towards him, plunges his hand into his right hand jacket pocket and agitates it as if searching for something. He draws it out and contemplates the back of it. "Nothing at all to be seen there." Then he turns the hand over and looks at the palm. That is holding at a bizarre little apparatus, which, in steel wire painted in flesh-color, is scarcely visible. The wires seem to be maintaining several phalanges of the digits.

"Another one of my inventions! It's a clever expert graphologist who can find a single common point between my normal writing and the one this little toy obliges me to produce, opposing all the habitual reflexes of my hand and fingers!"

He takes the open and on the second page of the Terrick letter he signs, in crude handwriting: *Joe Helly*.

The letter is sealed.

At that moment the magistrate speaks, to indicate that after that, Charfland goes to post he letter at the nearest post office.

Then the wretch, having returned to the room, is heard to murmur: "Let's prepare for tomorrow."

From a compartment with a secret lock contained in one of his valises, he takes out a bowler hat and a suit of the same dark cloth as the one he is wearing, and places his manual deformer in one of the inside pockets, and his packet of incriminating evidence in the other.

"Now it's the following morning," declares Monsieur de Landré.

The curtains are drawn and the light is switched off,

Charfland gets dressed, putting on the clothes from his valise.

He opens a crack in the door, cautiously, and stands watch.

"It's eight o'clock. Madame Durand is going out; her instructions to the maid prove that she won't be back until late."

The examining magistrate speak again:

"Messieurs, we're going to follow Charfland in his peregrinations."

The accused, his features drawn by anguish, because he cannot explain by the maid's spying the discovery of the apparatus modifying his handwriting, says nothing, and meekly accompanies his guards in the middle of the group following his double. The latter, as he passes the concierge's lodge, remarks aloud that everything is fine for the moment in the service stairway.

Without hesitation, taking a complicated route, Charfland arrives at a fairly busy street situated between an investment property devoid of a shop and a small café. He stops in the courtyard; the magistrate immediately explains that, because the audience cannot all witness what the murderer did in the actual location, the scene will be reconstructed in the courtyard.

Charfland resumes his monologue: "It's as I anticipated; that this time, the concierge isn't in his lodge and the café doesn't have any customers yet. No one will notice my comings and goings. Let's head for the lavatory, which—as my enquiries determined a long time ago—is that the end of this little corridor."

The bandit, operating then as if he were in the little redoubt, makes the gesture of throwing the objects of the crime into the bowl one by one; then he pulls the chain and murmurs: "Adieu, incriminating evidence!" Then he takes of his jacket, and, by means of two cleverly-dissimulated catches, he makes two pleats in the back, which gives it the form of a garment pinched at the waist; he increases the length of the lapels, which pieces of silk, hidden until then in the lining, soon ornament. He draws back the extremities to the top of his trousers, exchanges his long tie for a bow-tie, puts on a pointed back beard and a moustache, dons a pair of spectacles, pins a decoration to his buttonhole, takes a tube out of his trouser pocket, which, when deployed, forms an elegant cane, and exchanges his brown gloves for bright yellow ones.

The metamorphosis is the affair of a moment. It is successful; in spite of the general hue of the garments remaining the same, the silhouette is so transformed that it would never occur to anyone to connect the man of calm aspect and a slightly heavy tread who came in with the one of slim and elegant appearance who emerges.

By means of an itinerary that we shall spare our readers, but representative of a plan ripened well in advance, Charfland arrives at a large clothing store. With a strong Spanish accent he asks for a light overcoat, chooses one in dark neutral gray, pays for it, and leaves, with the overcoat over his arm.

The real Charfland is becoming very unsteady on his feet; one of his guards thinks he hears him murmur: "Who saw me, then?"

But it is not him on whom eyes are fixed; the leading actor takes possession of the general attention, save for that of Monsieur Landré, who never takes his eyes off the accused.

The scene terminated, Charfland does not hesitate, and more than in the precious scenes; he chooses a direction deliberately and takes the whole group into a large café, in which the time for aperitifs is beginning to create movement. He sits down at a table near one of two staircases descending to the lavatory. He orders a drink, for which he pays immediately, of which he drinks half. Then, partly hidden behind a newspaper, he watches the staircase attentively.

A woman in black with an apron and a white bonnet—the attendant from downstairs—appears and heads toward the cahier.

"You'll notice that she has the habit of doing that; it's the time for a chat," remarks the bandit, for the benefit of the witnesses. With a natural stride he heads for the lavatories and then mimes the scene that passes in a more discreet location; he undresses, turns his garments inside out, and comes out again dressed in bright gray; he changes cravats again, folds up his cane, puts away his gloves, crushes his fake bowler in his hands and puts on a soft felt hat with a dent in the middle. He removes his false facial hair and replaces it with a graying beard, puts on a wig of the same color, dons the overcoat and, with slight limp—which he does not abandon so long as he has that appearance—he goes up the other staircase and goes though the café again, keeping his distance from the cashier, who is absorbed in her conversation with the lavatory attendant.

"It's going well," he murmurs. "Joe Helly has anticipated all the difficulties. One change might leave a trail; two are utterly deceptive!"

He goes to a shop near the Bourse where he buys a large briefcase with two pockets, the dimensions of which he checks with a meter rule that the shop assistant lends him.

A few moments later, he goes into the hall of the financial establishments of the Universel Crédit and goes up a beautiful staircase leading to the luxurious rooms of the foreign service. He heads for one of the ushers and says, with a strong American accent: "Will you announce Mr. Joe Helly to your chief of service."

The usher holds out a notepad and pencil, but, as if he has not seen the gesture, Charfland slowly spells out: "J-o-e

H-e-l-l-y" to the man, who obligingly writes the letters on the pad.

"Reason for the visit?" the usher asks.

"Your chief of service ought to be informed; I've come to cash a check."

A few moments later, the usher returns, seeming slightly dazed. He bows profoundly to Joe Helly, who is negligently sitting on a sofa, saying to him: "If Monsieur will do me the honor of following me, Monsieur the Director General, who is the head of the foreign service, will be pleased to welcome you."

A few moments later, the entire group was in that chief's office.

"Monsieur Joe Helly?"

"That's me, sir."

"You've come to cash a check..."

"For ten million francs signed A. H. Terrick; you should have been informed—here's the check." And the beneficiary held out the precious piece of paper in question.

The chief of service examined it, then passed it to two employees summoned especially when the important visitor was announced; in view of the large sum, it is, in fact, necessary not to proceed lightly. The concordance of the check with the details in the letter was carefully verified, as well as A. H. Terrick's signature."

"Would you care to cash it immediately?"

"Exactly; it was also agreed with Mr. Terrick—for you'll agree that one can never take too many precautions, that I would sign the acquittal in front of you."

So saying, Charfland put is right hand in his jacket pocket and withdrew it immediately; he took the pen and, on the acquittal form put on the back of the check by means of a stamp, he applied the famous signature of Joe Helly before the very eyes of the Bank employees.

During the new verification, the murderer briskly rid himself of the encumbering implement with which he had equipped the palm of his hand.

"Very good, Monsieur; the ten million francs are at your disposal. Would you like a part of the sum in cash? I hope that you'll do us the honor of permitting us to open an account for you; the house terms are favorable, in particular..."

"No, I regret, Messieurs, that for the moment, at least, it's not a matter of that; I have precise orders from Mr. Terrick, who honors me with his confidence and his amity, and I need to proceed today with a distribution of the ten millions. If, therefore, you will give me that sum, in thousand-franc bills, in order that it's portable, I have what I need to take it away. Look."

And he displayed his morocco bag.

The director and the chief of service started, but they thought that before a client, as the man in question might one day be, it was necessary not to permit for a single instant the thought that the Universel Crédit might experience any shadow of embarrassment at paying out such a large sum on demand.

"Very well, Monsieur; you shall be satisfied." And the instructions were given by telephone.

A few minutes later, two cashiers appeared, and deposited the piles of bills on the big desk.

"Here, Monsieur: a hundred wads each containing a hundred thousand-franc bills."

With that, the so-called Joe Helly stands up, counts the wads, takes a few of the at random and verifies the number of bills in the packets. He even goes so far as to open a few to verify the contents.

Unhurriedly, he arranges the wads in his briefcase, making six piles on each side; as he closes the fastenings of one of the two pockets he experiences a slight difficulty in making the tongue of the strap go into its buckle.

He folds up the briefcase, which then presents the dimensions of forty-five centimeters in length, thirty-three in breadth and twenty in thickness, takes the large parcel under his arm, bows, and heads for the door.

All the witnesses, at that point, observe that the accused is livid. The examining magistrate remarks to him: "You see, Charfland, that everything has been reconstituted. You're continuing to maintain silence? If so, we'll follow you with the product of your crimes."

As he emerges from the office, Joe Helly is the focal point of all the gazes in the hall, and the reflection is heard: "He must be mad to walk around with a fortune like that!"

Without emotion, the bearer of the six millions goes through the entrance gate and resumes following a bizarre course. While walking, he takes off his overcoat; he goes into an alleyway where he rapidly slips the briefcase into a kind of brown kit-bag, and passes the strap over his shoulder in order to carry it. In another alleyway, leading to a hair-dressing salon situated on the entresol, he gets rid of his false beard, converts his deceptive cravat into a conventionally-knotted tie and transforms his soft hat into a bowler. He deposits his overcoat on the staircase that goes up to the hair-dresser's, after having ripped off the name of the shop from which he bought it. "It will be astonishing if it gets from here to the Prefecture."

He is outside again, with an appearance in which no one would have been able to discern the previous Joe Helly.

In a large café he confides his precious haversack to the cashier. "I'll come back to collect it in two or three hours." To himself, he adds: "Now it's necessary for Charfland to be reborn!"

He hails a taxi and has himself taken to a place not far from the family boarding-house, to which he goes on foot. Having arrived at his destination he enters deliberately, goes upstairs and opens the door softly with a duplicate key. In his room, he proceeds with a new transformation and appears as at the moment of his departure.

He rings to ask Thérèse whether any post has arrived for him. After the negative response he goes out, passes the lodge slowly, and makes sure with a glance that he concierge has seen him.

At a tranquil pace he heads toward a restaurant where he lunches frequently.

He sits down, while the accused, still framed by the two inspectors, takes a seat with the other witnesses at a neighboring table.

It is there that the lunch announced by Monsieur de Landré is served. It is an intermission; everyone eats with a good appetite, with the exception of the real Charfland, who is trying in vain to keep a straight face.

That intermission is followed by another; coffee is taken in a nearby establishment, where Charfland passes ostentatiously before the cashier and the regular customers, to whom he is certainly known.

The examining magistrate then speaks, saying: "Messieurs, on leaving here, the murderer spent the afternoon in a cinema to which he often went; as he went in he took care to exchange a few words with the cashier, the porter and the usherette. To save time, we'll skip over that step; we'll suppose that dusk is approaching and transport ourselves to the said cinema in order to continue the reconstruction following the end of the representation."

The accused does not seem to be listening any longer, concentrating all his strength on remaining upright.

In the vestibule of the cinema Charfland resumes his monologue.

"Almost everyone has left."

Then he hides behind the ample curtain that closes the hall, and observed: "All gone; that's good." He goes back into the hall, undresses again, turns his garments inside out, and in a matter of seconds becomes once again the man who was carrying the kit-bag. He goes out, wiping his eyes and stretching his limbs. The porter, who is putting out the lamps in the vestibule observes: "Another one who fell asleep; the usherettes never think about anything but decamping at the first signal of retreat!"

Charfland returns to the café, asks for his haversack, which is given to him, puts a silver coin in the tray on the counter, thanks the cashier and goes to the lavatory, where he checks the precious contents of the modest bag, and then leaves.

Then—"It's dark now," the examining magistrate observes, in a loud voice—the murderer heads for the quais. He stops under the pile of one of the new bridges, makes sure that no one is looking and accompanies what he does next with a verbal commentary

"What a good idea I had to note the remark made by a comrade in the Invisible Gang, who worked as a mason on this bridge, that there's a void that could serve as a good hiding-place. I've worked here frequently by night, for periods of half an hour or an hour; no one has ever disturbed me, so the stone is now completely unsealed. I remove the painted rods that imitate the joints; with the aid of this flat chisel I remove the stone... Oh, it's heavy, but I'm strong... Now, to avoid any deterioration of these precious pieces of paper, let's surround the knapsack with this rubber sheet; with this solution let's stick it down so as to render the package watertight... There it is, in place, but when will I see it again? If it's necessary to wait for months, even years, I'll have the patience; the stake is worth the trouble. Let's put the stone back. With the cement that I've taken care to store in the hiding-place, a little Seine water and this dainty trowel, this is all that's necessary to make a new joint... There—it's done. Finally!

"Now let's clean the place up. The rest of the cement, the trowel, the signing apparatus and the cane—into the Seine!

"Still no one around? Good I can change costume…

"Here I am, the placid Charfland again!

"Now, the Law can come!"

On arrival under the pile of the bridge, the guardians were obliged to sit the accused down on an old crate that had been left there; he could no longer stand up; he was livid, and large drops of sweat were running down his face; increasingly tremulous, his face gave him the appearance of a beast at bay.

When his double had pronounced his final remark— "Now, the Law can come!" Monsieur de Landré, addressing the accused directly and pointing his finger at him, cried: "The Law has come, Charfland! It is here, and it demands that you account for your crimes!"

The murderer went even paler. On the point of fainting, he could only murmur: "But who saw me, then? Who turned me in? But I didn't have any accomplices!"

"Clerk," said Monsieur de Landré, "write down the accused's confessions."

And the clerk, without any protest from the wretch, who was no more than a human rag, noted down the long-awaited confessions.

"Charfland, do you recognize the reconstruction that you have just witnessed as exact?"

"What would be the point of denying it now, since you have all the proofs?"

"Good! Inspectors, take the accused back to prison."

VI

Thus concluded the sensational reconstruction of a crime that had, with just entitlement, greatly impassioned public opinion.

In spite of all the advocate's requests, the magistrate refused to inform him or the accused of the means that he had employed to discover all the details of the affair.

"The rights of the defense have been respected; nothing remains now but the confessions of the guilty party," the examining magistrate limited himself to replying.

On the evening of that epic day, Max Semper visited Charfland in his cell. He succeeded in giving birth in his mind to the belief that the Invisible Gang had something to do with the discovery of his crime. The Gang, when the crime was reported, had easily divined that he, Charfland, was its author and that, in consequence, he had ten millions in his possession. The Gang had then dispatched two acolytes to Paris to demand a share, but Charfland had refused to recognize his associates and had not responded to the rallying signs they had made to him.

Judging that Charfland wanted to appropriate the whole of the stolen money, the Gang had opened an investigation, the results of which had been communicated anonymously to the magistrate; that investigation had been the departure point of the reconstruction that had just concluded.

Charfland, sure of what awaited him, then surrendered to Max Semper, in a spirit of vengeance, everything he knew about the Invisible Gang, and the delighted American detective crossed the ocean again, certain this time that the famous gang would fall into his hands.

If the reader desires to know the epilogue to the drama, let it be known that Charfland, condemned to death, paid his debt three months after the reconstruction of the crime.

Almost at the same time, Monsieur de Landré, taking advantage of an exceptional promotion, obtained a seat as a counselor in the Appeal Curt; that was the recompense of the Government, which, thanks to him, was able to respond victoriously to an interpellation lodged some time before regarding the "poor administration of justice." That interpellation, although conceived in general terms, was fundamentally aimed at the Charfland affair, but the very generality of its terms obliged the author to debate it. The interpellator had envisaged a scandal capable of opening a ministerial crisis; the Charfland affair having been set aside by the guilty party's confession, nothing remained but trivia of which the Garde des Sceaux had rapidly disposed. Then, turning against his adversaries the weapon of which they had tried to make use, the Minister had exposed the formidable endeavor undertaken by the Law to succeed in confounding the one and only guilty party in a frightful drama, executed in conditions so mysterious that it had required veritable genius and enormous labor to bring forth the truth.

Epilogue

Ten years after the closure of the Charfland affair, an exceptional session brought together the members of the Académie des Sciences and that Académie de Médecine. The convocation, entitled: "Communication of Messieurs Chasselan and Lavrille on the life and works of Nounlegos," bore an underlined annotation: *Exceptional importance.*

Needless to say, the meeting hall was full. The Academicians, somewhat intrigued, were wondering who Nounlegos, unknown to them, might be.

The president of the session, the longer serving of the two Academic presidents involved, made the following speech:

"My dear colleagues,

"About two years ago, the Académie des Sciences and the Académie de Médecine were informed by a notary in Bondy that Monsieur Nounlegos, recently deceased, had instituted the said Académies, jointly, as his legal heirs; he made us the inheritors of his fortune, of which he gave us free disposition, his instruments of study, and all his works.

"After having fulfilled the necessary formalities, our administrative services entered into possession of a certain sum of money, encumbered only by an annual income to an old domestic servant, and a marvelously accommodated laboratory equipped with items of apparatus bearing no resemblance to those of which we are habituated to making use. Our colleagues Messieurs Chasselan and Lavrille were charged with making an inventory.

"During their very first visit to the domicile, their attention was attracted by a series of stout hardbound volumes whose spines only bore serial numbers. Those records, all manuscripts, with numerous diagrams and calculations, bore as a title: *The Work of Nounlegos.*

"It took our delegates a year to familiarize themselves with them, and several months to verify for themselves some of the advertised results, which explains the delay to which the communication you are about to hear has been subject.

"We think, Messieurs, that we are informed as to the research of a truly superior order that the scientists of the entire world are pursuing relentlessly in order to enable science to participate in the greater wellbeing of humankind. We believe that we are particularly familiar—because we follow it step by step in our sessions—with studies made in our own dear land of France; we interest ourselves in it; we encourage it, attempting, by means of our discussions, to stimulate the genius that brings them to a conclusion. And yet we had no suspicion that, in a small detached house in a suburb of Paris, an unknown man was working, for more than forty years, on a problem whose mere exposure was an unusual audacity.

"That unknown man, Messieurs, before whom we ought all to bow down respectfully with veneration, and who is about to give us, in revealing him to the world, a glorious immortality, is Nounlegos.

"Yes, Nounlegos, the man whose science makes all of ours pale: the modest individual who has tackled on his own one of the most troubling aspects of physiology, who has conceived innovative apparatus, invented a method and new means of examination, the application of which to other subjects will revolutionize all of medicine and surgery!

"Nounlegos, who—listen carefully Messieurs—has succeeded in reading the human mind!

"Do not think that it is a matter of a few improvements of any psychological methods or the reasoned observation of the nervous reflexes that accompany certain impressions. No, Messieurs, Nounlegos has arrived at reading within the human brain, without taking any account of external phenomena, as we might read a book.

"He sees thoughts stirring within the brain as one can see the blood flowing through the arteries, as one can see nerves contracting under an electrical contact. Yes, he has seen thoughts; he has grasped them; he had read them; he has written them down.

207

"His work is not finished; what he wanted was to succeed in reading them at a distance, recording them mechanically and fixing them in an indelible fashion.

"Death has not permitted him to find the complete solution to the vast problem that he posed himself, but the road is traced out; others will have the honor of bringing the task undertaken to a conclusion.

"It is not without a profound emotion that I announce this discovery publicly, which places its author in the front rank of all the scientists of his century—what am I saying?—of all the centuries!

I do not know what the philosophers will think, confronted by the perspective of a humankind so new, in which sincerity—not apparent but real—will be so easily verifiable. Many will doubtless estimate that life would be better if the black veil that separates thought from speech and action were to remain intact. Others will be enthused by the idea that hypocrisy will henceforth be unmasked, that it will always be possible to know the true motives of human actions. But that is the affair of the philosophers. Let us leave them the care of envisaging the discovery from that point of view. For us, whose only love is science, it is from the scientific point of view that we ought to try to perceive some of the innumerable consequences of the miraculous work of Nounlegos.

I have told you already that the reading of what is happening within the brain can only be obtained with the aid of previously-unknown apparatus and mechanisms; these means permit the easy vision and the examination of what is happening in any part of the human body. We shall be able to follow, in the course of an illness, the various alterations of the organs and tissues; we shall be able to track the alterations made by any medicament or any treatment—and you can appreciate that a new therapeutics is now on the eve of being born.

"When a surgical intervention is judged necessary, the operator will be able to work with precision, since he will have seen in advance the milieu in which he is operating, and will have no fear of any surprise.

208

"I shall limit myself, Messieurs, to those few remarks, but I cannot restrain myself from adding that in addition to these repercussions on human medicine and morality, Nounlegos' discovery of genius, by virtue of the knowledge that it will permit of the movements and transformations of the various cells of the organism, will doubtless allow science to make inappreciable progress.

"Thus, you will permit me, Messieurs, on your behalf, that of all the scientists of France and the entire world, to render to the memory of Nounlegos the very profound, respectful and grateful homage that is due to him!"

Colonel Royet: *On the Brink of the World's End*
(1928)

Introduction

For long hours, I have mediated before these pages, hesitantly, with a heavy heart, my head vertiginous, as if on the edge of an abyss...

Ought I to make public these memories of one of the most anguished and tragic periods through which humankind has passed, without being aware of it?

Was it permissible for me to evoke the terrible threat that the future might reserve for us?

Oh, what perplexity was mine before the ultimate decision!

However, I have decided. The terrible secret is choking me. For more than twenty years I have kept it, having sworn to do so to Monsieur Luissant, the venerated President of the Republic. Today, my oath is no longer binding, because the illustrious Statesman summoned me to his deathbed in order to release me from it—me, the last survivor of *those who knew*. More than that, the great and good citizen engaged me to publish my notes and memories.

"Now that panic is no longer to be feared," he pronounced, in a voice already faint, "it's necessary for people to know how close they came to Oblivion. Perhaps the frightful vision of the accident that nearly destroyed life on our globe will render them better."

In delivering the lines to the printer, it is, therefore, a terrible will of which I am the executor.

It is also a confession, for which I glimpse the appeasement of a dolorous remorse. Although entirely virtuous, a responsibility weighs cruelly upon my life. Too sensitive and

210

too pusillanimous, I lacked decision. I allowed a frightful peril to grow before me, without denouncing it. My determination stood up just in time to prevent the definitive catastrophe, but too late to obliterate the effect of frightful misfortunes already consummated.

Perhaps people will consent to absolve me on imagining the heights of alarm and terror that I was obliged to scale. But above my imperishable dolor, crushing my weak personality, *the Fact* will be imposed, colossal in itself, disconcerting in its causes.

The Fact!

The World nearly perished.

The cause?

An unforeseen cosmic phenomenon? A cataclysm of the physical order? An unleashing of natural forces?

No.

Terrestrial life was threatened by a single man, simultaneously a genius and a madman.

And the reason for that monstrous aberration?

An amorous despair!

I. Roger Livry

The fifth of August 192*.

That date hammers my skull, an ineradicable obsession that marks the point of departure of the fantastic adventure in which I was involved.

That morning, I was very happy. In agreement with my principal, I had organized the syllabus of my course in philosophy for the next scholarly year. With a light heart, I had just saluted the gold-lettered frontispiece of Louis le Grand. For two months, I was departing on vacation, bidding farewell to my Lycée, and to noisy and agitated Paris. I was finally going to take refuge in a "retreat" that I had chosen some time before: a hemicycle of high mountains in the Savoy, with the blue line of an Alpine lake in a valley.

My suitcases buckled, and my ticket in my pocket, I call in at Fontenay-sous-Bois to bid farewell to Roger Livry, perhaps to make one last attempt to drag him along with me. But will he break with his need for isolation? Will he consent to abandon his laboratory, interrupt his research as an alchemist of genius?

I ring the bell at the gate of his villa. Little Tourte, Livry's "laboratory assistant," comes to answer it.

"Is Roger here?"

"Yes, M'sieur, in the laboratory—but we're leaving soon on a journey."

"On a journey!"

Why has Roger not told me about that project? Slightly anxious, I hasten my steps, heading straight toward the glazed roof of the laboratory, which is shining through the girdle of trees, in the filtered sunlight.

I knock discreetly and go in, as is my habit, without waiting to be invited.

As soon as he perceives me on the threshold, Roger looks at me suspiciously. He interrupts his work momentarily, which consists of arranging bottles of blue glass in the padded compartments of a black case with copper corners—a case similar to those used by commercial travelers.

Others are arranged around him, waiting to be loaded.

"Secret keeper! You didn't tell me you were leaving!"

Under that amicable reproach, which I try to clothe in a jovial tone, I cannot entirely hide my perplexity.

For a moment, Roger hesitates to reply, but then snaps: "Well, yes, I'm going to the Camp de Châlons."[29]

---

[29] The Camp de Châlons, or Camp de Mourmelon, was a huge tract of land transformed into a military base in 1857, which became the showcase of Napoléon III's Imperial Army, employed for vast parades. In the early twentieth century it also became an important center for experiments in aviation. During the Great War it had close links with the nearby Camp de

"The Camp de Châlons? You want to see Suippes again, then, the chalk trenches, the frightful mud where we suffered and fought?"

Roger does not reply. He checks the stopper of one of the blue bottles. Abruptly, a suspicion grips me. The Camp de Châlons! But that is where Capitaine Berjac is garrisoned—the husband of Mademoiselle Thiérard-Leroy!

Does Roger intend to inflict the futile torture on himself of proximity to the woman who, in his mind, ought to be his wife?

Perhaps—because, his eyes vague, he seems to have forgotten my presence by his side; a bitter crease purses his lip; he has plunged once again into the dolorous dream that that hunts him.

In my turn, once again, I evoke, angrily, the absurd and unrealizable amorous dream that has poisoned the life, to calm and so rational, of Roger Livry.

How could one imagine that that man of science, concentrated in study, rendered even more antisocial, almost misanthropic, by the years of the war, could have been struck by a thunderbolt? And yet, that was what had happened seven months before.

One day in January, an untimely hazard took Livry to the home of Monsieur Thiérard-Leroy, the director of the Observatory.

Irony! His visit had only one objective, to solicit some statistical information of a meteorological nature, but it needed no more than a brief appearance of the astronomer's daughter in her father's study to cast a profound and durable disturbance into my unfortunate friend's soul.

I saw Roger arrive at my home like a madman the next day, begging me to go incontinently to Monsieur Thiérard-Leroy's house. Without further ado, on behalf of my comrade, I was to ask him for the hand of his daughter!

Suippes, close to the Front, also used as a training ground and to store stocks of chemical weapons.

And, without any objection, I submitted to that irrational and precipitate demand, because I could not refuse Roger anything.

We had been united by the bonds of a fraternal amity since our first days at school; having entered the École Normale at the same time, we had lived side by side ever since. By virtue of delicacy, simplicity and modesty, Roger had been able to level our very different situations, and render a narrow intimacy possible between the multimillionaire that he was and a poorly-recompensed debutant schoolteacher like me.

In addition, in spite of its singularity, my embassy to Monsieur Thiérard-Leroy inspired high hopes in me. In spite of his rough exterior of a gangling and inelegant, almost hirsute man of study, Roger was, in sum, very presentable. After a session with the hairdresser and a lesson to teach him to tie his cravat, he would be able, like anyone else, to pay court to and please a young woman. Then again, in matters more serious than physique and costume, he offered what is conventionally known as a brilliant catch.

An orphan, Livry had inherited a colossal fortune from his uncle, a wealthy ironmaster, estimated at a hundred and twenty millions at least; and what was certainly better, in the eyes of a man of science like Monsieur Thiérard-Leroy, my friend had always made the noblest uses of his enormous income. A sworn enemy of luxury and snobbery, scornful of the idle life of pleasure that seemed open to him, Roger had been passionate about the study of chemistry since his adolescence. Exceptionally endowed with mathematical skills, he had initially gone into the Normale-Sciences, and had then resigned on graduating, desiring to devote himself more freely to scientific experiments and the experiments he carried out relentlessly.

Finally, during the hostilities, his conduct had been admirable. He had involved himself in the gas war, pursuing research at the front, under shell-fire, into the toxic substances employed by our pitiless enemies, inventing replies as he went along to their odious malevolence.

Five palms of his military cross and a red ribbon testified to his heroism.

Thus, I was beginning to count on the success of my comrade's project, perhaps a trifle eccentric and unreflective, when, as soon as I spoke, Monsieur Thiérard-Leroy placed a brutal impossibility before me; his daughter was engaged to be married to a childhood friend, Monsieur Berjac, an artillery officer; the marriage was arranged for the end of April.

What could I say to Roger's dolor when he learned about the abrupt termination of his first idyll?

It was so violent, so unmeasured, that I envisaged with anguish a morbid depression in that powerful brain, overtaxed by study and the terrible years lived since 1914.

Alas, since that fatal day, my friend's singular attitude had reinforced my fears. There was a series of furious crises, during which Roger uttered extraordinary threats, punctuated with phases of listlessness that were even more worrying.

Then, a kind of rage for work reassured me a little. Did not the laboratory where his perpetual effort was extended offer the best distraction from his troubles?

So, at that moment, my anxiety was perfectly legitimate, on seeing him abruptly quitting his elected refuge in order to go toward an indeterminate goal.

The Camp de Châlons! What projects might be lurking inside his head?

I wanted to reassure myself.

"You've chosen a singular place for a vacation," I said, taking advantage of a moment when he had interrupted his meditation in order to resume the organization of his strange luggage.

Roger raised his head. "A vacation? You're joking, Out there, I'll be better able to carry out the decisive experiments."

"Right! The war's over—and you've done enough in that accused region."

Roger clenched his fists.

"No, the war isn't over! Humans haven't ceased to be the shame of terrestrial life."

"You're very hard on your fellows."

The chemist laughed sardonically.

"Look at Jobert! Another serpent I've warmed in my bosom..."

Evidently, the example of Jobert seemed well chosen to support the rancor that Roger had against the human species—and my friend continued to evoke the disquieting physiognomy of his former assistant.

"I associated him with my work; I confided a part of my secrets to him—not all, fortunately. The rogue thanked me afterwards by stealing two centigrams of radium from me—which is nothing—and three hundred grams of Omega acid, which is more serious." Roger brandished one of the blue bottles that he was in the process of packing carefully into his case, and added: "Look! A phial like this one..." An excitement illuminated his gaze. "With this, I could turn the world upside down!"

Poor Roger. I judged it pointless to object to his startling affirmation.

"Fortunately, you're loyal to me, my boy," the chemist said, in a more placid tone, giving an amicable tap on the shoulder to young Tourte, who had just come in, his arms laden with packages.

"And me?" I said, in a tone of mild reproach. "You don't count me for anything?"

At that appeal, Roger relaxed. "Paul, my brother, take pity on my poor nerves, raked by suffering. Don't abandon me. You can—you ought to—help me in my great task. Look, come with me!"

He takes hold of my hands and pressed them feverishly.

A brief hesitation, an egotistical impulse, quickly strangled, and I renounce the snowy summits of the great Alps in order to go with Roger to the dismal plains of barren Champagne.

I don't have the right to leave him to struggle alone in the morbid crisis that he's going through.

I can see very well what he intends to do at the Camp de Châlons; if necessary, I can oppose his possible eccentricities.

Then again, perhaps he doesn't know about the presence of the Berjac household in that region.

"Go back to Paris quickly," Roger concluded. "In two hours, I'll pick you up with your suitcases."

Without resistance, I consented.

Little Tourte escorted me back to the gate. Opening the batten of the door, the boy stood aside; then, tugging my sleeve, he pointed in the direction of the Bois de Vincennes.

"Jobert! Again!"

I saw an emaciated and bilious face disappear; it was, indeed Livry's former laboratory assistant.

"Every time anyone goes out, he's there, watching."

While walking to the station, I tried to divine the reason for the surveillance exercised over the villa by that maniac. The idea occurred to me to alert the police—but what was the point, since, in a matter of hours, Roger would have left Fontenay. If Jobert manifested himself again when we returned, we would think again.

Why, oh why, alas, did I not yield to that first impulse by provoking the arrest of the radium thief that same day?

How many subsequent catastrophes would have been avoided!

II. Étienne Tourte, Apprentice Pastry-Cook

In the golden haze of the setting sun, the first military barracks raised on the edge of the Camp de Châlons emerged on the horizon.

Now we are penetrating the long street of the singular village that is Mourmelon-le-Grand: poor dwellings that the furies of the war have brought back to their origins as shacks weatherproofed with the aid of biscuit-tins, coiffed with tin-plate roofs, the debris of food-cans.

217

In the church square, the auto stops in front of a hotel that has remained almost intact.

The choice of our rooms is quickly made, because questions of comfort have never had great weight in Roger's preoccupations.

He is far more interested in the transport of the two cases secured to the roof of the limousine. There are a thousand recommendations to avoid collisions. He does not take his eyes off them until they are installed in his room.

They worry me, those cases with copper corners, which suggest the most fantastic reflections to the idlers assembled in front of the automobile.

"A photographer," suggests one.

"No, they're glider pilots," whispers another, with a knowing look—because, after a suspension, piloting gliders has become the order of the day again and the Camp de Châlons has become the terrain of choice for the pioneers of the new aviation; every new arrival is willingly seen as a seeker of wings.[30]

"That's the very thing," mutters Roger, who has overheard the comment in passing. "We'll be glider pilots. An excellent pretext for not exposing our flank to curiosity-seekers. Anyway, as soon as possible I want to be at home. Let's look for a house for sale."

I start in surprise. Now Roger is thinking of becoming a property-owner in this desolate place.

It's necessary to convince myself of that, when my friend drags me to see the village notary the next day. Roger asks for a furnished house, with the provision that it must be isolated and surrounded by large grounds.

---

[30] Gliding clubs proliferated after the Great War, when an intense interest developed in extending distance and altitude records. Activity was particularly marked in Germany because of the prohibition of training for powered flight there, and there was a competitive reaction in northern France.

Mention is made to him of a former brasserie situated outside the locality on the road to Suippes—but the buildings have been slightly damaged by the bombardments.

Roger wants to visit it immediately.

I still remember the painful impression that gripped me when the clerk serving as our guide opened the door of an enclosure surrounded by high but breached walls. In the middle stood a large building, half in ruins. The roof stripped of some of its tiles, the shutters worm-eaten and dislocated, a lantern sustained with great difficult by its rusty iron fittings: such was the unappetizing spectacle that one discovers on the threshold of the "property."

The interior of the building does not cede anything to the exterior appearance in dilapidation and dirtiness. Our entry has the effect of scaring away a band of rats, the sole masters of the dismal abode. In the rooms, there are broken windows, partly-collapsed ceilings and fractured floor-tiles.

"A few minor repairs will be made, on the entitlement of war damage," said the clerk, to clear his conscience.

"I like the place as it is," says Roger. "I'll buy it."

Two days later, it's done. Roofers have replaced a few tiles; glazers have replaced a few broken panes. The worst of the dust has been swept away by vigorous thrusts of a broom. A local merchant has provided "furniture." Not without audacity, he names thus some primitive camping material undoubtedly collected from the nearby trenches.

For his part, young Tourte occupied himself buying a stove and household utensils from a bazaar. With the best will in the world, the laboratory assistant offered to resume his original métier as scullion.

It was, in fact, by virtue of a singular misunderstanding that the boy found himself in Livry's service in the quality of apprentice chemist.

A few days after Jobert's abrupt departure, my friend had decided to look for another laboratory assistant. One Sunday, without realizing that he would find all the shops closed, he dragged me to the Rue des Ecoles, to his supplier of chemical products, from whom he was going to seek the necessary indications.

"In any case," Roger repeated to me, in a tone of mystery and mistrust, I want two hands, hands from which I demand neither science nor intelligence, which will handle my retorts without wanting to know what they contain."

We ran into closed shutters, of course.

Resentfully, the chemist stamped his foot on the asphalt; then he stated walking, mechanically following the sidewalk of a street going down toward the Boulevard Saint-Germain.

Suddenly, he stopped dead, his cane pointing to the front of a shop that more the sign: *Laboratory*.

He pronounced the word in a loud voice; I read it in my turn. Unlike the other shop-fronts, that one allowed its frosted glass windows to appear. On the door, a handle seemed to invite entry.

"Let's see," said Roger, who did not renounce his obsessions easily.

He crossed the road and opened the door of the shop.

We both had a moment of amazement; then our gazes met and we smiled. Before us appeared the preparation-room of a pastry-cook or a confectioner. Shiny pans were handing on the wall; on the shelves were molds of every form, bottles of candy, and to flatter or nostrils, the characteristic odor of chocolate mingled with vanilla and caramel.

In the room, with his elbows on the table, an adolescent was reading. He was little more than a child, clad in the classic costume of pastry-makers, a white hat and smock.

Ah, the hazard of destiny. Who could have suspected then that my life, those of our fellows, and the fate of the world, were going to depend on a heroic gesture on the pats of that apprentice pastry-cook?

At the sight of us the child got up and then advanced toward the threshold. He removed his hat politely.

"What can I do for you, M'sieur?"

"Nothing, my friend," said Roger, smiling. "We've made a mistake. Excuse us."

"No offense taken!"

"So, why did Messieurs the confectioners take it into their heads to baptize their back-kitchen a laboratory?"

At the slightly scornful expression "back-kitchen," the gamin raised his head, not without pride. "Well, M'sieur, we do chemistry here. We distill sugar, we manipulate perfumes and essences."

The statement took on weight primarily because of our interlocutor's attitude—that of a young cockerel rearing up—and by the moderated guttural accent of the Parisian slum-dweller. It amused us enormously.

"You're laughing, Messieurs," the contrite pastry-cook went on. "You're mocking me. Well, for sure, it's not chemistry as I'd like to learn it, true chemistry with bases, acids, met-alloids, so-called organic substances…chemistry as this book explains it." With a resentful gesture he indicated the book left open on the kitchen table. Then, ceding to the insouciant and cheerful philosophy that seems to be integral to the Parisian poor, he added: "Anyway, what do I care? I know it's not for me, the fine things one learns in lycées, and all the tricks I see through the windows of the Sorbonne when I pass by with my basket on my head. One isn't a prince!"

Livry seemed prodigiously interested.

"Would you like to learn chemistry, then—real chemis-try?" he asked, in a soft voice.

"Oh, M'sieur…"

The apprentice pastry-cook put his hands together, as if in adoration of a distant and fugitive dream.

"Do you want to come with me?" said Roger. "You can help in my laboratory."

"A laboratory like the one in the Sorbonne, with retorts and test-tubes and electric machines and microscopes?"

"Yes," said Roger, smiling. "A laboratory even better equipped than the one at the Sorbonne."

The gamin looked my friend straight in the eyes. "No! You're poking fun at a poor kid!"

"I'm perfectly serious."

I judged it appropriate to intervene. "But it will be necessary to consult your family, won't it, young man?"

A shadow of sadness veiled the boy's gaze. "My family! Well, Monsieur, unless I call the macadam Papa and the railings of the market in the Place Maub Mama, I can't name them for you, my family."

"You're a foundling?" I said, compassionately.

"Yes, since it's the custom to call children like that 'lost'."

He was decidedly interesting, that gamin, with his intelligent expression and his street-urchin repartee.

"By the way, what's your name?"

"Étienne Tourte, M'sieur…Étienne after the statue of the man in the square where they picked me up—you know, Étienne Dolet, who was put to death, back in the day, to teach him to live.[31] Tourte because that's the name, or the nickname, of the worthy woman who picked me up: Mère Tourte, well-known in the neighborhood—she sold fries at the Maubert market."

"Good! The good lady serves as your adoptive mother?"

"She served, M'sieur, but not anymore. She died last year—died of grief because her eldest, Gustave, died in the war. A strapping fellow Gustave—he was a roofer; he taught me to run over the roofs. Those were good times—you could breathe the air, not like here in the ovens. The Boches killed him; that changed my life, and to console myself, I took up science."

With the back of his sleeve, he wiped away a tear that was running down his cheek. Poor kid!

"What about your employer?"

"My boss? He's one who won't keep me back. I work in his house during the week."

---

[31] Étienne Dolet (1509-1546) was a French scholar and printer burned in the Place Maubert, along with his books, on the orders of the theological faculty of the Sorbonne, on a trumped-up charge of atheism.

Two days later, Étienne Tourte arrived in Fontenay. With an indescribable joy, he traded the white hat and smock of a pastry-maker for the grey smock of a laboratory assistant.

Today, without false shame, he declared himself ready to resume his place among the saucepans.

Roger was delighted with that solution. "That way we won't waste our time eating out, and we'll have no need to introduce strangers here. We'll be able to work in peace." Then, encouraging Tourte with an amicable tap: "Agreed, my lad; make us truffle sauces and champagne-style kidneys if it amuses you..."

"And desserts, of course!"

"Thumbs up for the desserts. In a few days, you'll be able to serve us *bombes glacées*, I can sure you of that."

The last words vibrated like a threat. The allusion to bombs plunged me into an anguish compounded from amazement and fear. What chemical work did he intend to do in this similar place?"

That same evening, Roger permitted me to glimpse the stupefying path into which his delirious brain was urging him.

III. Nightmarish Discourse

It was a heavy and sultry evening, with rumbles of thunder in the distance.

After dinner, well cooked, in truth, by little Tourte, Roger sent the boy away. When we were alone, with an abrupt gesture, he threw away a half-consumed cigarette and came toward me. A willful movement of his head seemed to drive away a final hesitation.

"Paul," he said, in a very calm voice, "you're a courageous man, and also a philosopher, so, you ought not to fear death?"

At that unexpected interpellation, I had a surge of anxiety, but since my friend was offering me the opportunity for a lesson in morality, I quickly recovered my aplomb in order to launch the reply: "Certainly, I don't fear death; like many others, I risked it for four years, at the front—but on the other hand, I don't fear life." Making my thought more specific, I went on: "Life is a duty that makes all the obligations of humanity concrete, and that duty sometimes requires more resolution and sacrifice. Because of that, all life ought to be sacred to us—our own as well as other people's..."

A fugitive irony traversed my interlocutor's physiognomy, but he hastened to approve: "I think exactly as you do. Suicide, like individual murder, is a cowardly and stupid act." He became strangely animated. "There's something better to do: radically suppress the cause of human miseries by suppressing the world, by stifling at a stroke the existences that trouble and poison the Earth's surface."

"Damn! You're lapsing into integral nihilism, my friend. Fortunately, you're not yet in a position to load the bomb that will blow this poor terraqueous ball to smithereens."

"How do you know? Have you ever thought about the end of the world?"

Roger looked me straight in the eyes. That fiery gaze re-ignited all my anxieties. To avoid a more serious excitation, I was obliged to follow him in his lucubrations.

"The end of the world?" I said. "Certainly, I've read all the scientific anticipations, all the fantastic presumptions, all the legends related to the question. Periodically, besides, amateur astronomers an hundred-sou astrologers take the trouble to announce the abrupt termination of our celestial voyage. This very day, if you search hard enough, you'll find, somewhere in the sky, the comet that's due to pulverize us. Since the year 1000 of sinister memory, prophets of that stripe have never shut up shop, but as the Earth isn't doing too badly..."

"Let's leave the jokes there, please, and remain in the domain of pure science. The Earth won't die from the impact of a comet; celestial mechanics are too well-regulated for that. The Earth will perish from cold."

"Yes," I risked, to temper the violence of Roger's words. "I estimate, like you, that when the Sun is extinguished..."

224

"The Sun!" My friend shrugged his shoulders in order to emphasize the scorn he accorded o my hypothesis. "The Sun! But my poor Paul, although it's true that in the first ages of the Earth, the Sun stored enormous quantities of heat inside our globe, at the present moment, it only contributes in trivial proportions to the maintenance of normal temperature. Look, it's as if you tried to heat the Place de la Concorde with a lighted candle. Oh, don't smile; it's not a laughing matter. Merely allow me to help you grasp the true—the only—reason that guarantees the terrestrial crust against the mortal cold of space."

"I'm listening like a docile pupil, happy to be instructed."

"Well, it's the 320 kilometers of atmosphere that constitute a gaseous mattress around us, impermeable to the cold outside. And do you know the indispensable agent of that impermeability?"

"Tell me."

"Water vapor." And, in a tone of complaint: "What! You didn't know, then, that water vapor regulates all terrestrial life? Suppress the water vapor, and you suppress life, because you permit the cold of space to penetrate all the way to the solid surface. Now, the cold of space reaches 270 degrees below zero..."

"Brrr! You're giving me cold chills in my back."

Without paying any heed to the interruption, Roger continued: "But to extinguish life on Earth completely, there's no need to envisage that extreme temperature. A great scientist, Charles Martins, has demonstrated that a decline of only six degrees in the mean temperature of France would bring the Alpine glaciers all the way to Paris.[32]

---

[32] The author adds a note at this point bearing the single word "Authentic." The reference is to Charles Frédéric Martins (1806-1889), a botanist and meteorologist who carried out extensive comparative studies of glaciers and concluded that

"I've calculated myself that a decline of forty-three degrees in the normal temperature of the globe would lead to the solidification of the oceans and transform the continents into vast deserts of ice."

"Fortunately, they're entirely theoretical calculations."

"No, it's been observed; it's a fact of our geological history. Millions of years ago, when the overheated surface was covered with gigantic flora, when fantastic animals, the bones of which we've discovered, pullulated on land and under water, when an intense life was established everywhere, the ice abruptly surged forth, stifling all creatures, animals and plants, and doubtless also the humans of those times—for there's no proof that, amid that exasperation of vital forces, human, civilizations and empires didn't exist in those distant ages.

"The result of it was an anesthesia of seeds, a destruction of species, a kind of end of the world, so abrupt and unexpected that science hasn't yet been able to offer a plausible explanation of the mystery." In a lower voice, Roger added: "Today, I believe that I've solved it, the mystery..."

He uttered a sigh, marking a pause. Then, with an ever-increasing tone of hatred, he went on: "After centuries, millennia of death, the resurrection came! There were other lives, other plants, other beasts and other humans. Was that life any better than the one swallowed up by the shroud of ice? It doesn't appear so, at least if I can judge by the odious spectacle of our present world."

Livry stood up; he strode back and forth, making broad gestures, and continued to emit his anathemas: "Today, what do we see, in spite of the apparent and illusory progress of civilization? Everywhere, the onslaught of base instincts and evil passions. Everywhere, lies, hypocrisy and fraud. Yesterday's atrocious war is only one incidence of that universal degradation. Half of humankind seems to me to be hell-bent on despoiling, torturing and destroying the other half. And if

---

the mean temperature during "ice ages" was only a few degrees lower than the present mean.

we look at the material signs, don't we find symptoms of decadence and decrepitude in all races and all classes? What is more abominable than the world of today?"

Roger stopped in front of me, his arms folded. His face was crimson with anger, his gaze fiery. He burst forth: "Paul, believe me, it's time, high time, to plunge the world that is coming apart and suffering—oh yes, suffering!—back into oblivion."

Poor Roger. At that moment, he was causing me a frightful pain, and a profound pity. Beneath the crazy words of an unhappy man, I sensed the distress of a grief-stricken soul, an exceedingly sharp dolor. I was, however, convinced of the impracticality of his hallucinatory threats; I was far more fearful of other, more direct, acts of violence against the Berjac household.

"I understand. You're meditating a book, a scientific work serving as the frame for a philosophical idea: a dream of the end of the world by cold, such as has happened in prehistory, such as occurred millions of years ago…"

Strident, demonic laugher cut off the thread of my speech.

In a harsh, metallic, arrogant voice-a voice whose tone made me shiver, Roger roared: "No, you don't understand! It's not a matter of a dream, but a reality; not contemplative philosophy, but imminent facts."

He made a violent effort to get a grip on himself.

"Excuse my nerves, Paul—but I want to finish where I should have begun. In this very place, I possess the substance that renders me master of lowering, as I wish, the temperature of the globe."

The chemist took me into the next room, where he had put the cases brought from Fontenay. He pointed to them with an emphatic gesture.

"This is the means by which we'll conduct the world to its final end!"

I don't flinch. He has just opened one of the cases. It contains the phials of blue glass that I've already seen, con-

227

tained in their felt sheaths. The chemist takes one out, removes the stopper, and pours a few drops into a saucer.

Without emotion, I gaze at the syrupy blue-tinted liquid that my comrade caresses—I can't think of a better word—and trickles between his fingers.

Obligingly, he explains:

"In the first box is my provision of the Omega acid. In the other, lined with platinum sheets, my radium is at the center of an asbestos mattress—for radium is a terribly inconvenient metal; it eats through everything, including glass."

Now he brandishes the ebonite case inclosing the strange substance discovered by the admirable Curie household.

"It's a big as a penholder! One wouldn't suspect that the contents are worth twelve millions!"

"Twelve millions!" I repeat, stunned.

"Yes, ten grams of radium…I have as much in my laboratory at Fontenay…and that's just a beginning. I've made a contract with the largest manufacturers of chemical products for them to procure me, within a year, the forty grams I'll need."

What point is there in protesting loudly? In his dementia, the poor fellow is multiplying, at the demand of his crazy imagination, the few particles of radium that he possesses.

He replaces the tube of radium and closes the two boxes carefully.

"Tomorrow, I'm expecting to receive at the railway station the glass tanks destined to contain the Omega acid, as well as the meteorological instruments that will enable me to observe the results. In four days, everything will be ready. While awaiting the definitive action, this first experiment will give an idea of the means at my disposal…"

It was heart-rending.

But once again, his grating laughter bursts forth in the silence.

"If the astronomer Thiérard-Leroy were able to suspect it, I think he'd have judged it futile to marry his daughter Hélène last April twenty-fourth to Capitaine Berjac of the three-oh-sixth artillery, eh!"

Those words make me shiver. Roger knows the names, he remembers the date. He's dominated by the obsession of that accursed marriage.

Doubtless spurred on by that reminiscence, the madman cedes to the cruel emprise of his distress. He becomes delirious.

"Oh, the blind lovers, they can't see Death. It's descending from on high, all white, as white as a bride... It's snow…it's ice... I'm summoning it, I'm attracting it, I'm guiding it…it extends its white shroud over them, over us, over the entire earth..."

"Roger, I beg you..."

The exhortations to calm remain stuck in my throat. I'm alone with the poor madman, in that remote house where the storm is rumbling, where the wind is howling, where the ground, beneath the harsh glare of lightning-flashes, seems to be carpeted with frost.

Truly, in that moment of alarming nightmare, I think I see around me the dead earth invoked by the demented vision, the crust of crystallized snows of the glacial epoch.

And Roger, his arms raised toward the havens, continues to vociferate:

"Tremble, beings and things...

"Dust will return to dust...

"I am the Man of the Apocalypse!"

IV. A Seeker of Wings

After that fearful evening, I knew the terrors of a night of fever and insomnia.

The next morning, Roger seemed to me to be fresh and well-disposed. In accordance with orders given the previous day, the auto, which had been put in the garage at the hotel, came to pick us up to take us to the station. In no time at all, we were there.

Numerous packages had arrived, addressed to the chemist. Roger arranged with the dispatch office for them to be transported and then we climbed back into the automobile.

Roger is driving; I am sitting beside him. A beautiful day is in prospect, tempered by an easterly wind.

That regular wind encourages trials in unpowered flight, for on the horizon, in the direction of the Ferme de Bouy,[33] two great white birds are furrowing the sky, alternately appearing and disappearing behind clumps of fir-trees,

On the road, we catch up with a strange machine being towed by a tractor.

"Well, well!" says Roger. "That's a new idea! Oscillating wings..."

In fact, by virtue of the speed of travel, the wings of the alerion[34] in tow, stretched over a supple armature, are beating the air regularly like those of an enormous bird.

But the auto of the seekers of wings turns right on to a side road, clearing the road ahead.

Roger was about to activate the accelerator.

"What if we go and watch?" I proposed

He shrugged slightly. "Poor inventor! If he knew, he wouldn't risk breaking his bones in a crude machine."

"If he knew what?"

My question must have seemed naïve, because Roger became irritated. "That we'll soon be dead, of course!" Then, after a gesture, he conceded: "But if it's agreeable to you to go

---

[33] The Ferme de Bouy, in the heart of the Camp de Châlons, was the training center for the Fourth Army during the Great War.

[34] An *alérion* [alerion] is a heraldic eagle; it was adopted by the designer Louis Peyret for the Peyret Alérion single-seat glider, which won the first British Glider Competition in 1922, piloted by Alexis Maneyrol; the two were fêted when they returned home. The term became briefly commonplace in application to gliders in general, and even to other small aircraft.

see at close range the attempts those larvae are making to crawl above ground, let's go!"

He turned the steering-wheel. Following the alerion, our vehicle reached the crest overlooking the plain, from which the machines were being launched.

We were soon on the fringe formed by the curiosity-seekers who were limiting the improvised aerodrome.

Two flying-machines were already in the air. Attention was, however, concentrated on the flying machine that had just arrived. In the circle of watchers, the name of the inventor was whispered: Guy Mayrol.

He proceeds with his preparations for take-off. The aides extend the "sandow" that is to project the alerion.[35] Guy Mayrol takes his place in the pilot's seat and utters a brief cry. That is the signal. The elastic cables relax; like an arrow, the alerion departs into space.

Almost immediately, alas, the apparatus stalls, descends in a spiral, and crashes on the hillside.

The crowd runs forward. Roger and I follow.

Fortunately, the fall has been gentle. The pilot stands up, unharmed.

In spite of his chagrined declarations of a short while before, my friend examines the flying machine lying on the grass with interest. Mayrol, a very young man with a sympathetic face, contemplates the injured machine with an expression of dolor and discouragement.

In the meantime, Livry has taken his notebook out of his pocket, and traces a sketch, while casting a glance over the various parts of the apparatus, measuring the inclination of the wings with the gaze, and then jots down equations.

I prefer to see him like that.

---

[35] A "sandow" was originally an elastic device used for exercising the arms, named after and marketed by the pioneering body-builder Eugen Sandow. The term was borrowed for application to catapults employed for launching gliders in France during the 1920s, but its fashionability was brief.

Suddenly, he approaches Guy Mayrol, and in a very soft voice, which I have not heard for a long time, he murmurs in his ear: "Will you permit me to give you some advice, Monsieur…?"

Mayrol looks at the unknown man with astonishment, but lets him speak without impatience. God knows how much advice he had heard!

However, the aviator follows the explanation, nods his head, and finally stuffs the piece of paper that Roger has just torn out of his notebook into his pocket.

After that incident, my friend rejoins me. We climb back into the automobile. Roger redirects the vehicle toward Mourmelon-le-Grand.

"You see, you're interested nevertheless in the future of unpowered flight," I say, to break the silence.

He makes a gesture of protest.

"Oh, don't exaggerate! I found myself in a position to procure that seeker some satisfaction. His wings are too narrow, the center of gravity of the apparatus is set too low. And yet, he understood the problem. If he listens to me, tomorrow he'll fly like a bird." Then, in an ironic tone: "Isn't it customary to grant small favors to those condemned to die?"

I keep quiet. What point is there is persisting?

In any case, we've arrived at our rickety château.

As soon as the threshold is crossed, Tourte, in a white apron, contrasting with the face, reddened by the fire of the oven, hands Roger a letter.

He opens it, scans it, and flies into a fury again.

"What is it?" I ask.

"Here, read it."

It's a letter from Philippe, the old domestic who serves as a concierge at the villa in Fontenay. Two banal pages to say that everything is in order, as at Monsieur's departure; one page of salutations. Then, at the bottom, a postscript that makes me jump.

I ought to tell Monsieur that Monsieur Jobert presented himself at four o'clock yesterday, asking to speak to Monsieur. I told him that Monsieur was absent.

The return to the scene of that individual caused me an indefinable malaise. But what could be the objective of that tireless pursuit?

"Perhaps Jobert wanted to solicit a re-entry into grace in your regard?"

My supposition provoked a shake of the head on the chemist's part—but the arrival of the station cart deflected attention to another object.

He supervised the unloading of various parcels. Until dusk, we were occupied in unpacking the crates sent from Paris.

First there were thick crystal tanks that Roger had placed in the middle of the empty space behind the house.

"This will be what I'll call our cold trap," he declared. "With four nuclei of that sort, I can bring the world to its end."

I let him talk, and helped him to install other apparatus of current usage in meteorological observatories.

Afterwards, it was necessary to distribute a whole series of maximum and minimum thermometers. One was set at ground level, another lodged in a shell-hole ten meters deep, which we were obliged to dry out first. It was hard work dredging the white mud of the calcareous soil. My pupils at Louis-le-Grand would have laughed if they could have seen their philosophy professor in his shirt-sleeves, like a well-digger.

"Now I need a thermometer on the roof, as high as possible," Roger murmured.

"I'll climb up," said Tourte, sketching a joyful caper.

Poor boy! Your destiny, to which ours was linked in an extraordinary fashion, obliged you to be an accomplished gymnast and daredevil!

The work took us until nightfall.

Surprised by the darkness, Roget consented to put off filling the tanks with the Omega acid, and the entrance on stage of the radium, until the next day.

For my part, I was exhausted. So, after a summary dinner, I wasn't sorry to go up to my bedroom and find my poor camp-bed.

V. Drama, Heroism and Folly

Roger's imperative voice extracted me from slumber.

"Quickly, get up!" my friend shouted. "It's four o'clock. The wind's favorable. If you want to, come and see Mayrol fly."

I got dressed in haste.

We arrived at the terrain just as the young pilot had finished his preparations for take-off.

At the sight of the apparatus, Roger's face brightened. "He's followed my advice!" he said. "His center of gravity seems appropriate, the wings are now aligned with the axis of horizontal stability. Ha ha! We might see some interesting things!"

I couldn't see any of the improvements mentioned, which might have existed only in Roger's hallucinated eyes, but I approved of what he said regardless.

To my great surprise, though, as soon as he saw us, the young man ran toward us. His extended hands sought those of the chemist.

"Oh, Monsieur, my dear Monsieur, how I thank you. Without great confidence, I confess—forgive me, but I've already had so many disappointments—I adapted my supportive surface to the mathematical points fixed by your drawing. I twisted my ailerons according to our sketch. Well, at dawn I made a trial; it seemed to me that my apparatus was a hundred kilos lighter, that it was supported in the air with an unusual force."

"It doesn't astonish me," said Roger, with amazing self-assurance.

Mayrol contemplated him, with a passionate admiration painted in his gaze. "But who are you, then, to have given me, without even knowing me, an idea from which I might obtain glory and money? For I sense that this time, I shall get there!"

"Me! My young friend, if you knew who I am, you'd doubtless lavish me with more execration than gratitude. I'm the Man of the Apocalypse."

For a moment, Mayrol was silent, disconcerted by those strange words. Without lingering any longer in astonishment, however, he installed himself on the seat of his apparatus, and made a gesture bidding the gawkers to stand aside.

The alerion was launched. To everyone's amazement, it rose twenty meters in an admirable fashion. Then the great white bird began to describe circles with a perfect regularity.

The spectators, whose number was increasing by the minute, were astonished and ecstatic.

The pilot seemed sure of himself. No oscillation indicted any disequilibrium. Occasional abrupt downward plunges were halted by a graceful upward curve toward the sky.

"One would think it were a seagull flying over the waves!"

That reflection by an officer rendered the appearance of that extraordinary flight exactly.

And I repeated the thought that Livry had a considerable part in the success that seemed increasingly certain.

It was marvelous—and how troubling!

Troubling?

Even more so than I imagined at the time.

Who would have been capable of foreseeing that Livry had just created, with his own hands, the supreme antidote, by which the Earth might escape the evil of death?

Time went by.

Large placards displayed on the ground in succession indicated to the pilot the results acquired.

One hour thirty. One hour fifty...

The alerion continued to rise and descend with a remarkable facility. One gradually got so used to seeing it soaring in the sky that at length, the spectacle became natural, banal, almost tedious.

Roger became impatient.

"Damn it! We're wasting our time. I'm sure the man will keep flying until his strength runs out. Let's go..."

He turned round, took a step forward, and then stopped, nailed to the ground.

His face had gone white; his hands were agitated by a convulsive tremor.

I shivered in anguish. Was Roger about to have a fit, there, in public?

Mechanically, my eyes searched the people surrounding us.

Many officers, sportsmen, chauffeurs, a few peasants—and, six paces behind, a group composed of two amazons and two cavaliers: a colonel and a captain of artillery.

Of the two women, the first as red-haired, her hair tight at the temples, her body roughly-hewn, with a mannish appearance. At first glance one divined a horsewoman, sacrificing all coquetry to the practice of her habitual sport. At any rate, I scarcely accorded a glance to the plain and graceless individual in question, who seemed to be there to serve as a counterfoil to the prettiness of her neighbor.

By a striking contrast, the other amazon gave the impression of a being all finesse and charm. A slim figure, as supple as a liana; an ideal face illuminated by large dark blue eyes, slightly sad; tufts of fleecy blonde hair escaping the edges of a straw boater. That ravishing creature almost inspired a sentiment of tender pity with her lily-like fragility.

It was toward her that Roger's mad gaze was directed. Abruptly, I understood.

The unfortunate hazard that, to all indications, it was necessary to expect at any moment, had occurred. It had brought before us Madame Berjac, the daughter of the astronomer Thiérard-Leroy.

Alas, I sensed then the extent to which the sudden and insane passion of my friend was justified.

That adorable woman was one of those predestined to charm and seduce at first glance. Others, like me at that moment, would have been able to admire, to love, such an exquisite work of art, a fragile item of Dresden china perceived in a display-case in a museum. It would have required a truly great assurance of one's heart and one's reason to remain insensible before such ideal grace.

An incident as rapid as lightning suspended my reflections. How can I describe the sudden succession of anguishes and fears with which those few seconds were filled?

Amid the acclamations of the increasingly dense crowd, the alerion was approaching the ground, ready to touch down at its point of departure as lightly as a bird. Mayrol had beaten the record for altitude and distance.

At the same moment, however, dominating all the other sounds, a loud cry of distress resounded.

I turned round, and horror gripped me before the imminence of a frightful drama.

Frightened by the large shadow of the apparatus sweeping over the ground and by the precipitate cheers of the spectators, Madame Berjac's horse has leapt sideways. Then, with a single movement, the beast has reared up on its hind legs. For an inappreciable time it remains in that unstable equilibrium, of which circus exercises only give a faint idea. It is a complete straightening, which horsemen have baptized with the significant expression "the candle." It constitutes the most redoubtable defense that a horse can oppose, because the weight of the rider and the instinctive action exercised on the reins combine to tip the mount backwards. Then the rider is crushed! A vice clasps the victim between the ground and the mass of the beast seeking a point of support in order to get up again. With the disposition of ladies' saddles the danger is even more horrible, for the amazon remains the prisoner of the forks sustaining her, and those forks intervene to produce frightful and mortal wounds.

Such is the perilous situation of the frail young woman. One senses, one sees, that she is doomed!

Cries rise up, horrified screams, in which impotence and dolor are mingled.

Pricking his horse with a furious thrust of the spur, Capitaine Berjac launches himself toward his companion, but, frightened in its turn, the animal swerves.

Among the pedestrians, people make as if to run forward.

Before all the rest, a man beside me has bounded forward.

With an incredible leap, of which only a professional acrobat would seem to me to be capable, he leaps at the horse's head, grabs the reins and clings on to them.

There is a violent shock, and under the effort of that counterweight, Madame Berjac's mount falls back to the ground. Other people have thrown themselves upon the beast, gripping it everywhere, immobilizing it. In the midst of the crowd I distinguish the savior who has fallen under the hooves of the horse, and then Capitaine Berjac, who carries his inanimate wife away in his arms.

All that, I repeat, has taken place so rapidly that the different phases of the scene have raced ahead of my impressions, my intentions and my movements.

Like my neighbors, I disposed myself to run, to bring help, but I did not have time to put one foot in front of the other before it was all over.

Only then did I recognize Roger as the man who had just been disengaged from between the horse's hooves. All at once, he is dusted down, asked if he is injured and congratulated for his coolness.

In my turn I approached my friend, and without a word, I squeezed his hands in mine.

"Let's go, quickly!" he murmured in my ear, in a halting voice. "I can't take any more!"

Poor Roger. At that moment, I was able to fathom the depth of his incurable wound,

He let in the clutch, and the auto sped away in fourth gear through the stony ruts of a scarcely-traced path, fleeing toward Mourmelon. The machine truly seemed to embrace its master's rancor.

There was a series of terrible jolts, shocks to break the springs. For a moment I feared that Roger, vanquished by sickness of living, might precipitate himself voluntarily toward a mortal catastrophe.

An abrupt application of the brake nearly sent me hurtling over the hood.

"Hold tight, there," muttered the driver, in the irritated tone that was the surest indication of his interior turmoil.

We had just stopped less than a meter from an immense haycart blocking the Rue de Mourmelon, into which we had plunged. With imperative blasts of the horn, Roger forced it to let him pass.

Before I had recovered from my emotion, the auto had traversed the village and stopped in front of the gate of our sullen dwelling.

Roger went up to his room and shut himself in. I judged that it was best to respect that grim isolation.

In any case, Roger reappeared against at lunch time.

Sitting facing me, he dispatched his meal without saying a word, and then, having swallowed the last mouthful, he said: "To work! I want the experiment to be in full swing by the end of the week, so that we're feeling the first effects of the cold.

With a sardonic smile, he added: "The lovers of equitation can enjoy the time they have left. Before autumn, I promise them a Siberian temperature. At least the amazons will remain by the fireside."

I abstained from any reflection.

VI. Jobert's Letter

The next day, from dawn onwards, the chemist applied himself to delicate and slow manipulations. As meticulously as if he were carrying out a real experiment, he distributed the

Omega acid. In successive layers, the syrupy liquid was spread out in the glass tanks. With scrupulous attention, Roger supervised the crystallization of the liquid, in such a fashion, he claimed, as to render the mass perfectly homogeneous.

My role was limited to following the chemist's work as a mere spectator. Roger had insisted on distributing the radium personally in the gelatinous mass formed by the aid.

With the aid of a long hollow platinum needle, he introduced traces of the precious substance particle by particle, in such a way as to impregnate the crystalline block. Eventually, the monotonous gesture seemed to make my skin crawl.

The ringing of the bell by the postman bringing the morning mail offered me a pretext to escape momentarily. I ran to the gate.

There was a letter addressed to me. I opened the envelope. A piece of lined paper escaped from it—vulgar letter paper of the liked that is usually offered in cafés to customers who ask for "something to write on."

At the first glance I deciphered Jobert's signature, a jerky, jagged scrawl with downstrokes interrupted by jumps.

In that scrawled page a graphologist would have discovered indications of envy, rage, pride and also a clearly emphasized cerebral derangement.

In fact, it was a veritable ultimatum that, via my intermediary, Jobert was addressing to Livry.

Judge for yourselves:

Monsieur Paul Lefort

Your friend Livry can hide at the Camp de Châlons, but I have penetrated the goal of the secret experiment he is preparing. I can foresee its incalculable consequences: to transform into arable land the chalky steppes of dusty Champagne, to change deserts into pastureland and heaths into forests. Now, having contributed to his works since their outset, it is only just that I participate in the glory of the grandiose results. Knowing that you are the only person possessing any influ-

ence over Livry, I am using your intermediary to make him understand his duty and to express my formal desires.

Either Livry will summon me and associate me with his work, not as an assistant but as a collaborator treated on a footing of absolute equality, or he will make me a gift in full property of the quantity of radium necessary to continue my research on the modification of calcareous matter on my own—a quantity that I fix at twenty grams.

My science is worth as much as his, and I cannot admit that his insolent wealth gives him the power to humiliate my poverty and arrest the impetus of my genius. In the scientific domain, as in any other, property is theft. Thus, equal shares, if he does not want to exhaust my patience and my resignation.

With best wishes, sincerely,

Jobert

The author of that statement was truly endowed with a strong dose of unconsciousness or effrontery. I judged that it was better to bring my friend up to date with the situation. I would see what he said.

More pensive than irritated, the chemist listened to a brief account of his ex-assistant's actions and movements since the day he had left the laboratory at Fontenay. He frowned on taking cognizance of the letter, and then nodded his head, as if those incoherent lines seemed perfectly normal to him.

In sum, the audacious pretentions of the rogue did not make him unduly indignant. He contented himself with pinching his lips, and they looked me in the face.

"Your Jobert possesses what we call scientific intuition, you know. I wouldn't have thought him that strong."

I couldn't help smiling at that unexpected appreciation. "Let's see—if I've understood correctly, Jobert intends to regenerate infertile soil, and become a benefactor of humankind. Now, it seems to me that you're marching toward an exactly opposite goal; instead of creating, you intend to destroy."

"That's true—but Jobert has nevertheless glimpsed one of the applications of my method, and that's not bad. Even so, it would be unfortunate if he took the theory too far, and especially the practice, for then..."

Roger left the sentence dangling.

"Then?" I prompted.

"Nothing. There's no need to develop my hypothesis, firstly because Jobert doesn't possess a sufficient quantity of radium, and secondly because you wouldn't understand a word of my explanations."

As the play of my features must have testified some resentment at that appreciation, however, my savant friend deigned to talk.

"Don't get annoyed! My research rests on theories so new, so troubling and so extraordinary that they almost escape our sense and reason. To make a palpable and so to speak, mechanical proof of them demands the help of higher mathematics, the integral calculus, because there alone can the notion of infinity be distinctly clarified. I'll spare you that demonstration, but in order that you can grasp it, I'll attempt a vulgarization by enunciating the as-yet-vague results in which the future laws of chemistry and physics are based.

"Inorganic ferments exist, which play in matter the role that microbes play in living beings. In consequence, large-scale effects—or, if you prefer, powerful reactions—can be produced by very small quantities of substance, possessed of an appropriate power of dissociation..."

Taking me by the arm, Roger led me to the tank in which the mixture of radium and Omega acid was crystallizing.

"Look! You have before your eyes a striking example of what I'm saying. What is nowadays known as radioactivity is, more simply, the dematerialization of matter." With a hint of pride, he went on: "The other evening, I reminded you that water vapor in suspension in the atmosphere opposes the intrusion of the cold of space, just as the panes of a window protect a room from the effects of the exterior temperature. Well, I'm breaking a pane of the atmospheric greenhouse in which we live like fragile plants. I'm shattering the glass of the sky—and this is my stone!"

He took a droplet of the blue- and violet-tinted liquid, and made the gesture of throwing it violently into the air. Then he went on:

"My Omega acid completely dissociates the water vapor with which it comes into contact, by fixing the oxygen and liberating the hydrogen—which, by reason of its weak density, rises up to the upper limit of the atmosphere and is probably lost there. But a remarkable fact gives my discovery its full range: after the adjunction of radium, the dissociation produced at ground level simply by exposing the liquid to the exterior air is transmitted from one particle to another. Every molecule of water vapor attacked decomposes its neighbors, and so on, with a speed proportional to the extent of the radiant surface. If you like, compare that action, of which radium is the principal agent,[36] to that of a trail of powder. Remember too that the extraordinarily intense phenomenon discovered by me, will be exercised equally from sea level all the way to the highest atmospheric layers.

"As an immediate consequence, no more evaporation of water! And evaporation, which constitutes the great thermic regulator of the globe, is as necessary to the life of the planet as respiration is to us. Conclude!"

But it was the madman who, in a tone without reply, provided the hallucinatory conclusion himself:

"Given the surfaces of radiant acid that I shall employ, six months will suffice to lower the temperature of the globe to a hundred and fifty degrees below zero. I estimate that no living organism will be able to resist such a climate.

"On the other hand, the surprise will be too abrupt for any organization to be made against such cold. All the heat

---

[36] Author's note: "An experiment by Marie Curie has demonstrated that radium decomposes liquid water, ice or water vapor with an extraordinary intensity." Marie Curie made this point explicitly in her Nobel Prize lecture in 1911.

and protection furnished by present habitations or vestments would become illusory. In any case, what would one eat? No more animals to butcher, no more running water. All movement impossible!

"From that moment on, after a brief struggle, life will disappear without there being any need to wait for the next year, when the temperature will drop a further hundred degrees, or the next century, when the advance of the ice will complete the covering of the entire globe."

In truth, it was horrific, that tale in the fashion of Edgar Poe, which Livry developed with an indisputable appearance of scientific precision.

Roger triumphed over my emotion. He had undoubtedly found the means to test my shaken suspicion.

"Have you grasped now the colossal phenomenon of the dematerialization of matter—a phenomenon characterized by an extraordinary liberation of energy? Here, I'm employing that energy to destroy the water vapor in the atmosphere, and indirectly, to produce cold. Jobert is thinking of using it in another way, to destroy chalk...but let's leave that; the energy can manifest itself in thousands of forms. You know at least some of them..."

As I opened my eyes wide in astonishment, Roger smiled ironically. "Of course! You must have heard mention of heat, electricity and light!"

"I understand," I murmured.

I could not help being gripped by the grandeur of those magisterial views; I completely forgot that the speech-maker was mad!

But I was troubled even more when Roger declared, in his modest tone: "After all, I only have the chance of putting these theories into practice, of giving them the consecration of experiment—and what an experiment! But I don't have the merit of having invented them; they were proposed by Gustave Le Bon. And let me just remind you of a sentence written by that great physicist in his book on *The Evolution of Matter*: 'The scientist who finds a means of liberating economically the forces that matter contains will instantaneously change the face of the world.'"[37]

And Roger sniggered.

"My insolent fortune, as Jobert puts it, has permitted me to pay the price—but I have found it!"

I lived a fearful moment then; a horrible conviction imposed itself on my mind: sound in body and mind, Roger was telling the truth! Had I not unknowingly witnessed the beginning of the titanic and mortal experiment of which the world was about to die?

No! It was too absurd.

If I had abandoned myself to it, I would rapidly have acquired the tremulous mentality of a man of the year one thousand, terrorized by legends and predictions.

Alas, my perplexities were, as yet, only at their beginning.

The next day I was woken up by Livry's triumphant shouting.

"Hey Paul! Come down quickly! Come and look: the temperature has already dropped three degrees since yesterday at the same time."

In fact, on setting foot in the courtyard, I felt a chilly wind strike me in the face.

He was exultant, and at eight o'clock he declared, with a proud joy: "Six degrees below normal. That's not bad for a start."

In truth, the weather seemed to be complicit with his mania. By the end of the day, we had the impression of a veritable cold snap. In the course of the night, I found myself obliged to add a traveling rug to my light bedcovers; I was freezing.

In the two days that followed, the cold got worse. A bitter north wind blew outside. That was abnormal for the middle

---

[37] Gustave Le Bon's far-sighted account of *L'Évolution de la matière* was published in 1905.

of August, but in sum, the seasons to which we have become accustomed in recent years have similar whims.

On the morning of the third day, Roger could not retain his joy on observing that the short grass was covered by white frost.

In the course of the afternoon, however, an unexpected blow put a brake on that enthusiasm. Roger was cheerfully getting ready to go for an excursion by automobile—in order to take temperature readings in the surrounding area, he said— when a telegraphist came to the door. He held out a dispatch. Roger broke the gummed seal with an expression of ill humor. "Why won't they leave me in peace?" he grumbled.

As soon as he had read the telegram, however, his physiognomy revealed a violent emotion.

"The wretch!" he murmured. "He's gone stark raving mad, then!"

As my gaze sought an explanation, he passed me the blue paper.

In my turn, I was choked by indignation and dolor after having read the frightful lines:

Public prosecutor, Seine, to Roger Livry, chemist, Mourmelon.

Property Fontenay burgled last night by unknown malefactor. Custodian murdered. Please return urgently.

"Jobert!"

The name escaped my lips, containing a formal accusation in itself.

"Yes, the rogue has put his threats into action. He's stolen my radium!"

"What are you going to do, then?"

"Return to Paris. It's necessary. I want to be sure about Philippe's fate. Poor fellow!"

His real affliction gave way to a burst of egotistical ill-humor. "To be disturbed like this at the most interesting point of my experiment!"

"You can interrupt it, to resume it later."

"No! Here, everything will remain in place. The phenomenon will proceed without us, for years if necessary. No one will suspect it, and the house can look after itself. All the same, it's vexing!"

Half an hour later, after having locked up the rickety château as best we could, we were speeding along the road to Paris.

VII. The Cold

The sad voyage is accomplished without a word being exchanged.

At six o'clock we arrive outside the gate of the villa in Fontenay. The house is full of agents of the Sûreté. The examining magistrate is completing his investigation in the laboratory.

All the luxury of the property is contained in that large low building behind the villa, in the middle of a veritable park that extends between the railway line and the Bois de Vincennes. There, Roger has realized a marvelous installation, equipped with the most advanced and most costly apparatus. To science he has been unable to refuse anything, not even an electric furnace that burns three thousand francs' worth of current an hour every time it is switched on.

We head in that direction, but as we approach the door, amazement nails me to the ground. The frame of carved stone—of millstone—in which the solid grille and the thick battens of the door were enclosed, has completely disappeared. The battens and the metal hinges are lying on the ground, leaving an opening excavated in the supporting brickwork; one might think it a construction at its outset.

"Walk!" whispers Roger, in a low voice. "And above all, stop looking astonished!" And as my bewilderment is not dissipated swiftly enough for his liking, he adds, impatiently: "Better than anyone else, I ought to understand how Jobert got in there. A simple dissociation of the calcareous stone sustaining the door, with the aid of the Omega acid. Have you forgotten my explanations already?"

Shivering, I followed my comrade.

Reciprocal introductions with the magistrate are followed by the latter's explanations.

"The door of your laboratory was being repaired, which facilitated the malefactor's intrusion" says the magistrate, without hesitating over what seems to him to be an evident observation.

Roger nods his head. At the same time, a glance instructs me to keep quiet. The magistrate continues is reconstruction of the crime.

In the middle of the night, the murderer climbs the wall of the property. Then he introduces himself into the laboratory through the open breach, goes straight to the strong-box; removes a steel panel with the aid of an explosive—a chlorated powder, according to the experts.

In spite of the care taken by the burglar to cover the front of the strong-box with blankets, the noise of the explosion is heard by old Philippe, the villa's guardian. He comes running, but on the threshold of the laboratory he falls, pierced with two thrusts of a dagger. The poor man is dying at the Hôpital Saint-Antoine. Nevertheless, thanks to the light of a lantern, he thinks he has recognized his attacker; he has designated Jobert, the former laboratory assistant of the master of the house.

"Everything indicates, in any case, that the crime has been committed by someone very familiar with the habits of your house," concludes the examining magistrate. "Had you, then, large sums of money in that strong-box?"

"Not a centime of cash, but ten grams of radium, representing a value of more than two millions."

The judge started. I stifled a cry of amazement. Had Roger really spent such a sum buying radium?"

Without excitement, however, the chemist proceeded with a rapid inventory.

"He has also stolen a demijohn containing twenty-five liters of Omega acid," he murmured in my ear. "And that's more serious..."

The last observations having been made, the examining magistrate retired, declaring that Jobert would be placed in the ranks of the most dangerous criminals; all the police forces would be launched on his heels.

"Will they succeed in arresting him?"

I formulated that question a few moments after the magistrate's departure, solely to break the somber silence in which Roger seemed to want to confine himself.

"I hope not!" he fulminated.

As I manifested a legitimate surprise in my expression, he explained: "I have no desire to see the Law doing chemistry on my back!"

"What do you mean?"

"That Jobert possesses a specimen of my acid, that he's divined too much of my work. I'd prefer that he doesn't talk, so, I want him to escape the searches."

"But he's a murderer! He merits a punishment!"

Roger shrugged his shoulders. "Like all of us, he's condemned to death. The Law can do no better."

I did not feel any desire to prolong that conversation, both idle and painful. I understood the urgent necessity of re-action.

To begin with, I wanted to liberate my mind from the doubt into which, reluctantly, Roger's extravagant claims had plunged me, on the subject of his purchases of radium.

That same evening, while my friend was at the Hôpital Saint-Antoine with his wounded servant, I went to the principal merchants of chemical products in the Latin quarter.

Livry had made large purchases from all of them.

From the very start, the merchants allowed me to discover that my friend's affirmations were still below the truth. Three months before, had he not concluded, in good and due form, an unusual contract for the supply of fifty grams of radium? At the current price of one million two hundred thousand francs per gram, he had thus engaged himself, with regard to the various producers of France and abroad, for a sum of about sixty million—a full half of his fortune.

On returning to the villa, I found Roger occupied with tidying up his laboratory. Without waiting any further, I could not master the impulse that drove me to try to talk some sense into him.

"Wretch!" I exclaimed. "Do you want to ruin yourself, then?"

He shrugged his shoulders.

"In a few months, we'll no longer be here. Do I still have to repeat that to you? So, tomorrow I'll go to my notary to tell him to sell my immovable property. Then, if necessary, I'll mortgage the villa at Fontenay..."

I let him talk. What was the point of countering such arguments? I would only try to see his notary, secretly, in order to prevent that irremediable eccentricity, which would put the unfortunate on the streets.

But would those officious precautions of a devoted friend be sufficient, against the obsessions of a willful individual like Roger?

No: at the rate things were going, very soon, circumstances would give me a duty to have resource to a dolorous extremity.

On the day when I found that it was impossible for me to defend Roger against himself, I would become culpable by keeping the secret of his folly; then, only one solution would appear possible: the internment of the poor fellow.

For some time already, would it not have been better to give the scientist the care required by his sick brain?

But our thoughts and our resolutions are truly submissive to strange oppositions!

From the moment that I began to encourage myself increasingly to take a decisive step, Roger seemed to be determined to adopt an absolutely normal attitude. And with regard to whom? With regard to the very people who might be called upon to judge his mental condition!

In the course of the Jobert affair he was summoned to numerous interviews with the examining magistrate, the head of the Sûreté, and the police commissioner of Vincennes. Was there an effort on his part to appear natural in order to remove any inclination on the part of the law to occupy themselves with his affairs? At any rate, I had never seen my friend Roger so amiable, such a brilliant conversationalist, so far from lunacy. The magistrates marveled at his logic and his intelligence. Behind his back, they addressed themselves to me to consecrate Livry as a superior man, a powerfully organized mind, a scholar of the first order.

He made the same impression on Dr. Revard, the celebrated surgeon and most prominent member of the Académie de Médecine. Roger had made his acquaintance at the bedside of poor Père Philippe, who was still battling between life and death. Quite naturally, the two men had allowed their conversations to stray on to scientific terrain. One day, to summarize his enthusiastic judgment on the subject of my friend, Revard, who was not reputed to be lavish with praise, whispered in my ear:

"Remember my diagnosis—your friend will be Galileo, Edison or Pasteur!"

After that, could one see me going to request the detention of Livry in an asylum? It would be me who was at risk of being treated as a madman and seeing myself locked up right away.

And yet, I retained the certainty that my friend was not cured. On the contrary, his strange ideas were becoming more profoundly rooted. Every morning, Roger came into my room brandishing the newspapers.

"I believe that's that, eh? Yesterday, fifteen degrees below normal. Winter temperatures at the beginning of autumn. The vines frozen in Champagne. Poor devils of vine-growers! If I could tell them how vain their lamentations are...

"And the meteorologists! Oh, it's necessary to hear them! They're serving us the cold wave, the perturbation of the regime of the winds, or even the sunspots! All the old ma-

251

jors are being worked to death. They're also accusing the Moon, of course. She has a broad back, the gentle Phoebe!

"Anyway, observe for yourself the unexpected activity with which the Omega acid is eating the water vapor. Since my cold machine has been functioning at Mourmelon, not a drop of rain—a sky purged of any trace of humidity."

In fact, a singular coincidence encouraged the extravagant fantasy of the destroyer of the world.

In the months since we had quit Mourmelon, the weather had cooled in a very abnormal fashion for the time of year. There was a veritable cold snap: a bitter north wind was blowing, as in December. Everywhere, that the popular sentiment could be grasped, on autobuses, at the restaurant, at streetcorners, the plaints burst forth. On the doorsteps, housewives were affirming that the seasons had "turned round."

Finally, there was one symptom that could not help but impress me forcefully: well before the usual date of their departure, the swallows were flying south.

I have always judged the instinct of animals to be superior to the anticipations of humans. Were we really threatened by an exceedingly precocious winter of exceptional rigor?

That fortuitous accord between Roger's hallucinatory predictions and the reality of facts ended up troubling me in a singular fashion. In vain I waited for a change in the weather, one of those abrupt releases of a soft warm humidity that normally succeed dry and cool periods—but the days passed without modifying the state of the atmosphere, the meteorological bulletins recorded increasingly sullen temperatures, to the great joy of the chemist and my increasing nervousness

It was then that, the following week, an event occurred that was to furnish a new aliment to my anguish.

VIII. The Sower of Cataclysm

I have omitted to say that, to Livry's secret satisfaction, all efforts to pick up the trail of Jobert had remained vain.

At one moment, it had been suspected that the murder had taken refuge in his mother's house near Algiers. The window of a farmer, the woman lived at Bouffarik. But a search carried out in the poor old lady's home had demonstrated that Jobert was not there. That he had gone there after the crime was possible, even probable if one put weight on certain indications. Perhaps Jobert had yielded to the desire to embrace his old mother before leaving the country, and the old woman's denials did not determine anything with regard to that particular point; a mother does not betray her son! At any rate, everything indicated that the criminal had reached Algiers and had succeeded in embarking for an unknown destination.

Such was the state of the information on which the police were relying when there were earthquakes in the vicinity of Douera and Bouffarik, which plunged the region into consternation and terror.

The newspapers of the epoch have described in detail the frightful panic of the first moment, the villages in ruins, the dead and the living buried under the rubble, and also the noble rivalry of the rescuers coming from all directions.

While deploring that public misfortune I would doubtless only have taken a distant interest in those events if Roger had not given them a truly singular interpretation.

"You haven't guessed what had happened?" he asked me, after having read the news relating to the cataclysm attentively.

As I did not grasp the significance of the question I remained silent.

"Well," Roger cut in, "I'm convinced that Jobert has certainly taken refuge in Bouffarik with his mother. There, consciously or unconsciously, he has provoked the catastrophe."

"The catastrophe?"

"Of course—the earthquake.

I was accustomed to my poor friend's mystifying speech, but that was truly beyond measure. Following the strategy that I had imposed on myself in such circumstances, I did not pick up the strange affirmation.

Nevertheless, Roger followed his train of thought.

"The suspicion occurred to me immediately. A study of the geological map has confirmed it fully. In the region tested by the cataclysm the ground is constituted by siliceous strata alternating with calcareous layers. Suppress or dilute the layers of marble, chalk or marl and everything collapses, dislocated. You've realized the conditions that engender earthquakes."

Mockingly, he unleashed a few darts at me: "No, however little versed you are in studies of chemistry, you must remember the fundamental experiment: chalk dissolved by acid... What am I saying? I blush to have to remind you of the Latin classics, in which you were taught that Hannibal, in order to cross the Alps, dissolved the rocks with vinegar![38]

"Well, I repeat to you, my Omega acid, amalgamated with radium, also enjoys the property of attacking limestone, but in proportions..."

This time, I pricked up my ears; a new horizon had been abruptly revealed to my troubled eyes: a horizon of which Livry took charge of fixing the lines.

"Of course," he said, in a jovial tone, "I'm preaching to a convert! You've even been able to observe that Jobert has been able to volatilize calcareous stone instantaneously, in the form of the millstone doorposts of my laboratory. His recent theft permits him to do things on a larger scale, and undoubtedly, the terrible consequences of his manipulations have escaped him, for they will have encountered the mirage after which Jobert is running inconsiderately—the so-called regeneration of the soil."

Roger laughed. "A fine regeneration of the soil!"

For myself, I shivered.

For a moment, Roger remained thoughtful; then, in a more serious tone, he said: "Which doesn't alter the fact that

---

[38] This myth originated in the work of the Roman historian Livy; Polybius makes no mention of the preposterous alleged feat.

the individual is now becoming very dangerous. I too would be able to ravage the earth, sow ruin, death and destruction here and there, but that would be local destruction, an absurd crime with no tomorrow.

"The end of the world, yes—that's a grandiose idea, as logical and ordered as a mathematical verity. It's an almost divine endeavor, in comparison with which a partial hecatomb appears to me to be abominable."

Full of his subject, Roger paced back and forth in the room, illuminated like a prophet. It was the first time that he had frightened me—really frightened, beyond any nervous sensation or imaginative shock. For the first time, my conviction was shaken.

Why? Because I had seriously envisaged the possible role that he attributed to Jobert. I had seen with my own eyes the solvent effects produced by the Omega acid. It was not unreasonable to calculate effects of the same sort multiplied to an extreme. At an infinitesimal dose, the radium had already determined extraordinarily energetic phenomena. What power could be attributed to the ten grams in Jobert's possession, to the eighty grams that Livry intended to employ one day? How could the limit be measured of the formidable reactions that might follow, since no laboratory had ever experimented with such quantities?

Thus, I almost admitted the thing that would have seemed insane a few months earlier: a man was able to provoke a cataclysm, an earthquake.

In that case…why deny another man the power to bring about an even greater upheaval, by imagining the destructive effect of the acid multiplied a hundredfold, multiplied almost infinitely?

Except that a doubt came to my rescue, to defend me against the definitive invasion of that frightful idea.

At its base, that reasoning depended on an entirely gratuitous hypothesis on Roger's part: the presence of the murder in Bouffarik on the day of the seismic shock, and the proven correlation between the phenomenon and manipulations of the Omega acid by his former assistant.

That doubt, to which my tottering reason clung, was to be cut away a week later.

There are dates that are landmarks in life. Thus, I will never forget that eighth of October 19 . It was my first lecture since the resumption of classes. In fact, I had been able to make Roger, who wanted to keep me with him, understand that it was necessary for me to resume my position at Louis-le-Grand, at least until the appointment of a substitute: a rule of decency that he could not make me violate, while awaiting the solicitation of a leave of absence that would permit me to devote myself to him.

Deep down, I experienced a secret joy at that resumption of contact with the academic world; for a few hours a week I would live in a saner and less troubling atmosphere than the one in which I had been plunged for two months.

Not that I begrudged the unfortunate Roger the worries, the difficulties and the tribulations. More than ever, I was prepared to sacrifice everything—my repose, my wellbeing, my career—in the attempt to free him from his terrible obsessions. There are duties of friendship that cannot be set aside.

By the very reason of my intentions, however, it seemed good to me to steep myself once again in my natural milieu. In teaching philosophy to others, it seemed to me that I ought to be the first to profit from my instruction.

Thus, I had devoted by initial lesson to Descartes, that great destroyer of preconceived ideas, that declared enemy of the imagination. Under the cover of admirable philosophy doubled with scholarly genius, I vituperated against the illusion of our senses, the tyranny of illusions, the false steps of reasoning.

In truth, I was speaking for myself.

With the fire of enthusiasm that sincerity gives, I uplifted my audience, I obtained a veritable success.

I left the class with my temples still throbbing, exhausted by physical effort but with a joyful heart, and a serene soul.

It appeared to me that I had reconquered my tranquility and my aplomb.

Joyful and resolute, I was leaving the lycée when someone tapped me on the shoulder.

"I've arrived in time to collect you," pronounced Roger's voice.

"You? Nothing serious, I hope?"

I had, in fact, left Roger in his laboratory, where he was ardently manufacturing further quantities of his acid, and I knew that the chemist was not easily distracted from his work.

He reassured me with a gesture. "Oh, simply a summons I received this morning from the head of the Sûreté."

"Ah! The Jobert affair again?"

"You've guessed correctly. According to the succinct note I've been sent, the blackguard has been found."

"You see!" I exclaimed, carried away. "Jobert had nothing to do with the earthquake, then, and everything you supposed the other day..."

With a gesture of his hand, Roger invited me to formulate my judgment with more reserve. "Gently—we'll see what they have to say to us at the Sûreté first. Thinking that the matter might interest you, I made a detour to pick you up."

He drew me toward his automobile.

Privately, I was counting in advance on a denouement that would complete the annihilation of the troubling suppositions of the preceding days. Already, I was muttering to myself inaudibly: "That will teach you not to get carried away in your hypotheses!"

We arrived at the Prefecture of Police. We were immediately received by Monsieur Régnaud, one of the deputy heads of the Sûreté.

"Well, Monsieur Livry," the functionary said, "you were right in opposing those who wanted to see Jobert as a thief attracted by the enormous intrinsic value of the radium. He has furnished us himself with proof that he's a simple madman...a dangerous madman, to be sure."

"He's been arrested?" asked the chemist, impatiently.

"No, but he undoubtedly will be, in a matter of days. He's taken the trouble to notify us of his presence in Messina."

"How?"

"An imprudence. He's written to his aged mother in Bouffarik. The letter was intercepted. The missive is sufficient for us to be convinced of his mental state, and also..." The deputy head of the Sûreté grumbled, in a lower voice: "And also the pitiful fashion in which the surveillance of the widow Jobert was exercised. Oh, the provincial police! In brief, by his own confession, our fugitive really did remain hidden in his home town until the day after the catastrophe. In the midst of the panic, without being recognized, he even helped with the rescue of his mother, buried under the rubble of her house. He made himself scarce as soon as he saw the old woman recover her senses. He went to Bougie, embarked on an Italian fishing-smack and reached Sicily. All of that, narrated in his letter, is instructive, but in sum, quite banal. Where the banality ceases is when he explains the cataclysm. In my profession, I've often had occasion to examine cases of delusions of grandeur, but rarely like this one."

And Monsieur Régnaud, his hands on his hips, slowly shook his head as he said what he judged to be an enormity: "Can you imagine that Jobert accuses himself of having provoked the earthquake by means of his imprudent experiments? He asks his old mother, who almost fell victim to it, for forgiveness!"

Roger said nothing; he merely looked at me with an indefinable expression.

As for me, I had become livid.

"After that," the functionary concluded, "the wretch seems to require alienists rather than the court of assizes. In the meantime, we've taken steps to alert the Italian police and request his extradition. In a few days, I hope, we'll have him in Paris."

As if in a fog, I saw my companion get up and take his leave of the deputy chief.

I stiffened myself in order to imitate him, and stood up.

In the broad administrative corridor, cold and bare, I was prey to a veritable vertigo. I had to lean on Livry's arm in order not to fall.

"Why, what's the matter?" said my friend, solicitously. "Are you feeling…faint?"

What was the matter!

For the first time since the beginning of the affair, the wall of incredulity that had protected me against definitive terror had been split; through that fissure, the last resistance attempted by my reason in revolt was about to drain away.

The veil of doubt had decidedly torn, allowing *the fact* to appear.

Mad, Roger undoubtedly was, in everything connected with his amour for Monsieur Thiérard-Leroy's daughter, but as soon as he was lodged in his scientific domain, madness gave way to an admirable clarity of sight—as witness the prodigious result of the advice given, off the cuff, to Guy Mayrol.

Amid the disorder of my thoughts in distress, that was the first proof that presented itself. A few days before, departing from the cliff of Boulogne, the aviator had made child's play of traversing the Channel and landing in a suburb of London. Then, only the day before, the newspapers had been full of his new exploit: Mayrol had launched himself from the summit of the Ballon d'Alsace, and after reaching an altitude of more than fifteen hundred meters, and flying over the valleys of the Saône and the Rhône, a blast of the mistral had carried him beyond Avignon.

In the course of the interviews to which he was obliged to submit, the hero of the day reported that a great part of his success was due to a mysterious unknown man, who had appeared and disappeared like the good genie of a tale, leaving behind him only a phantom name: the Man of the Apocalypse. And the press continued to discuss, to comment on and enliven Mayrol's confidence, surrounded henceforth with the Hoffmannesque attraction of the fantastic.

But I knew the truth: the Man of the Apocalypse was Livry.

Then, to complete the foundations of my judgment, came those striking coincidences—more than coincidences, *realizations*—corresponding to events announced by the chemist: the increasing marked lowering of the temperature; the duly-explained sorceries that were narrowly attached to Jobert's actions.

After that, how was it possible to persist in a blind negation?

Now, Roger, the friend of my childhood, the companion of my joys and troubles, appeared to me as the superhuman genius of annihilation and Death!

The simple role that I had attributed to myself was finished. It was no longer a matter of watching over a madman with prudent and compassionate attention. I had to enter into a struggle with a Force whose immeasurable power I already suspected.

No matter! The situation was revealed in such a way that I was condemned to march over my heart, to strangle my nerves, to stifle my self-esteem. Everything was effaced before a new instinct, which I discovered in my inner depths in those minutes of fearful suggestion: the instinct of survival—but an instinct enlarged beyond the interests of my own individuality.

Does Nature act, unknown to us, at opportune moments, to defend her creation and her creatures?

When a poor head allows itself to be invaded by such thoughts, there is nothing astonishing, is there, in seeing the body that supports it collapse?

The keen air outside whipped my blood. I straightened up again. I breathed out dely.

"There—that's better!" said Roger, as he installed me in his automobile.

"Yes. It was so hot in the offices of the Sûreté..."

260

Roger smiled in a Machiavellian fashion. "They've turned up the heating—and but that's only the beginning!" And in a tone of triumphant satisfaction: "In the plain of Châlons, for two days, it's been cold enough to split stones."

IX. The Release

"Are you asleep, Paul?"

It was the morning of the fifteenth of October when Roger came into my bedroom on tiptoe to murmur those words in my ear. His voice was grave; it was not accentuated by the amicable familiarity with which he came to wake me up when he needed me before the time I normally got up.

"I'm not asleep," I said. "What's wrong?"

Before replying, Roger turned the commutator placed at the head of my bed. The electric bulb lit up.

Then I was able to look at my friend. He was very pale; his tremulous hands were holding an unfolded newspaper.

In a muted tone that revealed a profound emotion, he pronounced: "You know, my projects might be modified completely..." He waved his arm in a veritably solemn gesture. "The world might live!"

To that colossal affirmation, I opposed a banal interrogation: "Why?"

"Because Capitaine Berjac is dead!"

Dazed, I was voiceless.

Roger held out *Le Matin* to me, which was delivered to the villa every day at six o'clock. With his finger, he indicated an article headlined: *Icy Autumn*.

First there was a sequence of dispatches coming from the eastern region, all signaling the disastrous precocity of winter cold. At Epernay, the thermometer had reached seventeen degrees below zero. At Sillery, the docks of the Vesle canal had been icebound for two days. Then a subheading made me shiver: *First victim: an officer drowned while skating*.

My heart constricted, I read the item:

261

Reims, 14 October, 9 p.m.

A serious accident has just plunged our region into consternation...

I read on without reading, my eyes only retaining the conclusion:

Capitaine Berjac leaves a young wife, the daughter of Monsieur Thiérard-Leroy, director of the Observatoire de Paris.

We salute with respect the grief that has struck that honorable family, as well as the officers of the 306th artillery.

I remained petrified. And as I kept silent, Roger's timid, almost ashamed voice murmured nearby: "Now she's free."

"Oh, Roger!"

I could not repress that exclamation, vibrant with indignation. What! My friend had arrived at that barbaric unconsciousness! Was not the poor officer, in sum, the indirect victim of the chemist's enterprises? He had died of the cold that the other had created.

At that moment, Roger horrified me.

To efface that painful impression, it was necessary for me to remount the current of our long friendship. It was necessary, above all, for me to tell myself that my judgment was iniquitous and absurd. One does not incriminate a madman. One disarms him.

Instead of playing the professor of morality with regard to Roger, it is necessary for me to take advantage of the lamentable event in order to render myself master of that powerful—and yet so feeble—mind. Rather than exasperate it further with vain remonstrations, I ought to encourage the fantasy that might deliver it to me.

Madame Berjac is free, so the world might be saved! Roger says so himself; he has shown me the terrain on which I must maneuver.

It was necessary to encourage his hopes but it was necessary above all to rein them in. My first efforts, therefore, were aimed at preventing him from making any inconsiderate move.

Straight away, I set aside the lugubrious shadow of Capitaine Berjac; I kept it for myself. And, in order to explain the critical tone of me exclamation, I did not recoil from a lamentable recantation.

"You're frightening me, Roger. You seem to me to be about to compromise, by an unreflective impatience, the happiness to which you might aspire one day."

"The happiness!" he murmured. The magic of that single word had cast a gleam over his sorrowful physiognomy. "Oh, tell me what I ought to do!"

"Wait! Let time, the great surgeon of the soul's wounds, do its work. That way, you'll show the tact of a man of heart, and that will be the supreme skill."

He listened to me with an extreme attention. Then, in a calm and resolute tone, he said: "I trust you; I'll follow your fraternal advice. But tell me again that I can hope!"

"You have the right to do so."

Oh, how dearly it cost me to formulate that affirmation, which hid a lie.

And in order to take immediate advantage of the scientist's good dispositions, I pointed at the frost that was covering the panes of the bedroom window.

"You can divine where it's necessary to begin?"

He passed his hand over his eyes, and, as if struck by a sudden revelation: "That's true! At Mourmelon, the Omega acid is continuing to operate. We'll go out there today; it will only take me a quarter of an hour to suspend the effect."

"Suspend? Why not destroy it permanently?"

After a hesitation marked by a contraction of his features, he said, in a dull voice: "I want to reserve the future."

At that moment it would have been maladroit to press harder. I attempted nevertheless to obtain an indication that might be of extreme importance later.

"You have a means, then, of stopping the effects of your cold?"

"Yes, a very simple means that renders the acid inert, just as gunpowder loses its properties of deflagration when it's moistened, and recovers them again when it's dried out."

"Will you explain it to me?"

Roger considered me with an expression in which I clearly discerned suspicion. Then, grimly, he said: "No."

But a first, enormous result had been acquired.

At ten o'clock in the morning we—Roger, Étienne and I—set off on the road to the Camp de Châlons.

Within two hours, the limousine drew up outside the abandoned house.

Since our abrupt recall to Paris, Étienne had returned there alone once a week, to remove the graphic recordings from the various meteorological instruments left at fixed points.

Nothing in the dismal dwelling had changed.

The sparse grass of the courtyard had disappeared under a layer of frost. The cold was biting; the sky had the dark blue tint of the great winter cold.

How could anyone suspect the colossal work of destruction that was being contrived there, in that square courtyard? How could one suspect those glaucous tanks, mimicking the appearance of bowls innocently set to collect rainwater?

One last time, Roger consulted the thermometers; the he came back to me. A melancholy smile wandered over his lips, and there was a hint of regret in his tone.

"As a scientist, I regret the action I'm about to take. I'm stopping an experiment at the moment when it's yielding prodigious results, more conclusive than those indicated to me by the calculations."

He shook his head, considering the receptacles.

"Now, let me cure this poor earth, which seemed so well lost. Give me ten minutes. Go and wait for me in the car."

I made no objection to the maniac's desire. I went away.

Faithful to his promise, the chemist reappeared a quarter of an hour later. As I interrogated him with my gaze he said: "It's done. In a matter of days, you'll be able to see."

After having relocked the door, my friend took his place in the automobile. He settled into the back seat. His eyes vague, his features relaxed, he smiled at his dream.

Poor fellow, I divined the vision that had just succeeded furious nightmares. That languor did not abandon him even when the auto came to a rather abrupt halt a few minutes after our departure. Roger continued to dream, while I leaned out of the window curiously.

We were near Mourmelon railway station and our vehicle had run into the tail end of a funeral cortege: officers and armed artillerymen surrounded the hearse, while other wore crowns with tricolor ribbons. I guessed the rest.

It was poor Capitaine Berjac that they were accompanying on his final voyage.

My heart constricted, I drew my head back in very rapidly, as if were guiltily ashamed to show myself.

Shivering, I looked at Roger.

He was still smiling at the angels.

X. The False Quietude

In the days that followed our journey to Mourmelon, Roger behaved with an admirable sagacity.

A radical transformation seemed to have taken place in him. No more of those monologues full of muffled and terrifying threats, no more of those fits of fury followed by phases of depression. He worked reasonably, applying himself to being and living, like everyone else.

Was it the force of his renascent passion that gave him such an empire over himself? Was it the abrupt change in the atmospheric conditions that was having a good influence on his temperament?

For, extraordinarily—and for me, conclusively, the dry cold had given way to a misty humidity. Everywhere, the thaw was announced: mild, rainy weather—"rotten weather," to employ the expressive term of the common people—set in. Then the sun began to shine, bringing with its radiance an Indian summer that contrasted in an exquisite fashion with the frosts of the previous days.

That remarkable relaxation, in accordance with the anticipations of the chemist, appeared to be the direct consequence of the visit to the house at the camp.

For me, it was a supplementary proof, and how suggestive!

So, in an undeniable fashion, Roger seemed to be on the road to recovery.

I congratulated myself and I trembled at the same time, because the divine amorous deception to which my friend was lending himself, and of which I had become the fearful accomplice, might well be doomed to end lamentably.

And when the moment of disillusionment came...

In the near future, I glimpsed the brutal end of the idyll on which Roger was building the future city of his happiness. Of what would he not be capable on observing for a second time the bankruptcy of his adorable and naïve confidence?

Fortunately, Roger opened up to me at the same time the hope of stopping future threats—and is such a prosaic fashion!

"Paul," he said to me, abruptly, "I want you to do something for me."

"Isn't that what I'm here for?"

"Oh, don't engage yourself so lightly. I know in advance that you have no liking for the task I want to confide to you. You're not a businessman."

Before knowing what he was getting at, I smiled, nodding my head.

"Bah!" Roger went on. "Out of friendship for me, you'll do it. You're to substitute for me in all matters concerned with the administration of my fortune. You're to deal with my suppliers, to do what's necessary to make the payments...because I have obligations to them. In any case, you'll only have to follow the indications of Sencier, my notary; I have every confidence in him. As for you, I don't need to tell you that I give you *carte blanche*. You'll act as I would."

And, putting his poor fiery head in his hands, he confessed: "I need to pull myself together, you see—a time of repose. For some time, I've been caressing a mad desire to lock the door of my laboratory; I no longer want to think about anything but my amour. So I'm asking you to be my steward, Can I count on you?"

"Can you doubt it for a moment, my friend?"

As I spoke those words I had a slight shudder, for already, the depths of my mind were pierced by the vague sensation that Roger had delivered himself to me.

He pushed me into the automobile himself, and gave the order to Julien to take me to his notary.

My head seething, I arrived at the offices of Maître Sencier, in the Faubourg Saint-Honoré. I received the most amiable welcome, which immediately put me at my ease.

My designation as substitute brought an unanticipated solution.

"I'll draw up a power of attorney for you," said the notary. "Then, furnished with the most extensive powers in all things, you can substitute yourself for the unfortunate scientist. In all conscience, we have the right to save his fortune. The purchases of radium…well, they'll fall of their own accord; we're due to pay on delivery of the merchandise; we won't pay, and the radium won't be delivered."

Thus spoke Maître Sencier.

That same evening, Roger signed a duly drawn-up power of attorney. Henceforth, I had free disposal of his wealth; I had him, bound hand and foot. He would no longer have a particle of radium, except for the few grams he already possessed.

This time, an immense relief invaded me entirely. Whatever might happen subsequently, Roger was no longer in a position to pursue his dream of ending the world.

And, sure of the future—oh, what an imbecile presumption as mine!—I let myself lapse into the pitiful, paltry and surely ignoble, but very human, observation that the world would not be saved, as I had believed momentarily, by the adorable tenderness of Amour, but thanks to the implacable and vile force of Money!

Roger kept his promise. He deserted his laboratory.

And that epoch marked, for him, more than a repose; it brought about a radical modification of all his anterior habits.

It was thus that Roger spent his days running around the tailors, shirt-makers and boot-makers most renowned in elegant society. One morning, he arrived with his beard trimmed and pointed, his hair parted from forehead to nape by a savant stripe. Another time, I surprised him abandoning himself to the care of a manicurist.

A manicurist in Roger's house! That small fact alone said a great deal to anyone who knew that antisocial seeker.

Then he turned his application toward various methods of physical culture. His dressing-room was garnished with the most complicated items of apparatus: exercisers, adjustable dumb-bells, electric masseurs. Within two weeks, my friend was unrecognizable. Instead of the tall, gangling, more-or-less hirsute fellow, almost neglectful in his attire, I had before me a veritable gentleman in a well-cut, dark-colored suit in perfect taste.

It had certainly required an extraordinary effort of will on Roger's part suddenly to become a man of the world in the accepted sense of the term.

That transformation accompanied a new and entirely unexpected way of life.

Roger dragged me to fashionable cabarets, passed in review the season's new plays, even strayed into dance-halls.

Poor Roger! That new twist to his ideas ought to have delighted me, but it caused me an unbearable malaise. Without any great effort, I guessed why he was so determined to strip away his old self. Oh, he didn't confide in me—what tact, what scrupulousness he put into never mentioning his amour!

However, a few days before the end of the year, his almost grim reserve gave way to an impulsive desire, prompted by an unexpected occurrence.

Since dinner, Roger had seemed to me to be nervous, very distant from the conversation. Once or twice, he began to say something, and then stopped. Then, as we were going to our rooms, he abruptly retained me by the arm.

"Listen to me, Paul. I'm haunted by a project. In advance, I beg you not to turn me away from it. You've been able to observe with what discretion I've conducted myself with regard to Hélène Thiérard-Leroy." He had returned her maiden name to his beloved! "During her mourning, I've never sought to see her, to place myself in her path. And yet, I haven't been able to constrain myself to remaining without news of the person to whom I've dedicated me life. I'm made use of Étienne to keep me informed, in order to maintain a link with her, however tenuous."

I made a gesture.

"Oh, don't worry, it's not a matter of any indiscreet investigation, any untimely step. The child has limited himself observing from a distance. By means of servants' gossip, he's kept up to date with her health and a thousand petty details of her life: trivia for others, very precious things for me.

"Thus, I've learned about a voyage planed by Monsieur Thiérard-Leroy. With the aim of making her forget more surely the great emotions that have assailed her, the worthy man is taking his daughter to Biskra until the end of winter. He's using the pretext of a slight illness to take her to that marvelous oasis. It's a good opportunity!"

That blind optimism disturbed me. The name of Biskra, associated with illness, evoked before my vision the extreme winter station to which those consumptives who can no longer even support the Mediterranean climate are sent as a last resort. And the slender, transparent silhouette of poor little Madame Berjac traversed my memory...

I carefully refrained from communicating such somber apprehensions to my friend.

"So, I thought that we could also go to Biskra...oh, remaining in the shadows, I swear to you. I'm sure of myself. I won't risk my happiness by making an untimely move. But to be close to her, to breathe the same air, to love her without her suspecting it—what harm do you see in that?"

"None," I murmured. Oh, I didn't reveal my sentiment. What would have been the point? I could see that Roger was only consulting me for form's sake. Nothing in the world could have modified his resolution.

He seemed delighted by my acquiescence.

"We have no more to do than pack our trunks," he concluded. "Thiérard-Leroy is leaving on Saturday. I'll give him a start of one steamer; we'll take the next one. You can see that I'm being reasonable. Is that all right?"

The question was settled.

The next day, Roger was occupied with the preparations for the departure. I had to accompany him to the suppliers and complete a wardrobe for myself as becoming as his own.

"You understand," he had said to me. "You need two white flannel suits, and a dinner-jacket—that's indispensable for dinner at the hotel."

"Thumbs up for the dinner jacket."

Fundamentally, I was beginning to lend myself to his childishness.

After having seen everything in black, Roger now perceived everything rose-tinted—but through what a prism of illusions! How was it all going to end?

A new whim of Roger's reawakened my alarm momentarily. Among the numerous items of luggage, I distinguished the two famous cases that had served to transmit the Omega acid and the radium salts to the Camp de Châlons.

"What!" I exclaimed. "You're taking that dangerous paraphernalia to Biskra!"

He looked at me, smiling. "La la! You're not going to get excited about a few decigrams of radium and the bottle of acid that I have to hand? Out there, on the burning threshold of the desert, I can doubtless determine certain details that will be useful later."

"You intend to work, then?"

"No. Is it necessary to repeat to you that I've too many things in my head and I my heart to abandon myself to any serious work. I don't call work the two or three meteorological observations that I'll have the leisure to make in excellent conditions."

Truly, without ill grace, I no longer had the right to suspect my friend's intentions. Wasn't the presence of the young window the best guarantee henceforth against a possible reawakening of the chemist's frightful designs?

A few remarks exchanged with Étienne enabled me to glimpse how precarious that guarantee was.

It was the day of the departure of Monsieur Thiérard-Leroy and his daughter. Roger had insisted on dispatching his young factotum as a scout. Under the pretext of preparing for our installation in Biskra, Tourte was going to accompany the voyagers, in the shadows.

Needless to say, the most important part of his mission consisted of sending dispatches bearing news at the principal stages of the journey.

Faithful to his discretion, Roger did not want to appear. He charged me with embarking the boy at the Gare de Lyon.

While the car was going through Paris, I was struck by the child's sad expression.

"You're not looking forward to making a magnificent voyage?" I asked.

He shook his head. "No, Monsieur Paul. And now I can tell you why..."

He recounted the story of his petty intrigue, which I knew already by virtue of Roger's confidence.

"I'm afraid," he added, "because I think that Madame Berjac is very ill. A bad influenza."

Ah! My presentiments!

Four days later, Livry and I departed in our turn. Roger had the appearance and the manner of a happy man. The telegrams sent by Tourte said that the Thiérard-Leroys had arrived safely after an excellent crossing.

With a fine confidence, Roger, the implacable and terrible scientist, the Man of the Apocalypse, set forth on the road to happiness.

Personally, I had a heart bruised by an indefinable sadness. I was still assailed by the most somber presentiments.

Those presentiments crystallized in Marseilles, in the most frightful and unexpected form.

While traversing the great city to go to the boarding jetty of the transatlantic liners, we had the impression of a city in turmoil. The crowd was agitated by the frisson of anguish characteristic of great misfortunes. On the streets people were snatching the newspapers. In the tumult of overlapping cries, over the racket of the autobus rolling over the cobblestones, we could not discern the words being howled by the newsvendors.

"What's happened, then?" Roger asked, when we arrived at the port.

"What! Monsieur doesn't know?" said the loquacious southerner to whom my friend had addressed himself. "Alas, the news arrives more rapidly in Marseilles than in Paris, especially when it comes from Messina."

"Messina!" I exclaimed, seized by an emotion and a reminiscence.

"Terrible, Monsieur, terrible! Worse than in Japan... There's been an earthquake. There's no more left of Messina than a handful..."

A hasty reading of the first dispatches convinced us of the extent of the terrible disaster. And among the confusion of news transcribed as telegrams arrived and precipitate special editions were published, Roger indicated to me with a thrust of his fingernail a small item found in the *Petit Provençal*:

A bizarre prophecy

A few days before the catastrophe, the Crown Prosecutor received a strange letter sent by a certain Jobert, a French subject. Wanted for a crime committed in Paris, the individual

had been arrested by the Sicilian police, and had then suc-
ceeded in escaping from the municipal prison.

In his letter to the magistrate, this Jobert, who is be-
lieved to be an anarchist madman, complained of various de-
nials of justice committed in his regard, demanded the imme-
diate restitution of papers and notes seized from him, and the
cessation of the pursuits instituted.

If these conditions were not accepted and fulfilled, he
threatened to destroy Messina from top to bottom before the
end of the week.

"He's kept his word!" pronounced the chemist, with a troubling gravity.

"What! You judge the wretch capable of having un-leashed such a catastrophe!" I exclaimed, fearfully.

"He had the means to do it, given the subsoil of the north-eastern tip of Sicily, disrupted by a series of anterior catastrophes: volcanic eruptions, earthquakes…a chaos of rocks in unstable equilibrium. I only hope that this time, Jobert has exhausted his supply of acid, or that he's perished." Then, in a tine of determination: "No matter! I'll clarify the matter. I want to know whether the man is dead or alive!"

Seeing me distressed, shivering with horror, he made an effort to chase away an importunate thought, perhaps of re-morse. In a casual, almost scolding tone, he added: "What do you expect, my friend? It's a great misfortune, but any pro-gress is costly, As soon as I'm a billionaire, I'll help to recon-struct Messina. But in the midst of all this, let's not miss our boat!"

XI. The Death's-Head

We are in Biskra.

About the first part of our voyage I shall say nothing. It only left me with vague and painful impressions. The terrible events in Messina had plunged me into a dire state of mind. Pitiless sea-sickness accentuated those evil dispositions by

273

keeping me bed-ridden in my cabin from the emergence from Marseilles to the landing in Philippeville.

Then there was a frightful day of jolts on the railway across a sullen landscape beneath a soot-black sky. That gray weather, which lent the high Algerian plateaux the aspect of the black plains of Artois, minus the towns, was worth the magic of a marvelous contrast when the train crossed the threshold of El Kantara.

Through the breach pierced in the somber rocks the golden vision of the sun-bathed desert appeared to our dazzled eyes, revealing palm trees and the gardens of the celestial paradise.

An hour later, our enchantment came to an end. Bikra offered itself to us, in its whiteness and its verdure.

Étienne was waiting for us at the station.

Roger's first words were to enquire about the Thiérard-Leroys. With a joyful animation, the child hastened to satisfy his master's anxious curiosity. The astronomer and his daughter were installed at the Villa el Blod—the White Villa—rented for the season; the young woman did not appear to have suffered from the fatigues of the journey. She spend long hours in her garden; she went out in her carriage.

"She's better, much better!" little Étienne whispered in my ear.

Good! The reassuring news was only designed to soothe Roger's confidence, about which I had begun to be slightly anxious. Things were arranging themselves in a better fashion than I had dared to anticipate. For the moment, therefore, there was nothing to do but abandon myself to the fortunate influence that emanated from the marvelous land, to take advantage in mid-December of the delightful temperature of a fine month of June in France.

We allowed Étienne to guide us to the Imperial Hotel.

It was an immense caravanserai responding to the uniform model that luxury hotels offer to well-off travelers everywhere.

With his habitual intelligence, our little courier had been able to choose a most agreeable apartment for us. Our bed-rooms overlooked the palm trees of the oasis, with an extended view over the immensity of the desert. Another room destined to serve as a drawing room and study overlooked a gallery with arcades, beyond which was a Moorish courtyard paved with mosaics, ornamented with spurting fountains and orange-trees in tubs. It formed a delightful décor.

It is nearly seven o'clock. We dress for dinner; we are both inaugurating our dinner-jackets. I cannot help smiling on seeing us decked out as snobs when the immense mirror on one of the monumental lands reflects our image.

We penetrate into the vast dining-room: white table-cloths, flowers and green plants everywhere; crystal scintillating under the caress of the light. Waiters with felted footsteps circulate silently, like black phantoms, crossing one another's paths, avoiding one another, hastening in a perpetual farandole. In a corner, "lautars," or imitations thereof, their rounded torsos stuffed into embroidered jackets are picking out more-or-less Rumanian rhapsodies.

The diners are various: a few young women in bright pretty dresses, a few angular old women; the men are unobtrusive, dissolved in the same uniform blackness. How much I prefer the frame and public of our Parisian restaurants to that conventional luxury, those sad, extinct people with faces like those in a wax museum.

But what's the point in quibbling? All in all, the milieu isn't unpleasant. Everything invites me to live and let live, to chase away preoccupations and bad memories. I have only to take my inspiration from Roger, who seems to be enjoying his new existence with the amused astonishment and happy insouciance of a child.

Already he has chosen a table near a glazed bay window.

"That's Monsieur Barnett's table," remarks a maître-d'hôtel, in a tone that says a great deal about the importance he accords to that individual. Then, with an obsequious smile:

275

"Here…the next table is free; the Messieurs will be very comfortable here.

We sit down. Soon, the Barnett in question, our neighbor, arrives. His advent suspends conversations and the sound of forks. There is good reason; never has such a strange spectacle been offered to my eyes.

Barnett certainly "makes an entrance," as the phrase is understood in the circus.

First, him: a skeleton in a black suit. Impossible to trace a more exact portrait of his ensemble. Oh, that frightful head with the bald cranium and the glabrous face, the ivory-tinted skin stuck to the bones; those frightfully hollow orbits, in which glaucous eye glimmer, immobile and expressionless; and those bloodless lips, drawn back to expose a double row of excessively white teeth. Then, to complete the hideous effect, a thin nose with hints of violet, which, seen from a certain angle, designs a hole in the wan face.

A death's-head!

Slightly behind that macabre individual comes a little man with an olive complexion and a face like a ferret, certainly a half-breed. Finally, closing the march, a negro of colossal stature with a horrible bestial visage, covered in scars.

The negro is wearing a somber livery overladen with silver ornaments, the outfit of a undertaker in full regalia. And, a contrast between the hideous and the pretty, his huge black paws are respectfully holding a rose-wood tray surmounted by a perch, on which are set two ravishing hummingbirds, two living jewels.

Open-mouthed, we watched that incoherent stage-setting. The continuation of the performance was to reserve further astonishments.

Barnett sat down in front of the only place-setting. Opposite him, the negro placed the perch, and then remained frozen a pace behind it, in the attitude of a vast, well-trained valet.

The half-breed took up a position to the right of the birds; from a leather case he took out a kind of little metal

trough, perhaps silver-plated. He placed that bird-table accessory in front of the little creatures, and the hummingbirds set
about pecking the minuscule seeds contained in the trough.
Sometime, the attentive half-breed helped them by lifting a
delicate ivory spatula to their beaks. With an imperturbable
gravity, Barnet took his meal in parallel with that of the birds,
while addressing gracious and encouraging words to them.

After a long moment of stupor, Roger and I ended up
smiling at one another with our eyes. Then hypotheses flowed
between us in whispers:

"A conjurer."

"A necromancer."

"A lion-tamer who's going to give a performance at the
hotel,"

"A hypnotist."

We were mistaken. Barnett was none of those. After dinner, Étienne, who had been invited by Livry to take coffee in
the hall in our company, revealed the quality of the extraordinary individual.

Barnett was simply a rich American, and an utter eccentric. After having been a master of the strange and redoubtable
sect of the Ku Klux Klan, he belonged, it appeared to one of
the "suicide clubs" that exist in the United States. At dates
fixed by solemn engagements the members of those associa-
tions have to pass over to the afterlife by the most expedient
means.

Oh, Franklin, Grant and Washington, what would you
have said if someone had told you that some of your descend-
ants would sink into such morbid extravagances?

Barnett still had a year to go before the supreme date. He
was employing that period of grace traveling in the company
of the only two beings for which he experienced a human sentiment, his birds.

He possessed about two hundred birds belonging to the
rarest and most magnificent species in the New World. That
winged population occupied three-quarters of the ten-room
apartment retained for the season at the Imperial Hotel. With

the aid of trellis, the rooms had been transformed into aviaries. Three people were attached to that little society: an avian veterinarian—the half-breed we had seen during diner—and two negroes. Every day, at the whim of his fantasy, Barnett "invited" some of his pretty boarders to dinner. That evening, it had been the turn of the hummingbirds.

"What a crackpot!" I exclaimed, shrugging my shoulders

"Bah!" said Roger, with a serene indulgence. "Everyone's free. At least that one's not harming anyone."

And by a natural association of ideas, he returned to the other madman, the criminal and terrible madman. "Oh, I was thinking about Jobert. I think I've found a surer means than police searches of laying a hand on him." He took a piece of paper out of his pocket. "Look, read this advertisement that I intend to place in the most widespread newspapers. Tell me what you think."

I scanned the paper, on which was inscribed:

Monsieur Jobert may address himself in all confidence to Roger Livry. In the interests of science, Monsieur Livry will forget the past and invite his ex-assistant to reach an understanding with him.

"You're making a pact with that murderer, then?" I exclaimed.

Roger smiled. "There you go with your fine words. Above all, I want to be practical, and render Jobert harmless, by taking away his teeth.

"How?"

"By making him a proposition: either I'll buy the acid and the radium he stole at a price fixed by him, if he has any left, or I'll offer to let him work with me."

"With you? Père Philippe's murderer!"

"First of all, Philippe is out of danger; when he comes out of hospital in a few days' time I'll ensure him an income."

"But Jobert's a dangerous madman!"

"In that case, isn't it preferable to have him close at hand? You see, I intend to settle that matter before Mademoiselle Thiérard-Leroy becomes my wife. My responsibility is engaged, after all!"

Apart from that alarming confidence in the conclusion of his matrimonial projects, Roger seemed to the reasoning accurately; on analysis, his idea was perfectly defensible.

"Place your ad, then," I ended up saying. "We'll see whether Jobert reveals himself."

Glad to have convinced me, Roger took me out of the hotel,

"This magnificent might invites a stroll," he said. "Étienne can show us where the White Villa is." And, rapidly, to take away a suspicion that was already pricking me: "Oh, understand me clearly. If I want to know where she's living, it's to be sheltered from any involuntary indiscretion." In a lower voice, he pronounced, religiously: "For the moment, it's sufficient for me to breathe the air she breathes, the air charged with delightful scents."

Roger, the cold calculator, turned to lyricism: I couldn't help admiring the touching sincerity of the passion that guided him, and also the perfect delicacy with which it constrained his conduct.

So, that evening, we only saw from a distance the clump of palms and orange trees behind which the White Villa was sheltered. Roger resisted the desire, innocent I sum, to approach the wall. It was like a sacred terrain on to which he, being profane, could not stray without offending the divine creature who had captured his soul.

After a mute contemplation, during which his poor heart must have been singing a love song, my comrade took me back to the hotel.

In the hall, we encountered the macabre appearance of Barnett again.

The American is lying back in a rocking chair. In front of him there is a table laden with partly-emptied bottles. The ugly fellow isn't on a diet of orange-blossom water. He has fled the rigors of "dry" America, and is pouring himself draughts of whisky, which he mixes with champagne.

279

As we pass by, he makes an effort to salute us, and even to smile. Oh, that death's-head rictus! It's enough to give one nightmares.

Roger bows courteously; in the phase through which he is passing, he can draw upon immense indulgence for people and things. Personally, I only lift my fingers to the brim of my hat. I find him repulsive, that alcoholic with his counterfeit eccentricity. Our idlers ought to react once and for all against the blissful admiration of these Anglo-Saxon so-called eccentricities. On tracing them back to their source, one invariably finds a cerebral breakdown caused by the abuse of strong liquors.

And our friends from England and America enabled us to know, in the course of the Great War, real men veritably worthy of our admiration.

At any rate. I'd like to see that skeletal individual a hundred leagues from Biskra. Is that a presentiment? Barnett doesn't only cause me a disagreeable impression, he scares me!

XII. The Idyll Begins

What had to happen, has happened!

A fortnight ago, Roger entered into relations with the Thiérard-Leroys, and I needed that entire fortnight to determine the exact impression that the unexpected coup-de-théâtre made on me.

Unexpected? On reflection, I might, on the country, have calculated the probability of an encounter in a social circle as narrow as Biskra's as a virtual certainty.

It occurred, inevitably, at an intersection of two narrow streets in Old Biskra.

We had gone as far as that agglomeration of clay houses and walls of dry mud enclosing garden of palm trees a few kilometers from Biskra, to which tourists go in search of a sensation exactly similar, so the colonials say, to a village in the Sudan.

We were following one of the alleyways, where the high cob walls are prolonged by the branches of palm trees overhanging the enclosures. Thus are formed shady, profound and silent corridors full of mystery.

Suddenly, in a patch of light that was plastered on the ground by virtue of an intersection, a few paces away from us, I saw the astronomer Thiérard-Leroy and his daughter appear.

We had to back up against the wall to allow the young woman to pass, leaning on her father's arm. I experienced a horrible embarrassment. As for Roger, he was as pale as a corpse.

By virtue of an instinctive propriety, we saluted. With a mechanical gesture, the old man returned our salute; his eyes were vague and dolorous, doubtless fixed on distant preoccupations.

Madame Berjac looked directly at us, with a tranquil and gracious assurance. On discovering Roger, however, she experienced a shock. A pink tint appeared in her cheeks. She leaned more forcefully on her father's arm. Then, after having passed by, white and frail, she turned to look back.

And I saw that she was speaking animatedly to the old man.

Roger continued to lean back on the earthen wall, doubtless in order not to fall. Taking him gently by the arm, I led him away.

"My God, how I love her!" he murmured, in a breath. "How beautiful she is!"

Yes, more than beautiful, touching. She appeared to me as Dante's imagination invoked the shade of Beatrice walking amid the flowers of eternal gardens.

I drew my comrade outside the checkerboard of shadows, into the dazzling light of the sun.

We were getting ready to walk slowly in the direction of Biskra, when a slightly quavering voice behind us made itself heard.

"Pardon me, Messieurs..."

We turned round, and found ourselves face to face with Monsieur Thiérard-Leroy.

"You will excuse, Monsieur, a step that is doubtless inconsequent, when you know that it is dictated by an invalid who is very dear to me, my daughter."

"Cover yourself, Monsieur," said my friend, with profound deference, perceiving that the old man had remained bare-headed. "The sun..."

"The sun scarcely shines for me," replied the astronomer, with a sad smile.. He replaced his broad-brimmed panama. "I was saying that my daughter, Madame Berjac, doubtless under the suggestion of an invalid's illusion, thought she recognized in you a person who had saved her life last summer at the Camp de Châlons. She will continue to be eaten away by anxiety so long as she does not know for sure that her memories are playing her false." And in a more tremulous vice, the father added: "Now, Monsieur, my child's state of health does not permit any preoccupation. That is why you see me before you."

While Monsieur Thiérard-Leroy was pronouncing these words, I was watching Roger, anxiously.

He was biting his lip until it bled. Then he appeared to make an immense effort to regain full possession of himself. He succeeded.

"Monsieur," he said, in a tone of perfect modesty, "Madame your daughter is not mistaken. It was indeed me who, at the Camp de Châlons, last August, made an impulsive gesture, perfectly natural, with the aim of avoiding a serious accident."

The astronomer seized Livry's hands.

"You...you...! The unknown man about who she has spoken to me so often...! Monsieur, will you tell me your name?"

"Roger Livry."

The old man passed his hand over his forehead, searching for a memory; but the light was immediately extinguished. The name of Livry did not recall anything...

I preferred it that way!

He introduced himself in his turn. Then, in an imploring tine, he said: "Monsieur Livry, may I ask you for a favor?"

"Please do."

"I believe…I am sure…that my daughter would like to thank you herself. Excuse me, but I'm trying to do everything possible to help her get better. She has passed through such rude ordeals…that slight satisfaction... She's there, nearby, in our carriage..."

"Your desires and those of Madame your daughter are orders for me. In my turn, I would be very glad to salute her. But Madame Berjac should not exaggerate the gratitude she believes she owes me. At Châlons, I arrived before the others. All my good fortune was there!"

I marveled at my friend's good grace, the tact and the urbanity. At a deliberate pace, he followed Monsieur Thiérard-Leroy. Fifty meters away, behind a cactus hedge, the carriage was waiting.

How can I describe the expression of profound joy that illuminated the pale and charming visage of Madame Berjac when her "savior" was brought to her. In that joy, there was doubtless a little contentment at having divined as accurately, at having rediscovered "the unknown man" floating in her memory like an enigma, sometimes sweet and sometimes irritating. Perhaps there was something more!

The poor child was entering that terrible phase of tuberculosis in which life wants to blossom regardless, hastily, because it senses the threat at short range.

The word "frightful" came to mind. Alas, it was written in her waxen features, engraved in the overly blue veins of her diaphanous hands.

To confirm the lugubrious presages that I had formed since the departure from Paris, there was not even any need for the throaty cough that she tried to stifle in her lace handkerchief.

She was better, it had been said. A very relative better, which ordinarily accompanies the reaction consequent on a change of climate.

At the first glance, I acquired the cruel certainty that, barring a miracle, she was doomed.

As for Roger, during that first introduction, he remained the gallant man, full of reserve and attentiveness, that he had become.

How did he succeed in strangling the devouring passion that was setting him ablaze? Undoubtedly by developing an extraordinary will-power.

How, on the other hand, was he not struck by the mortal pallor spread over the face of the poor creature? Perhaps he had elevated his love into spheres so radiant that his dazzled eyes could no longer discern anything.

But I, who could see, was struck by a tragic horror when Roger said to me, pointing his finger at the cloud of dust raised by the carriage carrying Madame Berjac away: "Oh, my friend, I am so happy!"

I mentioned a miracle.

Is the miracle about to be produced?

For two weeks now, Roger has been an assiduous guest of the White Villa, and Madame Berjac seems visibly reborn. The presence of the "savior" has brought a little joy into that dwelling, which seemed consigned to desolation.

The charming woman chats, is agitated, is clutching on to life again, to hope.

And Roger has such a delicately exquisite fashion of paying court to her!

In his expressions, in his gaze, there is nothing of the misplaced levity of a flirtation. Nor is he playing the role of the tenebrous beau; he has been able to avoid the slightly ridiculous romanticism of the petrified lover. More simply, he has made himself a friend.

Beside the chaise-longue in the garden, where the still-plaintive convalescent is lying, he talks about frivolous or serious things; he is cheerful without extravagance, attentive without insistence. His stories are interesting, and stop in time not to become wearying.

With regard to Monsieur Thiérard-Leroy, Roger exhibits a deference, a modesty and an affability admirable in a scientist of his stripe—for everyone knows that two scientists in one another's presence quickly fall into controversy, which degenerates into dispute.

Here, nothing of the sort! To the slightly incredulous surprise of the director of the Observatoire, Roger offered to help him in his astronomical calculations—for the worthy man has not refrained from installing a telescope on the terrace of his villa in order to search the ever-pure sky at his leisure. And the astronomer's joy equaled his amazement when that unknown of the day before, not content with bringing hope to the soul of his dear invalid, set about resolving the most complicated problems as if they were child's play.

That amazement changed into profound admiration when, little by little, Roger revealed his theories to him, and his work on the Omega acid. A few laboratory experiments effected with the aid of the extraordinary acid ended up convincing the eminent astronomer of the immensity of the discovery.

The old man was so impressed that the following day, he opened up to me. "Oh, Monsieur, Monsieur, what a man your friend is! Once, he saved my daughter. Today, he seems to be restoring her to life as if he were pouring out a mysterious philter. Now, he's in a position—he has proved it to me—to revolutionize the face of the world."

He took his head in his hands. "You see, by virtue of living in the commerce of the stars, by virtue of scrutinizing Infinity, one becomes something of a visionary, and one acquire the soul of a mage. Now, your comrade causes me to marvel and frightens me by turns. I see in him an angel descended from Heaven, a supernatural being incarnating formidable forces unknown to our humanity. My God, may he protect my daughter!"

I calmed the old scientist's excitement by means of conventional words; I carefully refrained from identifying the terrible antecedents of the "angel." What was the point, now that "the Man of the Apocalypse" had become a man like others?

At the present moment, Roger was showing himself to be the absolute master of his will and his common sense.

I arrived at the conclusion that Roger had been subject last summer of a temporary crisis, of which no symptoms any longer subsisted. The cure might therefore be considered radical and definitive.

After that, nothing more remained for me to do but to associate myself wholeheartedly with my excellent friend's future projects, to sustain his joy and his confidence.

There is only one cloud on the horizon—decidedly, I shall never succeed in chasing them all away! Roger has made the acquaintance of the frightful Barnett.

The first contact was made by virtue of an absurd wager that we had unwittingly caused the American to lose. The manic has an obsession with betting on anything, every time he encounters people stupid enough to take up his incoherent challenges. And he finds them! When he doesn't find them, he falls back, it seems, on his domestic and his bird doctor.

In brief, the third evening after our arrival, when we were at table, the Death's-Head approached us, and without any preamble, said: "I owe a thousand dollars, Messieurs."

Astonished, we waited for him to explain himself.

"I owe a thousand dollars, exactly—you've made me lose them."

What was he saying? I suspected that he was drunk.

"I owe a thousand dollars," the fellow repeated, for the third time, "because I bet the maître-d'hôtel that no traveler would consent to remain my neighbor for more than five meals…and I'm paying for it. The sixth meal is commencing now, and here you are. I've lost the bet. Thank you, Messieurs."

And, bowing with all the grace of which he was capable, he went back to his place.

"He's amusing!" Roger declared.

"You think so? Personally, I have a horror of drunkards."

He smiled indulgently.

"How severe you are! Perhaps the poor fellow is drowning in alcohol the chagrin he has at being so ugly."

In the meantime, whether I liked it or not, it was necessary for me to suffer the salutations and smiles of the Death's-Head, and exchange polite banalities with him. But when Roger was already an assiduous guest at the White Villa, a circumstance placed him in a more intimate relation with the American.

One evening, we were admiring the two marvelous hummingbirds that were in service at our strange neighbor's table.

In response to a compliment by my friend, Barnett said: "They please you, and you please me. I give them to you."

"I'll accept with gratitude, if you'll permit me to dispose of them in favor of a lady friend."

"I give them to you," he American repeated.

The next day, the two ravishing little birds drew cries of joy from Madame Berjac.

"Render him this justice," Roger said to me, when we returned to the hotel. "That Barnett, whom you can't abide, isn't a nasty fellow. Personally, I'm thinking of appropriate means to cure him of his suicidal mania."

"Try to stop him drinking," I muttered. "Yesterday evening he was dead drunk again."

"Come on! You're becoming as intractable as a member of the Temperance League. Personally, I'd be sorry if any misfortune overtook that inoffensive eccentric."

No, in spite of all arguments, Barnett remained deeply antipathetic to me; I could not accustom myself to his terrible visage. Unlike Roger, I was not going through a phase of universal tenderness.

"After all, you're neither malevolent nor stubborn," Roger conceded. "I've convinced you with regard to Jobert; in the end, I'll destroy your prejudices with regard to Barnett…"

How sensitive I still was, deep down! The name of the former laboratory assistant, dropped into the conversation, renewed my malaise.

At that moment, in any case, the inventor of the Omega acid was not thinking very much about Jobert. He was no longer living for anything but his amour. Losing sight of the earth, he was allowing himself to be carried away under full sail toward the land of Tendre.[39]

XIII. The Day of Joy

Oh, the beautiful, unforgettable day!

That morning, as was his habit, Roger had been to obtain news of Madame Berjac, a little after the daily visit of the physician.

Before lunch, he came to find me in the garden of the Casino.

"I've seen the doctor!" he shouted from a distance, as soon as he saw me. "He's lifted all detentions; henceforth, Hélène is no longer an invalid, so far as he's concerned, and scarcely a convalescent. He's only going to come twice a week in future. He's authorized tennis, the piano, walks in the town—in brief, all the distractions of which the poor child was deprived.

"From today onwards, she's resuming social life, and to begin with, we're going to the Biskra races."

I could only rejoice with my friend; the physician's indications dissipated my last anxieties. We were both able, therefore, to put our hearts in harmony with the echoes of the festival that as commencing—for in that Saharan city, the races

---

[39] The reference is to the allegorical *Carte de Tendre* [Map of Tendre, or Tenderness] drawn up by several female hands in 17th century salon society, and printed in Madame de Scudéry's novel *Clélie* (1654-51). It represents the course of an amorous pilgrim's progress to the not-entirely-celestial abode of love.

have become a solemnity that agitates the whole of the sur-rounding desert.

Already, since the morning, the Arab chiefs have been performing caracoles in the city streets, followed by their goums. Trains are pouring out travelers coming from Constantine: white burnooses, and the uniforms of zouaves and rifle-men are cutting cheerfully through the European crowd.

In the midst of the hubbub we head for lunch. We're dying of hunger.

At table, Livry is as joyful as a schoolboy on vacation. To give Barnett pleasure, he bets him that the first woman who comes into the restaurant will be blonde.

Damn! It's a negress!

With a burst of laughter, he pays his two thousand francs, and for the champagne as well.

I allow myself to be carried away by that child-like joy. I feel slightly intoxicated, drunk on intimate contentment, mental quietude and also deliverance. Perhaps egotistically, I think that Roger has no more need of me; soon, I shall be able to go back to my small abode on the Quai des Grands-Augustins, my dear books, my lycée! I can resume my life!

I am allowing myself to float among those sweet thoughts while a landau carries us away toward the White Villa, where we are going to pick up Monsieur Thiérard-Leroy and his daughter.

Madame Berjac appears on the threshold. She is a joy to behold.

The lily has become a rose. Her complexion has lost the waxy hue that squeezed my heart. This time, the blood is flowing beneath the transparency of the skin. The face is fuller, the lips are red, the eyes, finally, have the expression of wellbeing and vivacity that appears to certify a complete return to health.

Our carriage stops at the entrance to the passage. Roger offers his hand to the young woman to help her down, and then his arm, to lead her to the grandstand. They form a handsome couple, at whom everyone looks.

I abandon myself to the intoxication of the spectacle. How far the two of them are from the Biskra racecourse!

The races are over; the multicolored crowd breaks up in an indescribable confusion.

We climb back into the carriage and take the road of return.

But they do not want that first festival of their hearts to end yet.

"Father, what if these Messieurs were to give us the pleasure of dining with us this evening?"

Madame Berjac had uttered that remark with a spontaneous innocence that testified adorably to certain premeditation.

Roger played the worldly comedy of conventional protests, the fear of disturbance, the dread of imposing fatigue on the hostess; in the end, we accepted.

The dinner was all that a charmingly intimate repast can be.

Afterwards, we went on to the veranda to take coffee.

On the insistent plea of her father, Madame Berjac consented to remain in the drawing room; in spite of the mildness of the temperature, the old man was fearful on her behalf of the humidity of the evening.

While we were smoking a cigarette, the young woman sat down at the piano. Quietly, her fingers picked out a delightfully melancholy melody; I recognized a Chopin nocturne.

Roger has stopped talking, and then smoking. Perhaps without being aware of it, he has risen to his feet. He walks toward the drawing room at a somnambulistic pace; the music attracts him, hypnotizes him. Through the partly-open bay window, I see him lean his elbow on the corner of the piano.

Then the melody falls silent. Monsieur Thiérard-Leroy and I remain sunk in our rattan armchairs, contemplating he magnificent night. The astronomer seems happy.

In a low voice, he tells me about the immense, definitive relief that the day that has just gone by has brought him. He confides in me the fears and anguish he has passed through since his friend Destule, the great specialist in maladies of the lungs, had let him know the gravity of his child's condition, advising the voyage to Biskra as a last resort. Then, by way of excuse for the idyll that has been knotted so rapidly—too rapidly for the proprieties of society—he tells me the story of his daughter's marriage to Lieutenant Berjac. It was one of those unions arranged long before by the families, between childhood friends; a last wish expressed by his dead wife, who had died three years ago. Perhaps imprudent, that fashion of uniting two destinies with links formed by the passivity of mind and custom!

In my turn, I sing Roger's praises: his heart of gold. I touch lightly on the magnificent situation of his fortune. Then, on those mutual confidences, we return to the drawing room.

Roger and Hélène are no longer talking; they are holding hands.

They have the superb surprise of pure souls. On our arrival, they do not make a movement to release their clasp; they dispense with blushing and lowering their eyes.

Their two faces are radiant with a calm happiness, forged of certainties

"Come on, Roger," I say, in a tone of affable authority. "It's getting late. It's necessary not to abuse Madame Berjac's amiability."

He smiles benevolently.

"You're right, my Mentor."

With his usual correctness, without insipidity or foolishness, he takes his leave of the young woman.

"Until tomorrow!"

"Until tomorrow…!"

They were never to see one another again on this earth!

XIV. The Day of Woe

Alas, a day of tears was to follow the day of joy.

The next day, Roger was up early. Full of a juvenile ardor, he occupied himself with realizing a desire expressed the

day before by Madame Berjac. We went to all the shops looking for equipment for a game of tennis.

It was in vain; the bazaars of Biskra possess many of the
knick-knacks typical of Oriental countries—copper vases,
carpets, embroidered gauzes and so on—which come directly
from Lyon, but to procure tennis equipment, it is necessary to
order it from Constantine, or even Algiers.

"That's annoying," said Roger. "Hélène would have been
glad to play this afternoon."

"Bah!" I said. "Game postponed for forty-eight hours."

"At least I want to inform her. No disappointment, however slight, ought to be caused to her by me."

"Perfect!" I joked. "You'll be a model husband."

For want of tennis, he ravaged the greenhouses of a hor-
ticulturalist to put together a marvelous bouquet of camellias.
Then, after having scribbled a few words on a card, shortly
before lunch, he charge Étienne with taking the flowers and
the note to the White Villa.

A quarter of an hour later, the boy came back. Roger had
the impatience common to all those in love.

"Well, did Madame Hélène give you a good welcome?
What did she say?"

"I didn't see her. She hasn't come down this morning.
She's slightly indisposed."

As was appropriate, I calmed the keen annoyance experienced by my friend. "A little emotion and fatigue. After a day
like yesterday, it's necessary to be expect that."

"Yes," Roger conceded. "It's a lesson."

Without allowing anything to show, I was anxious—and
Tourte took advantage of a moment when I was alone to whis-
per some brief news into my ear that turned my anxiety to
anguish.

"Oh, Monsieur Paul, it's not good at the Villa. At the end
of the night Madame Hélène had a coughing fit. The doctor no
longer leaves her..."

During lunch, Livery sought to mask the worry that was
devouring him. I perceived it in the volubility of his conversa-

tion. He passed from one subject to another without transition, carried away by a flood of words, absent-mindedly, for he made no response to the few questions I asked him. When we left the table we went to the White Villa.

Monsieur Thiérard-Leroy came down to receive us. His head was shaky, his eyes haggard and his voice tremulous.

"Oh, my friends, my friends... She's not well...fever...coughing blood. The doctor doesn't understand it. All day yesterday she seemed so normal! I've telegraphed Algiers and Chanel for a specialist...and also Tunis, where Professor Maggio, the King of Italy's physician, is passing through, it seems. I've begged them to come. Let's hope that it's an alarm without consequence...let's hope!"

The old man held out his arms, with a tormented physiognomy that belied his appeal to hope.

Devastated, we left the Villa.

Until five o'clock Roger wanders around the town, with me by his side. That aimless course procures us the moral interval after which we can, without indecent insistence, return for news.

It is not good. The poor child has fallen unconscious; she has only emerged to fall into an ardent fever.

Roger says nothing, but his mute dolor is grim. Forgetting dinner time, we resume our aimless wandering through the streets that open before our feet. It would be impossible for us to wait at the hotel; walking is a means of expending our nervous energy.

Roger has violent impulses, fits of tension that recall the bad days of the last year. Sometimes, large tears emerge from beneath his eyelids. By the exasperation of his self-regard, however, he masters the despair that is gripping him.

Several times, I hear him murmur: "No, it's impossible...it can't be...I don't want it."

Twice more in the evening, at nine o'clock and midnight, we return to the Villa. Each time, on crossing the threshold, an indescribable anguish grips me, so keenly do I sense disaster suspended overhead.

293

If it were to fall…!

It does not. Madame Berjac is torpid, the fever having retreated before injections of quinine. That prostration, following the crisis, does not tell me anything worthwhile.

Roger has refused to go back to the hotel. He wants to sit on the edge of a ditch close to the White Villa.

With his head in his hands, he stays there.

He dreams and he weeps; sometimes, too—and that is more frightful—he laughs.

My God! What am I going to do with the poor fellow if fatality takes its course?

At dawn, he consents to follow me, on the assurance that nothing has changed in the young woman's condition.

Nothing has changed, except that she is growing weaker hour by hour, according to what Étienne reports, having remained in the servants' parlor at the Villa. But I don't add that detail.

The two practitioners summoned by Monsieur Thiérard-Leroy arrive that afternoon by the four o'clock train. Immediately, we run to the Villa.

In the drawing room, where the presence of the woman he loves floats everywhere, Roger awaits the result of the ultimate consultation.

Arms folded and head bowed, he marches back and forth like a beast in a cage.

He approaches the piano where the first oath was exchanged, and recoils, as if stuck in the heart. On the music-stand he has recognized the Chopin nocturne that she played two nights before.

He goes back to the door, which stands ajar; he recoils again, seized in the throat by the odor, insipid and bitter at the same time, of ether, camphorated alcohol and creosote: the odor of houses in which someone is dying.

Finally, a noise of footfalls is heard on the stairway.

In silence, the physicians descend, followed by Monsieur Thiérard-Leroy, who accompanies them to the door.

From where we are we witness a terrible mime, far more expressive than words. The doctors shake the father's hand effusively; they keep their eyes lowered, inclining their science before that heart-rending dolor.

They have gone, and the astronomer is still there, collapsed on the bench. He is sobbing convulsively. It is frightful to contemplate the affliction of that old man, weeping like a child.

It is necessary for us to approach, however. I take Roger by the arm and push him toward the vestibule.

Our presence stems the excess of tears. Monsieur Thiérard-Leroy shakes his head, and in a distant voice, murmurs as if speaking aside: "My dear child…a few more hours and it will be all over…a rapidly progressing pneumonia…she's just entered her death-throes."

And addressing Roger, he raises his voice, enclosing in his cry a rage, a blasphemy and a reproach: "And to think that nothing…no one can save her…not even God…not even you!"

Then, exhausted by that effort of violence, in a tone suddenly softened: "She loved you. Before losing consciousness, she wanted your flowers by her bed, close at hand. Do you want to see her?"

"No!"

Roger's exclamation emerges hoarse and brutal, and also heart-rending.

And without saluting the desolate father, without a word of condolence, he flees outside.

I addressed to the astronomer a gesture and a gaze that implored forgiveness and pity in favor of the distraught, and, quitting the lugubrious villa in my turn, I threw myself on Livry's trail.

I caught up with him at the hotel.

He had locked himself in his room, next to mine. Through the door, I heard the whistle of his labored respiration, and also the scratching of his pen running over the paper. Feverishly, he was writing letters.

I had the fearful thought that he was drawing up his last will, that he had formed the project this time of ending his existence. One fact reassured me: he did not have any weapon to hand, no razor, nothing that could procure him an immediate means of attempting to kill himself.

Close to the partition, I therefore remained on watch, prostrate in an armchair.

It was seven o'clock when there was a light tapping at my door.

I went to open it.

Little Tourte appeared before me, his eyes full of tears.

For a long moment, the child stood there without articulating a word, the sobs stuck in his throat. Finally, he stammered: "She's dead!"

I put a finger over my lips, designating Roger's room with a glance.

"Yes, Monsieur Paul, but...it's still necessary that he knows. Then, what will he do?"

Ah! I put off until later the examination of that terrible question. In my head, too, the ideas were clouded.

I threw myself back into my armchair and wept recklessly, all the tears I had. I wept for the poor little flower, scythed down, I wept for Livry and I wept for myself...

My chagrin was interrupted by the abrupt opening of the communicating door.

My friend was before me. His icy calm and his livid pallor seemed terrible to me. I thought my eyes were deceiving me...but no...he had put on his dinner-jacket!

He looked at me with an indefinable expression in which I read anger and scorn, and then said, in a curt voice: "You're weeping? What are you waiting for to get dressed? The dinner bell has rung."

Was I hearing correctly? Roger intended to go to dinner, in the glare of lights and flowers, to the music of violins, when nearby, his beloved, rigid on a white bed...

In spite of all the self-control that I had promised myself to maintain, I could not master a revolt.

"You're talking about dinner downstairs with every-one…but you don't know…"

He interrupted me with a furious snigger.

"Yes, I know…I knew before you. She died at exactly five-forty. At that precise moment, my heart burst, my terrestrial life stopped there. Imbeciles will tell you that it's telepathy—the donkeys! They know nothing but words... But if I no longer have a heart, I still have a stomach. For a little while, at least, I shall be obliged to satisfy it... This evening, I'm hungry!"

Those clashing words caused me to shudder. They opened my eyes to the verity that I had been simple enough, culpable enough, to cover up. Roger had never ceased to be mad.

For a few months the dementia had simply been dormant, manifest in another form. It still existed, and today, by virtue of a frightful shock, it had awoken again, more violently, like a volcano returning to activity after a long repose.

I knew what Roger, insane, was capable of doing. Fortunately, I had taken my precautions. His reign of terror was over.

Now, the Man of the Apocalypse gave way to a poor lunatic, neither more nor less dangerous than all the others, and worthy of an immense pity.

Unfortunate Roger, my pity would not fail him! But for the moment, my head and my heart were reeling. I did not feel strong enough to follow him to the restaurant.

"Excuse me this evening," I said to him, in a plaintive tone. "I have an atrocious headache."

"As you wish!"

With that brief remark, Roger left.

For some time afterwards, I remained slumped in my armchair.

Then, suddenly, the sentiment of a duty to fulfill brought me to my feet. It seemed to me to be appropriate to take my condolences to the old man who was weeping out there all alone. Similarly, it was a charity to put myself at his disposition in the cruel circumstances. Roger had the excuse of his madness. I had none.

I went downstairs in order to go to the White Villa. As I went past the restaurant I cast a glance through the windows. It was to collect a painful impression. Roger was finishing dinner at Barnett's table. The two men were exchanging words with an animation full of enthusiasm.

I fled.

At the sad house I fund Monsieur Thiérard-Leroy in conference with a man clad in black, who bore on his face the stereotyped conventional grief of undertakers.

Once, through tears, I had seen those faces gliding around me when my poor mother died.

As soon as he is free the astronomer comes toward me, his hands extended.

"Thank you, thank you! It's good of you…and Monsieur Livry?"

I represent my comrade devastated by such grief that he is under the threat of going mad, in no condition to accompany me. A pious lie!

"Poor fellow!" murmurs the old man, his shoulders drooping, crushed by his immense unhappiness. An in a soft, almost tender voice, he murmurs: "Would you like to see her?"

There are cruelties that one cannot avoid.

I see her again, the poor and charming creature. A further metamorphosis; the rose has become a lily again, a lily so white, so pure, that I fall to my knees. In smiling expression fixed by death, she seems to be asleep. Between her knotted hands, Roger Livry's bouquet of camellias has been disposed. Oh, those smiling lips, which will be veiled by a shroud tomorrow!

I withdrew, my head empty of sensation, my body exhausted as if in the wake of an immense effort. Like the dim-witted oxen that, abandoned to themselves, return to their stable, I found myself back on the threshold of the Imperial Hotel.

As I penetrated into the hall, though, I was offended by an unexpected, terrible and odious spectacle: Roger, his face illuminated and his voice loud, swilling champagne in the company of Barnett.

He perceived me, ran toward me, and, shoving me by the shoulders with a violence and a force that only hysterics, in their crises, possess, he said: "You're just in time…we're having a good laugh!"

And the other, the frightful Barnett, takes up the theme in his transatlantic jargon: "All right! No more perfectly joyful fellow than Master Livry! He's just bet me a million of your money that within a week, there'll be frost in Biskra!"

"A million!" I exclaimed, almost in spite of myself.

"Yes!" And with the insolent pride of those Americans parvenus, he added: "Oh, I could get more."

Imagine! Barnett of Cleveland, "worth" fifty million dollars!

The horrible individual uttered a demonic snigger, with which Roger mingled his strident laughter.

Between the two men I remained inert, enervated, impotent.

Then, Roger questions me in his turn: "You're not drinking?" And, as if traversed by a glimmer of light: "Oh…I get it...the dead woman. Do as I do, damn it—I'm not weeping!" His voice became muted, menacing and prophetic: "We'll give her, I swear to you, a beautiful funeral!"

XV. The Wind of Madness

For a long time, a very long time, I stand on the platform of Biskra railway station, watching the train draw away that is carrying Hélène Berjac's coffin.

Without any pomp and without any fuss, the young victim of pitiless destiny departs northwards, in accordance with her father's wishes. He has refused to display the spectacle of a cortege of mourning to the indifferent curiosity of strangers. How well I understand that! Alone, with a retired general, a comrade and Polytechnique classmate of Monsieur Thiérard-Leroy, I accompanied the old man on the first stage of his calvary.

Livry has not come!

And, my soul drowned in bitterness and sadness, I continue to follow with my eyes the black caterpillar of carriages crawling toward the darker confines of the sunlit plain.

The train has disappeared into the mist blurring the limit of the northern horizon.

I go away. I feel terribly alone and abandoned. This country, which had conquered and charmed me, now appears grim and hostile. How and when will I get out of it? What resolution is stopping Roger?

When I return to the hotel I find him hard at work.

"I'm busy setting up my batteries to win Barnett's million," he murmurs in my ear, in a confidential tone.

No allusion at all to the frightful drama that has just traversed his life: a complete indifference with regard to the last sad chapter that has closed the idyll of the White Villa. I can't hold it against him, any more than his scandalous attitude on the evening of Madame Berjac's death. He is irresponsible, alas, and if a respondent exists in this horrible adventure, it's me

Without appearing to perceive my presence, Roger is pursuing on the terrace manipulations analogous to those I witnessed in the building in Mourmelon. Fortunately, he only has a small quantity of radium at his disposal, too weak, in my opinion, to produce an appreciable result.

The first experiments, however, have proved to me that I ought to be ready for any eventuality. If necessary, I shall remove and hide the photographic baths in which he is mixing his terrible compound.

But in themselves, those suspicions and anxieties dictate my duty. The time has come to make it absolutely impossible for Roger to harm himself and others. Depriving him of the usage of his capital is only a palliative; complete assurance is necessary, and that assurance can only be obtained by the frightful but necessary extremity of his internment.

Is it not, in any case, the sole fashion of giving him the care that he needs?

At that moment, I make the dolorous decision.

Alas, Roger's attitude in the days that follow oblige me to hurry things.

He has lost his discretion as a man of good society. Now, he comes down to dinner in a flannel jacket spotted with acid-stains. Every evening, the poor fellow stays up late in the company of Barnett. The overstimulation of alcohol adding to that of madness might produce a furious crisis at any moment.

I could sense it rumbling, that crisis, in the rare words that my comrade addressed to me, for he now showed himself, with regard to me, suspicious, acerbic and almost coarse. In vain I tried to get him to tell me to whom he had addressed the numerous letters and no less numerous dispatches that he sent every day. With equal futility, I tried to discover the purpose of his frequent excursions. Several times, he instructed me brutally not to accompany him outside, arguing his desire to be alone.

In brief, I felt that he was barely tolerating my presence.

Almost in the same fashion, he began to keep Étienne at a distance. For that reason, the boy could only procure me very obscure information—for example, for several days Roger had a bunch of keys, which were certainly not those of his apartment at the hotel or his luggage. Also, in the course of his mysterious excursions, Roger often met an Arab in rags, who looked like a beggar, with whom he had long conversations.

"Poor Monsieur Roger," the child said, in reporting these incidents to me. "It's time to think of taking him away, or he's going to do something bad."

Yes, it was time.

One last blow came to spur my desire to act without losing any time. For two days, the temperature dropped in proportions absolutely abnormal for the hothouse that Biskra is. The winterers were buttoning their overcoats all the way to the collar, and the ladies were wearing furs to go out. The drop on temperature was explained by snowfalls in the nearby Aurès; there were precedents—but personally, I immediately gave the event its veritable and disquieting significance. The Man of the Apocalypse was on the march! Roger was setting out to win his bet.

Well, no, he wouldn't win it.

That same evening, while the lunatic was helping Barnett to empty bottles of gin and whisky, I went straight to the terrace where I had seen him set out the vats of acid. I was fully determined to remove the dangerous compound, to disperse it, to bury it in some corner of the desert.

But I searched for the containers in vain; they were no longer there.

Roger had certainly transported them outside to a location of which he alone was aware.

I swore that that would be his last experiment, but this time, I needed help. Incontinently, I wrote to the Public Prosecutor of Batna, the administrative center to which Biskra is attached. I explained Roger's case, recounted the lamentable story of his amour, insisted on the clear cerebral breakdown that had been manifest in him since Madame Berjac's death. A false shame prevented me from going to the end, of revealing the terrible and disconcerting things that might happen if Livry remained at liberty.

In addition, I would not have been understood.

By virtue of my own experience, I sensed clearly that ordinary minds were unable to accept such conjectures right away, without revolt. In the very interests of my request, it was better to keep quiet and not risk becoming a madman in the eyes of those I wanted to convince.

When I had finished my letter it was very late; I wanted nevertheless to put it into the box at the station myself.

When I got back, I had to submit to a furious scene on Roger's part.

"Ah, finally, there you are!" he roared, as soon as he heard me go into my room. Almost brutally, he dragged me into his, and stood before me, his features contracted, his gaze hostile.

"Look! Can you explain this letter that I've received from my stockbroker?"

He threw the piece of paper in my face rather than handing it to me.

I scanned the missive rapidly.

In substance, the stockbroker informed Livry that it was impossible for him to realize the six millions in cash demanded urgently, for the good reason that all his clients movable assets had been transformed into bonds with a long expiry date.

It had been necessary to expect that coup-de-théâtre one day or another, but it had arrived at a particularly deplorable moment.

Roger exploded. "So that's how you take care of my interests! By doing the opposite of my instructions and my desires!"

"Calm down, Roger," I replied, determined to weather the storm. "You knew in advance that I'm not a businessman. I did my best."

He threatened me with his fist, at the paroxysm of his fury. "You're lying! You're lying! You couldn't be unaware that I needed funds disposable at the end of February to pay for the delivery of fifty grams of radium. Your operations should have been limited to collecting that money. Instead of that you've lent yourself to I don't know what swindles..."

"Oh, Roger!"

The insult appeared to me to be so abominable, even in the mouth of a demented individual, that I did not have the strength to submit to it without protest.

Insensible to the cry of my offended soul, however, the poor fellow continued, with an atrocious snigger: "Of course! I can see your game clearly! You wanted to stop my arm, raised to accomplish an act of justice, an act of reason, an act of regeneration. You've attempted to preserve the rotten world, because you were afraid for yourself. Yes, afraid, afraid, afraid..."

He marched toward me, his arm raised, his eyes bulging. For a moment, I thought he was about to drive me into a corner, seize me by the throat, and strangle me in a fit of furious madness.

In that moment of anguish I felt so miserable, so bruised, that I almost wished for that frightful end. It would be a conclusion!

But his hoarse breath drew away from my face. He took a step backwards, and, pointing his finger at me, said: "Well, you won't succeed! You can do what you like, I shall have my radium. And instead of eighty grams, I'll buy the half-kilo that the Krafts of Nordlingen are offering me. Here, look at their letter! And I'll pay cash...

"Then, with the hundred and thirty liters of Omega acid I have, the Earth won't be so heavy!"

Mute with horror, I followed that rising tide of terrible arrogance. But Roger suddenly abandoned his comminatory tone, and with an accent full of bitterness, he expanded in reproaches.

"You have no backbone, little Paul. Instead of remaining my ally, you've taken it into your head to set ambushes for me. What do you expect? I've replaced you in my confidence and my affection. Today, I have other allies, more faithful, who have associated themselves more courageously, without a hidden agenda, with the goal I'm pursuing...

"I forgive you your treason, because the strong are ignorant of vengeance. But henceforth, I no longer know you. Go! You're free!"

His gesture was broader than the walls of the room—his gesture of expulsion.

That was too much.

Dejected, my head bowed, I head for the door. I'm about to reach it when I feel myself seized around the body. At the same time, I hear Roger's voice, imploring: "Paul, Paul...don't go! Don't abandon me!"

I turn round. Even more than the heart-rending timbre of his voice, the dolorous expression of his physiognomy stirs the very depths of my soul.

And the hands retain me.

"You don't see, then, that I'm mad…you don't sense my burning heart, my exploding head…oh, if you knew how I'm suffering!"

With his closed fist, he hammered his forehead.

"There, there, I feel something like a rasp passing back and forth through my brain. It's horrible…"

For a moment, I gazed into his eyes with a profound pity. "Why don't you want to let anyone care for you?" I said to him, in a very soft voice.

He smiled bitterly, and shook his head. "Care for me! My illness is incurable."

"Try anyway…I'll help you with all my might." I put the maximum of persuasive affection into the affirmation.

"What's the point?"

Roger let himself fall into a chair, wearily. In my turn, I had the impression that I was about to render myself the master of my friend, when I heard galloping footsteps in the neighboring corridor, and then a frantic hammering on the door.

"Hey, Master Livry! Gee up! Hurry!"

Without waiting for anyone to open the door, the odious Barnett shoved the batten. He stuck his horrible face through the gap. I had the sensation that behind the death's-head, madness and woe were mounting a triumphant offensive return.

"Hurrah!" the monster continued, his green eyes gleaming like those of an owl. "Hurrah! You've won the million! Outside in the Oasis, the seguias are frozen.[40] Ah, Monsieur friend of the Devil, tomorrow you're going to show me the little device…then I'll give you a check for as many millions

---

[40] Author's note: "Seguias are little streams that are contrived in all directions around the feet of the palm trees, the cultivation of which requires irrigation."

as you please for the other affair, the great *chambardement* of the world, as you say in France."

At the first word, Roger had straightened up, his face blossoming. With an expression full of assurance and pride, he looked at me, and his gaze seemed to be saying: *You see!*

Oh yes, again I saw the gulf opening under our feet.

I was going to see many others. That frightful night had not yet tested me enough. After responding to Barnett's vigorous handshake, Roger made a proposition: "No need to wait until tomorrow to show you how I produce the cold. Would you like to see now, Barnett?"

"All right! You're expeditious, worthy of being born American."

"Let's go, then."

"Is it far?"

"A few steps."

"Right! I'll get Jim to follow with a basket of champagne. It's perfectly appropriate to celebrate an event as sensational as the end of the world, in fact!"

"Very true. Get Jim to bring a lantern too." Turning to me, he said, in the most natural tone in the world: "Are you coming with us, Paul?"

Since Barnett's irruption, Roger seemed to have lost the memory of the violent tirade he had just inflicted on me. In the same way, his mind no longer conserved any trace of the moment of sane reason during which my poor friend had exhaled his dolorous plaint. In his brain on fire, the ideas and impressions were whirling like dead leaves whipped up by a storm wind.

For my part, I was ashamed of having abandoned myself to a momentary weakness. Before the immense peril that Barnett's intervention had just revealed to me, that weakness had become cowardice. Fortunately, Roger had not let me go!

Now we're outside, Roger, Barnett and I. A few paces behind, the negro Jim is following, with a basket full of bottles under his arm.

It's three o'clock in the morning. In spite of my overcoat, buttoned up to the neck, the cold penetrates me.

Where is Roger going to take us?

As soon as he takes the direction of the march, a suspicion invades me and causes me an indefinable malaise. A few paces more and the suspicion is confirmed. Another hundred meters, and it changes into a certainty.

We're outside the White Villa.

XVI. Trinity of Demons

Serenely, Roger has taken a bunch of keys out of his pocket—the keys glimpsed by Étienne. He opens the gate and goes into the garden. We follow him.

For my part, I have the impression that night-prowlers and grave-robbers must have. How powerful my friend's will-power or aberration must be, for him to dare to commit what I, personally, consider to be a sacrilegious violation.

Without slowing down he scales the six steps of the per-ron, and puts the key in the lock of the vestibule. On entering the house of the dead, instinct makes me remove my hat, as in a tomb.

This time, Roger wouldn't be lying if he accused me of being afraid. In spite of the people surrounding me, I can't rid myself of the grip of that nervous, irrational, stupid fear. It's the "nocturnal terror" classified by physicians, which attacks children neurasthenics, the weak and the expressed. It's the fear of noises and glimmers of light, the imprecise anxiety that evokes the abrupt intrusion of specters and phantoms, the ex-pectation of *something*.

Now, the *something* is there!

Behind one of the doors that opens on to the vestibule—that of the kitchen—I can hear a slight rustling, a barely per-ceptible friction. Someone is there, moving with infinite pre-caution. Who can that someone by, if not a shade?

Now the handle of the door is turning, slowly, slowly...

A second, a century, and the door opens...

My blood freezes in my veins.

Through the gap, I white form presents itself, a head advancing with a feline prudence…a head…no, a fabric enveloping the appearance of a head. Can there be a material head within that white specter?

"Don't disturb yourself, it's me."

From the passage, Roger has just directed those words at the specter. Then, a ray of lantern-light projected in that direction completes the breaking of the detestable spell. What my unhealthy imagination has mistaken for a phantom is an Arab enveloped in a burnoose, coiffed with a hood that prevents his facial features from being discerned.

In any case, the Arab has stepped back, closing the door again.

Who can that indigene be, chosen by Roger to guard the dead woman's house? Undoubtedly, the one with whom the madman held the long conversations observed by Étienne. But where has Roger found that man of confidence?

Those questions, I pose without having the clarity of mind necessary to fathom them. The chemist is already going upstairs, bringing my thoughts back to the cruel memories that haunt this place.

On the first floor landing, he passes without pausing the door of the room where *she* died.

I breathe!

He continues going up to the door that gives access to the villa's roof-terrace. We set foot on that terrace.

On the concrete, the vats of acid that I saw being prepared are set out.

With a gesture, he indicates them to the American. "There!"

Barnett has the lantern moved closer. He gazes as the pale opaline substance formed by the mixture of the acid and the radium. A joyful grimace appears on his face; he puts out his hand…

"Go on! You're straight, Master Livry, and I'm your servant. I'll write the check…"

But the madman is able to resist that first success.

"One moment! I want your conviction to be entire, absolute. Before accepting your word and your money, I want to give you a tangible proof of the power of my Omega acid."

"The cold's falling on my shoulders; that's sufficient for me."

"No. Cold is felt, it isn't seen. I'm going to show you another application of my product, visible this time, and no less terrifying."

"All right! I'll open my eyes wide."

"Help me to take the basins down, then. You too, Paul, please."

Like Barnett, I obey without knowing what Roger is going to do."

We each take hold of one of the porcelain receptacles by the edges. Trembling, I considered the frightful substance. Apart from a few phosphorescent gleams that are escaping from it, it seems inert; one might have thought it the kind of paste used for making impressions, for low-cost molding.

On reflection, do not gun-cotton, melinite and all the most terrifying destructive agents offered to humankind by modern chemistry offer the same perfectly-inoffensive appearance?

The vague anxiety into which Roger's new determination has cast me at least has the effect of chasing away the specters prowling in my mind. We go back to the ground floor of the lugubrious house.

Having reached the vestibule, Roger knocks on the door that opened before, and the white silhouette appears again.

In a low voice, Roger exchanges a few words with the man in the burnoose. Afterwards he says to me: "Pass me the basin."

I still obey. He takes the object from my hands, hands it to the Arab, and does the same with the receptacle held by Barnett.

"Two will be enough. Let's keep the other two."

In a muffled voice, the Arab has murmured something.

That voice! It seems to me that I've heard it before. An illusion, no doubt. What common point can exist between my memories and that indigene? In any case, all my attention is now attracted by the Arab's maneuvers.

He has just lit a lamp. Then he places an oil-heater on the floor-tiles of the kitchen, lights the wick, and sets a saucepan on top of it. With the aid of a ladle, he transfers the contents of the two vats of acid into the saucepan.

What does this infernal cuisine signify?

"Let's go outside!" says Roger, who has thus far watched the strange preparations in silence.

Now we're in the garden.

The Arab has followed us there, but he stays in the shadows, outside the zone of the radiance projected by the lantern. He is beginning to intrigue me greatly, that individual who persists in hiding beneath the hood of his burnoose.

But Roger places a hand familiarly on Barnett's shoulder, and in a tone pierced by a grim bitterness, he says: "You see this house…well, I condemned it to disappear on the day of my departure from Biskra. To show you my power, I'm going to destroy it immediately…

Inside the house, a kind of sizzling is audible.

"It's starting," said the chemist, becomes more excited. And with the dramatic tone of an evil genie in a fairy tale, he proclaims: "One…two…three…accursed dwelling, return underground!"

That theatrical declamation might seem ridiculous but it sounded terrifying.

At Roger's invocation, a strange phenomenon occurred before our eyes. The white façade of the villa, made of stucco and molded plaster, suddenly vanished in the midst of a cascade of broken glass, and the noise of beams and furniture smashed to pieces.

There was scarcely anything to be seen but a light mist, like vapor rising toward the sky.

Abruptly, I understood. I had just seen a repetition of the terrible destructive process that hazard had delivered to Jobert.

Thus had the millstone supports of the doorway of the Fontenay laboratory disappeared; thus had the calcareous foundations supporting the soil of Bouffarik and cemented the volcanic rocks of Messina disappeared.

It was frightening to think that such a power of subversion might fall into human hands—and what hands! Those of madmen.

With his arms, Roger indicated the formless heap of debris that lay on the ground. "Wood, a few bricks, a few bits of metal—not one stone! As soon as the Omega acid boiled, its vapors acted on the chalk like a spark on a powder-keg.

"And now that you've seen Monsieur Barnett, I await your decision."

Without saying a word, the phlegmatic American took out of his pocket a supple red morocco folder containing his check book.

Armed with a fountain-pen, he filled in the blanks of the printed forms.

"First, the million of the bet. It's yours." He made as if to detach the check.

Roger stopped him. "No need. Add that million to the two hundred others that you're going to place at the disposal of the Kraft Company of Nordhausen for the first of March."

Barnett does not blink. "Time to cable New York, and the Krafts will be able to withdraw what they indicate from the Bank of Germany."

"I'll take charge of the rest."

Then the terrible man utters a snigger of joy. "I was right just now—you're the Devil."

"No, I'm the Man of the Apocalypse." That was like a roar, in which an exacerbated pride was mingled with an atrocious dolor and a furious overexcitement.

With a feverish movement, Roger takes hold of Barnett's hands and shakes them frenetically. Then, running to the Arab, he seizes him in his turn and draws him toward the Yankee. He unites the hands of the two men.

"Barnett, this is our other companion. We shall be three to work without fear and without weakness on the destruction of abominable terrestrial life.

Instinctively, I had retreated two spaces. I remained the mute, horrified witness of that diabolical pact.

And, the hood of the burnoose finally having been removed, by the faint light of the lantern, I discover the features of the third demon.

That emaciated face, bistre by virtue of being earthen, those eyes illuminated by the gleam of folly, that mouth contracted by a rictus of hate, all belonged to Jobert.

I had before me the murderer and thief of Fontenay, the irresponsible author of the catastrophes of Bouffarik and Messina.

I say "irresponsible" because it was not possible to be mistaken about the advanced degree of mental alienation that was eating the wretch away; it was only necessary to look at him.

And without difficulty, I explained his presence. He had come running in answer to the appeal launched by the advertisements placed by Roger in the newspapers. Hidden under that Arab disguise, he had arrived in Biskra at the very moment when my unfortunate friend was sinking into the crisis unleashed by the death of Madame Berjac.

He arrived in time to complete the frightful trinity of dementia.

Such is the truth that my reason imposes.

At least I have an advantage over Jobert!

As soon as possible, I'll notify the police of the location of the murderer of Fontenay. I'll put an end to his dangerous exploits.

Why not immediately? I'm now invisible, outside the circle of light.

In the crisis of excitement that has taken possession of them, the three madmen seem to have forgotten me. Without attracting their attention, I can reach the extremity of the garden and climb over the low wall that surrounds the villa.

Another step backwards and I can escape.

Involuntarily, however, a spectacle perhaps even more poignant than the collapse of the building nails me to the spot.

Roger brandishes his fist menacingly at the rubble. "Before leaving," he proclaims, "I want to leave nothing behind. Everything here belongs to me...even the memory." And, turning to Jobert: "Bring me the gasoline."

The fake Arab runs toward a shed that contains garden chairs and tools. A few seconds later, he comes back, his shoulders bending under the weight of six cans of gasoline.

"What are you going to do?" asks Barnett.

"Burn the last vestiges."

"Hurrah! A fire of joy!"

"Of joy!" Roger repeats, in a frightening voice. "That's right!"

Followed by Jobert, he runs toward the heap of beams, furniture, fabrics and the debris of household equipment. In order to proceed more rapidly, the two fanatics stave in the gas cans with a hatchet and spread the contents over the rubble.

A light shines, a flame shoots up as high as the treetops. In the blink of an eye, the conflagration is red, crowned by fuliginous smoke.

"Jim! Champagne!" cried Barnett, transported by delight.

The negro takes from his basket some of the enormous bottles knows as jeroboams, which only find grace with the clientele of Anglo-Saxon bars. Illuminated by the red glow of the conflagration, sometimes drowned by swirls of nauseating smoke, the three madmen and the negro gesticulate, sing, shout and drink in turn.

It is a demonic Sabbat, a vision of Hell!

Shivering with fear, I flee; I jump the wall, pursued by Roger's hoarse cry, which rises up like a war cry and drowns out Barnett's hurrahs:

"I am the Man of the Apocalypse!"

XVII. Alarm Call

The Marseille express has just passed through Ville-neuve-Saint-Georges station with a thunderous din. Another twenty minutes and I shall be in Paris.

Oh, that return voyage lived in fever! It is always thus when one deplores lost time, time that one can never recover.

When I think of those two days, completely wasted, searching for Roger! When dawn broke, after the terrible night in Biskra, my poor friend had disappeared, in company with Barnett and Jobert. A rapid automobile had carried them away toward the coast.

I had an idea that the fugitive would head straight for his villa at Fontenay. That is why, as I approached Paris, my anguish bordered on sharp suffering.

As soon as I arrive, with Étienne, I leap into a taxi.

Finally, we're outside Roger's dwelling. Through the trees, I can see the closed shutters.

Trembling, I press the bell-push. A long wait, a minute, a century...

Obedient to my nerves, I ring again. Dragging footsteps are heard on the gravel; the little door opens cautiously, framing the head of old Philippe.

"Oh, it's you, Monsieur Paul."

"Roger has come back, hasn't he?" On my part, it's more of an affirmative cry than a question.

"Of course! Monsieur came back four days ago."

"Is he alone?"

"Yes."

"What is he doing?"

"That, I can't tell you, as Monsieur arrived at night and sent me to sleep at a hotel. Well, he is the master. This morning, when I came back here, he'd gone again. I only know that a large automobile must have come into the garden—I saw the tracks of its wheels in the gravel."

My anticipations were realized. I went pale.

"Philippe, go fetch a locksmith."

For a start, I was determined to get into the laboratory.

It took a full hour for workmen to reckon with the powerful locks replaced after Jobert's burglary. Guided by Étienne, I ran to the cupboards where Roger kept his provisions of Omega acid. The doors of the cupboards were wide open; the acid was no longer there.

One more confirmation of the impending danger!

One can, it appear now telephone cities in Germany. Incontinently, I go to the central office at the Bourse. After extreme difficulty and a wait of more than seven hours, I eventually obtain communication with the Kraft Company of Nordhausen.

It's done! The Krafts have delivered the radium, a hundred grams—an enormous, extraordinary quantity that represents almost half of the stock existing in the world. And in the apparatus, the Teutonic accent of Kraft inflates with mocking joy and blissful pride to add that the settlement of forty million dollars has been made in cash, by Mr. Barnett, Monsieur Livry's authorized agent. Since the armistice, no industrialist has completed such a colossal deal..."

I left the Boches to their imbecilic satisfaction.

Oh, yes, they had done a wonderful dead! Thanks to them, humankind would be called upon to defend itself against circumstances that were doubtless unique in the history of the world. It would be far more devastating that the world war and its consequences.

To engage in that extraordinary struggle, it would be necessary to appeal to the united resources of all governments, all social organizations and all individual and collective energies.

Would even that be a sufficient guarantee? Where should the effort be applied? Where should the battle be joined? How could the point of the globe be discovered at which the trinity of monsters, Livry, Jobert and Barnett, intended to install the secret factory of death?

All that, others would determine. My own role was limited to sounding the alarm call.

But would that call be heeded?

Where is the man capable of accepting, coolly, the monstrous idea that the end of the world might be imminent?

That man, I believe I have found: it is Monsieur Thiérard-Leroy. The cruel loss of his only child disposes his soul more fully to envisage the worst eventualities with serenity. Then too, the great scientific worth of the astronomer eliminates any suspicion of folly or trickery. Finally, he knows the essence of Livry's discoveries, and has even determined their extreme consequences. Furthermore, his position as director of the Observatoire gives him the ear of the public powers. He will be heard where a teacher like myself would have every chance of being sent away, or even directed straight to the special infirmary of the remand prison.

My resolution is made; I shall place the fate of the world in the hands of Hélène's Berjac's father—and after that, to the grace of destiny.

The old scientist welcomed me with the affable mildness that is the foundation of his character. In addition, the bond of common dolor favored my bitter confidences.

I told him everything that he still did not know. I insisted particularly on the terrible results of Livry's procedures: the experiment at Mourmelon, confirmed by the experiment at Biskra. Then I revealed the no less troubling aspects of the problem revealed by Jobert: the crimes against humanity affirmed by the days of fear and mourning at Bouffarik and Messina.

The old man listened to me without interrupting. When I had finished, he headed toward a filing cabinet, pulled out a dossier, and brought it to me.

"My dear friend," he said, with a serene gravity, "on the basis of the data furnished by poor Livry, I calculated the effects of the Omega acid for myself; I did not know that these theoretical calculations had been anticipated by experiments." He shook his head. "The Earth is going to traverse a frightful crisis. I can even glimpse the means that might be employed to bring about the catastrophe...oh, this leaves far behind cometary collisions and other imaginative prophecies."

Then, tucking his dossier under his arm, he said: "It's necessary, even so, to seek advice."

We went together to see the President of the Council.

Monsieur Luissant, the head of the Government, was then the Minister of the Interior.

We met the Minister at the exit from a session in the Chambre that had been very stormy. There had, it seemed, been much verbal abuse with regard to a pending conflict between a gamekeeper and a mayor. How miserable those petty village squabbles were going to seem to Monsieur Luissant when he heard the extraordinary revelations that we were bringing him!

And what effect might those threats of total annihilation produce on the mind of that Statesman, still young, loving life for the satisfactions that it accorded him, and those greater still that the future seemed to reserve for the future of his powerful intelligence!

With an impressive coolness, he followed my explanations, corroborated by Monsieur Thiérard-Leroy's; he examined the evidence. After that, he showed the most magnificent kind of courage: that of credence. How many others in his place would have recoiled before the fear of ridicule by refusing to take the terrible prospect seriously?

I can still hear him pronouncing, in is calm but determined voice: "Well, Messieurs, we're going to act. But above all, I demand absolute secrecy from you. Think of the wind of terror, frenzy and dementia that would blow over the world if it knew...

"Against this trio of madmen we shall make use of the weapons given to us by the international entente regarding the anarchists. We shall track them everywhere without weakness, and without false sentimentality. It is no longer merely a matter of protecting a people, a race or a fatherland but humanity entire! This evening, my secret orders will be given, and the Sûreté Général will commence the search."

With a pale smile he added: "The Sûreté Général will never have better merited its title, will it?"

In the days that followed, the measures taken by the Government became more precise.

To begin with, Monsieur Thiérard-Leroy and I made a rapid journey to the abandoned house in Mourmelon. It was possible that Roger had passed that way in order to reactivate the acid disposed in the vats, or perhaps to remove the receptacles.

We were mistaken. The vats were found as the chemist had left them after his last trip. He had not returned to Mourmelon.

Our first concern was to bring the dangerous apparatus back to Paris.

Thanks to the indications that Roger had given the astronomer in a moment of expansion, it was possible to dissolve the unknown product that neutralized the Omega acid. The terrible substance became active again. A series of experiments with it could proceed, with which were associated Monsieur d'Arsaumont, the celebrated chemistry professor at the Collège de France and Dr. Manrichoff, the great biologist of the Institut Pasteur.

The President of the Council had judged it possible to share the secret of universal death with such men.

I remember those experiments as if it were yesterday, carried out in great mystery in the garden of the Observatoire and Professor d'Arsaumont's research laboratory behinds the Butte Montmartre.

Two events forgotten today relate to that exciting research: a powerful frost that descended unexpectedly in the middle of March 19   and a collapse of the ground that happened in the Rue Tourlaque in Montmartre and claimed a innocent victim, a poor woman surprised by the collapse of the roadway. To the terror of the three scientists, the vapor of an infinitesimal dose of the Omega acid had provoked the accident; no one apart from us ever knew the veritable cause.

After that, we had a clear comprehension of the role of Jobert, the evil genius of cataclysms, and we determined more exactly Livey's fantastic power.

It was terribly simple. With the quantities of acid and radium at his disposal, in less than three months, the drop in temperature would reach a hundred degrees below zero; another three months, and water vapor would no longer exist on our globe; the cold would be that of space.

It was a fortnight after our first visit that the scientists brought the terrifying results of their experiments to the Minister. I was there. I listened to those men of courage and science examining and rejecting means of preservation, one by one, like useless weapons.

"So," Professor d'Arsaumont summarized, "I can see nothing that can be done to prevent the diffusion of the cold. The action of the Omega acid spreads successively through the molecules of water vapor in the air. Very rapidly, the evaporation of the ocean will be nullified. Every day, the fissure through which the life of the earth is escaping will grow larger. First the oceans will freeze, and then the mountains of ice formed by the seas will flow over the continents. But well before that, all movement will be suspended; houses and stocks of combustibles will soon be impotent to defend humans against the bite of the freeze. The animals will perish first, then the plants. No more drinkable water, no more food. The soil, hardened by the frost, will even refuse to receive the bodies of those who succumb first. The others will follow soon after."

And with the most admirable stoicism, the great scientist added: "After all, the life of the humans who exist today in very little in space and time; if we make a leap of hundred years they will all have disappeared. What we have to preserve is the work of humans, the creation rather than the creature.

"Now, this Livry, holed up in some unknown corner of the globe—a forest, a mountain or a desert island—will suffice for that task of destruction if no one succeeds in stopping him in time."

At that point in the tragic conference, the President of the Council—I can still see him—shrugged his wrestler's shoulders in a movement of desperate impotence.

"We're searching, moving heaven and earth...we haven't found anything yet."

XVIII. Barnett's Hummingbirds

It was true.

Two weeks after the beginning of the search, the problem remained as obscure as it had been on the first day.

Only a few clues had been picked up, and they related to the American Barnett. Thus, it was known that he had embarked at Philippeville on a Spanish steamer. Several people had accompanied him; doubtless Livry and Jobert had been among them, but it had been impossible to establish that with certainty. Then Barnett had been seen in Paris at the Hôtel Majestic at a date that coincided with Roger's appearance at the villa in Fontenay, and the following day in Nordhausen, where the Krafts had placed the enormous consignment of radium in his hands.

Three weeks later the American had arrived in Biarritz in an immense automobile; there, all trace of him was definitively lost. What was certain was that neither Livry nor Jobert had accompanied him in those peregrinations.

Where were they hiding? A mystery!

At any rate, Monsieur Luissant estimated that the ten carboys of Omega acid—Étienne Tourte had given him that number, representing 250 liters, would have had difficulty escaping the investigations of the customs at terrestrial or maritime frontiers. Now, no chemical product of that kind had been identified in the frontier zones, where surveillance is particularly rigorous with respect to liquids. The Minister therefore found himself led to believe that the fatal carboys had not left French territory. That was, however, a theoretical deduction; did not Barnett's enormous fortune give him the means of purchasing a great deal of silence and complicity?

In brief, in spite of the efforts of all the police forces in the world—efforts stimulated by the promise of considerable rewards—nothing had come to dissipate the darkness. And those who knew expected from one day to the next to feel the first wave of cold passing over the Earth, the precursory sign of the terrible cataclysm.

Is it the heroic calm of the scientists surrounding me, or habituation to the terrible? In any case, the idea of the event no longer brings me the same terror.

I wish I could go to sleep one night and not wake up again, since there's nothing more to do.

In the mechanical life that was mine in those weeks of waiting, I could no longer even find the strength to devote myself to any kind of intellectual task. Every day I went either to the Tuileries or the Luxembourg, and mingled with the old rentiers, the retired, warming themselves in the early spring sunshine. Like them, I read the newspapers from the first line to the last—which is to say that my eyes scanned the printed symbols…but my mind was far away.

However!

It as the fourteenth of April in the Tuileries; my poor eyes abruptly pierced the fog through which, a absent reader floating in the unreal, I was scanning the text of my daily.

What news was capable of shaking my unhealthy apathy? Oh, nothing but, at first glance, an item of provincial gossip, one of the silly things that the occasional correspondents of small towns believe themselves to be obliged to send from time to time.

Tarbes, 12 April 19 . The fauna of our picturesque Pyrenean region has just been enriched by a rare species what has so far escaped the attention of naturalists. And when we say "fauna" it might be more appropriate to say "flora." Shepherds grazing their sheep on the edge of the Bois d'Astruc perceived marvelous birds flying through the low branches: dwarf birds with plumage iridescent with all the colors of the rainbow. They succeeded in capturing a few. The

*small birds, sent to Tarbes by courtesy of Monsieur Loubestal,
a schoolteacher, were recognized as hummingbirds of the
most delightful and purest species. How did these charming
guests of the tropical forest been acclimatized to our woods?
Such is the palpitating problem offered to the sagacity of the
ornithologists of our region...*

I uttered a cry, and bounded from my bench, offending
the quietude of my placid neighbors.

"Barnett's birds! Barnett's birds!"

Like a leitmotiv I murmur that phrase, nothing more: by
itself, it encloses the tyrannical suggestion that has imposed
itself on my mind. At the same time, I run like a madman in
the direction of the Concorde. I cross the Champs-Élysées and
arrive at the Place Beauvau. I go into the Ministry of the Interior. I must have a troubling and bizarre appearance, because
the Cabinet usher hesitates to pass on the request for an audience that I scribble in haste. Eventually, without having to
wait too long, I am introduced into Monsieur Luissant's presence.

"Why, what is it?" the Minister says, benevolently. At
the first glance, he has divined by emotion.

"Barnett's birds...there can be no question that they're
Barnett's birds..."

I pass him the newspaper, indicating with my finger the
article lost in the miscellaneous news on page three.

"We'll see!"

The Minister has pronounced those words with the serene tone of a man who effuses any hypothesis a priori; doubtless the frequentation of men and things has taught him that
the negation of principle and he preconceived idea are the
flaws of inferior minds.

In quick succession he demands telephonic communication with the Prefecture of Police in Tarbes, exchanges a few
remarks with the director of the Sûreté and then with the Prefect of the Hautes-Pyrénées.

Turning back to me, he says: "No individual answering Barnett's description has been seen in the vicinity of Tarbes. There is a foreigner recently installed in a former Franciscan convent on the Montagne d'Ossat, close to the wood where the hummingbirds were found, but it's a matter of a South American by the name of Manuel Porfirias...so, no sign of the Yankee Barnett."

"Oh, if only I could see for myself!"

"Do that. Go down there, conduct an investigation yourself. To facilitate your actions, I'll attach an inspector from the Sûreté to you." And in a voice of infinite sadness, the Minister concludes: "In the present circumstances, we have a duty not to neglect anything, even mirages.

I depart the same evening, in the company of Étienne Tourte and the agent adjoined to me, a tall, modest and sympathetic fellow answering to the name of Martin.

As soon as we arrived in Tarbes we collected some initial information. The Franciscan convent of Ossat, the property of the Peruvian who excited my curiosity, has recently been put up for sale. It was a very old monastery dating from the fourteenth century, with the appearance of a fortified château. It was perched on the summit of the Montagne d'Ossat, an isolated hill four hundred meters high, which stands in the plain of Tarbes five kilometers from the first foothills of the Pyrenees. As for the new owner, according to rumor, he proposes to establish a sanitarium in the large buildings disposed for fresh air cures. Arrived three weeks before with his domestics and his luggage, he had proceeded with an initial summary installation. He had just departed on a journey to bring back the large furniture and other objects destined to complete the accommodation; he was expected that same evening at the Hôtel des Espagnes.

Those details were contrary to the entirely instinctive arguments that had brought me from the other end of France. Before returning to Paris, I wanted at least to follow the vain trail traced by my imagination to its end. Installed at the Hôtel des Espagnes I awaited the arrival of the Peruvian doctor.

He arrived at nightfall in an automobile truck laden with luggage. First, two negroes got down from the vehicle, in the midst of the wide-eyed admiration of the idlers of the sidewalk. My heart beat faster; in one of those negroes I seemed to recognize Jim!

But now the doctor gets down in his turn: a small thin man with stooped shoulders. He advances into the light of the electric bulb suspended above the portal. Then I utter a hoarse exclamation, repeated by Étienne beside me.

In the so-called Peruvian Manuelo Profirias, I have just recognized Barnett's mulatto veterinarian.

A pressure exerted on my arm by the agent Martin recalls me to prudence.

"Let's go," he whispers. "It's necessary that they don't see us."

Half an hour later, we held a meeting at the Prefecture, in which the Prefect, the Public Prosecutor, the Commissaire of Police and the Capitaine of the Gendarmerie take part.

The immediate arrest of the doctor and the negroes was decided.

At nine o'clock in the evening, as they were about to board a train for Bayonne, the mulatto and his two acolytes were apprehended.

At the first interrogation the individuals continued to lie; the mulatto claimed to be named Porfirias, was astonished when mention was made to him of Barnett and birds; he was visibly reciting a lesson learned. But the scene changed when I came into the Prosecutor's office.

At the sight of me, the frightened mulatto told everything he knew. Obedient to Barnett's orders, he had bought the convent of Ossat. He had arrived there three weeks before, coming from Spain in the company of his master and the two Frenchmen from Biskra. Rendered unrecognizable by make-up and wigs, they had passed for domestics. Since their arrival *the three* had been working night and day on chemical manipulations about which the mulatto knew absolutely nothing. Then, four days before, Barnett had given the order to set the birds free. Finally, the day before, the master had told him that he no longer had any need of his services. Well ballasted with money, he had intended to leave for America in the company of the two negro servants. Only *the three*, therefore, still occupied the monastery of Ossat.

That coup-de-théâtre left me stupefied. I glimpsed the incalculable consequences attached to the discovery of the three madmen. The others were bound to the supposition of an anarchist plot, but I knew the truth!

By virtue of the confidences extracted from Manuelo, it was learned that they possessed weapons, ammunition and food supplies for six months. Those precautions implied the idea of resistance, further encouraged by the very particular disposition of the location.

In that regard, the Prefect provided very curious details regarding the topography of the Mont d'Ossat, a kernel of granite embedded in a mass of marble. In eruptive eras, that granitic jet had traversed the calcareous sediments already formed and broken through the exterior to constitute the summit of a hill. It was on that needle of hard rock that the Franciscans had constructed the buildings of their monastery, extracting the materials from the granite itself, as people for whom time and trouble were of no account. The convent had thus been conceived as a fortress; it was, in fact, designed to withstand the assaults of the Saracens. It formed an ensemble of massive constructions, surrounded by a wall fifteen feet thick. Oak doors edged with iron and enormous grilles commanded the entrance to the various quarters established between the interior courtyards. In order to become masters of the ensemble, besiegers would therefore have to take those veritable redoubts successively.

But before thinking of taking it, it was necessary to reach it. Now, with the exception of a poor goat track traced by the monks, which the people of the region called "the marble staircase," the mountain rose up in a series of sheer escarpments.

The Prefect did not hide his perplexity. If the three men really had ideas of resistance, it would be necessary to expect a murderous combat, all the more terrible because the President of the Council, kept up to date from minute to minute, telephoned instructions to take possession of the Three no matter what the cost, and to employ extreme means if necessary: cannons and bombs.

Poor Roger! Now that the other danger seemed to be on the eve of being thwarted, my heart bled with fraternal pity. But how could I reach out a helping hand to that furious maniac?

So long as the diabolical trio had not been reduced to impotence, all compassion had to be effaced before the superior interest of humankind.

Finally, I extracted a little hope from the resolutions that were made. Before launching a frontal assault, a surprise attack would be attempted.

Two battalions from the garrison at Tarbes would leave in the dark of night in automobile trucks; a detachment of artillerymen would accompany them with a wagon of explosives. Those troops would surround the Mont d'Ossat; in all probability, they would be in place by three o'clock in the morning. Before daybreak, a group of volunteers, reinforced by artillerymen equipped with melinite petards would climb the marble staircase silently all the way to the door of the former convent. Without any preliminary warning, they would blow it up, and try to capture the three inhabitants as quickly as possible, taking advantage of the disturbance that the surprise attack was bound to cause.

The plan was wisely contrived to avoid bloodshed.

But alas, this time, once again, wisdom was obliged to recoil before folly, and the surprise would be ours.

XIX. The War of Oblivion

Today, with the passage of years, the memory has almost been lost of the tragedy that unfolded around the Mont d'Ossat

326

in the middle of April 19 . At any rate, even rereading the newspapers of the epoch, it is very difficult to form a clear idea of those obscure and variously reported events. The imprecision of the accounts, the unexplained events—because they were inexplicable—and the malaise into which unsatisfied public curiosity was thrown, all contributed to thicken the mystery and favor the formidable secret, the prerogative of a handful of people.

One could not, however, cry to the crowd that, in that corner of land, the life or death of the world was in the balance.

But I shall resume my story at the moment when an automobile was carrying me through the black night in company with the Prefect, the Public Prosecutor and General de Lozières, commanding the garrison of Tarbes. By virtue of a special favor, young Étienne had been admitted to huddle next to me in a corner of the vehicle. It would have cost me dear to separate from that child, who, after all, was able to give useful information about Livry.

Following in a second vehicle were gendarmes escorting the mulatto Manuelo and the negro Jim; they had been brought along at hazard, even though it was understood that little help that could be expected from those accomplices, the first human rag sweating fear to the point of losing his memory and the second a colossal brute incapable of furnishing the slightest explanation.

We were heading for the Mont d'Ossat, a journey of some twenty-five kilometers.

It was two-thirds of the way along the route that a singular phenomenon occurred, of which we were to have the explanation a few hours later. I say "phenomenon," although the occurrence itself was perfect simple; in the very calm night, in which the absence of any wind contributed to the silence, a powerful gust passed by, agitating the trees that bordered the road: a whistling that seemed to be the result of a giant aspiration was audible in the higher layers of the atmosphere. Then, for the duration of a minute, the noise of a distant collapse was heard. And that was all; nature reentered into silence.

In the vehicle, the conversations stopped. All of us had shuddered, as if at the first clap of thunder presaging a storm.

"An avalanche in the high mountains!" murmured the Prefect.

No one replied. It might have been true, and yet, for my part, I had the intimate presentiment of something much more redoubtable.

The spectacle that was offered to us at first light justified that presentiment.

According to my companions, the panorama of the Mont d'Ossat had been completely modified, and in what a strange fashion!

Instead of the butte in the form of a pyramid with a wide base, a needle of granite with a vaguely triangular section stood up vertically above the plain. At the summit of that natural tower was the Franciscan convent, whose walls overhung the abyss at an altitude of four hundred meters. Only a granitic table bordered the enclosure toward the eastern apex of the triangle, forming a sort of esplanade, only a few meters across, literally suspended above the void, outside the entrance grille.

Around it, keeping a respectable distance from the base of the enormous monolith, the troops arrived during the night and peasants from the surrounding area were contemplating that fantastic décor with a stupor mingled with fear.

No more "marble stairway," no more escarpments, however steep: a smooth wall, without a ledge. The mountain of marble that wrapped the primitive rock had vanished without leaving a trace. At ground level, there was the alluvial terrain constituting the plain of Tarbes, but a chaotic terrain, pitted by potholes, sown with moraines and the debris of uprooted trees.

For educated individuals that change of view remained incomprehensible. An earthquake? An abrupt collapse of the subsoil? Nothing in familiar notions could help to construct an acceptable explanation. As for the others, the villagers and the soldiers, they were not far from attributing that magic to divine or diabolical intervention. Quite naturally, those simple souls cried either miracle or sorcery.

I alone was in possession of the truth. The strange upheaval was due to Roger's maneuvers. The Franciscan convent had not been chosen at random.

The curious geological particularity of the Montagne d'Ossat lent itself marvelously to the madman's frightful projects. Already very difficult, access to the convent became impracticable after the disappearance of the calcareous mass that constituted the mountain's slopes. Roger knew in advance that his acid gave him the means to upset nature by suppressing the marble at a stroke.

Then, a terrible deduction was imposed.

After Barnett's action in releasing his birds by virtue of one last incoherent impulse of pity, and the dismissal of the servants, the collapse of the mountain clearly indicated that the scientist was ready.

In effect, the scientist had cut the last bridge linking him to the earth. The Man of the Apocalypse was about to commence his work.

"Good," said General de Lozières, beside me. "At least this inexplicable phenomenon has the result of simplifying the phenomenon. If we can't climb up to the rogues, at least it's impossible for them to come down again. They're in prison." And, moved by a natural sentiment, he added: "At any rate, my brave soldiers won't have to risk their lives in an imbecilic struggle!"

Poor General! I did not take charge of dissipating his generous illusions. I did not have the right to divulge the terrible secret.

He would find out soon enough, alas.

I judged that there were better things to do than contemplate open-mouthed the eagle's nest from which death was about to spread over the world. As soon as possible, Monsieur Luissant needed to be brought up to date with the new situation, of which I alone possessed the key.

In haste, I had myself taken back to Tarbes. My head was so full of fearful thoughts that I was quite surprised when the auto deposited me outside the town's telephone office.

Addressing myself to the postmaster, I was able to obtain immediate communication with Luissant.

By the tremor of his voice in the receiver I sensed how distressed the Minister was by my revelations, even though, fearing the indiscretions of the telephone, I sought to filter the truth.

"I'm coming," Luissant said to me. "I'll bring the most eminent scientists engineers and army chiefs; I'll give immediate orders to have materiel of various sorts sent to Tarbes. We'll try everything that's humanly possible."

The President of the Council arrived at midnight on a special train. With him were the Minister of War, the Commander-in-Chief of the Artillery, the Chief Engineer of Explosives, the Director of the Meteorological Bureau and also, naturally, Messieurs Thiérard-Leroy, d'Arsaumont and Manrichoff.

Circumstances brought me, an obscure petty schoolteacher, to take my place in that cenacle of the highest notabilities of France.

The Council of War—and what a Council!—was held at daybreak before the somber mass of the Ossat.

"Messieurs," pronounced the Minister, with an anguishing gravity, "it's absolutely necessary that we find a means of reaching the summit of the peak and the people occupying it. Give me credit for the immense reasons that motivate the necessity; tell yourselves that they surpass reasons of State, that they concern, if you wish, what I shall call humanitarian reasons.

"And if you judge that my emotion, my efforts and my extreme determination are excessive and ridiculous by comparison with the goal to be attained, I beg Messieurs Thiérard-Leroy, d'Arsaumont and Manrichoff to contradict me. I make you the same plea, Monsieur Paul Lefort, who is sacrificing to these superior exigencies a close, quasi-fraternal friendship."

After the great scientists whose indisputable testimony the Minister had invoked, I nodded my head. Then, it seemed that a frisson stirred the epidermis of the others: those who did not yet know.

Then we debated. And in the course of the arguments exchanged, it was necessary to allow a few rays of extraordinary verity shine through. All the methods of scaling were examined in turn. None gave satisfaction. To climb up by means of ladders along the flanks of the rock was theoretically possible, but such work would require the establishment of successive landings. Even with the employment of the most advanced electric drilling equipment, the engineers judged that the enterprise would take more than a month, even supposing that the madmen at the summit would do nothing to oppose it.

In any case, the trenchant voice of the Minister put in: "It's necessary for us to be up there within a week, isn't it, Monsieur Thiérard-Leroy?"

"It's necessary," the astronomer repeated.

"I thought immediately of airplanes," Monsieur Luissant pronounced then, "but on the advice of the Commander-in-Chief of Aeronautics, it would be madness to think of landing on that pointed spur of rock or in that chaos of roofs. Dirigibles, on the other hand, floating above the Ossat, might be able to deposit a few resolute men in one of the interior courtyards."

The chief of military aeronautics made a sign of assent.

"Within forty-eight hours," the Minister continued, "our six available dirigibles must rally at Tarbes, whatever the weather." The statesman added: "But it goes without saying that before then, we'll have rendered the monsters incapable of doing any harm. That will be the task of our air force. General Hochtheim can explain that to you better than me."

The Chief of Aeronautics then set out a very simple plan for the employment of airplanes.

First of all, a few light aircraft would fly over the Ossat, for an initial reconnaissance that would permit photographs to be taken. Then a squadron of bombers would intervene, which would drop tons of explosives and gas shells on the building. We could count, on the one hand, of the destruction—or rather the dispersal—of the chemical substances produced by Livry, and on other, of the certain asphyxiation of the three wretches. Afterwards, a squad of specialists equipped with gas masks could be disembarked at leisure to verify the effects.

All that seemed very logically conceived.

An impression of immense relief ensued.

After the emotion of the first moment, it appeared to the most timorous eyes that perhaps we had exaggerated, if not the danger, at least the difficulty of warding it off in a manner as sure as it would be rapid.

I alone lowered my head; Roger's death sentence had just been pronounced. I would so much have liked to save the poor follow. But how could I have implored in his favor?

The orders can be launched immediately. An automobile radiotelegraphic apparatus has just arrived from Tarbes. It can easily communicate with the large station of the Croix d'Hins near Bordeaux; from there, the air force camp at Istre can be reached by telephone, where everything ought to be set in motion during the night.

However, the wireless telegraph apparatus, when switched on, does not work.

Is it a fault of attunement, or a breakdown in the transmission apparatus? At any rate, the waves are not transmitted.

After several fruitless attempts, the decision is made to send a dispatch by motorcycle to the nearest telegraph office.

"A bad start," murmurs Monsieur Luissant.

No one says a word.

The hours pass, with what slowness!

I'm cold.

Is it an unfortunate predisposition of my physical being, deprived of sleep, or a fallacious impression of my nerves by which I'm experiencing the expected sensation is advance?

No. Others than me seem to be suffering the uncomfortable effects of the atmospheric freshness. There is no doubt that it's accentuating. It contrasts strangely with the sun, which is rising over the horizon and ought to be better able to warm us with is rays.

At Monsieur Luissant's invitation, our group goes to seek shelter in a tawdry wagoners' inn at the intersection of two roads.

The common room has already been invaded by soldiers. We take refuge in a room with primitive furniture. An armful of vine-branches produces a bright flame in the fireplace and chases away the odor of mildew reigning in the room.

Eleven o'clock: our anxious impatience finally finds a diversion.

XX. Disappointment and Disaster

Three airplanes are spotted in a north-westerly direction. They are the reconnaissance aircraft.

They are flying at a low altitude, in spite of the sonorous purr of their engines. They pass over the needle of the Ossat and immediately veer away in order to land behind our position, a mound that overlooks the bifurcation of the two roads.

The aviators make their report.

They have fulfilled their mission. Several photographic views of the Ossat have been taken. They have not, however, distinguished any human being within the walls of the convent. They complain about the cold and the poor performance of their engines.

Another hour goes by.

Here comes the squadron of large bomber aircraft. The machines are flying very low, a hundred and fifty meters at the most; abrupt signals appear to be given by the squadron leader to regain altitude. Everyone divines that they want to pass over the needle.

But it seems to us that they cannot succeed in flying over the obstacle, because they disperse to the left and the right in order to go around the strange obelisk at mid-height, scarcely two hundred meters.

What does it mean? Machines that can normally reach seven thousand meters! That, at least, is the figure cited by the professionals that surround me.

Heavily, the large aircraft reach the neighboring landing-ground indicated to them by beacons.

Twenty minutes later, the commandant of the squadron, Capitaine Tenan, an ace among aces, presents himself to his chief, General Hochtheim.

"It's incomprehensible, General," he says. "About twenty kilometers from the place, our machines suffered a regular loss of altitude, as if they were falling along an inclined plane. If it had been a matter of one or two aircraft out of my six, I would have put the decline down to engine failure or a lack of fuel, but the whole squadron…!" He made a gesture of chagrin. "Explain it if you can! My planes have a ceiling of two hundred meters, and that with difficulty."

A disconcerting observation.

"Give me a report!" mutters the chief of aeronautics, deeply grieved to see the initial failure of the plan he had so judiciously explained that morning.

"You'll succeed better with your dirigibles," says Monsieur Luissant, to appease that disappointment.

"In the meantime, I want to ensure that the people up there sense our surveillance weighing upon them," says the General. "I'm waiting for observation balloons, and before our big dirigibles come on the scene this afternoon, we're going to be able to watch a captive ascent. The aerostatic fleet brought from Bordeaux is disembarking as we speak at the nearest railway station. Within an hour it will be in the vicinity of the Ossat."

We go to lunch.

Without waiting for the end of the meal, served with despairing slowness by the staff of the inn, the Minister gets up from the table. We all follow him

On foot, we go to the edge of a little wood. The ascent is to take place from there.

A captain who has come on ahead of his column examines the location. Nothing will be easier, he declares, than to float a "sausage" a hundred meters above the needle of the Ossat. Thus, we'll be able to complete the reconnaissance of the airplanes, and perhaps discover with binoculars the emplacement of Livry's "refrigerators."

That first ascent, therefore, promises very important results. Who can tell? Perhaps the solution vainly sought might suddenly appear.

Tenuous as the hope might be, it imposes itself even so; it brightens our expressions.

Now the captive aerostat appears; its baroque silhouette is bobbing a few meters above the vehicular winch around which the metallic cable is wound.

The "sausage" has been inflated on the way. Insufficiently, no doubt, for it seems flaccid; its ascensional force is very weak. That won't last! Behind comes the truck with cylinders of compressed hydrogen; in a quarter of an hour it can be reinflated properly.

The tubing is fitted, the taps opened—but the gas doesn't flow. Nothing! No pressure..."

"The hydrogen cylinders have been damaged," declares the vexed captain.

We are all nervous, disappointed by that further failure.

Fortunately, good news arrives to palliate the annoyance caused by that unfortunate incident. The Minister is summoned to the improvised telephone installed in a tent. After a brief conversation, Luissant returns to our group.

"A success, Messieurs," the Minister says, "The *Colonel Renard* and the *France* are floating over Tarbes. The Commandants of the dirigibles are requesting orders by optical signals, because it definitely seems that we'll have to go into mourning for wireless apparatus. It's no longer functioning."

General Hochtheim orders the *France* to press on to the Mont d'Ossat and carry out the reconnaissance that it has not been possible to effect. Within half an hour the airship is in sight.

We begin to hope again.

This time, nothing appears likely to trouble the dirigible's maneuvers.

As often happens at sunset, the breeze has dropped; the air is admirably calm. Already, the watchmen posted on a hill are agitating, sending signals in a northerly direction.

Preceded by Étienne, who is running as fast as he can, I climb up there.

Luissant joins us. He communicates the supplementary information he has just received about the large aerial units—for the alerted dirigibles have been taking off since the previous evening. With various fortunes, they are all attempting to reach the Pyrenees.

The *Ville de Paris*, departed from Toul, has come down in the Duchy of Bade. The *Ville de Nancy*, from Mayence, has been drawn north-eastwards; the balloon has been signaled passing over Utrecht; perhaps it is lost in the North Sea. The *Patrie* emerging brand new from the workshops of Moisson, has been obliged to turn back by an engine breakdown. The *République* has called in at Clermont-Ferrand; it will resume its south-westerly route in the evening.

In sum, only the *Colonel Renard* and the *France*, two navy dirigibles departed from Toulon that morning have been able to accomplish their aerial voyage without a hitch. In spite of the westerly wing blowing persistently, the two airships, traveling in convoy, have crossed the Cévennes and then continued their route as far as Tarbes, where the façade of the corn-market has been demolished in order to permit them to take temporary refuge there.

Already, the long gray spindle of the *France*, an ex-zeppelin, is a patch in the blue sky. The balloon is visibly increasing in size. But is it an illusion? As it gets closer, one might think that it were getting heavier.

Around me, comments underline the same impression: the balloon is losing speed, and losing altitude.

Now it's no more than two kilometers away, but its altitude must be less than a hundred and fifty meters. Is it a landing maneuver?

"No!" declares General de Lozières, who is following its movement with his binoculars. "The envelope is deforming; the balloon appears to be breaking in two..."

He utters a cry. "Damn! The balloon's falling."

That cry of anguish is repeated by all the spectators. With a vertiginous rapidity, the *France* spins on her axis and hurtles toward the ground.

My respiration halts. Instinctively, I close my eyes in order not to see.

A dull sound; that is the crash.

A horrified exclamation rises from the plain. Everyone runs toward the lamentable wreck. The immense envelope covers the nacelle and the martyrs enclosed therein like a shroud.

I don't have the courage to assist in the horrible recovery of the cadavers.

I retrace my steps as far as the inn. I collapse, prostrate, at a table, my head clasped in my hands.

The Minister has followed me, accompanied by his general staff. As if in a dream, I hear the plaints of General Hochtheim and the strange and despairing observation to which he has proceeded of his own accord.

Aircraft can no longer rise above the ground!

What incredible sorcery is retaining the aerial apparatus conceived by human genius, marvelous machines that have proved their worth?

The fact is there: those machines can no longer fly.

"No matter," says the Minister. "We'll try other means. Cannons, mines..."

We return to the terrain of the strange battle.

After the incredible failure of aviation and aerostatics, the floor is given to the artillery. Certainly, a bombardment of the convent is possible, on condition of bringing special engines. To make projectiles fall at an altitude of four hundred meters in a relatively narrow zone, one could not think of using field cannon; the projectiles would only produce insignificant scratches on the granite walls. At the very least, it would be necessary to employ much greater firepower: mortars capable of plunging fire, able to fire large explosive charges.

That operation will involve the transportation of extremely heavy materiel, the installation of platforms and, in sum, the extension of the railway line and the establishment of a spurs far as the location chosen for the establishment of the batteries—hence, extensive works and adaptations of the route. One would therefore run into the same inert factor, impossible to force: time.

The director of the artillery estimated at more than a week the necessary interval before the first cannon shot could be fired.

"And then," the General added, doubtless to the great mortification of his self-esteem, "thousands of shells might fall on the convent without producing appreciable results. Certainly, we could burn all the combustible materials—but what then?"

"It won't be sufficient to destroy!" Luissant interjected, almost violently. "The problem won't be solved is we don't succeed in setting foot up there!" He waved his fist at the abrupt summit. "Understand me well, my friends, we're engaged in a struggle for existence." Luissant emphasized the final phrase in a dramatic fashion. Full of grandeur, the gesture of his open hand ran around the entire horizon, encountered the sun and broadened out toward the sky.

As if in response to that mute invocation to the earth and the Universe, up above, on the accursed mountain, at the top of the squat bell-tower that emerged from the crenellated walls of the monastery, a flag in the form of a pennant slowly unfurled.

"The black flag!" murmured General de Lozières, who had directed his binoculars toward the summit.

Then, at the moment when the sun disappeared behind the gold-rimmed mountains, a sudden cold breath descended from the sky, like an invisible cold shower.

On that splendid spring evening, the Man of the Apocalypse declared war on Life.

XXI. The Tide of Terror

Another late night of terror and tears.

The Minister, the generals, the scientists and I were entrenched in the low-ceilinged room of the inn. An infinite despair weighed upon us. In spite of the decent meal that the Prefect had summoned from Tarbes, the white tablecloth and the harsh light cast by two automobile headlights serving for illumination, our spirits could not overcome the prostration that was gripping us.

Never, even in the most critical hours of the war, on the eve of attacks, under bombardments, had I witnessed such depression.

After the semblance of a dinner in which the food was barely touched, everyone sought his corner in order to think or sink into torpor. The Minister refused the camp bed that had been prepared for him.

Vanquished by fatigue, I surrendered to a heavy slumber.

Abruptly, toward midnight, a loud detonation caused me to sit up, at the same time as all my companions.

The window-panes had shattered into smithereens.

Most of us found ourselves hurled to the floor, struggling in a profound obscurity.

By the light of a pocket electric torch, we were able to look around. Those who had been knocked down among the overturned benches and chairs got up again.

Apart from a few cuts caused by broken glass, no one was wounded.

"What now?" asked the Minister.

"Undoubtedly an explosion nearby," General de Lozières supposed.

339

"In the direction of the air fleet!" exclaimed General Hochtheim, on the threshold of the door, partly open. "Oh! That light! Out there, everything's on fire!"

We race outside on the heels of the head of the air force, guided by the red smoke rising toward the sky.

Detachments camped in the vicinity come running, but imperative cries are heard dominating the tumult: "Stay back! Stay back! The gases!"

An officer, his eyes haggard and his clothing in tatters, gives us the explanation.

The bombs brought by the aircraft and sheltered under tarpaulins have suddenly exploded, setting fire to the airplanes and scything down the fleet's personnel.

Murder!

He does not form that thought precisely, but everyone understands, and with an instinctive movement, turned toward the mysterious Ossat.

Again, a profound silence reigns over the plain.

We go back to the inn in order to avoid the bite of the cold. As best we can, we block up the openings of the windows devoid of glass with the aid of bundles of straw and blankets.

Large log fires render the room a semblance of heat.

I continue to shiver until dawn, always expecting a further disaster.

Finally, daylight appears.

On reading the mental distress of those surrounding him in their dolorous faces, Luissant searches for words of comfort, which ring false.

Oh, Roger, Roger, if a vengeful God exists somewhere, will your dementia earn you forgiveness for your crime?

During those dolorous reflections, I walk instinctively toward the Ossat, my eyes fixed on the terrible mount.

But what is that white thing falling along the mass of black granite? Something draws away from the wall, gently pushed by the breeze, descending slowly toward the plain.

One might think that it's one of those paper parachutes sold in bazaars as children's toys.

Soldiers run toward the object that arrives from the sky. They take possession of it, and assemble around it.

Then the circle breaks. A sergeant comes toward me. In his hand he holds an envelope of gummed cloth.

"A letter, Monsieur," says the sergeant. "It must have come from up there. Perhaps you'll take charge of giving it to Monsieur the President..."

"Give it to me, my friend."

I shiver. At the first glance, I've recognized the firm handwriting of Roger Livry.

The madman has traced the unusual inscription: *To the World's Heads of State.*

What can the nature be of that communication, whose address alone denounces the wretch's arrogant madness?

More than anyone else, Monsieur Luissant seems to me to be qualified to take cognizance of it.

I find the Minister at the inn at the intersection. He has taken refuge in a poor room that has been reserved for him In spite of all the power of self-possession that he has, the courage of the statesman is visibly under stress. His finger trembles as he indicates a poor wicker chair. Then he passes his hand over his brow.

"Excuse me, Monsieur Lefort, but what I've just seen is terrible. The explosion has torn some apart; others have been killed on the spot by the asphyxiating vapors. Oh, the poor fellows, the poor fellows!" He makes a effort to chase away the funereal scene that is haunting him. "Well, what is it?"

"A message from Livry."

In a few words, I tell him how the letter reached me.

The Minister breaks the seal. Frowning, he reads. A mask of dolor and resignation descends over his energetic face. He seizes my hands.

"Oh, my friend! This time, I believe we're doomed." The assured tone of his calm voice veils the superhuman anguish against which he is stiffening himself. "Here, read it for your-self."

I take the letter and read it in my turn.

I am neither a barbarian nor a torturer. As a scientist and a Frenchman I profoundly deplore the catastrophe of the dirigible that attempted to reach me, and similarly, last night's explosion, which must have claimed victims. I regret not having warned you that the radiations emitted by my acid attack hydrogen and modify its density within a radius of five thousand meters, which will increase by the hour.

In the same way, your aircraft can no longer fly in the vicinity of the Ossat. The air, the density of which is modified, will no longer support them.

Renounce, therefore, attempts to reach me with the aid of balloons. Similarly, do not count on destroying my frigorific installations by means of a bombardment. Firstly, they are shielded from your attacks; secondly, my radiations can decompose your explosives and provoke their deflagration. Do not bring explosive materials within fifty kilometers if you want to avoid further misfortunes. In any case, what could those means of attack achieve?

No power in the world can henceforth prevent the suspension of terrestrial life within a period that cannot surpass two full months. In consequence, your duty as governors is to avoid spreading alarm. Allow beings to sink slowly into a sleep that will be eternal.

After centuries, new life will flourish on the earth. By virtue of the law of progress, for the future humankind, that life will be adapted to an improved organism. The new beings will not have the terrible flaws that come from the lamentable imperfection of our organs and our rudimentary senses. Among those evils I will only cite those whose horror I know by virtue of having experienced or recognized them during my existence: war, tuberculosis, alcoholism, madness, and lovesickness, the greatest of them all.

Above all, I dream of a humankind that will only have one sex and no heart. From that will emerge the veritable superhuman.

In order that my work should be judged sanely, I am not a Power of Evil, and I am not a Maker of Oblivion. I am conscious of determining a leap in progress, for time is nothing, the centuries scarcely mark the hours of the history of the World. I am the Annunciator of the New Era. I am the Man of the Apocalypse.

Alas, I had been familiar with the lunatic's theory for a long time. But a nuance that struck me in that ultimate profession of faith was the bitterness and disenchantment that was visible beneath the superb declarations, and the need or self-justification that surfaced several times.

As or Monsieur Luissant, he shook his head sadly, his gaze lost in a distant dream. And in a low voice, he murmured: "From the philosophical point of view, this madman is perhaps a sage, preaching resignation for the present and hope for the future."

But in that poignant moment, it was me, the weakling, who drew from my sharp remorse the courage and the ardor necessary to bring the strong man round.

"Listen to me, Minister. I've penetrated the depths of the unfortunate Livry's soul. Well, in the tone of his letter I seem so glimpse a fissure through which a little pity has slipped into his sickness-exasperated brain. Oh, if only I could reach him, if only I could cry to him: *Have mercy on the World!*"

Luissant made a gesture indicating the extent to which he judged my desire illusory. In a dull voice, he said: "Haven't you read the newspapers, as I have? Haven't you seen the dispatches from the agencies?" And with is hand, he indicated a pile of printed papers scattered on the rickety table. "Well, in spite of all the means I have of imposing silence, within a few days, the terrible truth will burst forth. The press won't be content for long with the stories I allow to filter it, the rumors that my offices have refrained from denying.

"Quite naturally, people are beginning to get excited by the unusual movements taking place in the region of Tarbes. The opposition papers are talking about a vast anarchist plot, a kind of Mafia whose base of operations is situated on the Pyrenean frontier, receiving orders from Barcelona. The socialist papers are uttering loud protests, saying that the government is proceeding with a secret mobilization, denouncing our intention to declare war on Spain over Morocco..."

The Minister could not help shrugging his shoulders

"And our dirigibles dispersed to the four corners of the sky, one broken down, another lost! But what will the exasperation of opinion be on learning of the catastrophes of yesterday and last night? Already, correspondents from everywhere are laying siege to the press office that it's been necessary to set up in Tarbes. Tomorrow, In spite of my efforts, they'll be here, in our midst. What am I going to say to them?

"In Paris, the Chambre is becoming stormy; on the Bourse, the index has already fallen ten points." With a smile of bitterness and scorn, the Minister added: "If only it was just the stock prices!"

My resolution did not buckle before that profound and reasoned disenchantment. And an idea emerged, which had been sketched confusedly in mind since reading the letter.

"Minister, there might perhaps still be one means of reaching the summit, of which we haven't yet thought."

"What?"

"A glider."

Luissant recovered his bitter smile. "My God, Lefort, you heard General Hochtheim's declarations yesterday. If that man, the most audacious of all, has renounced employing that weapon, it's because your idea isn't practical."

"Look at the new Icaruses, though! They're now flying at heights that far surpass that of the Ossat! Hasn't Guy Mayrol reached fifteen hundred meters recently?"

"That's true—but those are exceptional exploits. Then again, it's not only a question of altitude. In the present case, where do you see the possibility of a landing for an alerion supported by the wind, which can't suspend its progress?"

"Mayrol accomplishes marvels of audacity and skill every day. Why shouldn't he be able to let himself down into one of the convent's three courtyards?

"Let's admit it—but do you believe that the madmen up there would let him land? They'd kill him."

"I'm still holding to the hypothesis of disembarking a passenger; I'm also assuming that the disembarkation would take place at night.

"Oh, my dear chap, you're straying into the implausible."

"At the point we've reached, as you've said yourself, everything ought to be attempted, even the impossible."

"I agree, but where is the audacious man ready to risk the adventure, without him needing to be brought into the terrible secret in order to convince him?"

"I believe that Guy Mayrol would accept. I know arguments capable of convincing him."

Rapidly, I retraced the scene at the Camp de Châlons in which Roger, by an impromptu stroke of genius, had so fortunately seconded the efforts of the young seeker.

"Summon Mayrol, then," said the Minister, in a disenchanted tone.

I ran to the telephone.

Within ten minutes, I had picked up Mayrol's trail. He was at Juvisy aerodrome, where he was trying out a new model of alerion. Within half an hour, my desire was on their way to realization. I did not have to say very much to decide the hero of unpowered flight; I simply told him that it was a matter of saving the mysterious unknown man, the Man of the Apocalypse, who had traversed his existence like a good genie never seen again. In giving him that reason I was sincere; while trying to save humankind, why should I not think also of saving one human being who was particularly dear to me?

I still have present in my memory the noble and simple words by which Mayrol made his acceptance known: "I owe your friend everything: my success and my fortune. Count me in!"

The details were quickly settled. At Juvisy, by order of the President of the Council, a special train was formed to bring Mayrol to Tarbes, with his crew of assistants and his best two machines. He would leave at four o'clock in the afternoon, and would reach the Mont d'Ossat the following morning.

In spite of the rapid success of my step, I was too agitated to savor the peace of any relief. Incapable of remaining in place, I had myself taken to Tarbes. I took Étienne Tourbe with me in order to take the child away from the sinister ambience of the Ossat.

I was able to get a few hours sleep in a hotel bed. Nevertheless, three hours before the arrival of the special train. I was at the station waiting for Mayrol.

XXII. The Savior

Mayrol arrived at eight o'clock. Immediately, the young man took care of unloading his alerions. Their long fuselages were carried on two trucks; with their wings folded, the marvelous gliders resembled, on a gigantic scale, the yellow dragonflies that pose on reeds in marshes.

A crowd had gathered along the barriers, in spite of the cold, to watch the maneuvers. I noticed that the people did not have the verbose and noisy agitation characteristic of southern idlers. What I read on those closed faces was an anxious curiosity and an ill-defined anguish. I remembered having once seen such a crowd near Douai, in the black country; its members were standing at the entrance to a mine to which the rumor of a firedamp explosion had brought them.

As the Minister feared, the comings and goings, the troop movements and the mystery that surrounded the Mont d'Ossat—the whole ensemble of occurrences—was beginning to excite public opinion.

Great God! What would they do if they knew? Mentally, I formed nightmarish scenes of the terror that the possible proximity of universal panic might evoke.

Yes, Luissant was right when he deployed all his energy to maintain silence. It there anything more pitiless and more cruel than to allow an invalid to understand that he is about to die?

And I admire the stoicism of little Étienne, who *knows*, and is nevertheless cheerful as he watches the disembarkation of the apparatus.

But the alerions have already been hoisted on to flat-bed motor-trucks, like those employed to transport tanks.

I take my place in an automobile with Mayrol.

The trucks and the mechanics follow.

In order not to give any warning to the madmen of the Ossat, it's agreed that we shall stop out of sight of the summit.

The alerions are garaged in two large barns on the edge of a large pastureland. Mayrol and I, still flanked by the boy, continue our route toward the granite needle.

Until now I have not given any elaborate explanations. I have understood that the imperturbably phlegmatic young man would first want to see and then judge with his own practical sense.

Without saying a word, smoking his cigarette, Mayrol makes a circuit of the tower of black rock. He examines it from different angles, and scrutinizes the bake-like rock that protrudes outside the convent wall. He compares the evidence of his eyes with those of a plan I have given him, labeled with altitudes and dimensions. He reflects for some time, and then comes back to me.

"Monsieur Lefort," he says, in his natural voice. "It's not a matter of a trial but a realization, isn't it?"

I make a sign of assent, and my features lit up with a sudden hope. "It's possible, then?"

"Yes thanks to the wind, which is steady, and the mountains that surround the lain of Tarbes. I'll find a point of departure in the foothills of the Pyrenees that will permit me to arrive above the needle. There, I can calculate my movements to descend on the convent in an ever-decreasing spiral, like a sparrowhawk. In the final circle the radius is so sort that the alerion turns on its axis and remains almost vertically above the landing-point."

"And you'll go down then into one of the interior court-yards?"

"No, because then I'd drop like a stone; it would be a mortal impact, which wouldn't get us any further forward. But a passenger cold take advantage of the precise moment of ver-tical descent to slide down a rope about…let's say fifteen me-ters long; He'd be able to reach the ground of the Ossat while giving me enough scope to reset my apparatus and take a tan-gential route, brushing the roof. The end of the descent toward the plain is nothing. Except…"

"Except?" I say, slightly dazed by the audacity of the maneuver so calmly explained.

"It's indispensable that my companion should be an ac-complished gymnast, immune to vertigo. Finally, in order for me to retain full mastery of my controls, the passenger must be very light, fifty kilos at the maximum."

"No more?"

"Not is you desire a realization."

I am devastated. The hope, albeit vague, that I had forged since the previous day, collapses lamentably. And why? For a small difference of a few kilos! I weigh sixty-seven and Maytol cannot take more than fifty. Thus, the fate of the world depends on seventeen kilos, more or less.

Oh, it would be hilarious if it were not so frightful.

I shake the hand of the courageous pilot, with a desolate expression.

"Excuse me for having disturbed you unnecessarily, my dear Mayrol. Since, in fact, no one can reach the unfortunate Livry…"

"No one! What about me, M'sieur Paul? You're not counting me?"

Who said that?

It is little Tourte.

By voice of seeing him close by, an inseparable companion of these days of suffering, I had, in truth, forgotten him.

And I discover beneath me that little spindly figure, his intelligent and determined eyes gleaming.

"Me, I weigh forty-two kilos," he says, with assurance and pride.

Mayrol and I look at one another without saying a word. The gamin has stunned us with the unexpected proposition thrown into the midst of our impotence and distress.

Well, no, neither one of us had thought of him. And already, the idea of accepting the help of a child is causing us to shiver. But in a tone that seeks to be convincing, he now makes his generous offer precise. In order to argue, he recovers the mocking loquacity of a child of the slums.

"Monsieur Mayrol said fifty kilos, right? For that, only an anorexic or a kid like me is good for the stunt. It's almost as if I were made to measure. It needs someone agile—you know me, M'sieur Paul! I have the feet of a goat mounted on the body of a rubber doll. Me, who can leap down from a wooden horse on a steam-driven roundabout, I have what it needs to get down from the alerion. And vertigo—ha! Don't know it. What if I told you, Monsieur Mayrol, that I used to amuse myself sitting astride the pulley of a crane perched at the top of the scaffolding surrounding the church of Saint-Étienne-du-Mont? The roofers said that that was seventy-five meters high. You see, Monsieur Lefort, without wanting to offend you, that it isn't you who's learned to do as much."

And by way of conclusion, he brings out another argument: "Do you think that Monsieur Roger would seek to harm me, the little starveling he pulled out of the mud to make a Monsieur of me? Look, Monsieur Paul, without bragging, I've become a member of the family even more than you. Oh, I know what you're going to say; Jobert and Barnett, two dirty beasts. But then, lions don't eat rats. Then again, in that regard, Monsieur Roger must be something of a tamer: he'll protect me.

"And finally, it's necessary to tell you that it would amuse me a great deal to go up in an alerion."

What a flame of desire is shining in Étienne's eyes when he pronounces those final words! Then he blushes and murmurs a remark that shows us the depths of his soul: "One day, perhaps they'll talk about me in the newspapers."

The entire psychology of the Paris gamin is contained in that.

In spite of the poignancy of the situation, Mayrol and I can't help exchanging a smile. And by the play of his physiognomy, I sense that the aviator is leaving me the responsibility of making the decision.

In ordinary circumstances, the idea of discussing the child's heroic proposition would have seemed monstrous to me. But we are going through a crisis beyond the natural, in which questions of life and death cannot be posed from their habitual angle. Certainly, dangers will lie in wait for the boy at every step—but is not the other danger, the silent danger, affirming itself more terribly with every passing hour?

At midday, in April, in the middle of April, in that region, renowned for the mildness of its climate, the puddles formed in depressions are covered in a sheet of ice. Even more than the very judicious arguments put forward by Étienne, it was perhaps the abnormal sight of that frozen water that acted upon my decision.

"So," I said, in a grave voice, "you're sure you're not afraid?"

Astonished, Étienne affirms his bravery: "Afraid, Monsieur Paul! Of what and whom? Not Monsieur Mayrol, not Monsieur Roger. So?"

My only response is to seize the former pastry-cook in my arms, and say, after kissing him on both cheeks: "Well, go then, my brave lad!"

Emotion grips my throat, and I have to make an unusual effort in order not to weep.

Alas, I was later to shed the tears held back at that moment.

The decision taken, as a man of action, Mayrol does not lose a minute to make arrangements for the adventurous attempt.

I take him to Monsieur Luissant and General Hochtheim. When they know the plan as a whole and the role to be played by little Tourte, they accept it without objection, without a word of pity or affection. They simply give the accolade to the little fellow. For them, the child is a man, running to sacrifice.

Mayrol settles the details of the execution in concert with Hochtheim.

At first he thinks of taking off at dusk; then he decides to depart in complete darkness. At midnight, the moon will be low enough on the horizon to prevent the alerion being distinguished, while permitting the silhouette of the convent to be discerned in a perfectly sufficient fashion.

In any case, four powerful searchlights will concentrate their beams on the squat bell-tower of the chapel. That will be the beacon that will guide Mayrol in his flight.

The choice of a launch-site for the apparatus is quickly made; various items of information coincide in indication an ideal terrain: a platform situated on the crests that rise up between Pierrefitte and Cauterets. It is seven hundred meters above the valley of Argelès and dominates the plain by about a thousand meters. From there the sliding skips departed that served for the exploitation of an abandoned mine.

That point of departure is twenty kilometers from the Ossat as a bird flies; the pilot thinks that he will arrive over the needle in half an hour.

Finally, one of the great advantages of the chosen point is that it is in the immediate vicinity of the electric railway line to Cauterets. Transportation of the alerions will thus be effected with ease.

A rapid reconnaissance permits Mayrol to take account himself of the excellent conditions offered by the platform of the mine.

Similarly, General Hochtheim will prepare him a landing-ground that will be illuminated from midnight on.

The material details having been duly settled, the pilot sets out to utilize the remaining hours of daylight to carry out a trial. A hillock masked from the Ossat by a pine-wood is selected. Little Tourte takes his place on the saddle placed behind the pilot's seat. A rope fifteen meters long is solidly fixed to the framework of the apparatus.

Launched by the sandow, the alerion rises without difficulty. Lightly and easily, it rises above the plain, aided by the strong breeze.

Mayrol suggests to the child that he set down in a farmyard, on a heap of straw capable of deadening the shock in case of a fall.

And several times, the exercise, perilous in itself, is carried out with an ease that renews our hopes. At an agreed signal, emitted by Mayrol by means of a shrill whistle, Étienne lets himself slide down the cable at the precise moment when the apparatus passes over the heap of straw.

"It's nothing—less than nothing!" the boy says, when we congratulate him on his agility. "Like descending from a moving autobus."

After those encouraging trials, we go back to the inn for dinner: a sad meal that reminds me of those we had at the front, on the eve of an attack, when we and the chiefs were griped by the terrible responsibility. Risking one's own life is a little thing, once one gets used to it, but leading, *driving* others to death...

Isn't the present case similar in every point?

Mayrol is silent by temperament; I'm too emotional to talk; in any case, as soon as I attempt a remark, an interior thrill quivers within me and prevents me from continuing.

Fortunately, Étienne has coolness enough for two; his nose in his plate, he eats with a hearty appetite; he regales himself on a cream desert concocted by our hostess.

Oh, those hours of waiting that separate us from the supreme attempt! They seem all the more cruel to me because I'm alone now.

Luissant has been obliged to go back to Paris, recalled to the Council of Ministers; the Prefect is at his post in Tarbes; General de Lozières is supervising the installation of the railway track. The three scientists have gone to the observatory on the Pic du Midi to study the progress of the atmospheric refrigeration.

I have told Tourte to rest for a few hours before the great departure.

Mayrol has returned to his hangar to check the bodywork of his alerion one last time. In addition, he has given orders to paint the wings black, in order to render the apparatus invisible at night.

I am, therefore—I repeat—alone, horribly alone beside the smoky lamp.

Oh, that frightful vigil!

My apprehensions return in a host. Then night falls in my spirit and I fall back into my intellectual lethargy.

"Well, Monsieur Lefort," are you sleeping awake?"

Guy Mayrol is before me, shaking my shoulder.

It's true; I had seen him without seeing him.

"It's time," he says, simply.

I shudder. On the morning of his execution, a man condemned to death experiences what I'm experiencing at this moment. And yet, it isn't my life that is at stake,

I go to the next room, where the child is asleep. Before I wake him up, a sharp dolor traverses me. In the final analysis, it's necessary. Undoubtedly, there exists, beyond the immaterial wills that prowl around us in order to weigh upon us, if necessary, our own intimate will. I must be going through one of those psychological phases, because, when I shake the little sleeper gently, I am acting like the obedient subject of a hypnotist.

The gamin leaps out of bed, like a soldier hearing the alarm sounded.

I dress him in a fur jacket for which I've sent someone to search in Tarbes, because the cold outside is very sharp; the thermometer is marking seven degrees below. What a fall in three days!

We take our places in the automobile that will take us to Pierrefitte, a journey of thirty minutes. There, the electric train is waiting for us; a truck is carrying the glider. The train climbs the slope rapidly. Now we're at the alerion's launch-site.

The moon is due to disappear at about one o'clock. Mayrol will take off at about twenty past twelve. Everything is ready. The sandows are stretched by the aides.

In haste, I renew my instructions to Étienne. Once again, I hug the dear boy to my heart. Mayrol installs him on the saddle, and then seizes the controls.

The apparatus shudders, lifted by the winds but retained by the military engineers. My heart has stopped beating.

"Hup!"

That's the conventional "let go." The rubber bands contract. The black bird bounds into the void and disappears into the night.

The die is cast.

XXIII. Life is Stronger than Death!

In haste, I make the return journey to Pierrefitte. The auto brings me back to the Ossat.

Followed by the engineers, I climb the wooded slope that masks us from the needle.

Now I'm at the crest. I stop dead; the soldiers accompanying me do likewise. The vision that is offered to our eyes breaks our momentum.

Illuminated by the white light of the electric projectors, the granite summit is outlined against the sky, an immense black tower with a bizarre crown formed by the tapering of the rock and the silhouette of the roofs, steeples and turrets of the Franciscan convent.

One might think it a fabulous animal crouched on the tower: a unicorn, dragon or chimera with trenchant claws and a crested spine.

Down below, all around, troubling glaucous glimmers rise from ground level, as if to prohibit any approach to that place of terror and mystery; they are low-lying pools of frozen water whose surface is iridescent in the moonlight.

The appearance is so fantastic that one can scarcely place it in the real world. It is a scene of Walpurgis Night, and one searches the air for phantasmal shadows, for deformed larvae.

I dig my fingernails into the palms of my hands in order to rid myself of the emprise of those hallucinations.

But now the moon has disappeared behind the western hills, plunging the plain and the base of the cyclopean giant into blackness. I fix my eyes on the darkness rising along the granite like a sea of ink. I prick up my ears. Will I discern the strident blast of a whistle that ought to mark the decisive moment? Or will I hear the racket of the fling machine crashing into the rocky wall?

My nerves are stretched to breaking point as the seconds succeed one another, as the tide of shadow gets closer to the summit.

A time elapses that must be quite short, but seems to me to be a century.

And through the night passes a light, distant sound that quavers like the call of a cricket in the hearth.

There is no doubt about it; it's Mayrol's signal.

Behind me, a bright light sets the curtain of trees masking the aviator's landing-ground ablaze; I divine that it is composed by acetylene beacons, lit at the agreed moment to facilitate Mayrol's return.

The lights go out abruptly. Perhaps Mayrol has already landed. Nevertheless I march a hundred meters and stop at the limit of the first potholes. With all my strength, I resume listening to the silence.

This time, toward the foot of the bluff, I hear a distinct sound. It recurs at regular intervals. One might think that it were the crystalline sound of glass breaking as it falls. What can it be?

I don't have time to forge hypotheses. From up above, I hear a cry.

In the muted echo, I rediscover the shrill, child-like timbre of a voice that has not yet broken, and also the heart-rending anguish of someone calling for help.

Horror! Only little Étienne could have uttered that cry.

I think I'm about to faint. My ears buzz, the blood beats in my temples with a staccato rhythm.

I truly think that at that moment, I was on the brink of collapsing under the sledgehammer blow of a cerebral congestion.

"Monsieur Lefort? Are you there?"

Perhaps it was that intervention by Mayrol that saved me, by provoking an instinctive reaction of my reflexes.

It is only at the third appeal, although the young man is almost within arm's length, that I can articulate: "Yes...I'm here."

I cling on to him, in order not to fall.

"Hey! Monsieur Lefort, you've allowed yourself to be gripped by the cold."

By the light of a lantern, I can vaguely distinguish other shadows moving around me. I feet a bottleneck introduced between my lips.

"Drink!"

I obey. A sensation of wellbeing invades me. Now, I've recovered my aplomb. I can now hear the pilot, who declares in his tranquil voice: "I succeeded. Little Étienne has set down up there. Before I prolonged my flight over the rooftops, the brave boy called: 'It's okay!' Except, it was time for me to come down to earth. I was gripped by the cold. Then I experienced a bizarre impression: the air was no longer supportive. When I reached the ground, I broke the machine...eh? What's that?"

A second apart, two detonations have just sounded on the summit of the Ossat: two gunshots.

356

I seize Mayrol's hands and in a breathless voice: "My fried, a frightful drama is in play up there. I'm a criminal, yes, criminal, for having let that child…to what? My God, what to do?"

I give signs of the most violent despair; I march, I totter, I weep with impotence and shame.

In vain, the pilot tries to calm me down.

I am obliged, however, to yield to the evidence of the arguments he enumerates. There is nothing we can do until daybreak.

How will the hours go by that separate us from the dawn?

I know nothing about them. There is nothing there in my memory but a dead time.

Except that, at the first light of morning, I have returned to a state of sluggishness, in much the same condition as when one emerges from a faint.

I can no longer feel much of anything, neither physical inconvenience nor mental anxiety. My bare hands are not suffering from the sharp cold that is powdering the earth with a white frost; my eyes rediscover the sinister stele of the Ossat indifferently.

My nerves are decidedly torpid.

Perhaps fatality wanted to have pity on me, by permitting me that anesthesia of my sensitive being, before pushing me toward the frightful calvary that still remained for me to climb.

Mechanically, I follow the officers and soldiers who are hastening toward the foot of the rick. They too are impatient to piece the mystery of the successive sounds that troubled the silence of the night of anguish. They have all heard the fall of broken glass, the supreme cry for help and the gunshots in the course of their guard duty—and also another sound, much duller and more muffled, that came from directly below the granitic spur, shortly before daybreak. That sound, I did not perceive.

With agility, those brave fellow run through the potholes and crevasses of collapsed earth. They give no thought to the possibility that the madmen might greet them with rifle fire from their lair.

As best I can, in follow on the heels of the nimble group—and suddenly, I see the soldiers stop, lean over toward the ground, step back, and then form a motionless circle.

I approach in my turn.

On the hardened ground, there is the cadaver of a man, a body folded in two, the limbs dislocated, the skull open.

Blood, the debris of viscera and cerebral matter have splashed the surrounding area.

At the exhortations of a lieutenant, the soldiers overcome their horror and lift up that miserable human wreck. They uncover the face, left almost intact. I throw my hands over my eyes; I have just recognized Roger Livry.

It's too much.

I move away a few paces in order to get further away from the abominable vision. I go around the granite base. There, other soldiers are considering curiously the debris of black glass that stews the ground, and also the gelatinous plaques extended here and there by splashes. The sight of those things forces my dolorous brain to think again.

That paste with the opaline tints is the terrible mixture of radium and the Omega aid.

In a host, question marks assail my mind. But I am decidedly empty, annihilated. The power of reasoning and the sense of observation have abandoned me.

By myself, I remain in no condition to untangle the tragic thread of events.

Someone has to come to my aid.

That aid, the dead man will bring me himself.

Before my distracted eyes the silhouette looms up of the lieutenant who substituted just now for my routed courage by occupying himself with the collection of Roger's mortal remains.

"Monsieur," the officer says, "this letter was found on the cadaver. I believe it's addressed to you."

I take the envelope that he hands to me. Indeed, the sub-scription, in which I recognize the handwriting of my child-hood friend, is in my name.

I stammered a thank you.

Then, sitting on a large boulder at the foot of the sinister mountain, I took cognizance of the unfortunate's final missive.

Such as it is, I am copying that document, in which, in a flash of lucidity, the madman retraces the final act of the dra-ma, crying his pain to the universe, imploring its pardon.

My dear Paul,

Have pity on me. I've suffered so much.

By virtue of the suffering of the last year of my life, more than my voluntary death, I have commenced the expiation of my crimes.

For a year I have lived in a fog of death and desolation, scarcely illuminated during the few days that you know. I have seen so many things that you could not see. Mad—I was mad!

That dream of the regeneration of the world by the de-struction of present Life, I made in good faith, I swear to you. Never, at any moment, did I believe that I was yielding to an egotistical rage or an amorous despair. Never, before tonight, have I perceived the enormity of the sins of which I was the unconscious cause.

In order to remove the scales from my blind eyes, it has required one final sacrifice, that of an innocent, that of poor little Étienne.

By the time you read these lines, all those who were on the Mont d'Ossat will be dead. It is necessary, therefore, for me to tell you...

First of all, Barnett killed himself the other night. The wretch met a frightful end. Since our arrival in this convent he had not ceased drinking and getting drunk. In a fit of delirium tremens *he became fearful of the mortal cold that was increas-ing and wanted to protect himself from it. Soaking his gar-ments in gin, he set fire to them. For a few minutes he ran, a living torch, uttering the cries of a damned soul. In an interior courtyard of the convent, a heap of calcined bones and black ashes will be found. That is what remains of Barnett.*

I remained alone with Jobert. As I got to know him better, the man filled me with horror: a sanguinary madman who exulted in the memory of his crimes. In the last few days, I have been obliged to use my authority to prevent him shooting with a rifle at the soldiers who appeared in the plain. Yesterday, he manifested a savage joy when the dirigible crashed.

This evening, he claimed to hear suspicious noises from the direction of our vats of acid—for my refrigerators are installed outside the convent, in an old vaulted cistern only receiving daylight from outside through long and narrow ventilation shafts; by that means, they were sheltered from the most powerful shells.

Alas, I judged it materially impossible for anyone to reach our eagle's nest by any means whatsoever. However, little Étienne was there. Guided by the radiation of the radium, the child had discovered the stone staircase leading to the cistern. He had had the idea of taking the sixty vats one by one—they only weigh fifteen kilos each—and throwing them to the foot of the rock.

He had reckoned without Jobert.

Surprised by the wretch, Étienne tried to defend himself, but the other, like a coward, plunged a dagger into his heart.

Drawn by the martyred child's cries, I ran. I recognized Étienne, my pupil—almost my son—lying in a pool of blood, and standing over him, Jobert, his dagger red, laughing ferociously, uttering threats and insults.

Then, a veil was torn in my poor head. I discovered the abominable truth. I was horrified.

Without saying a word, with two bullets from my revolver, I slew the monster.

After that execution, in my turn, I decided to die.

It is necessary for me to profit from that hour of temporary lucidity to protect the world from the inevitable return of my horrible folly. Before then, I wanted to write you this letter, certain that you would find it in the vicinity of the Ossat.

What more is there to say?

Before disappearing, I want to beg forgiveness from my victims, from all those I have harmed.

First of all from you, my very dear friend, my brother, for the mental torture that I've imposed on you or more than a year. From Capitaine Berjac, whom I killed indirectly. From the people of Bouffarik and Messina. From the unfortunates who were manning the dirigible lost yesterday, the victims of last night's explosion. And above all from poor little Étienne. Was the blood of that child necessary, then, to redeem the supreme crime meditated against humankind? Finally, from the pure and gentle soul of Hélène Thiérard-Leroy.

A cruel punishment might await me in the afterlife: the reprobation of the woman in memory of whom I have perpetrated the most terrible of designs. That will be justice.

To you, Paul Lefort, I bequeath all my worldly goods; I know that you'll make noble use of them. May they serve, in the measure that is possible, to repair the damage I have done to others.

Before hurling myself into the void, I shall halt the effect of the mortal effluvia. I shall neutralize the vats of acid that still remain. You will find a formula included herewith; it will permit the separation of the radium from the Omega acid.

As for the formula of the acid itself, I shall take the secret with me. It is necessary that no madman or wretch can ever take up the destructive dream again.

May the world live in peace.

The Man of the Apocalypse is dead, killed by Eternal Life.

Cover of the 1932 Spanish edition of
On the Brink of the World's End